affinity

Chris Dias
Dias Ex Machina
129 – 6807 Westgate Ave
Prince George, British Columbia
V2N 5T8
DiasExMachina@gmail.com

Written by Chris Dias
Affinity: The First Book

Cover by Nick Greenwood

CHRIS DIAS

Affinity

The First Novel

ALSO BY CHRIS DIAS

Amethyst: Aiden's Way
Amethyst: Controlling Chaos
Amethyst: Hallowed Kingdom
House of Skye

PREFACE

(Minor spoilers if you know nothing of the story)

Affinity was a project I stared at for nearly a decade. At the end of this book, you'll find a postface (which I admit is a word I can't stop smiling at) detailing the history of inspiration and how this work finally manifested. I don't believe novels are written in a vacuum, and I am honest about this one's astonishingly long development time.

I wanted to detail some elements for readers to consider before diving in. You'll quickly discover the three different narratives at play, separated by their individual titles *Paradise*, *Conestoga*, and *Torus*. The decision to present these stories simultaneously will become obvious relatively quickly. Still, I'll admit that the average reader that polishes a chapter a day may grow confused given the switching perspectives.

Ultimately, I couldn't solve this one obstacle, and I did my best not to repeatedly exposit for those tackling this work in less than a few sittings. I discovered that repeatedly elaborating on the same subjects grew tedious and wouldn't serve the novel's already protracted word count. Given that challenge, I decided mid-way through the development not to offer *Affinity* within the YA genre I had approached with *Amethyst* and *House of Skye*. *Affinity* is unambiguously adult-orientated, with mature descriptions and themes outside its complex storyline.

One solution to this interpretive challenge would be to follow each story independently, reading all the chapters of one setting in sequence before restarting the book with the second and then the third. Personally, I believe this significantly reduces the quality of the overall story as specific plots are paired or spaced apart to accentuate their narrative weight.

The other issue when reading the stories independently is determining which one to read first. Despite the opening chapters indicating a preferred order, there is no "first" or "last," especially given the lack of definitive times presented.

Finally, I wanted to discuss some aspects of my writing style. To cut through the miasma of ambiguousness, I'll come clean and admit that as someone who suffers from OCD and ADHD, I have issues reading fiction that focuses more on the setting and the scenery than the characters and their actions. I am less interested in what a character thinks and more in what they say.

While I subscribe to the classic adage of show don't tell, I enjoy imaginative and elegant dialogue. My experience, while beginning with novels, turned quickly to screenwriting. I began in college with courses involving classical literature and creative writing. I then migrated to a second-year screenwriting course, a rare offering at a school of that size, a course I subsequently repeated.

I later became an advent follower of dialogue-focused storytelling. Readers will find that represented here, as frequently the background descriptions and internal motivations will take a back seat to the banter the characters will have found themselves in.

So, if you're looking for a poetic digression in the political environment of a fantasy world, perhaps you should check out the appendices where I placed most of that content.

Chris Dias
15 August 2021

We believed quantum nonlocality only applied to the microscopic level. On the scale of a single universe, that would be correct.

What we didn't know was that entanglement reaches beyond this, into the expanse between realities.

When related events occur, it could lead to a self-amplifying chain of events. If unresolved, one possible outcome is that of a waveform collapse, at which point the realities will be effectively indistinguishable.

Script Gamma
Verse 34
Plex Codex

PROLOGUE

"To begin a story, one must first design the universe."

Given the elaborate puzzle lock occupying the whole of its foredge and the lack of any label on its spine or cover, the old book refused to surrender its secrets. Flourished with wood, stressed in etched copper, and bound in thick black leather, it sat undisturbed upon the granite pedestal alone within the vault. One wall was transparent next to a locked safe door. Without an atmosphere within the chamber, the smashing of melee weapons and the firing of small arms outside was muted to deep thumps.

The massive tome rested on a rolling library cart, distinctive given its heft and ornate embellishments. It was the only one with corner protectors and a locked clasp requiring dials to be rotated, pistons to be pulled, and combinations to be solved. It was sandwiched out of place within a set of color-coded encyclopedias of equal height. The cart laid within an immense archive with a million books stacked on multiple floors within an octagon-shaped chamber with branching hallways.

A five-pointed star, known as a Godhead, inset within an ever-increasing spiral of mathematical perfection was the volume's only embossment, radiating from the corner. Dust had worked into the impression, blown across the cover via a light breeze from empty windows. The castle solar was fringed in weathered murals depicting battles clashing sword and shield. Rotted wood paneling hung under the crumbling ribs of a vaulted granite ceiling. The book waited upon a ripped blue tufted chair.

A splash of blood tarnished the transparent partition as a pair of communion rustlers left their felled and nearly decapitated comrade by the vault door. They loosed a volley of gunfire, one from a pair of flintlock pistols and the other from a 12-gauge trench rifle. The two men retreated from the oncoming mashing of steel teeth and razor claws. Shots connected were ignored as the monsters advanced.

A lean body passed by the library cart, disregarding its contents and focusing on more pressing matters. A moment passed before she stopped and returned. The figure leaned gracefully, revealing a thick sleeveless green robe over a white and black form-fitting, padded and pocketed jumpsuit. A pastel, three-fingered hand reached down to remove the errant book from the cart.

The wind tossed his unkempt white hair and three-month beard as he scaled the broken stairs leading to the precarious drawbridge. It had been raining, and he cautiously walked under the portcullis hung by only a few lingering unbreakable strands. The Aelon Ziggurat, built by the kingdom of Aurago, was two centuries old and abandoned a decade ago after the pogrom of Volani. The red-stained star-shaped fortress had been overgrown with vines and trees, and legends of restless spirits had discouraged reoccupation.

The lone survivor climbed out of the shaft and fell onto fresh snow. He turned sharply and dragged the grate back over the entrance. He frantically reloaded his decorative copper and silver flintlocks as he scaled the hill. Upon reaching the crest, he took a brief opportunity to remove a brass coin pierced with a gold necklace stamped with the spiral-shaped symbol of his faith. He kissed it and wrapped the chain around his fist. He marched, battered and bone-weary through the ruins of a devastated cityscape.

The alien hand placed the book gently on the desk, caressing the elaborate mechanism occupying the foredge. Fingers found a dial that rotated, ejecting a rod that freed a gear connected to a handle that, when twisted, revealed a combination of ciphers easily solved. A few more steps finally returned a reaffirming click, and the latch unlocked. The hand caressed the edges before slowly flipping open the cover.

The older man pushed through the rusted wrought iron door to enter the solar. Clearly exhausted, he stopped to find his breath, appreciating how well preserved this chamber was compared to the rest of the castle. It matched what he had been shown, including the details on the frescos and the mesmerizing pattern of spars crisscrossing over him. And there it was just as predicted, despite every doubt he had. He pondered how anyone could have missed it, like it was placed waiting just for him. He reached down to the tufted chair and retrieved the book.

The survivor stumbled and fell to his knees upon emerging from the devastated city weathered from over a thousand years. A lattice of crisscrossing train tracks extended out before him. His train waited at the periphery, marked by its polished steel windsplitter-pointed nose. Porthole windows speckled the streamlined chain of a half-dozen cars. The survivor's relief only lasted a moment as the locomotive started to peel apart, with fragments spiraling into a snake-like torrent of debris. It possessed a circular mouth of twisting blades made from scraps of metal. As it expanded from the mechanical chrysalis, leaving little of the train behind, the survivor could almost see through the entire length of the monster. The whirlwind's bellow came from a tempest of grinding metal—cooing that followed birth pains. The survivor could only gape in awe at the spontaneous creation of a living storm, curious if it noticed him.

"To tell a story, one must confront its end."

PART ONE

AWAKENINGS

TORUS

Despite the oddity of the world itself, life within was relatively normal. Nature existed within a range of acceptable expectations. The engineers and scientists of Iokon developed great machines to serve man. These were straightforward constructs designed for functionality rather than aesthetics. The state police of the Metropolis enforced control with magnetic or energy weapons. Life appeared normal.

However, either before or after the Collapse, something changed. Illogical breaks from reality emerged. Machines not built by man roamed the land. Ethereal beings appeared. The dead awoke. Eventually, man discovered how this was occurring, a strange black mist materializing around beings and bestowing them with supernatural abilities. Even to this day, no one knows where smoke came from…

…but it is here.

Ethaniel Collianthus
A History of Lies,
1339 AC

The train was a rusted black-iron extended boxcab with a dated cowcatcher and a single car trailing behind. It couldn't manage more than fifty kilometers per hour at notch eight, but the contractor had limited funds. The train carried an unusual name, the Loch & Serpent.

The desert sands churned as the beast approached a rusted steamrunner wrecked on the tracks. It was a six-wheeled vehicle powered by a front-mounted hydrocell engine and once represented the artistic whims of a flamboyant owner, boasting chrome fender flares, wooden spokes, riveted polished iron, and copper accents. It had been stripped of anything of value decades previously and sat as a reminder of how unforgiving the badlands could be.

The Loch & Serpent neglected to slow as it slammed into the automobile, splitting it in two and tossing the halves from its path.

*   *   *

"Wake up, woman!" Machus said. His scarred face was coated with soot from the dirty engine wrapped around them.

Sloan slowly opened her amber eyes and focused on the conductor. Her red hair was cropped short on the sides and back with additional length atop her head. Her eyes looked old under arched brows within a younger face

"I have a name," she said.

"Which is not worth remembering," he said. "I thought your kind didn't sleep."

"I'm very much human," Sloan said. She had been sleeping on a bench with a moderate cushion. The train afforded little ration for comfort.

"Your weapon claims otherwise."

"Last I checked, it doesn't speak. If you thought it did, you probably should see someone."

"Regardless, we've reached as far as I'll take you."

"Implying we're not at our destination."

"Close enough."

"Which is how far?

"An easy walk," Machus said, belligerent.

"For you or me?"

"What does that mean?"

"Simple question," Sloan said as she sat up. "Is our destination an easy walk for someone like you?"

"And who's someone like me?"

"Someone who doesn't care about the details of our contract."

"I thought you were going to say *an old bigot who isn't paid enough to care.*"

"I needed to take a breath."

Machus turned his back on Sloan and reverted to servicing the locomotive. He was its CIC (conductor-in-chief) and only crew member. Sloan's blade had been resting on her chest. She held it firmly; its numerous charms, lockets, trinkets, and other keepsakes hanging off the pommel, guard, and fuller rattled off one another as she stood. The exquisite ornamentation gave off the impression it was a ceremonial accessory.

It was not.

The train slowed, and a peek outside confirmed impending dawn as shadows slowly stretched across the arid desert. She strolled to the rear cabin. She had on her leather, boned corset with matching black collared bustier and opened ruffled paisley skirt over leather pants.

She departed the locomotive and crossed the umbilical to the slightly corroded iron door leading into the car. She knocked once and pushed it open without waiting for a response.

"This is far he'll go," she said. "I imagine we'll have a walk."

* * *

Sloan pulled the outside door to the stopped train open and felt the morning's heat. She looked to the dawn and forced her eyes to adapt.

The desert was a salt pan littered with mud quagmires and covered with a lattice of crisscrossing train tracks. Unlike most territories Sloan had visited in her life, the Mare Dagos lacked many of the ruins of the once-encompassing empire that ruled this land.

The sun emerged from behind the column at the center of their world. This close to Nimbus, the night lasted just under six hours. It would get considerably hotter as Uno orbited this way.

She dropped her boots heavy on the dirt, blowing dust up her face. She brought her weapon up and laid it across her shoulders.

A man followed her, taller with steel flecks in his beard under a generous brow and a balding head. He wore his weathered military jacket over a double-breasted vest and ammunition sprawled across belts and bandoliers. A flat palladium ring on his finger was visible.

"As far as he'll go," Agosta said. "Not like there's anything out here." He looked across the expanse and the lack of anything approximating civilization save for the iron network.

"Do you have a direction?" she asked.

Agosta nodded.

"Thirty *'k'* plus," he said. "Six hours walking."

"Seven. We should get there before Uno passes. If we get stuck, we'll need to find shelter from the heat."

They made off, away from the diminishing shadow of the train behind them, each footfall kicking up the loose dirt covering the pan.

"Thirty kilometers…god damned coward," Agosta said.

"If you were being contracted for a mission such as this, would you risk everything?"

"Yes."

Sloan waited for him to continue, but he didn't.

"…Well, that was a gripping speech. How long did you mull that one over?"

"You're sticking your neck out more than him."

"Well, he's right there behind us. Go back, offer that riveting speech, and convince him to carry us the rest of the way."

"He's probably hoping I'd dip into my reserve."

Sloan glimpsed up at him with an eyebrow raised.

"Wait, you have a reserve?"

"I saved every coin for you."

"Well, not every coin. Ohhh…" Sloan trailed off as she came to understand the details of Machus's contract. "He doesn't know, does he? You couldn't trust he wouldn't drag us to the middle of the desert and extort what little you had left."

"Take that as proof of the faith I have in you."

"You've known me less than forty-eight hours."

"Prove me right."

"Not a matter of proof. You've no choice but trust me, which anyone, including our pleasant CIC back there, would say is misguided. I could read his bigotry the moment he laid eyes on me."

"Well, fuck people like that," Agosta said, which Sloan was dumbfounded to hear. "Trust is assumed until betrayed. Call that naïve all you want, but there are certain qualities I seek…so…like I said…Prove. Me. Right."

* * *

Uno was beading down, and the temperature was increasing. The Loch & Serpent was still in sight, given the lack of hills in this part of the world. It was a dot kilometers away, with their destination still hiding in the distortion of desert heat.

"Does the temperature bother you?" Agosta asked.

"It bothers me as much as I'm obligated to keep you alive."

"Point taken. We should have enough water to get us there."

Sloan gave a half-nod, then stopped dead in her tracks.

Agosta stopped to stare back.

"Meaning you lack enough for the return," she said.

"It's a risk."

"A significant one." She approached him. "You do have enough for the return; for how many?"

Agosta held his ground and gave her a smirk.

"One," he said. "Our destination should have enough."

She nodded.

"So, if we fail…" she said.

"Then there won't be a need to take more."

Sloan glared at him, knowing what he meant. She broke the uncomfortable silence.

"Under normal circumstances, I'd take that as a threat," she said, "but given the details of the contract, I'd call it more…gallant."

Agosta offered Sloan a wave to the open desert.

"Shall we?" he asked.

They walked abreast. Agosta removed, double-checked, then holstered his single-action revolver. Revealing it exposed flamboyant alien engravings, golden plating, and a pearl-plated grip.

Sloan took note.

"Brass inscriptions," she said.

Agosta smirked, unclasped his holster, and offered her the weapon. She examined it, more advanced than a percussion revolver and less eccentric than the pinfires and pepperboxes she had seen. The alien glyphs pressed in the metal glinted with only a few strands of auburn smoke lifting from them as she handed the weapon back.

"You could have sold that and paid for an army," she said.

"You devalue your talents."

Sloan stopped again, causing Agosta to throw up his arms and pivot back to her.

"Now, what is it?" he asked.

Sloan shook her head and walked past him.

"Nothing," she said.

"It wasn't nothing."

"You kept them because you know how this will turn out and because you trust your aim over those of brainless grunts. I'm partial to agree; I'd wager quality over quantity any day. Plus, it reduces the number of potential betrayals…to one."

Sloan stowed her blade on her back. Agosta paced her, noting how she wasn't sweating while wearing such an opulent outfit in this climate.

"We should go over the plan," he said.

"The plan is fine."

"No, we're going to go over it again…and again. And just for kicks, we may go over it again."

Sloan sighed.

"I guess we have several hours to kill," she said. "I'm not particularly incentivized to talk about the weather."

"We could talk about our lives?"

"Rather not."

"I know jokes."

"Let's go over the plan."

Agosta smiled as Sloan diverted away from his playful prodding. He let another uncomfortable silence pass before he spoke again.

"I do have expectations, by the way."

"What I expect is that someone is going to die," Sloan said without giving him a look. "Let's make sure it's not us."

Sloan kept her attention on the desert in front of her. In truth, she could feel the heat; it was only slightly deadened by her nature. It's not like she could change. Part of her curse prevented her from altering her appearance. Others like her were not as blessed with fashion. She had gotten used to the wardrobe, aware that the only aspect of her person she could change was affixed or dangling from the weapon strapped to her back.

Before Agosta reiterated the plan he conceived, he scanned the terrain stretching from them.

There was no horizon, no vanishing point outside what clouds blocked. What remained was distorted from the desert heat. His eyes arched up, following the curving landscape as it reached hundreds of kilometers over them and fell back to form the column behind called Nimbus.

The Convex. To others, it held a different name. Given the bowed terrain, they could almost make out their destination.

The ring's interior was peppered with lakes, forests, mountains, and valleys, but this was a fraction compared to the apocalyptic remains of a dead empire, leaving not only ruins but an insane mesh of train rails, dense enough in some regions as to call them tracklands. It was the culmination of an insane forgotten industrial machine that someone forgot to deactivate.

"Quick aside, how good are you with those weapons?" Sloan asked.

"Are you inquiring about my accuracy? I can set out some rocks."

"I'm thinking of a more immediate assessment," she said as she frowned at the silhouette emerging from the heat distortion ahead of them. They had previously assumed it was a rock or an old Iokon ruin until it shifted.

Agosta noticed the giant copper wheel forming most of the creature's torso. Rounded plates of rusted armor slid around the body, occasionally exposing the clockwork assembly of gears, pistons, and synthetic muscles held together by a brass exoskeleton. As its metallic, canine-like jaw opened, it coughed a gust of yellowish smoke. Its six insect-like legs seemed carved from ivory as it drove them into the hard dirt of the desert floor. The hair growing from its back resembled broken wires.

"Plagurwocky," Agosta said as his shoulders slumped. The beast's central wheel spun before it dropped its torso upon the ground. It accelerated towards them. "What a lovely start to the morning."

Sloan readied her blade, the charms echoing around them.

"Vulnerable at the joints," Sloan said.

"Landing a round in its mouth may connect with the brain cavity, sever its neural processor."

"How do you know that?"

"Not my first go around," Agosta said as he drew his firearms and rolled the drums to ensure every chamber was loaded.

* * *

Given the angle, Machus could still observe the two via his copper-plated spyglass mounted to the edge of his cab window. It was difficult to discern the shape that was moving towards them. It could be a lupus or a phachogoerus, or even a manticore.

The conductor took a slow bite from his salted fish and pickle sandwich and looked again, shifting focus from combatant to combatant. He assumed Agosta was military by the man's attire. The woman was a mystery, though his prejudice hoped she would take a hit. The creature came into sharp detail for only an instant.

"Heh. Plagurwocky," Machus said. "Badlands not going easy on ya."

Machus figured if the monster dispatched the pair of them, he would wait until it had moved on before he would sweep in to salvage, see how much brass Agosta was holding back. Machus was more interested in Sloan's weapon. A dispirited effigy totem fetched a high price on the black market.

Machus took another bite, followed by an extended wash from a black bottle filled with ochre liquid, before peering through the scope again. He saw a puff from Agosta's firearm and a finishing move from Sloan seconds before the concussion wave from the gunshots finally reached the train.

Machus's heart sank.

"Ahh shit," he said.

* * *

Sloan pulled the entirety of her sword from the jaws of the plagurwocky. A final flurry of golden smoke spewed from its nose. Agosta had shot out both its eyes, and the mechanical abomination collapsed. Steam and murky water spilled from its wounds.

Sloan stepped back and inspected her pristine blade. It, along with the charms dangling off, was forged from sterner metals; it would take a lot to chip, let alone break.

"So…what'd you think?" Agosta asked as he reloaded his weapons. "Impressed?"

"Yes, I handled myself with distinction," Sloan said.

"My thought's exactly." Agosta holstered and examined the beast to ensure it was dead.

"Considerable salvage in a creature such as this," Sloan said. "Care to rummage for brass?"

"Perhaps on our way back," Agosta said, "assuming our conductor hasn't stripped it bare by then." He loathed this aspect of life in the badlands and had no intention of tearing the animal apart upon their return. He resumed his march. "To our earlier topic—will I be able to depend on you when the need arises?"

"I'm more concerned about you. Emotion clouds one's skill."

"You implying my weakness resides in me investing in this operation's success."

"I used fewer words," Sloan said as she followed him.

"Heaven forbid I should get attached to anyone."

"My performance won't be obscured by irrationality. Even your plan comes off as impulsive."

"You're right; I should've taken a week to think it over."

"I fear it wouldn't change anything even if you had."

"What does that mean?" Agosta stopped.

"Care to pick up the pace?" she asked.

"What does that mean?"

She stopped and saw his firmed lips and aggravated appearance.

"Do you want to have this conversation?"

"I will take on this responsibility right now, alone. Take the half you have and head for the train. Easiest money you'll ever make: a few days from a city that didn't want you there to begin with. If I underestimated your commitment to what's being asked, that's on me. But I can't have someone accompanying me if they sincerely believe this to be a waste of time. I never wanted mindless mercenaries. I need someone who'll be invested and desire success despite no penalty for failure in their eyes. I need you…to be angry if we fail. I need you to hate the idea of losing…hate it…more than your desire to win. If you can't feel that, then I was wrong in my opinion of you and should stop now."

Sloan considered her response. He was forcing her to be invested, something she hadn't planned on doing.

"I won't fail," she said.

"Are you taking this personally?" Agosta asked.

"Should I?"

"Yes."

"Then I will."

"I'm unconvinced."

"Then ask me again tomorrow." Sloan continued walking, passing Agosta, and taking the lead, ignoring whether or not he was following. He eventually would but kept a few steps back.

"When you're back home, safe and sound, wondering why I didn't turn around," she said. "*Well, fuck people like that,* was when I decided to see this through to the end."

CONESTOGA

The erids arrived on a small outcropping of rock with few supplies and no boats. Somehow, they crossed The Fearghas to reach the black cliffs and then were able to scale them all the way to King's Table, where The Waking Ruins awaited them.

How did they cross that expanse? They must have had help; someone took pity on the refugees, as some biblical allegory.

Those initial immigrants failed to record how they managed it or how they wandered through the catacombs for over a year without being completely wiped out. The only logical conclusion was that they stumbled upon something in their journey, an artifact so powerful that it could hold off the watchers and ferry a population across a torrential ocean, an artifact they still employ to ensure their technological edge over others.

Keid Rana
Editorial
The King's Herald

Terri Zahn opened her violet eyes, and they darted as she attempted to discern where she was. It was that fleeting instant when dreams and reality enmeshed, and she was unsure which was which. She felt the weight of Candace's arm over her naked chest. Terri's shoulder was nestled between two breasts, and she arched her head to sniff auburn hair.

Candace rolled to face Terri, who was still reorientating herself. Candace stroked her fingers across dark skin, a light touch that forced follicles to perk and nipples to stiffen. Terri smiled, temporarily distracted by her palm-sized mobile lighting up. She didn't bother looking at it.

"Are you okay?" Candace asked, her accent pointing to her local birth in Eridius. Terri responded with a fiery kiss, intertwining their tongues.

"Yeah," Terri said as she pulled away. "Just one of those…"

"Nightmares?"

"I nodded off for only a few minutes. When you nap, dreams are formed from your surroundings, like your imagination doesn't have time to visualize something interesting. You dream of yourself right where you should be doing what you're supposed to, with only a small part trying to tell you something's wrong. And yet, no matter how outlandish your surroundings, you're always convinced it's reality. So much so that when you wake, for a split second, you're not sure if you're still dreaming."

"So, you dreamt of yourself being here? What was different? Was I here?"

"Of course. Kind of hard to explain. I felt that…I…was different somehow."

Candace continued stroking Terri's lines around her shoulders and neck until finding a fresh groove below her collarbone.

"Is this a new scar?" Candace asked. "Scabs, jackers?"

"Chicken. Piccata."

"So, that's my fault."

Terri extracted herself from Candace's embrace and left the bed. She sported more scars on her back, blemishes upon a beautiful, sylphlike ebony body.

"Something to remember you," Terri said as she glanced at the mobile illuminating the same message as before.

"You can't be leaving already," Candace said.

"Staplegunners say jump." Terri began with her socks, then made for the nearby dresser to find her uniform shirt.

"You proctors are an enigmatic sort, aren't you?" Candace said as she sat up on the bed, pulling the sheets over her naked body. "Got your handshakes and language. What is it, cryptolect?"

"It's more of a code than a language," Terri said as she started donning her shirt, with the ends falling below her waist.

It was an entirely manufactured language fashioned by the proctors as a way for them to communicate secretly between their kind. The tongue originated within the guild hallmasters and passed down the membership. The language was meant to be fast, communicating as few words as possible. Although not a complex language to learn, given its almost mathematical approach, it was continuously revised. Proctors knew their language eventually would be cracked by outsiders, so secret communications go out often, instructing loyal proctors of changes. The alterations can be minor or significant, forcing everyone to adapt to the new vernacular.

"Just another level of secrecy," Candace said. "Anyone not of the guild is a pariah, even me." She touched a hidden button on the dresser next to her bed, and a portion of the blank wall became transparent, revealing a breathtaking grass-covered plateau dotted with ivory buildings and canals of blue water glinting in the morning sun.

"You're not an outsider."

"People ask about us. If I'm one of those…girls in every port. They ask if you have a wake of broken hearts."

"I don't work that way."

"Then why do it? Why go out there? What are you trying to prove? It's not like you're an ex-pat. You have a place to pitch your tent."

"Some people want to build a home," Terri said as she finished the last button. She had misplaced her jumpsuit. She remembered tossing it but wasn't aware of her apparent strength. "They want that foundation. I wanted adventure. To move. Explore. Find answers. The guild offered groundwork. They gave me footing."

"And big guns."

"We're not mercenaries."

"Sure look like hired muscle. I don't see proctors building communities."

Terri stopped searching and leaned against the dresser to address Candace as the conversation grew more serious.

"We are one," Terri said.

"You're more connected to them."

"That's clearly not true."

"You could stay."

"You could follow. Proctors could use doctors."

"That's not my life."

"And staying isn't mine."

"When you leave, I never know when you'll be back."

"That's the price."

"Which I pay."

Terri stepped back to the bed and sat on its side. She reached out for Candace's hand and held it.

"Patterns have been in our favor," Terri said. "Eridius never deviates far from the Mare Tharsis. I may be back within two or three weeks."

"Why?" asked the impassionate Candace.

"Because that's how the exclaves migrate."

Candace pulled her hand away, annoyed at Terri's sarcasm.

"No, I mean, why do we do this?" Candace asked.

"Because we have…amazing sex?"

"That notwithstanding."

"Don't I come back with the best stories?"

"Until you don't come back at all."

"And on that day, you'll be the only one with the broken heart…as I'll be certainly dead."

"You know that's not better…right?"

"This may come as a shock, but my propensity to travel doesn't preclude emotional connections. I have a family, one I chose. I have brothers, sisters. And you give me a reason to come back. Haven't you ever heard the proverb absence makes the heart grow fonder?"

"Whoever said that certainly didn't consider the world in which we live…and the careers we chose."

The door to Candace's single-room apartment buzzed. It was a reinforced steel door opposite a small dining table cluttered with dishes and across a kitchen equipped with a stovetop, microwave, and sink, though no oven. Terri looked towards the door, aware of who was outside.

"Go ahead," Candace said. "Probably your work wife."

Terri jumped off the bed and made for the door, ignoring that she was half-naked. She opened to a shocked Noah Bennet.

"Hey—God damn it, Terri!" Noah said, keeping his aim on Terri's face. Noah was heavier, taller, and the older of the two, marked with eye wrinkles and drooping cheeks. He wore a flat palladium ring on his index, which Terri never asked about. He was casually dressed in faux leather and denim marked with his proctor chapter.

"I trust your eyes to stay up," Terri said as she departed from the door. She found the rest of her clothes in the bathroom and diverted as Noah entered the apartment. He passed halfway into the dining area, noticing the covered Candace on the bed.

"Noah," she said.

"Hey Candace," he said.

"You look good."

"So do you."

"I'm naked."

"Beyond that."

"I gave her the adventure speech," Terri shouted from behind the door. Noah addressed the bathroom.

"Adventures are reserved for fiction," he said. "There's nothing bold about killing or being killed.

"See?" Candace said.

"You're not helping!" Terri said.

Noah stepped closer to the door and whispered in cryptolect, "Commissions are in. Our names are on them. Word has it we lost a chapter somewhere in the void." Noah only spoke a few seconds to convey that message.

"Totally not a language," Candace said.

"Still not helping," Terri said.

Noah turned away from the bathroom and browsed through the nearby kitchen.

"Have any cookies?" he asked.

"Noah!" Terri said.

"What, she's a good cook."

"I'd say come back tomorrow, but we both know neither of you will be here," Candace said.

"I'll make sure she comes back," Noah said with a wink. "How's the clinic?"

"Clinical. The only death I see comes from people like you. I spend the rest with locals patching cuts, prescribing painkillers, and ensuring the brothel hands don't have venereal disease."

Noah stopped and considered the implications of what Candace said. He tried his best to appear inconspicuous.

"Is that…a…severe problem?" he asked.

"Damn it, Noah," Terri said, squirming as she emerged from the bathroom. She was fully adorned in her jet-black, skin-tight, full-body proctor flight suit, blessed by numerous pockets and mechanical interfaces affixed to ankles, elbows, and other joints. Her gloves were off and shoved in a pouch.

"I'm just asking?" Noah said, noticing Terri was fitted perfectly as she zipped up her chest. "That was fast."

"Don't ask what I skipped," Terri said.

"Unlike you," Candace said, "Noah probably should have a girl in every port."

"That requires too much effort," Noah said. "I can't even manage one."

"Just waiting for the perfect girl isn't enough, Noah; you have to put yourself out there."

"I literally do that every day."

"You two caught up?" Terri asked.

"Suddenly in a rush?"

"She hates long goodbyes," Candace said.

Terri approached the bed.

"Well, pardon me for catching up with a friend I've known longer," Noah said.

Terri crawled onto the bed and offered a long kiss, which Candace accepted. Noah stood back and waited patiently, averting his attention, staring at a kettle on the stove.

"I'll be back," Terri said. Candace grabbed Terri's flight suit and held her.

"Don't promise," Candace said.

* * *

Noah and Terri approached the exit of the housing block with light spilling from the door. Passing windows revealed the marginal utopian paradise beyond.

"You going to tell her," Noah said. Terri glared at him. "Eridius is bound for the Techna Planitia. Probably six months, at least."

"She's used to distance," Terri said.

"No, she isn't. You assume. One day, she won't wait. Frankly, I think it's a miracle she put up with you this long."

"Why is it that family waits, friends wait, but love can't? Is it really that delicate?"

"I wouldn't know." Noah stopped short of the door. "Look, Candace is a friend, but I've steeled myself to the eventuality that one of us will deliver the bad news. And honestly, I do hope it's me for purely selfish reasons, but that does come with the added responsibility of repairing the damage left behind. I even had a speech memorized."

"Oh? Enlighten me?"

Noah shrugged, trying to recall what he had written.

"It puts the fault of everything entirely and appropriately on your shoulders and that she's best to grieve in portions when away from the rest of her fruitful and productive life. She's seen her share of death. She'll get over you."

Terri took a few seconds with a nod to consider what Noah had said. She smirked.

"You summarized," she said.

"Yeah, it's a lot longer; I didn't feel the need to itemize a list," Noah said as he pushed open the door to the outside.

"I'd do the same for you," Terri said.

"My family, such that they are, have acknowledged the reality of my eventual and expected abrupt demise long ago." They emerged into the brightness of morning, and both took a second for their eyes to adjust. "And I don't know much about relationships, but I do know that love's connection is both fragile and destructive when broken. But we consign ourselves to it…because…I don't know; we're sadists, I guess."

Eridius was home to over a hundred thousand, one of the first exclaves colonized after humans awoke within the vessel. Refugees fleeing Pyxis took their chances within the superstructure and were soon set upon by watchers. Though many died, the survivors eventually found Eridius. It was another three hundred years before the Union rediscovered it. By then, the new nation was booming under a stable democracy.

Noah and Terri took a minute admiring their domed colony. The most striking element of Eridius was King's Table and the Black Cliffs of Erid—the latter a towering drop-off surrounding the single central city. Laced with flint and chromite, the obsidian-colored cliffs rose a quarter of a kilometer from the surrounding waters of The Fearghas that encircled the mainland, forming King's Table.

The sole gateway sat on the only other landmass, Lochlann Island, a kilometer from the Table. Over the centuries, the erid dug into the hard stone and tunneled out a network of roads leading to the coast. The excavated debris was heaped to form the exclave's solitary beach where the waterfront was located.

The waters of the Fearghas were notoriously rough, forcing most of erid to resort to aircraft when fishing and when moving to and from Lochlann Island.

Terri and Noah walked through the capital city of Erid, passing by the Living Stone—the transparent, crystal monolith constantly projecting a bright white light with no apparent energy source.

Initially, the city was relatively small as the remaining land atop King's Table had to be rationed for agriculture. As it grew more advanced, eventually, stacked greenhouses were erected to feed the population, and the city expanded further.

Erid was a majestic city with rounded edges, parks, and mirror-like roofs covered in photovoltaic cells. The city's twinkle could be seen from any spot within the exclave.

They approached the proctor guildhall, trying its best to fit in with the rest of the city and failing somewhat. It lacked the solar roof, replaced with an immense skylight to release crutches in an emergency. The stone wall was marred by the large opened garage door leading into the bay.

Terri's attention arched towards the transparent lattice dome that peaked fifteen kilometers over them. Twenty-six kilometers across, the space was cavernous enough to carry its own climate. An artificial sun attached to the interior provided the simulation of a day cycle.

Beyond the dome lay an ocean of stars, along with Trinity—its supermassive black hole, neutron star, and red supergiant rose over the near-invisible second crest of the peanut-shaped monstrosity they lived in, what the exclave of Eridius sat upon.

Terri was astonished at the scope of the universe, but only for a moment. Noah joined her in admiring the landscape.

"Was fun being home," he said before resuming his pace towards the guildhall.

"Well, they say absence makes the heart—"

"Don't fucking start with that."

* * *

Terri and Noah stridently entered the stadium-seated conference room half-filled with other proctors from other guild chapters. Coulter, the only ordermaster in residence, sat behind a podium in front of a large digital screen that displayed this section of the Mare Tharsis—the flat, featureless region connected to other flat, featureless regions on the skin of the vessel.

"Staplegunners in the house!" Noah said to herald their entrance.

"Wow, somewhat empty turnout," Terri said.

"Who died?"

"Proctors of Macer," Valco of the Covenant Regulars said.

"How many?"

"All of them?"

"They found pieces," Mattias of the Company of Irregulars said. "Identified by DNA."

"Watchers?" Noah asked.

"Have to assume."

Coulter waited patiently as Noah and Terri took two adjacent seats near the front of the room. The illumination was subdued and the walls shrouded in shadow. It made Coulter appear even more ominous in his red and black cloak and scared face.

"As a result of recent losses, the local chapters are spread thin," he said. "We've also received requests to fill out other open contracts." Coulter opened a computer panel on the podium and read from it. "Dogs of Abercrombie?" Three individuals wrapped in green and white raised their hands. "You got Betaden-456, a supply transport. Covenant Regulars?" A half-dozen bound in blue nodded. "Jackers have been hitting up trade routes between Fornas and Aquino. Gammaden-709."

"Some excitement," Valco said.

"Brotherhood of Phylax? We're splitting you four between two active contracts. Have to fill in their ranks. Alphaden-643 and 777."

"Same chapter?" Evora from that chapter asked.

"Of course. Staplegunners. Same deal. A couple of your fellow chapter members are requesting master journeymen to assume command for two active operations. Crate retrieval and personnel escort."

"Spreading thin," Terri said after nodding.

"Most members are still opposite of the Cavin Vallis. Good month before we can even out the ranks. Proctors to ready!"

Everyone stood. Coulter made a fist with his right hand, then covered it slightly with his left.

"*Sentinels in Dark*," he said.

"*Sentinels in Dark*!" Everyone said except for Terri and Noah.

"Wait," Noah said. "When did it stop being *First and Last*?"

"I thought it was still *Who Dares the Void*," Terri said.

"That was last week."

"I liked that one."

"Okay, shut up," Coulter said. "In the absence of other ordermasters, I'm lead. Take your contracts, uphold the oath."

* * *

The two entered the crutch bay of the guildhall—three stories of scaffolding, cranes, assembly cubicles, robotic arms, platforms, and hoists. It was coated in ivory paint with splashes of red and yellow within warning signs. The two descended a short flight of stairs and rattled the grates topping the drainage canals.

"Feels counterproductive to split us between two contracts," Terri said. "They must be thin on stewards."

"Count yourself lucky," Noah said, "Philokalia is beautiful."

"Wait, when did you see the contracts?" Terri asked. Noah reached into his pocket, then removed and offered a personal tablet.

"Coulter was a formality. I checked them before picking you up," Noah said.

"Why didn't you open with that?"

"We got to talking about feelings and relationships like a pair of teenagers, then the potential of cookies filled my thoughts, and I got distracted."

Terri scrolled through the proctor contract. Who was hiring them? Where were they going? What would they be asked to do? The proctors served multiple roles as scavengers, engineers, and explorers. Initially, it was unsanctioned, lacking an official designation as the first expeditions ventured out to brave the catacombs. At that time, local militaries had taken on such risks.

As the number of excursions increased, so did the demand for those trained to handle what would be encountered. As official government-run caravans carried the banner of a nation, a market emerged for independent contractors required to venture deeper in search of the precious technology required to develop a nation.

Eventually, a charter emerged to publicly sanction and designate these contracts. Before being official, and to placate the negative opinion of the human race becoming vultures, these non-governmental expeditions would also be tasked with various other responsibilities, including escort, rescue, retrieval, and exploration. The primary purpose of scavenging would be an informal supplementary responsibility, enabling these contractors to earn extra money and acquire needed technology to make their jobs easier.

These mercenaries were given a name, a common vocation for ex-military or combat-trained personnel. Between the proctors, a new culture emerged. This subset of civilization traded amongst themselves, creating a secret language and guarded guildhalls only they could access.

"Escort from Bythos to Corvos—" Terri said.

"That's mine," Noah said, "yours is the next one."

Terri scrolled further as they walked.

"Harvester retrieval from Philokalia? Never been there," Terri said.

"Maybe fun," Noah said. Terri continued scrolling.

"What, you're not looking forward to chaperoning a scientist," Terri said.

"Got no problem with that. Have you seen the company?"

Terri reached the section detailing assignments.

"Aww crap," Terri said. "Those two. Shameless bigots. You're going to be doing all the heavy lifting. Somewhat relieved you're steward for that one."

"That's what I figured," Noah said. Terri read further.

"Synfallin," she said.

"What?" Noah asked.

"The endolon's name," Terri said. "Is that female? Can never tell." Terri handed back the tablet, and they increased their pace. "They're weird. Got that mask they have to wear all the time."

"Imagine how we look to them."

"Oafish and ugly. Sorry, you got stuck with it."

"What makes it worse is that I'm probably going to be the one stuck listening to some conceited alien snoot ramble on about how important their job is and how much more important they are." He diverted to their crutches in a nearby cubicle. "I think endolons are vegans, so that's going to be a nightmare."

The value or capacity of one's crutch didn't translate to rank or authority. Some were inherited, others purchased. Many were assembled from the parts of fallen allies or scavenged technology.

Terri owned a cage, an enfolded exoskeleton augmented with armored plates and prosthetic extensions. Hands were articulate and slightly larger than her own. The suit walked on its toes; digitigrade was a common feature of most crutches. It wasn't an all-encompassing machine, though vulnerabilities were infinitesimal.

The dominant characteristic of her cage was the second set of additional arms connected to the shoulders. They extended almost to the ground and were tied to a subcutaneous wireless neural processor implanted behind Terri's ear. As she climbed into the cage and activated its systems, she tested one of the secondary limbs; its three-fingered hand spun in place and clapped a few times like a pair of cooking tongs. A weapon hardpoint on her shoulder flaunted a plasma cannon which blossomed like a flower before refolding itself to her back.

Noah owned a more expensive and comprehensive shell—a complete full-body exo-suit—specifically known as a dodger. The digitigrade legs added a few inches like Terri's, but the lack of secondary limbs or prosthetic extensions made his suit appear smaller. It was undoubtedly more flamboyant, with dashes of chipped red metal matched with dark carbon fiber and orange stripes across the chest. A handheld plasma launcher was folded on his back, next to a smaller javelin pistol, both between the numerous flight thrusters scattered over his body. Hidden within his arms sat a set of blades sharpened to an atom's edge.

They each carried small packs with whatever they could fit, be it a change of clothes, snacks, or alcohol. Noah followed Terri out of the bay, and they approached the city's edge, waiting for transport. It arrived quickly, a sizeable wingless aircraft with a cavernous cargo bay that ferried them across the water to Lochlann Island. Its inharmonious stone building dominated the otherwise lush landscape. The transport didn't bother landing, and the two crutches stepped off.

The building was featureless save for granite doors twice their suits' size and an oblong alien access panel that Noah addressed.

"Rhode, Fignas, Klypso, Etaden, Fignas, Fignas, Coro," Noah said as he keyed in the code on the panel. A strange resonance rang out with each press, an alien tongue repeating the command in its indecipherable dialect. The door creaked slowly open. There was always the chance something was waiting for them on the other side, and both crutches trained their weapons. Fortunately, they were spared conflict, staring into the vacant platform. Noah punched in a similar code on the inside, and the platform descended before the doors closed.

The lift brought them to a short tunnel leading to another larger gateway. The hallway behind them moved as they walked, cutting access to the platform.

Lighting was nearly non-existent within the catacombs as the gateway creaked open. Noah came around and took the lead, assertively casting a powerful light down the immense hallway. The walls felt like stone. The ceiling towered ten times their height above. Noah rolled his light about, gauging the dimensions of the corridor.

"There's the shutter," Noah said as he darted down the dimly lit corridor. He pushed in a section of stone, revealing a handle, then removed the panel easily, exposing a hand-crank generator in the wall. "After you, ma'am."

Terri stepped forward, and she commanded one of her spare limbs to grasp the crank. The crutch's immense strength jostled the stuck lever free and spun it faster than any human could. The crank was connected to a generator that supplied power to this section of the ark. Previously hidden shutters coughed as they unlatched, cracked their seal, and lifted, revealing the colossal geodesic dome they had just exited and the space beyond.

The vessel's skin the exclave was attached to continued hundreds of kilometers past, arching down over an artificial horizon. Beyond, the second crest of the hourglass-shaped other half emerged. Distances were deceptive without a frame of reference, but they both knew the crest was thousands of kilometers away.

Their attention shifted to Eridius as it crawled slowly and silently away. It never made sense why the exclaves moved. There were many theories, and most of them were probably wrong.

"Six months," Terri whispered.

Noah grimaced and walked away.

"Should have told her."

PARADISE

At the conclusion of that assembly, a cardinal of the Ahkdanate, Kuni Reklaws, brought forth a young woman. She was barely an adult and clearly terrified. The excubitor pinned her to the table as the cardinal proceeded to cut her skin. The act was obscene; no intelligent being deserved to be treated that way regardless of what would follow. That being said, it did appear to have the desired effect.

From the wound poured out the most brilliant white light. Then we discovered her fear was from being located, not from any pain that might have been inflicted, proven moments later as, before the covenants, the excubitor proceeded to flay the flesh from the creature's body. There was only a breathtaking, luminescent being instead of blood, muscle, and tendon. Such radiance was fleeting as her head was parted from her body seconds later.

The light immediately faded, leaving a shriveled creature that turned to dust before our eyes. The act was barbaric. Admittedly, the truth had been revealed, but I was expecting evidence that such a creature was a threat. I'm still waiting.

Fallah Ellan Palak
Corvos

Kaiden Sivoy jolted, gasping for air as he flailed under the woven cotton animal blanket he found himself under. He nearly fell off the battered wood and iron freight wagon he rode upon. Sacks of wheat, radishes, and tree nuts resting within the bucket-shaped vehicle provided little comfort, with one particular spiny bag embedded in Kaiden's lower back through most of the evening. He grunted upon impacting the side of the wagon and swiveled his head to gauge his surroundings. Kaiden's white hair was unkempt, as was his three-month beard. Various colored stains ran down his once clean traveling clothes.

"Let me guess, you're not a married man, Mr. Sivoy," The wagoner said without bothering to look back. Kaiden orientated himself, noticing the fields of tall amber grass they were passing through. He was borderline impoverished and desperate for transport, wanting to return to the capital before Passover. The wagon was towed by a single kip, a beast that crossed a bovine with an equus in a lean body connected to a feathered frill atop a horned skull that was popular as a beast of burden given they had no known top-speed.

"Was…" Kaiden said as he sat up. His vision was limited to only a few meters, and he rummaged through his boiled leather rucksack, searching for his glasses. "Bizarre point of trivia."

"No one sharing a bed wakes like that," the wagoner said.

"Have we arrived?" Kaiden finally found the case and carefully donned his nearly broken glasses.

"Well, considering we're still in motion, I think the safe assumption is no."

Kaiden felt the hump in his rucksack to confirm he hadn't been robbed while he slept. They were the only ones on this path as few merchants traveled from the south.

"In my profession, assumptions can often be misleading," Kaiden said.

"We'll arrive a good day before the festivities; don't you worry."

Kaiden reached over the car to catch the tops of blades fluttering in the breeze, a tell-tale indicator that they were soon to arrive.

"Been away long?" the wagoner asked.

"Some days…I sincerely wish I had," Kaiden said.

A trio of men clad in tunics, cloaks, and tattered trousers emerged surrounding them, with one blocking the path of the kip. They had ineffectively tied bundles of dried grass around their cloaks to feign some measure of camouflage. Each was brandishing a different primitive blade save one outlier wielding a rather ornate spadroon.

"Hold your positions," the lead bandit shouted as he slowly circled the cart.

"Oh, you've got to be fucking kidding," the wagoner said, hand still firm on the reins. Kaiden did little more than perk a brow.

"Just a random raid, merchant," the lead bandit said. "You got the day's misfortune."

"You can't possibly be that desperate for roots and seeds," Kaiden said as he slowly stepped off the back of the cart, leaving his sack atop a bag of wheat. "He's on the way to market, you imbecile; rob the man when he leaves the city."

"Not the most convincing argument," the wagoner said.

"Can't feed my family on faith," the bandit said. "Aurago has taxed the southern villages into poverty on the Ascension's behest."

"On that, you have my sympathies," Kaiden said.

"We can't make by on that, but the wagon and its cargo will do."

"Peasants robbing peasants while the affluent laugh. You should direct your ire towards those who oppress you."

"Enough of the history lesson, old man!" the bandit said. The other two stepped cautiously forward, and Kaiden noted their apprehension. "Hand over the sack."

"Just three of you, eh?" Kaiden asked, sizing the two men approaching. Kaiden shrugged, though he was just testing his shoulders. His back also felt weird. He wasn't as sprightly as he used to be.

"With weapons," the wagoner whispered.

"Weapons?" Kaiden said with a slight chuckle. He pointed to each bandit. "He wields a harvesting sickle, him a scythe. These are farmers, not bandits."

"And him?" the wagoner asked about the outlier.

"Ceremonial. Not even sharp."

"Step away from the cart or die on this worthless road!" the lead bandit said.

Kaiden rolled his eyes, then reached under his rucksack and removed a one-handed hardwood sword. The three bandits laughed.

"You mock our weapons while wielding a waster!" the lead said, nudging the sickle to advance.

The moment the bandit stepped within reach, Kaiden flicked his sword against the bandit's arm, knocking the sickle from his grasp to Kaiden's, who then drove the blade into the side of the wagon.

The ornamental sword charged.

Kaiden grasped the blade of his weapon with his other hand and blocked the downward slash.

He then wound his blade around his opponent's, rotating the bandit's hand and pulling his weapon free.

Kaiden then kicked the man to the ground.

The now unarmed sickle moved to intercept with a scream, only to catch the tip of the waster in his mouth.

He stood there, jaw filled with wood and Kaiden looking unimpressed before twisting the weapon, knocking out two of the man's teeth.

He recoiled back as the lead bandit finally came around the wagon with his intimidating scythe.

"Make sure not to hyperextend," Kaiden said. "It's a common problem when handling such a weapon."

The bandit lurched forward with a slash, which Kaiden easily avoided, allowing the blade to embed into the wagon. Kaiden drove his palm onto the shaft, attempting to break the weapon, only for an infective slap which still caught the bandit off guard.

"Damn," Kaiden said, "I'm out of shape." He then rolled up to the stem of the sickle, offering the broadside of his waster against the bandit's ear. The man fell back. "I'd offer consolation, but this wagon is the man's livelihood, and I barely have enough copper to get past the gates and buy lunch off my favorite butcher. So, take your weapons and your friend's teeth, and off you go."

The three bandits obliged. Kaiden tossed the ornate sword back and let the group abscond back into the grass. The wagoner never left his perch atop his cart. Kaiden stepped on board.

"You an errant?" the wagoner asked.

"Was never one for chivalry," Kaiden said. "Let's just say traveling necessitates certain talents."

"Well, this doesn't mean you're getting a refund," the wagoner said.

"Wasn't expecting one."

* * *

Kaiden's eyes focused on the trodden path the wagon was following, the closest thing to a road coming from the south. From this vantage, the walls of Sadatoni were the city's singular dominant feature. The land was relatively flat with few nearby mountains, making the cylindrical capital visible from the horizon. At over a hundred meters in height, it cast shadows on the impoverished housing radiating from the barrier.

The southern barbican enclosed a gateway that reached almost to the top of the wall. It was an intimidating cavity wide enough to accommodate a small village. Kaiden always wondered if the city wall had been constructed by giants, as that could be the only justification for its scale, given it dwarfed the buildings inside.

Legend claimed a gate of stone and wood once filled the expanse, having disintegrated centuries ago. Attempts to rebuild resulted in doors collapsing under their weight or impossible to move without employing technology the Aegis prohibited. This forced the construction of a smaller wall and gatehouse under the shadow of the larger one. Barred culverts every wall segment ejected water that flowed into natural rivers surrounding the city. The water would eventually flow to the Kalian channel north of the wall.

The scale of Sadatoni's barrier became apparent as the wagon passed under the gateway, with Kaiden estimating the keystone itself weighed over two thousand tons and measured longer than two galleons end to end. There was a queue as crowds pushed into the city. Each carriage or cart boasted banners trumpeting their kingdom of origin, marked by icons connected to their royalty—the whale of Velora, the compass of Pyxis, or the chisel of Kaelum, to name a few.

"Quite the gathering," the wagoner said. "I imagine every kingdom on Bythos has sent envoys. Will there be jousting, you think. A hastilude?"

"I imagine everything and more," Kaiden said. "Three days of darkness. Competitions. Carousing. Crime. Three days…without the eyes of gods to judge them."

"Is that why they do it?"

"It's why I would."

The wagon cleared the, passing under a pair of portcullises, and entered the city. Kaiden dismounted and retrieved his rucksack and waster. Blades were banned in the city; thankfully, a wooden training sword wasn't sharp.

"Sure you don't want me to take you further?" the wagoner asked.

"Quite all right; I have responsibilities before heading home." He also didn't want the wagoner to know where Kaiden lived. He emerged into a bustling section of the market next to a nearby Ascension cathedral. The cobblestone roads were heavily trodden on by wains and wagons.

Four kips pulling a two-story carriage rolling on six oversized stagecoach wheels blocked Kaiden's committed pace, forcing him to sidestep. The road offered little ration for such vehicles, with some bending overhead signs and forcing passers to duck into nearby stores. The sheer walls of buildings hugging the road stacked multiple levels of houses and shops with walking bridges crossing over the main streets. It was a maze few knew by hand. From up high, the curves and loops of the roads made the city resemble a fingerprint, with red roof tiles occupying every crevice.

A rounded shadow crept towards the city. Dozens of kilometers across, it was blotting the Body of Tyrus and was due to envelop the city in only a few days.

Kaiden entered one of the market squares, with all attention directed on preparations for Passover. Cafes expanded into the plaza. Market carts set up shop. Unfortunately, it also brought the city militia and the local knights into the mix, feeling they had something to prove. The locals flaunted mismatched plates under the flag colors of Aurago and the chariot emblazoned on banners. Soon, the arrogant and ornate members of the Episcar order and Seraphim Torus would sweep in from the Ascension Exclave searching for heretics and those possessing forbidden knowledge.

Kaiden wandered through the crowd, attempting to look inconspicuous and going about it badly.

"Ainsley!" he shouted and waved to a local wheelwright. He then passed a weaver working a loom. "Nicolette, good morning." And then a tanner. "Harbor. How are you?"

"Good…I guess," the tanner said confusedly.

Finally, Kaiden reached a butcher he knew.

"Samuel," Kaiden said as he perused the selection.

Poor town cutters often butchered mouflon and grunter; game was reserved for kings. This one offered minced meat in a bladder, kip legs, whole tied and boned racks of swine, and salted beef from the previous day before sold at a discount. Trussed fowl had been cut and killed that day.

"Kaiden…I'm Harbor," the butcher said.

"Oh," Kaiden said.

Harbor nudged behind Kaiden.

"That was Samuel," Harbor said. "You didn't get any of them right."

"Sorry," Kaiden said as he inspected the fresh hand pies made that morning. Salted meat set with day-old jelly from stew making filled a hot swine fat crust. Kaiden found roasted mustelid and swordbills wrapped in grunter belly hanging smoked and cooked. Unlike other cutters, Harbor used ovis skins to create basic sausages stuffed with wheat, jellied conger, and a profuse amount of herbs.

"Where've you been?" Harbor asked.

"Surprised you noticed I was gone," Kaiden said.

"We miss those we love and hate with equal passion."

"I'm fairly certain that's not true. I was south."

"Missionary? Crusade?"

"Scavenging."

"Thought the royal host and mercenaries would have picked that land clean by now."

"Paradoxically, no," Kaiden said. "After they wiped out a civilization, they did little with the land they claimed. Almost as if it wasn't about the prize but of murder."

"You know, your unabashed opinion of history—"

"Facts; they're called facts—"

"—Is the reason why you're unpopular. People look at you…people who talk. You'd do everyone a favor learning a little discretion."

"Well, that'll be easy next week. You getting ready?" Kaiden asked.

"Three days of dancing, merriment, and revelry," Harbor said.

"Sounds fun—"

"Arrogant knights, religious fanatics, thieving outsiders, political dissidents, wandering adventures that think they own the world, and tax collectors insisting the celebration benefits us more than them. Pinch me."

"Lot of tourists expected," Kaiden said as he was abruptly pushed aside by one of the garish and colorful imperial guards that forced his way to rip a freshly plucked and gutted galliform on a rope he subsequently tossed over his shoulder. The guard's armor was all-encompassing, covering his face, leaving a strip of colorful animal hair jutting from the closed helmet. The guard moved on without so much as a peep.

"You know he should pay," Kaiden whispered, ensuring he wasn't overheard.

"He should, but he doesn't," Harbor said.

"There should be oversight."

"There is," Harbor said with a point to the sky.

"Gods don't count. If you can call them that…I don't."

"Keep that dissenting discourse to yourself for the next week, lest you answer directly to those deities you deny."

"They're coming?" Kaiden asked.

"Worst kept secret. A dying king, a popular regent, timed perfectly to Passover."

Kaiden took a hand pie and tossed a copper towards the butcher before running off.

"Thanks, Samual!" Kaiden said.

"I'm HARBOR!" the butcher said.

* * *

The only chemist Kaiden knew, Ward Marshall, operated a pharmacy dead center in the Milhall District. It was cocky, given the goods sold in the back. The storefront was a nearly empty set of shelves leading to the counter and its plentiful lineup of goods stacked floor-to-ceiling behind the pleasantly plump elderly pharmacist in a white lab coat that recognized Kaiden as he approached the door. Kaiden handed the rest of his meal to a beggar and entered.

"Marshall," Kaiden said.

"Sivoy," Ward said as Kaiden browsed the spartan selection of teas and herbal remedies, a requirement of most apothecaries.

"All set?"

"Philokalians don't have deep pockets," Ward said, "but we'll see. You look like shit, by the way. Correction, you look shittier than the norm. Are those traveling clothes?"

"I haven't been home yet," Kaiden said.

"From where?"

"The Aelon Ziggurat."

Ward's eyes popped.

"That far south?" he said. "Is it still haunted?"

"I wouldn't know," Kaiden said.

"What possible reason would you have to rummage through old bones?"

"Kind of difficult to explain. I found myself in possession of information that compelled me to take matters into my own hands."

"Must have been trustworthy to coax out of your cellar. So why come to me first? Looking to procure some hartshorn?"

Kaiden stepped up to the counter and spoke softly, "I need your library."

"No."

"…and your brain…to analyze an artifact I found."

"Thousands of tourists will be flooding the streets in a couple days. Word speaks of an Ascension caravan. That's Silantine Knights—"

"I know—"

"And purgitans—"

"I know—"

"Meaning every city guard and monitor will be walking like their genitals are clamped in the jaws of a kip."

Kaiden skimmed his fingers along the counter, refusing to step back.

"Nag convoy on the way as well," Kaiden said.

"Exactly," Ward said.

"Which is why this couldn't wait. Best get it out of the way. Trust me. It's worth it." Kaiden scanned the passing crowds outside while Ward ensured his business was empty. "Please..."

Ward firmed his lips, then removed his lab coat, revealing dual leather bandoliers brandishing pipettes, dispensers, syringes, tweezers, razors, scissors, tongs, and thermometers all meticulously cleaned. Ward threw his coat over the counter and pointed to a door beside it.

"And yes," Kaiden said, "hartshorn will be lovely."

Ward's library was hidden behind a false wall in a medical office sparsely populated by state-approved medical books, those supporting natural remedies over ones utilizing technology and proven by science to work. According to city plans, the room beyond was part of a warehouse next door. Beakers, brushes, burners, clamps, flasks, funnels, and tubes ready to brew various concoctions sat on the central table. The prohibition mentioned not the tinctures but the labels and tags affixed or hung from the bottles.

The very words inscribed were outlawed.

Alchemists like Ward would parade their selections openly under the guise of legitimate merchants, only opening their secret safe when needs arose. The outcome of these amalgamations pointed to the malleability of reality, that certain exceptions existed within the logical order of the universe, proving it was imperfect.

This observation was not a popular one within religious circles. The Ascension did not prohibit the production, importation, transportation, and sale of alcoholic beverages, especially if merchants paid their taxes. The same applied to pharmacists and snake oil salesmen. The irony that the Ascension would prohibit the sale of magical potions but allowed frauds to sell nonmagical ones with claims of magical abilities was not lost.

It would be decades before the purgitans would get wise to the practice and attempt to curtail these merchants. The issue that arose came from a potion's nonmagical application. Most potions could be passed off as alcoholic cocktails or tinctures. Many purgitans could not effectively scrutinize a pharmacist's selection to ensure a legitimate solution was not a potion in disguise. Instead, a merchant's store would be searched for a cryption safe, and many alchemists were routed in this fashion.

Ward's knowledge was proudly displayed within ten thousand books surrounding his lab. Kaiden admired his private collection, the forbidden knowledge contained within the pages. Ward observed Kaiden as he orbited the library.

"We're hardly friends…best acquaintances, so this won't be free," Ward said. Without any other acknowledgment, Kaiden removed and offered a small crystal of glowing red and gloss black. Ward accepted and gawked at the stone.

"Is this…you have painite?" Ward asked. "How long have you been sitting on this?" Kaiden ignored him as he toured the collection, occasionally tapping on a tome's spine before moving on. "You son of bitch. You know you could have opened with this."

"I like talking to you," Kaiden said.

Ward admired the stone.

"I can make an invisibility tincture with this," he said.

"If they ever found this," Kaiden said, admiring the books.

"Thirty years and counting."

"To the grave, I'll keep it safe."

Ward watched Kaiden as he scanned the spines of the collection.

"Let's get to it; I can't have the business closed long."

Kaiden approached the table and took note of the equipment, identifying the arrangement of devices and materials; it spoke of a pattern.

"What's all this?" Kaiden asked. "Bismuth, agarwood, spinehorn heart…incanetics?" Ward shrugged. "You're not trying what I think you're trying? Starting small, I hope."

"Everything does."

"Well, like I always said. If you're going to sin, might as well go for a big one," Kaiden said. "Doesn't matter if you forge a potion or a life out of clay; the purgitans will still burn you." Ward nodded while Kaiden sat down next to the table. "You're the best maker I know."

"I'm the only maker you know," Ward said as he cleared the table. "So, come on, let's see what the big deal is."

Kaiden dropped his rucksack on the table. He opened the flap and removed the book occupying almost the whole of its girth. Flourished with wood, stressed in etched copper, and bound in thick black leather, beyond a small symbol in the corner, the tome's most distinguishing feature lay with its elaborate puzzle lock that occupied its entire foredge. Kaiden let it drop with a thump that toppled a glass.

"That's a…" Ward said.

"Big deal," Kaiden said.

"Big…son of a bitch."

"Cover is exactly fifty-five centimeters tall and thirty-four centimeters wide. Adding in the clasp, it's twenty-one centimeters thick."

Ward studied the book. The metal corners were lightly scored, the copper components suffered some tarnish, and the leather cover was weathered slightly.

"Those are…familiar," Ward said.

"Sequence numbers," Kaiden said, "where each is the sum of the two preceding. Twenty-one plus thirty-four is fifty-five."

"That is familiar."

"Only one book has ever been recorded to be that shape."

"An Iokon Apoc."

"Exactly."

"But this can't be one."

Ward stroked the symbol on the corner of the cover, then rolled the book over to examine the blank back.

"Why?" Kaiden asked.

"Well, I've never seen an Apoc."

"No one outside of the proctors has."

"But the description in Karak's book never mentioned a puzzle lock."

"Karak?"

"Karak Rastaban. A relatively infamous Ascension proctor that made searching for the Apoc an obsession that devoured the latter half of his life. Supposedly, the old testament of the Ascension was only a muddled translation of an even older book that he claimed in his diary to have located. But he sidestepped discussing details." Ward spun to return to his library and pulled a smaller book without checking the title. "Spent most of his published journal talking about the history of the Apoc and its prohibition by the church in favor of the newer Opus. He made retrieving an Apoc for the Crypt a lifelong obsession. Ended up finding three. Well…four, he claimed the last was an oddity, an older book that looked nearly identical but exhibited certain…variations."

"Is this storytime?" Kaiden asked. "I thought you had a store to run." Ward opened the smaller book and placed it beside the monstrosity.

"It can wait. The promise of this book drove Karak mad. He followed a trail for three decades. The initial account was pulled from the manifest of a Forthwind Guild sailing vessel as part of the personal library of a Corvos abecedarian who subsequently lost the book when the ship was sunk off the coast of Thalim. Somehow the book managed to wash ashore without water damage where it was recovered by the alchemist Enoch Naraka who attempted to decipher it."

"Naraka is dead."

"Yeah, killed himself; burned his lab before the purgitans got to him. The story claimed this fourth book, in flawless condition, was recovered from the ashes by a local law enforcement officer who donated it to the Royal Library of Patala in Alshain."

"Naraka died a thousand years ago."

"The Ascension confiscated it from Patala."

"Then it's locked up in Altair."

"It was stolen," Ward said, laying back in his chair, "...by a rector apprentice, Algol Almach...who, if you can believe it, was captured and summarily executed, but the book wasn't located."

"Okay," Kaiden said inquisitively.

"Five centuries later, a fishing vessel in the Falkland Firth caught a giant decapus," Ward said. "They cut its innards, and the perfectly preserved book fell out matching Almach's."

Kaiden laughed and stood.

"This is fiction!" he said.

"Likely...probably still true, though. The captain handed it to the curia at the village of Castor. He called the church, and Karak Rastaban arrived. He locked the tome within a wrought iron box believed to suppress magical radiance and took it personally back to the proctor crypt of Altair. Of course, it never arrived. When you find yourself part of a growing myth, one can't help but get involved."

"And with all of that, he never described this book?"

"Only that he believed it was a rogue, extant copy of the Iokon Apoc, but estimated it was far older, potentially pointing to it be an original manuscript—a proof ancient Aegis employed to build their bible."

"Ironic that they would label that book heretical a millennia later. Did Karak ever find the book again?"

"Fifteen years later, in a library in Kaitos. It was returned to the crypt upon orders of the church. Karak was never heard from again."

"How did his journal get published?"

"It was found stuck in a tree. Taken to Corvos, distributed, and subsequently declared profane by the church. Kinda saw that coming."

Kaiden slid closer to Ward as they both admired the tome.

"Is there…anything else?" Kaiden asked.

"Not much. Makes sense now in retrospect why every report lacked information on the book's contents."

"No one's been able to open it. They only assume it's an Apoc because of its resemblance. And this symbol…" Kaiden's finger tapped the cover. "The Godhead."

"The what?" Ward asked.

"Star inset a spiral. This part, I know. It's in Natal Tojilfenias's book, *Deciphering the Impossible*. She's the one that cracked Proto-Script. Ninety consonants, forty vowels, and three tones. A syllabary written form. The Godhead is one of those symbols. A five-pointed star inset within an ever-increasing spiral of mathematical perfection…a ratio matching the sequence numbers."

"Tojilfenias was branded a heretic," Ward said.

"Bastard purgitans torched every lead we had, burning any evidence that they altered scripture. Too bad Natal couldn't continue her work."

"You think this book is indestructible?"

"Surface wear points to the contrary. I just think that it wants to be read." Kaiden fondled knobs, rods, and levers.

"If that's true…then…open it," Ward said. Kaiden didn't respond. "You can open it, right? Should I get a locksmith?"

"There's no key. It's entirely a subject of skill."

"Meaning you haven't."

"I'm not good at puzzles."

"You're an academic."

"Who's bad at puzzles."

"Okay, let me see it?" Ward imposed and slid the book in front of him. Kaiden pushed closer and loomed over a shoulder as Ward worked the mechanism, first checking for what moved and what wouldn't.

The first step was easy—a minuscule hidden dial required fingernails to rotate, pulling a rod out of place. He twisted the handle, popping out a piston on the spine. Ward worked on it before revealing a four-dialed combination lock overlaid in various symbols.

"Yeah," Kaiden said. "I got that far. But this glyph cipher is a real brain buster. The complexity should compromise the lock."

Ward noticed a sliver of steel wedged between two pieces he flicked out.

"Did you try to pry this open?" Ward asked.

"Broke a knife," Kaiden said. "It's quite strong."

"Savage."

"I got desperate."

"This will take dozens of steps."

"The arithmetic is an interesting touch," Kaiden said, which brought a confused look from Ward. Kaiden pointed. "These symbols can be deciphered as numbers. It's a very complex way to indicate a three-digit figure with a single symbol."

"I don't see it."

"Trust me, that's one thing I'm good at. 347, 555, 241 along this one side. Two of those are primes, but I can't figure out a relationship."

Ward pushed himself from the desk, walked to a nearby cabinet, and removed a pen and a pad of paper. He laid them next to the book and scribbled equations.

"What are you doing?" Kaiden asked.

"Math," Ward said. A minute later, after an entire leaf of numbers, functions, and variables, he returned to the puzzle. "It's not a pattern of primes, but of multiples of primes…that's way more complex than I thought." Ward worked the combination lock, and after another minute, the book clicked. Kaiden's mood perked, but that lock only exposed more elements to solve—a slide puzzle, more levers, and a rod eventually pushed, which unlocked the book.

"Fantastic," Ward said.

"It's a test," Kaiden said. "It's not meant to lock people out. I imagine only about one percent of the population would be able to figure this."

"What a voyage for it to be found here," Ward said. "In my life, I never thought I'd ever set eyes on Karak's obsession."

They both just stared at the unlocked book. With the latch open, they could see the foredge and the hundreds of rough pages within. Kaiden ran his finger around the outer edge of the cover and lifted a crack; it groaned like a never-before opened book.

He slowly drew the cover, but it was cut short as several loud thumps resonated from the shop's front door.

Both men jumped, with Ward letting out a quick yelp.

"Gods damn it!" Ward said.

"Yeah…" Kaiden said. "I knew that was going to happen."

Kaiden closed the book without locking the puzzle and slipped it back into his rucksack.

"What are you doing?" Ward asked.

"You have a store to run," Kaiden said. "Can't draw attention this close to Passover." Kaiden stood and slung his pack.

"You're not going to leave me hanging like this," Ward said.

"I'll bring it back after the festivities. I'm going to devote considerable time." Kaiden made his way to the lab exit.

"How did you know?" Ward asked.

"What?"

"Where to find it? The Aelon Ziggurat—that monstrosity. It's abandoned, cursed, and off the beaten path. No one casually goes there, and if there was an account of this, whoever wrote it would have taken it. What prompted you?"

"As I said…difficult to explain, and as you stressed so eloquently, we're not technically friends."

"Then we'll make it a financial agreement," Ward said loudly, the rapping on the door getting louder. "PISS OFF! ONE MINUTE! After Passover, let's work together. I'm the only one smart enough to be trusted with something like this."

Kaiden thought about it, nodded, and then addressed Ward one last time.

"I appreciate the candor," Kaiden said, "…but that's not true."

*   *   *

Several customers spilled in as Kaiden exited Ward's apothecary. He shuffled through the crowd and diverted to a set of stairs to an upper level lined with colorful shopfronts and crisscrossing bridges. He navigated past clothes vendors and cafes toward another set of stairs he climbed. Atop a terrace, several painters were taking inspiration from the view. Kaiden appreciated that the city supported the arts; it was the rest he found deplorable.

He was awash in a sea of red tiles, with a bridge connecting this roof to a taller guard tower, part of a network soldiers used to avoid the crowds on the ground level. Kaiden approached a railing and confronted the inevitable…the encroaching darkness still outside the city.

He looked to Philokalia, the miniature world a hundred kilometers across connected via a pillar only three hundred meters high.

Passover.

During the celebration, thousands would cross via dozens of makeshift cable cars. When it blocked the sun, artificial darkness would fall on the city. Even from this distance, Kaiden could see hills, lakes, and the Castle Kurzel built around the umbilical connecting it to Bythos. Towers built upon mountains were so tall they could pass by similar buildings in Sadatoni. Their capital sat opposite the globe, facing the sun.

On this cloudless afternoon, Kaiden could almost see the entire planet, though most was obscured by the glare, atmosphere, and curvature of the globe.

Security would be tight given the number of tourists, not counting the influx of native aliens from roaming caravans.

Kaiden admired the unique construction. He owned scale models of how the universe operated, the worlds connected via rings or umbilicals to the core world of Bythos he resided upon.

Philokalia was the closest, with the mirror-like planet of Abraxas, where godlike Aegis governed everyone below, the furthest out. But there was no interpretation with Kaiden's scale model, no loss of function or appearance. His orrery matched how the universe worked.

A full-scaled mechanical model of a geocentric solar system, where most planets were hundreds of kilometers apart rather than hundreds of millions.

The gears and motors were locked under the crust of Bythos and controlled everything, including the heaven rings, one of which supporting their sun of Uno. The other worlds, Argose, Kerberos, Grimaldi, Kenoma, and Machina, all smaller than Bythos, were visible this morning, though their connections, either to pillars or rings, often vanished in the haze of the sky.

Philokalia's gravity was the same as Bythos, counteracting its larger rival just off the surface before Bythos took over despite distance or size.

The official name recorded in books referred to it all as the Solokring. In open conversations, it went by a more straightforward name.

Kaiden took time to admire it before realizing what he would need to do, and he marched back down. He found the telegraph station down another block. Messengers, bird or kip, took to their duty every afternoon, and Kaiden hoped to get a letter out before the deadline.

"I need to compose a message," he announced to the clerk.

"To where," the employee asked.

"Corvos. I have the specifics here." Kaiden handed a filled form over.

The employee examined the paper.

"The message, then?" he asked.

Kaiden hadn't written it yet; he frantically grabbed the form from the clerk, flipped it over, and began writing.

* * *

Kaiden ducked into the alley next to the Ascension church. The manhole cover was hidden in an alcove, so no one observed the scholar pulling it off and descending into the catacombs. His lab was built out of an unlabeled basement with a forgotten access door to the sewer. There were no windows, so Kaiden fumbled for a pack of matches he remembered were sitting by a counter but had fallen on the floor.

A curse and a stubbed toe later, he threaded a struck match into the lantern. His library appeared ransacked, but that was part of Kaiden's organization.

He was surrounded by unused trinkets and mechanical inventions, including microscopes and equipment required to grind a lens. Garbage was thrown everywhere from unused or broken creations, and sketches plastered the walls.

Kaiden knocked over one stack of precariously balanced books as he approached his desk. He placed his rucksack on it and removed the unlocked codex. He admired the finish and the Godhead radiating from the corner.

He didn't want to reveal to Ward how he knew the book would be in that specific room within a cursed castle on the border next to a destroyed empire.

Kaiden twisted his head to glimpse the drawing he kept nearby, the one with the bipedal but inhuman figure. Kaiden stared at its oversized head and broad smile exposing needle-like teeth.

"You were right," Kaiden whispered.

* * *

The distance between the capitals of Aurago and Corvos was only a few hundred kilometers, with the latter closer to the planet's northern pole. Such a journey once would take weeks; now, a speedy land whale could cross the gap in less than two days.

Occupying and spreading over eight islands, the College was the southern seat of Corvos royalty. It was the highest-level university on Bythos and operated as the lighthouse and dockhouse for most boats coming into the Corvos capital of Sineotok, one of the greatest manufactured structures in the known universe.

An uncaring hand slammed the knocker on the door forcefully. Within a generous dorm room within the College, a dark-skinned hand pushed through white linen sheets as she stretched. The knocker thumped again before the messenger frustratingly tossed the letter under the door.

The woman stood and staggered towards the door to retrieve the letter. She ran a finger through the envelope and removed the message.

Still stuffing clothes into a pack, the woman fell out of the room. She laced up her black trousers and tucked her tunic before buttoning her suede vest. Her old mentor would not have sent such a message thoughtlessly.

She navigated the generously lit hallway with one wall occupied solely by arched windows separated by pilasters and topped by entablatures. She ignored distractions such as orators, artisans, and musicians.

The woman descended stairs in front of a row of columns supporting an imposing pediment and entered the main square outside the campus. Colonnades ran up the sides of the plaza.

She lamented Kaiden's choice to return home to Sadatoni. They had not spoken in years, and now, she was racing to the station to catch the first whale out of the only home she had ever known.

By any luck, with the increase in traffic given Sadatoni was due to celebrate Passover, finding a free seat wouldn't be an issue. Despite its size, she wouldn't be able to see Philokalia from here, but after a few hours of travel, it would eventually rise from the horizon to mark her approach.

There was one final seat unclaimed, a whale that would set off immediately and travel through most of the night. Perfect. She paid a premium and secured her transport.

As she waited in line, the woman took a moment to read the letter from Kaiden to verify she hadn't missed anything.

…My Friend Terri Zahn, please come to Sadatoni at once…

CONESTOGA

What else can be said—this place makes no sense to us…because it is designed not to.

It wasn't intentional. We assume the weavers were bipedal, with big brains or thin bodies. We thought they looked like us because, in our search for answers, we did not expect anything else.

The other races encountered are as close to mirrors of our own kind as possible. The weavers are the opposite in every way, so how could we understand them? We live in an impossible construct, but to them, it's a shipping container, a suitcase. They pick things that interest them, nothing more. We've been discarded, tossed from their reality back to ours. Reality?

Yes…it only makes sense if you accept that at least at some point, this "container" existed outside of our perceptions and, at one point, extended into a fourth physical dimension. Occasionally, we'll find a door, an access point to their perception, and reality around breaks down. The technology they leave…it was all intended. Those trying to understand this place will go mad.

It will never make sense, so stop thinking about it.

Nekau Weninoff
Aurago Cryption Academy

In 776 AC, Aurago attempted to establish a military base within the exclave of Philokalia to expand interests in the region and extract resources. A legion of five hundred medics, engineers, and other military personnel commanded by Colonel Justin Price established a base within the habitat, which felt like a utopia compared to where they came from.

No one knew at the time that the migration routes of Philokalia and Aurago rarely passed, and the two exclaves wouldn't reencounter one another for another one-hundred and twenty-five years.

Within five, realizing they were isolated, Price officially abandoned his military rank and declared the colony of Ordanos independent from Aurago. When an expedition from Volani arrived in 791 AC, Price had proposed a peaceful relationship. Volani aided Ordanos with much-needed technology to better survive the unusual habitat along with two-hundred and fifty of their colonists.

It was 801 AC when a scab hive arrived. Thankfully, the Aurago-derived soldiers still knew how to fight, starting a conflict that raged for decades. The population of Ordanos grew, and its leadership switched to a republic in 805 AC after Price's death.

In 911 AC, the Aurago exclave returned and attempted to oust the population upon discovering the situation. By then, those in Ordanos were entrenched. As the Aurago military poured out of the Kalian Monument, they were not met by humans but by a well-armed and powerful scab force, eliminating the invaders. As it turned out, Ordanos and the scab colony had formed a non-aggression treaty in a unique situation seen nowhere else.

The exclave was twice the size of Eridius. Given the still limited population of Ordanos, their ability to extract usable resources from the environment, be it minerals, food, or salvaged technology, was limited. Before the *Rough Raid*, Volani had offered Ordanos harvesters—gargantuan, automated walking machines shaped like wine barrels that navigated the lush landscape, searching for anything of value without damaging the ecosystem. Ordanos subsequently contracted the proctors to maintain these machines. In exchange, all the proctors asked was one crate of whatever the machines found.

It was like a kid opening a birthday present. There could be food, rare chemicals, or even errant technology. A proctor chapter once opened their crate to find a logic-marker, a half-dozen transducers, a zero-speed manipulator, a blast driver, three bags of poultry heads for some reason, a perfect chrome sphere, a live grenade, and a necklace of severed toes. Safety policies dictated that crates could not be opened unless within a guildhall.

The four proctors stared at the five-ton metal crate as it was slowly ejecting from the harvester onto a six-legged walking platform known as a carryall. None of them were wearing their crutches.

Deven was a scrimm. Based on their appearance, human scientists initially assumed they were either derived from an avian background or were an evolved chiroptera mammal. It was discovered that although scrimm were more closely related to the latter, they were neither.

Deven's patagium—a membrane between his arms and legs—was barely visible, overwhelmed by a fur body and spines. A small snout protruded under a pair of large black eyes from his canine-like face fringed by massive diamond-shaped ears.

Sloan was human and not nearly as conspicuous with cherry locks and amber eyes. Kaiden was the oldest by at least two decades, implied by the frayed grey hair sticking out from under his helmet. Agosta was younger but taller, with silver strands in a beard under a near-shorn head and a thick, furrowed brow.

"Anyone want to take bets?" Deven said, staring at the crate.

"Corpse," Kaiden said.

"It's not designed to—"

"Unless it can't separate it from anything useful, then it takes everything. Corpse."

"Safe assumption," Agosta said.

"A negative driver," Sloan said.

"Numatter cores," Kaiden said. "Been short on those for weeks."

"Fruit," Deven said.

"Grasping for the brass ring there," Agosta said to him.

"My desires are achievable. After three weeks on dried rations, fresh fruit is worth its weight in gold."

"Touché."

"Well…looks like some lost souls are seeking leadership!" a distant female voice said. The group collectively rotated to find a tall, multi-limbed armored cage approaching them.

"*Who Dares the Void*!" Deven said.

"Hey," Terri said. "that's catchy!" She reached their position atop the hill, noticing the assorted shells and cages at the nearby camp.

"They sent you?!" Agosta asked with a smile. Terri sent a silent neurological signal to her cage, and it outspread to release her from the suit. As she stepped down, the suit folded and compacted itself to an assembly a quarter of its size.

"Only the best!" Kaiden said boisterously as he sprung forward to embrace his old student. "Missed you, sweetie." She held him back.

"You've aged well," Terri said.

"It's been four months."

"Seven, maybe I was wrong."

He released her and stroked the fresh groove below her collarbone. "Is this a new scar?"

"Chicken."

"Those fuckers can be nasty."

"Good to have you, steward," Deven said.

"We had it under control," Sloan said. There wasn't jealousy in her tone. It was more out of frustration they had to wait for Terri to show up.

"Of course, you did," Terri said.

"Ordanos insisted on a master journeyman. Had it practically wrapped until they changed the details of the contract."

"Someone will raise hell in time." Terri then acknowledged Agosta. "And why aren't you in charge?" They shook hands.

"I need sponsorship," Agosta said. He was one of the most respected senior fellows in the chapter. Unlike Kaiden, who despised authority and resisted endorsement, remaining a senior fellow for nearly three decades, Agosta's hardnosed attitude had made him unpopular with certain hallmasters.

"Well, let's make sure that happens at the end of this."

"Our apprentices, Sloan Katona and Deven Serenda." Agosta motioned to the two younger novices.

"Scrimm," Terri said.

"Yes, lucky guess," Deven said.

"In that case, I'm truly superfluous." Deven smirked at that comment. Terri approached the oafish robotic harvester. "Is that it?"

"Ugly little fuck, ain't she?" Agosta said. "Gleans anything it can find, minerals, technology, food. Crams it into the crawler. Any bets on what you think is inside?"

"Fruit, hopefully."

"Thank you!" Deven said.

"Agosta, you're my deputy given rank. Let's talk."

Terri and Agosta separated from the rest of the group, hiking over the crest of the hill near a pristine brook.

"Why isn't Bennet with you?" Agosta asked.

"He's steward on a personnel escort to Corvos," Terri said. "How long before the module is ready?"

"Two hours."

"We can't bring that carryall through the route I took. We're going to have to circle the Altair Basin."

"That'll take two days just to get out of the exclave. Half of us can fly, but the carryall can't. Won't we be late for our rendezvous?"

"I'll keep us on point!" Deven said. Terri acknowledged the distant scrimm, nodded, and offered an upward thumb.

"I forgot how good their ears are," she whispered to Agosta.

"Hey," Agosta said. "Glad you're here."

"Wasn't lying, by the way. You're older than Noah and me. You're not required to genuflect. Just be less of a…hardhead."

"You meant to say asshole—"

"I meant to say…that you're brutally honest; you second guess orders you don't agree with; you refuse to accept raid contracts; you put people before the pact, and you cannot abide the favoritism imparted by those that kowtow to the masters."

"I won't apologize for being honest."

"And you shouldn't."

They continued circumnavigating the camp, noting the dimming of the day and the landscape around them.

"Scuttlebutt has you for headmaster," Agosta said.

"One more step and we can form our own chapter."

"We?"

"Noah, all you guys. Anyone else we want."

"Never liked the name anyway."

Terri unzipped and reached into her flight suit. She removed a flat plastic bottle and offered it. Agosta examined it, unsure of its contents.

"Barley-broo," Terri said.

"You serious?" Agosta said as he snatched the bottle and twisted off the cap. "I am very. Glad. You're here." He brought his nose close to the rim and drew in a deep breath. He closed his eyes and took a slow mouthful, letting the alcohol roll across his tongue. He swirled, then swallowed after every tastebud had its share. He savored the sensation before his outburst. "FUCK!! Me!"

"Been a while," Terri said with a snort.

"Ran out like three weeks ago."

"Well, ration it; I only got the one."

* * *

"I remember something about past assignments," Terri said.

"Yeah," Kaiden said, "you'd think with all the strange shit we've encountered, it'd all be locked in long-term. But see enough…and even the novelty becomes tedious. I've forgotten more miracles than I'd like to count."

They sat beside trees, gazing out through the habitat's transparent roof to the stars beyond. It was a new day, and the group was deep in the exclave's wilderness on route to its gateway. They were expected to suffer another evening within this opulent landscape before escaping into the dark catacombs of the Conestoga's interior.

"There has to be a few of consequence," Sloan said. "Best I got was hunting roche in Kenoma with this guy." She threw a wave in Deven's direction.

"I guess for me, it was Artifact 25-76," Terri said.

"I think I know that one," Kaiden said. "Pyramid?"

Terri nodded.

"Ominous black and topped with a lit pyramidion carved from solid quartz," she said. "My ancestors, the Proctors of Marathon, erred on the side of caution and avoided entering. The first excursion that attempted entry never returned."

None of them were garbed in their crutches and had let a moment of placidity pass as they enjoyed breakfast.

"Isn't the interior larger than the exterior?" Agosta asked.

"We never stepped off the platform at the end of the entrance tunnel, but I can tell you, it wasn't an illusion."

"What was inside?"

"Harsh angles, unnatural terrain, light sources behind floating objects, so we couldn't tell what was generating it. My guess it was a few kilometers across. What about you?"

"Egeria," Agosta said. "One of the captured planetoids. Just one big chamber. One hundred and fifty kilometers across. Maybe hollow, but we never found an entrance."

"This place is insane," Terri said.

"Any of you see a watcher?" Sloan asked.

An uncomfortable silence passed between them.

"Kiron's group tussled with one a few weeks back," Kaiden said, "Lost half their lance."

"Well, I'm sure they thought it was a good idea," Terri said as she finished a breakfast wrap. "Kirons aren't known to be intellectually endowed."

"I'm sure we've all seen our fair share of strange things," Kaiden said as he stood. "We should get ready."

"You guys…" Terri waited for the other two to focus their attention, "…ever have weird dreams?"

"In this world, I'd like to hear your definition of weird," Agosta said.

"I stopped dreaming years ago," Kaiden said.

"That's…another subject entirely," Terri said, "and not exactly healthy. You should see someone about that."

"I got hypertension," Sloan said.

"Atrial fibrillation," Deven said.

"You should…both see someone," Terri said. "Is everyone in this lance broken in some way?

"Appreciate people for their flaws," Agosta said, "not their strengths."

"Don't love a perfect thing," Sloan said. "A perfect thing doesn't need you to love it back."

Deven cracked its mouth to a smile and perked his ears.

"Oh, I like that one," he said.

"Thanks."

"Well, we can just stick a pin in this grade school study group," Terri said as she walked from the group. "Pack out your trash. We're not savages."

* * *

After breakfast, the five proctors approached their crutches. While Terri and Kaiden continued operating their augmented cages, Agosta climbed into a larger shell, a medium-weight jagger passed down over three generations. Like the dodger, it possessed a flight system manifesting as a dozen thrusters scattered about the body. It flaunted the same digitigrade legs but sported considerably more armor and firepower. Agosta's ancestors had slapped on a colorful striped pattern of blues and greens, which he maintained.

Deven required a specific model to conform to his biology. His people built the tanager for such a purpose, possessing a complicated grappling and cable-based transport mechanism in its arms and legs, allowing him to affix to nearly any surface. It also boasted enhanced wings that amplified his own and leg-mounted thrusters that could, combined with pneumatic pistons, launch Deven vast distances.

The absolute beast was owned by Sloan. Her massive rig was a colossus, three times the mass of Agosta's jagger and layered in thick metal plates. It was the largest crutch operated by the proctors. It shook the ground when it walked. Unlike Agosta and Deven's model, Sloan was entirely contained within the torso. Large forearm plasma blasters and a shoulder-mounted missile pack complimented her brute strength. The yellow and black-striped paint made it appear like a very angry pollinating bug.

The squad continued their journey through the domed habitat. The artificial lights above were still increasing in brightness, simulating dawn, and various distant animals could be heard waking with morning calls.

They marched in a line down the hill, across a field of tall grass, beside a waterfall that ran water through a creek before cascading off another edge in front of them. The group stopped as Terri stepped to the cliff edge.

Below her, she noted the reinforced artificial supports holding this upper level stable and the water falling to mist as it fell a kilometer below to a similar environment. Across the expanse, the landscape at this level continued into a forest and distant hills.

"What is it you see," Agosta asked. "A lake?

"Dropoff," Terri said. Agosta approached the edge and noted the second level of land beneath them and the rigid supports holding their level up.

"Why can't anything be normal?" Agosta whispered.

"We're on an alien spacecraft," Terri said.

"Scabs," Deven said over the radio. The team immediately took to cover. Terri and Agosta returned to the group. "I see two scrappers and a reaver."

Terri peered through a set of range-finding binoculars to observe their opponents. The scrappers were little more than a mishmash of salvaged armor in multiple colors covering the insectoid scab underneath.

The reaver was more comprehensively designed, with an array of lance-shaped aerodynamic appendages jutting from its back along with a jumble of thrusters to keep it airborne. The scrappers marched with primitive magnetic projectile weapons built from salvaged military repeaters, while the reaver floated above with a more powerful javelin launcher built from a flechette driver and an index ejector.

Everything technological in the open-world ran off a universal system of modules left over from those that created the vessel. One could build any number of devices from these components, though most of the time, they made weapons.

"Scouts," Agosta said, "we got a hive."

Deven brought up his sniper weapon and peered through the scope. He caught sight of the giant insects clad in porcupine-like armor down the next hill. One was floating upon a cushion of jet exhaust while the others stalked through tall grass.

"What about their treaty?" Agosta asked,

"Can't risk it," Terri said. "And their agreement doesn't extend to us. You got the duty, Sloan. Bring it down."

Sloan's rig lumbered forward. The missile system rotated from the back to the shoulder and locked in place. It opened, revealing its payload. She locked on the three targets, opened her weapon, and launched a salvo.

TORUS

Look to those old brass flagpoles, sculptures, vases, even blasted cutlery.

The old Iokons never knew of smoke and employed its conduit for the banalest of purposes.

It was ornamental to them, and they never knew its value.

According to history, they could not have made such a perfect metal intended for magic that didn't exist yet.

Something doesn't line up.

Ethaniel Collianthus
A History of Lies,
1339 AC

The rattle of the rail car jostled Noah. An empty steel teacup reverberated off the riveted floor panels, and he caught it before it could strike the floor.

Noah glanced out the window of the upper-level observation deck to the expanse of arid plains and the silhouettes of distant ruins barely perceptible from the miasma of acrid dust wafting around the perimeter of Jacob's Creek, which their train had departed from the previous day.

From the outside, their carbody-class train offered the impression of prestige with its uniform and near spotless bullet-shaped gold-accented red skin. The half dozen cars dragged behind matched the engine's external panache. Inside, it was an eclectic mix of luxury and utilitarian design. Large cabins afforded some comfort, intermixed with cluttered machines and exposed iron. The observation room featured oval windows fringed in copper that curved overhead, offering a picturesque panoramic view of the wasteland.

The engine cruised at notch-five, half-throttle, a brisk but still leisurely pace towards the ark of Corvos. Deep within the lower deck of the engine, the train's six tank-hydrocells vented steam to the outside, partially obscuring Noah's view of the decrepit landscape.

"Never the best of views, is it?" Terri asked. She entered without knocking and loomed over him with her short dark hair falling over violet eyes. Gilded sleeves accented her red tailcoat, contrasting against her sable skin. She looked towards the barren landscape.

"Go where the work is, I guess," Noah said as Terri offered a steaming thermos. "How far out?"

"Almost there," she said as she poured the brown brew into Noah's cup. He took in the aromas, following it up with a sip.

"Wow…that's…uh…that's shit."

"No respect for authority," she said, shaking her head.

"I respect you enough to drink it," he said as he did so.

"We're not dating, so you don't have to lie about stuff like that."

"No, but you are the CIC, so I kind of do about certain things."

"Like?"

"You're looking particularly ravishing this morning."

Terri firmed her lips, then shook her head. Noah was her best friend, and she allotted him more leeway with his remarks.

"Go fuck yourself," she said.

"Look to the others for gratification. They'll all take a bullet for you."

"And you?"

"I would gladly push them into the path."

"With such chivalry, I am surprised you're single."

"I'm single because the options out here are limited to you and a spitfire more in love with her machines."

"There's more to the world than this train."

"Funny that you, of all people, would say that."

"Yeah, I walked into that one."

Terri took in the barren landscape dotted with ferns, wildflowers, and islands of dried grass. She noticed one tree-shaped succulent shift a branch, causing Terri to focus on it. For an instant, she recognized the silhouette before refraction from the heat revealed it to be just a cactus.

Or was it hiding?

"See something?" Noah asked.

"Always do," Terri said. Noah was puzzled before Terri rolled from the window to open the door. She offered it to Noah so they could depart the observation deck. "Shall we?"

Noah stood, still wrapped in his weathered duster over a slightly swankier double-breasted charcoal-colored cotton vest and matching trousers. He was a larger man, with muscles concealed under a layer of childhood laziness. Noah stood and reattached an unfastened white suspender. He retrieved his matching pair of brass, silver, and oak double-barreled caplock pistols from the table and holstered them.

As they scaled down the steps, they reached a waiting Mannah, donned in dirtied coveralls with her stained face hiding perky cheeks and pulled blonde hair tied in a knot.

"By the way, we need service," she said to them.

"*By the way*?" Terri asked. "We weren't having a conversation."

"But you two were talking."

"I don't think it works that way," Noah said.

"We need service."

"We're on a schedule," Terri said.

"I'll remember that when we're dead on the tracks with a groundmover on our ass."

"I'll get you some yard time soon, I promise."

Mannah then faced Noah.

"You called me a spitfire?"

It took Noah off guard, and he looked to the stairs leading into the observation deck.

"Did you have your ears to the door?" he asked.

"You left the intercom on," Mannah said.

"WHAT—Wait…was everybody listening?"

Almost on cue, Deven, the youngest member of their group, garbed in his old blue and gold military tunic, passed them.

"Noah, the gallant hero that would hold up a pair of babies while running through a storm of gunfire screaming, SAVE THE CHILDREN!" he said.

Noah shook his head.

"No respect for authority," he said.

"Deven, how far from Corvos?" Terri asked.

"Five minutes."

"And our cargo?"

"Passengers are agreeable if not a little unexciting."

"Let's hope the next run involves something resembling an adventure," Terri said.

"Adventures are reserved for fiction," Noah said. "There's nothing bold about killing or being killed."

"I don't care what the contract is as long as we get paid," Mannah said.

Noah stepped down from the upper level and crossed the gap to enter the engine, only briefly taking in a larger landscape view. As he and Terri entered the locomotive, Noah confronted the conductor.

"Why are we on a schedule?" he asked.

"What?" Terri asked.

"You said *we're on a schedule.* We don't have anything lined up after we arrive. Did you just say that because we're broke and can't afford yard time?"

"We're not broke."

"Can't be rolling either. The last time, we dropped everything on modifications rather than maintenance. We have to replace the hydrocells when we hit the station. So, either we're broke, can't afford a yard ...and you lied...or you already have the next lead lined up."

"Well, to be honest," Terri said, then puffed her lips and exhaled. "If there's an option C—"

"Shit. it's both."

"It's both."

"Did you find it in Jacob's Creek?"

"No, it found me."

"Pardon?"

"Someone knew where we were and sent a message that was waiting for us."

Noah glimpsed to ensure they weren't being listened to. He ensured the nearby intercom was off.

"Can't be. Is it?" he asked. Terri stared at him, giving him nothing. Noah figured it out. "No...Terri." She still just looked at him. "No. No." Terri continued into the locomotive. "No. NO!" Noah watched Terri scale the steps to the cab. "FUCK!"

* * *

Within the wastelands of the Mare Dagos sat the towering fortress stone wall enclosing the ark of Corvos. The shimmering gold and red train crossed the open gate within the anachronistic barrier into an ocean of farmlands and roads interrupted by a dozen massive castles marked by stacked turrets, ramparts, and towers. Several bastions were modified to support smaller buildings that hung over the edges of ramparts or sat atop perimeter walls.

The railroads snaked between the castle blocks, over artificial canals, and under walking bridges. Corvos stood out as the most antiquated ark, given its function as an education center during the Iokon Caliphate, the empire whose ruins scarred the world.

The train passed by the castles Dexacol, Grijahu, and Reischall before reaching its destination at the keep of Scawhill. The half-dozen cars pulled alongside a steamliner of five times that number with an engine three times the height.

"Throw out the anchor, boys," Terri said.

“I’ll see to the unload,” Kaiden said in their digitized voice through a face seemingly made of garbage. “Corvos might be progressive, but I’d rather avoid the eyes.”

“That’s fine, Kaiden, but we’ll be here a day. Find something to enjoy.” Terri said. Kaiden nodded and remained on the train while the others exited.

The station was immense, with visible iron trusses overhead holding a glass roof under gilded stones. Walls of stained wood and copper-plated rails divided passengers.

Noah, Terri, Deven, and Mannah spilled into the crowds.

“Noah, you’re with me,” Terri said.

“Why?” Noah asked.

“Cause I’m a cruel and heartless leader.”

“I just don’t want to talk to her.”

Mannah shouted behind them, “Government commissions are often unspecific on details. How do you know who authorized it?”

“Another Communion fetch quest. It’s always her.”

Terri removed a bound scroll from her pocket and handed it back to the engineer. Mannah unfurled and read as the group crossed the yard, fighting through crowds trying to board the larger train looming over theirs.

“Alienist, paleographer, and church philologist,” she said. “Mouthful. Philologist?”

“Study of history in literature,” Terri said.

“All of this for a librarian?”

“Downplaying all those fancy words,” Noah said. The group emerged from the crowd and passed through the keep gates into an expanse of shops, halls, and schools. Students of various practices ignored the new arrivals as they rushed to and fro.

“I’m new here,” Deven said, “who?”

“Communion contracts are reserved for jobs too menial for their knights or…” Terri said while pointing to a distant tower as their destination, “often is the case, too dangerous.”

“This will be the latter,” Noah said.

Terri turned back to the group. She pointed to Noah.

“Let’s go; the rest of you break up. Take in whatever culture you can find. Certainly, won’t find much out there.”

Terri and Noah departed, leaving the rest to their own interests.

“And the pub is where?” Mannah asked loudly. Several passing students overheard, and all pointed in the same direction. Mannah nodded and followed their direction. Deven shrugged and trailed behind.

“Who’s buying?” Deven asked.

“I got boobs, so it isn’t me,” she said.

"Hey, don't get too boastful, your majesty; what I got is plenty good."

* * *

Noah and Terri entered the lavish circular office of the Communion Proctor in Corvos. Books lined the perimeter, interrupted by the odd artifact salvaged from the ruins of the old Caliphate. She was facing away from them, transcribing TYKOL inscriptions upon a whiteboard from an old unlabeled leather book held open in her other hand. An impressive black glass table dominated the center. The skylight hung two stories above them, and the light above oscillated from passing clouds.

Noah and Terri waited at the entrance.

"Hello?" Terri announced.

"Stand by?" she said while continuing her work. She lacked exaggerated feminine characteristics. Cropped bleached hair above a long neck extended her stretched, elven physique. Sharp, pencil-thin lips hung under a button nose.

"We're on time," Noah said.

"I never said you weren't."

"Behave," Terri whispered to Noah.

"It's a power play," he said.

"The box in front is the down payment," the woman said, still fixated on the whiteboard.

Terri approached the desk and unlocked the waiting crate. Bundled in paper packing sat six brass globes and a pouch of rattling coins.

"Six globe hydrocells and a thousand brass," the woman said. "Will have it delivered within the hour before you leave."

"Good start," Terri said.

"Says you," Noah said.

"Another dozen and ten thousand upon retrieval," the woman responded, finally rotating to face the two. She stopped upon noticing Noah.

"Oh," she said.

"Likewise…" Noah said. Terri glanced at her friend, who returned the look. "Yes, I know. Doctor...Syn Fallin"

"I wish you didn't," Syn said.

"That was three years ago," Noah said.

"Two."

"For what it's worth, I'm—"

"It's not."

"Well," Terri said, "we can just stick a pin in this touching interchange…I thought this was a legal or church matter...is this going to be an issue?"

"Perhaps I should consider another team," Syn said.

"We're here, Doctor Fallin. We're able and willing."

"It's not a matter of faith...it's a matter of…"

"It's the latter," Noah said. "You're not expecting us to survive."

"Aww, you do care," Terri said without sincerity. "You underestimate our abilities, doctor. Now, if you please, the contract?"

Syn stepped closer to her desk to place her book. She retrieved a pen and opened her ledger.

"Very well," she said. "Affiliation?"

"Independent Transport Union," Terri said.

"Train?"

"Vanderov Express."

"License Code?"

"RBX-888."

Syn paused.

"RBX is a privateer designation," she said.

"We're not pirates," Noah said.

"Of course," she said with a slight sarcastic tone, "legal pillaging only."

"Artifact retrieval?" Terri asked.

"Yes."

"Technology?"

"The details are in the contract."

"Generous compensation," Noah said. Syn circled the deck and handed a bound scroll to Noah.

"Note the destination," Syn said. Noah unfurled the contract and read the details. He centered on an important point.

"Oh," he said, then handed it to Terri. "It's the latter, skipper."

Syn's brow furrowed, and her attention shifted between the two.

"You're the conductor?" she asked.

"Sorry, I don't have my hat," Terri said.

"My apologies for being presumptuous. I rather enjoy the idea of him taking orders from you." Noah rolled his eyes. "Do you have faith in…the rest…of your crew?"

"Every one of them. Fully capable," Terri said.

"And they can manage any threat or situation presented?"

"Absolutely. I command a full complement qualified to handle any encounter."

"What's a full complement?"

"Us and four other people," Terri said as she rolled up the scroll.

"That's…it?"

"All we need. We got a railrunner," Terri said, "a tooley who's a real ballast scorcher, and our bug slinger is—"

"I'm sorry, ballast scorcher? Bug slinger?"

"Rail slang," Noah said.

"Our engineer is capable," Terri said, "and our brakeman is a loginoid."

"A loginoid," Syn said

"That going to be an issue?"

"On the contrary, it's a selling point. Are we settled then?"

"Not exactly," Noah said. "You sent a message specifically for us, but you weren't aware I was on board." It twisted into a confrontation, but Noah needed to know the truth, not that it was easy to come by with Syn. Not that she ever lied, only as an alternative to speaking the truth, she wouldn't speak at all.

"You were on record for prior Communion contracts," Syn said, "and you were the nearest on file. Seeing you among the crew explains why."

"How important is this?" Terri asked.

"Very," Syn said.

"So why not do it yourself?"

Syn didn't answer.

"She already has," Noah said. "How many expeditions preceded ours?"

"Two," Syn said.

"First one didn't return, so you sent another. Did anyone come back?"

Syn paused, delaying the inevitable. Noah was right; she wouldn't lie.

"Not…exactly," she said.

"Well, that instills me with confidence," Terri said.

"A compartmentalized report you're not privy to," Noah said.

"As you're no doubt aware. The church employs me; I'm neither indentured nor a priest."

"But you do pray," Noah said.

"They won't send another noble stock," Terri said, "so you went looking for the closest train on the list. You've not a clue what's waiting out there. Do you even know what we're searching for?"

"It's in the report," Syn said.

"…and how did it know?"

"Is that necessary?"

Terri took in a long breath and blew it out as a sigh.

"Technically…no…and we're not in a position to decline."

"Skipper?" Noah asked, but it wasn't a question.

"We'll accept. Have the payment delivered hastily, and we'll depart within the hour."

Terri offered only a passing glance to the other two, shook her head, and left them alone.

Syn took a step closer. Noah remembered her beautiful green-blue eyes.

"Be careful," she said, faking apathy and failing. "There's a part of me wishing you'd said no."

"Just do it," Noah said, changing the topic. "...I deserve it."

"You won't even try to make amends?" she asked.

"It wouldn't help."

"It'd offer the opportunity for me to disappoint you."

"You can and should take the opportunity to lash out. If you want, I can feign remorse and beg for absolution—"

"Doesn't work if you telegraph—"

"But don't think you ever had or could disappoint me."

"Then why—"

"I did what I did because I made a single critical error."

"I'm riveted by your sudden desire to expound. Do tell."

"I hated your religion more than I loved you." Syn's mouth opened to counter, but she stayed silent. "I had faith in you, but I couldn't absolve who you answered to. This is business, it's different, but if you wanted my heart, they couldn't have yours."

"So that's why; it wasn't out of selfishness?"

"That's how it manifested, and I admit it was misdirected. Your response was warranted, unavoidable, and unfortunately…expected."

"Complete the mission. Come back alive. Get paid. Like you said. Business—"

"You should've lashed out. Just as you should while I'm here."

"I took the—I'm taking the high ground."

"Your people DO like claiming they're above everyone else—"

Syn drew her hand back to strike.

"About fucking—"

Syn struck Noah across the face with an open palm as hard as she could, and it rattled his skull.

He felt it and let the pain sit.

"Feel better—" he said.

"Come back…and then I never want to see you again," she said.

Noah made for the exit.

"You're better than the people you follow."

* * *

"I didn't realize you had a fan club," Terri said to Noah as they left the castle. They crossed a courtyard populated mostly by better-dressed students. "Let me guess; you told her she was the only one until you shouted another's name." Noah kept silent as Terri practically orbited him. "Boomers do it all the time. Deven, Mannah…Hell, Kaiden would if they had any urges."

"And you?" Noah said. "You got that girl, Clara, in Aquino. And what's her name in Pyxis?" Noah snapped his fingers a few times, "Shatlo?"

"Sharlto."

"And here?"

"Candace, but you know that; you met her."

Noah's mood perked.

"Ohh, right," he said. "she's nice."

"She baked us cookies."

"She baked us cookies. Is your conscious clean?"

"Spotless. Everyone knows each other. As long as I keep moving, I never have to stop." Terri perked her brow to Noah, but he kept silent, forcing Terri to stop in the middle of the courtyard. "So?"

"It wasn't that?" he said. Terri remained motionless, her arms open. "Do you seriously need to know?"

"I can't think of anything else right now."

Noah continued walking, and Terri followed.

"She's not Communion," he said, "but she handles contracts for them in Corvos. I...stole a salvage lead off her desk."

Terri pulled on Noah to force him to stop and confronted him. She wasn't angry, more impressed.

"Wait, the job in Grimaldi!?" she said. "That's how you got it?!" Noah grimaced and continued walking. "I'd take my hat off for you if I had one. Still feels like an overreaction on her part."

"And Fellose Falling. Blind Hollow.

"Three times—"

"And…Jacob's Creek. Palatino. And Grimm's Crossing."

Terri was dumbfounded.

"I take it back," she said. "I hope she slapped you."

"She did."

PARADISE

Whoever he was, he knew everything about us, the Crypt, its contents, even what vestiges to avoid. He posed as one of us, employed the helm, walking openly until locating her. He drew chalk to vaporize the cell wall.

I don't believe she knew him; how could she? By her reaction, he had been a stranger until that moment. While the helm got them out of the Crypt, security had locked down the Exclave by this point. Then we located the cloak—they had already teleported, abandoning the chalk and the helm. He had spent a life's fortune to acquire precisely what was required to break out this single creature.

Subsequent decades entertained dozens of theories. This individual possessed one of Paradise's most powerful relics and squandered it, breaking out a living statue from the most heavily guarded prison in the universe.

A few of us believed he was a duke, some powerful lord hiding in plain sight. No, she was not a trophy, and no one gives up that much power in trade. And it was no paid mercenary working for another; else, he would have sold those relics and bought a small empire.

I read of legends speaking of knights slaying fantastic beasts hoping to rescue a princess. In this situation, she was both the damsel and the dragon.

Eighty-five years later, she returned to the Crypt of her own volition. She had given in to a moment's despondence upon the death of her lover. Her cell was upgraded in furnishings and security, and she has not attempted escape since.

Altair Account File
534e789s5ge4yt98nou6i
Untitled

"The episcopate requests your presence," Carthan said.

The obedient member of the Episcar order, adorned in ceremonial plates and banners, placed the scroll on the capacious wooden desk populated by lenses, display stands, books, and dozens of loose pages filled with notes. The knight rolled the scroll across the table, and it tapped a goblet of wine beside the sitting proctor.

The sacristy sat in an annex off one of the abbeys within the exclave. Noah employed the decorated cylindrical chamber as a provisional office when outside the vault as it contained numerous artifacts potentially fated to be sequestered.

Beyond the murals presenting the thin and smooth featured Aegis the world worshipped, illustrations of dubious accuracy, most of the room was dominated by display shelves, cabinets, and wardrobes, with Noah's desk dominating the opposite end from the door.

If Noah stood, the knight would still dwarf him. While appearing that Noah had let life behind a desk influence his slightly plump shape, it covered a later life of discipline and calisthenics. He was also older, with a few wrinkles beginning to show. His brown and gold boiled wool cassock covered much of his body.

"I think you have me confused with someone important," Noah said.

"They said to look for the elitist, arrogant snoot in the Altair sacristy," Carthan said.

"Okay, that does pretty much narrow it down."

"Noah Bennet, Proctor," Carthan said. Noah retrieved the scroll.

"By name?" Noah asked.

The knight stepped closer.

"You've been recognized as someone of authority within Altair," Carthan said. "According to record, you have personally documented the acquisition of vilon, zebul, and machon class vestiges. Your certification of the Spiral of a Thousand Suns was comprehensive. It was noticed."

"By?" Noah asked as he slowly pulled the seal from the scroll.

"Someone able to command you out of your tomb."

Noah held the scroll down with a stone on one end and his goblet at the other.

"Tombs are reserved for the dead," Noah said. He read over the directive. He saw the repugnant symbol of the purgitan order atop the paper, the inquisitors the rest of the church despised. "Purgitans…"

"Are you rejecting this?" the knight asked with an upturned nose.

"What's your name?" Noah asked as he brought his goblet to drink. The scroll rolled back up when he did so.

"Carthan."

"Carthan, I'm an Altair proctor, which affords a measure of tolerance. I'm not required to pass judgment or purge heretics. I'm not even obligated to pray."

"Regardless, the order is given."

Noah nudged the scroll back across the table to the rector.

"We don't associate with the inquisition," Noah said.

"I thought you'd be honored," Carthan said, flicking the scroll back to Noah. "Correction…you should be."

“I was raised behind these walls and focused my professional life on studying the universe,” Noah said. “I will not be a tool of the zealotry, thank you.” He stood and tossed the scroll when Carthan raised his hand.

“The purgitan leads the envoy; he did not put in the request.” Carthan threw the scroll back, which Noah caught. He opened it over the light and scanned down to read the details of the order. He found the critical detail he previously skipped.

“Aegis,” Noah whispered.

“As said,” Carthan said. “It was noticed.”

“Why?”

“Never question the gods,” Carthan said as he marched towards the exit. “We depart in the morning.”

“You’re going as well?” Noah asked.

“Full parade, obvious given the company. Settle your affairs; don’t be late. And…for your own health…don’t be seen.”

Noah sat back down on his desk and opened the scroll again. He confirmed his previous observation…that a procession of Ascension carriages was due to leave for the Auragon capital of Sadatoni from the Ascension exclave in Aquino, a caravan populated by purgitan inquisitors, members of a Silantine Guard, as well as several Episcar knights. Noah would be the only Altair proctor, a request transmitted from the Aegis Conestoga, which would be rendezvousing with the convoy just outside the destination, likely before the crossing of the Kalian Channel. Noah confirmed the unmistakable signet stamp pressed into gold candlewax representing the Aegis making the request. Each one possessed their own, though Noah wasn’t aware of who this one belonged to.

“Questions,” he whispered in an empty chamber. “they’re all I have?”

Noah’s fingers gently caressed the lump of flattened wax.

“Who are you? And why...would you ask for me?”

* * *

Noah exited the sacristy and crossed one of the many courts of the exclave—the city-state enclosed by the kingdom of Aquino. The walled metropolis was the sovereign nation owned by the Ascension, residing within the peninsula north of Aurago. The Prior Piazza was its largest square and one of the few open to the public who had been massing since that morning to ensure good seats for that afternoon’s execution.

Noah had no intention of lingering and briskly spanned the expanse connecting the sacristy with the Episcopal Library. The Seminary lay to Noah’s right, with the walls of the Caddel Gardens on his left. Beyond the nearby buildings, in the distance half obscured by low clouds, rose the Canton Obelisk, the half-kilometer hollowed monument that served as the home for the church's archbishops, a construct that dwarfed all others on this planet as per Ascension doctrine. Noah had never been inside. The entire exclave was built from heavy masonry, though with the obelisk, it appeared as a single uniform carving.

The formalities of the killing had taken up most of the day, starting with orations from Machus, the palatinus of purgitans, parading in his traditional garb. The oversized standing collar covered his lower face up to his ears, and pads accentuated his shoulders under flared sleeves. Buttons, ropes, and ceremonial chains hung off the cardinal as he proselytized.

A group of Silantine guards flanked him, marked by towering leather and steel hoods matching the shape of the obelisk behind them, adding nearly an arm's length to their height. Even this was shadowed by the purgitan enforcer, whose opaque helm was shorter but twice the width and topped by vents from which white smoke wafted. He was wrapped by an immense collection of perfectly matched plates and overshadowed by an intimidating executioner's blade marrying blade and axe. The man was herculean in stature, heightened by risers in his boots.

The whole of the spectacle was reserved for a single male individual tied to a post atop the raised platform. Noah guessed the victim was barely out of puberty. There was no visible ethnic difference between the prisoner and those watching.

"It is our sacred mission to preserve the purity of our species!" Machus said to the adulating crowd. "Never forget it's been only ten years since our deities commanded us to crusade, to bring about the fall of heretics, they who sheltered the chaff, who now flee scattered across this world. Do not be fooled by their diplomacy, their civility. They are the weaker people. By sympathizing, we make ourselves vulnerable. They see this as cruel only because it strips them of the power they'd willingly steal from you…and your children. Know that offspring is our most precious commodity, one they would draw from to make themselves mighty!"

The words were familiar to Noah, paraphrased from the Iokon Opus, the revised testament that replaced the apocryphal tome centuries ago, which few alive have read, not even Noah. The new book was turgid, pedestrian, meandering—simplistic propaganda to convince the masses. Yet, it was also skillfully demagogic, fashioned via an unsophisticated vernacular to sway the most elementary of readers, enforcing ultranationalistic and theocratic views. Indoctrination required a sacrifice. In lieu of ethnicity, the Ascension selected the perfect scapegoat, those who weren't human at all.

Noah found his objective sitting at a table outside a café that spilled into the square. Tyrel Corwin was a vice-dean at the Suburbicarian Holy College, and his tawdry attire pronounced that to everyone passing by.

"Coming out of your tomb, Bennet," Tyrel said as Noah approached. A waiting seat welcomed him, but he didn't accept. Sitting on his side of the table rested a weathered and unlabeled brown leather-bound tome with frayed corners and rough edges. A pair of mugs and a steaming pot sat in the center. Tyrel was drinking.

"Just to remind me the sun still shines," Noah said. Tyrel nudged a chin towards the book.

"Well, that's it. Was bound to flame in a day. Proctor prerogative, I assume."

"Exactly," Noah said as he accepted the book.

"Tea? I got a good spot here," Tyrel said as he drank.

"I have no desire to see this." Noah offered only a superficial glance at the inevitable killing. Machus was still pontificating on his platform, but to Noah, it was only a discordance of bigotry.

"Is it true," Tyrel asked, "that there are those of you born within the tomb who live out the whole of existence within it, and die without ever seeing the light?"

"I leave folks like you to deal with conjecture. Proctors involve facts." But yes, Noah knew of them, but it was a secret shared by only those that lived within Altair.

"Huddled in the darkness, surrounded by science," Tyrel said.

"You know the church once supported the pursuit of knowledge, the quest for truth. Someone that chairs the college should know that."

"I misspoke. I'm not criticizing the practice. Days like this…occasionally I envy what you do."

"Why are you here?" Noah asked. "If you disapprove…"

"I can't be seen disregarding tradition," Tyrel said. "That's another proctor prerogative. I've laced my tea with enough alcohol to cloud my empathy."

Noah tapped the end of the book on the wrought iron table and then slipped it into his satchel.

"Wish I was so easily swayed. Thank you for this," he said. "Every word saved from our past preserves our future." Noah turned to leave, hoping to clear the square before the inevitable occurred.

"You'd do well dwelling in darkness," Tyrell said. "Purgitans are growing popular. A day may come when they knock on your door. When the last heretic is put to flame, they won't stop; the circle of intolerance will only grow smaller."

Noah said nothing else and continued his steadfast dash to the opposite side of the square.

"Know that they seek no civilization, no faith, no desire to genuflect to the true gods of paradise!" Machus said. "The Aegis command we put them all to flame save only a few, to remind us why we killed them. They question our gods, and we…are that answer. Do not forget: they may appear like us, but it's a husk, a coat covering their hidden stain!"

Noah managed to reach an alley leading to a set of stairs descending into obscurity—one of the many entrances to the Crypt of Altair, all unlabeled to dissuade interlopers. He offered a final glimpse to the platform when Machus unsheathed a short single-edged blade and slid it across the victim's arm.

Instead of blood, a beaming white light spilled out, like the skin was only a sleeve masking a hidden star. The young man still screamed as a human should. The brilliance was enough to sway the crowd, and they lost all lingering sympathy, cheering the coming demise.

"Fucking barbarians," Noah whispered before exiting the square.

* * *

The thirty-meter wide circular crypt door weighed close to 60 tons and was locked by a six-point pressure system. The hinge, as large as a carriage, swiveled the massive gate outwards to a waiting Noah. He nodded in gratitude to the pair of proctors tasked with operating the ancient apparatus and entered Altair.

A ball of light floating via a pair of fixed stone wings drifted overhead Noah as he crossed into the massive chamber so large that the light couldn't reach the walls.

He descended further, glancing by a darkened annex. Similar floating balls slowly illuminated, basking the kilometer-long, four-level repertory in a soft glow. It was only one of a hundred different caches within the crypt. Noah considered the wisdom locked here, reserved for a small brotherhood within the Ascension, the knowledge he knew and was sworn to keep secret.

Within the Exclave existed the most secured vault outside of Abraxas, erected to accomplish one thing—to contain all the anomalous objects, entities, and phenomena that disobeyed the laws of reality.

Magic.

The number of these items pointed to the universe's incapacity to control every aspect of itself.

The use of these items was prohibited and, if discovered, had to be reported or disclosed to the nearest Ascension representative. According to them, vestiges, despite any positive effect they may offer, posed a significant threat to the stability of the universe. An item breaking the laws of creation may spread to infect others, resulting in the eventual destabilization of reality.

Vestiges included weapons, armor, books, clothes, furniture, rocks, statues, animals, and—very rarely—people. No one knew how a vestige came about—it appeared utterly random.

Patterns eventually emerged after centuries of documentation, all recorded later by the proctors of Altair. The more complicated the item, the better the chance it would break reality, potentially the source of the forbiddance of technology by the Ascension.

Only the upper echelon of the faith (outside of the proctors) was permitted within the Crypt of Altair. The actual vault existed several levels below the ground, within the superstructure of Bythos's interior, with deeper levels containing the more dangerous examples.

Hundreds of floating lights radiated outward from the four corners of the illuminated cube sitting in the center of the expanse. A counterweight, pully-augmented platform descended from an upper level, the clanking gears echoing off walls hiding in the darkness. The elevator was forbidden technology, but the rules put forth by the Aegis did not apply to the crypt or the proctors operating inside. The cube's walls were transparent and within sat three floors layered with bookshelves, display cases, and a bedroom.

The platform reached the floor, and Noah stepped off after locking the lift in place. He carried the pack under his arm. Reaching the perforated glass and steel walls, Noah pulled a simple chair from a collection stacked a few meters away. He dragged it across the stone, dispersing the echo across the chamber. A metal door and chute allowed the passing of items into the separate building. A single door forged from leaded iron weighed close to a ton and hadn't been opened in forty-five years.

A solitary woman sat at a desk within the transparent structure. She had shoulder-length red hair and was draped in an ornate and patterned fringed white and silver sleeveless cassock. And nothing else. She swiveled her chair to Noah and smiled. She didn't look more than thirty years old. Her eyes presented contrasting colors, blue and yellow.

"Evora," Noah said as he sat. He opened his satchel but placed it on the ground.

"Noah. Good afternoon," she said. Her voice was calm and soft. "Do you have anything for me?"

"Yes…but I'll get to that."

"Must be important for you to break up the pattern. You're not due until tomorrow."

"I won't be here tomorrow," he said. She closed the book she was reading. "Don't be concerned. I've been summoned."

"By name?" she asked.

"Yes."

"Then I am concerned." Evora stood, approached the glass, and tended plants growing in the corner.

"It's part of the profession, but I appreciate your regard for my safety."

"You're my friend."

"Again, that's appreciated. Regardless, we should tend to matters." Noah removed the unlabeled brown leather-bound tome with frayed corners and rough edges of his pack, placed it on the pass-through, and pushed it into the structure.

"Corwin told me this made the latest prohibition list," Noah said. "He offered it rather than put it to flame." Evora accepted the book on the opposite side.

"*Operatio Sphaerae Coelestis*," she said. "Figured its time would come. Did they kill him?"

"Corwin? No, of course not."

"Not him…"

Noah wasn't aware of how Evora knew. Perhaps another proctor mentioned it. He even might have offered it in passing.

"Yes," Noah said.

"They'd kill me if they could."

"You're immortal, not indestructible…thankfully, they don't know that."

Evora nodded, then opened the ledger and noted the entries. She wandered to a card catalog and pulled several drawers.

"Proctor Zeta Kennison recovered Item class machon, file number 543-Alphaden-456," Noah said.

"Yes…bands of ignorance," she said as she removed a card. "Locked in strongroom Venture-Aura M23."

"Says someone wearing the band is ignored by everyone and everything that can see, hear, or smell the wearer. Invisibility?"

"No, the target is still tangible and visible—we simply ignore the wearer's existence."

"Useful."

"It was…" she said. Noah smirked, knowing what Evora meant. "By the way, someone misfiled 645-Betaden-567. I corrected it."

Noah opened his ledger, flipped a few pages, and verified.

"Infinite Yarn," he said. "Just a vilon. No big deal, but thanks for the catch." Noah's brow perked up, and he reached into his satchel to remove two smaller softcovers. He tossed them into the pass-through and pushed them into Evora's chamber. "Oh…completely forgot. Two more recovered from the Volani crusade."

Evora removed them and inspected the near-featureless covers.

"You mean pogrom."

"Yes, I misspoke."

"Prohibited?" she asked.

"Of course."

"The best kind. Fiction?"

"About magic, knights, and monsters, sooo…probably not." Noah smiled and chuckled. Evora followed as she added them to a stack organized on a metal workbench next to her desk.

"Thank you," she said.

Noah removed his pencil and jotted a few notes.

"I've been beckoned to Sadatoni," he said. "Aegis are attending the Passover."

"Who requested you?" she asked.

"They did."

Evora took in a deep breath and pushed it out.

"My thoughts exactly," Noah said.

"They are prescient," Evora said. "If you don't know why maybe you will. Not for something you have done but for something you will do. You had to join the rest of the world eventually."

"If that's the case, why did you turn yourself in?"

"Because a life I had. You should try it." Evora returned to her chair.

"The dice were rolled at my birth," Noah said. "I was cursed with curiosity in a world that considers apathy a virtue. I was fortunate to find myself in a magical vault with every oddity the universe could spit out at my disposal."

"And the cost was just your soul."

"A bargain."

"You always found knowledge more valuable than faith."

"It's a staple of the proctors."

"And you're about to rub shoulders with purgitans. Ideological opposites."

"All segments feature two ends. Most lie in between. Maybe I should embrace this opportunity. Ensure they don't exploit the voice of gods."

Evora laughed and shook her head.

"You're naively optimistic," she said.

"This vault itself is a vestige, an aberration that breaks reality. Within holds an immeasurable number of wonders, both revolting…and beautiful. Dogma dictates Altair exists to sequester what we cannot destroy. But ask anyone here…not just me. We're caretakers, waiting for our time for enlightenment. I hope to be alive that day. When the vault is opened, and the knowledge contained within it floods the world."

"I wish I was so confident."

"Mark my words—one day, you'll be free."

"That was never in doubt," she said. "Freedom means to be unbound from fear. I'm freer here than I was when I was hunted. I've been asked why I came back, why I don't escape. I don't have to. Immortality begets patience. I'll wait for the locks to rust, for the stones to erode."

"You don't consider that ironic?" Noah asked.

Evora smirked, then slammed her fist into the metal workbench, buckling the legs, cracking the apron, and leaving an impression on the top. She held up her arm, revealing the skin of her hand had faded up to her elbow, replaced with lightly tarnished copper. Noah didn't jump from the outburst; Evora was proving a point and not articulating rage.

"I'm not made of iron or stone," she said.

"I forgot, you're forged of sterner steel," he said.

Evora chuckled. She had no lungs or vocal cords. The glammer covered her artificial body, and breathing was part of that illusion. Noah often wondered if she did it intentionally to appear human or if it was an automatic process like it was with him.

"Does nothing shock you?" she asked.

"Part and parcel of the profession—to react to everything like I was expecting it…no matter how crazy it may appear to others."

"One day, something will legitimately astonish you, and it's unfortunate I won't be there to see it happen."

"You and I have cataloged more items than anyone else, even those I call elders. Eventually, even the amazing can appear mundane. Besides, wonder precludes impartial analysis. We both know the universe is telling us something. One of us just needs to listen."

"In that case, may your gods guide you to your next great mystery."

Noah slipped his ledger back into his satchel and closed it.

"With that tone, are you worried I won't return?"

Evora kept her stare on Noah, exposing the wisdom behind her old eyes. She was one of the oldest things in the crypt, older than Viotto "metalman" Albertine, Mortal Mathew, Offensive Adam, and the magical tree Arbor Vitae. It had been decades since she turned herself in.

"Mabuza's Chordophone," Evora said after a somewhat uncomfortable pause.

"Excuse me?" Noah asked.

"Next on the list."

CONESTOGA

There's no greater example of how odd weaver tech is than looking at a hypersolid. It can resemble a cube, then, with the application of energy, change into a sphere without expending any power itself.

It opened so many questions involving the curvature of spacetime and the existence of higher planes of existence. We realized we could build devices that could reach outside of our visible universe, to become what they needed to be on a whim.

And what was the first thing someone did? They made one into a gun.

Proctor Nicol Corella
995 AC

The lance approached the three scab corpses, with only one of them even partially intact. Sloan's barrage had annihilated an acre of grass and destroyed all life within it.

"That was easy," Deven said.

"You need to shut the hell up with your baited responses," Agosta said as he stepped upon the scorched land.

Sloan used a foot to push the helmet off, revealing oversized eyes and a broken mandible.

"These things creep me out," she said. "Almost human from the outside."

Agosta knelt next to it and used his secondary limbs to roll the body as he examined it. He noticed something and motioned to Terri.

"Take a look at this," Agosta said.

Terri took a knee beside Agosta, immediately spotting the torus-shaped inscription on the beast's armor.

"How odd," Terri whispered.

"What is that you think?" Agosta asked.

Kaiden loomed over them.

"A tribe, a hive designation," he said. Kaiden offered only a slight shrug before helping Deven and Sloan in their attempts to salvage anything of value from the remains.

Terri ran her fingers along the groove. There was a familiarity with the shape, something she had forgotten. Agosta looked over Terri's shoulder. "You recognize it," he said, not asked.

For an instant, Terri held onto a thought, perhaps a memory—an image. But just as quickly, it faded, like the fleeting recollections of a soon-to-be-forgotten dream.

"Yeah," Terri said, "…but from where?"

Deven removed a severed tarsus from a scab's armored forearm. At the same time, Sloan cut into the pronotum of another corpse, gaining access to the internal workings of the powered armor. She knew the scab's awkward flight system was of some value, but it was far too large and unwieldy.

With all people in the Conestoga, be it scabs, scrimm, khitin, or endolons, technology was derived from the weavers, those who built everything and somehow left behind an easily comprehensible system of machines, devices, and power cores any civilization could use.

"We got chimeratanium," Deven said as he threw everything recovered in a pile, "a couple ounces of quasaline and a hypersolid."

"Average haul," Kaiden said.

"Have to cut the casimirite off their armor."

"Their weapons are a different story," Sloan said. "Precision chips, repeater indexes, and I think I can salvage the flechette driver from the reaver."

Terri nodded.

"Take everything; burn the bodies."

"Sir!" Deven said as he reached into one of the scab's armor. He removed what resembled a fabric-sewn toy doll of a small pet. Terri and Agosta approached.

"They hit someone," Agosta whispered. "…recently."

"Get everything loaded in the packs," Terri said. "Document it."

"That could take us all day," Deven said.

"You in a rush to get home? Take the casimirite as well."

Deven said nothing; he only resumed his work.

Agosta whispered to Terri, though Kaiden could hear, "Adding a day increases risk, longer journey back. Might not be economical."

"You're point?" Terri asked back.

"You're looking to pick a fight?"

"If they've broken the alliance with Ordanos, we need to know."

Agosta nodded.

"I'll prep for us to stay another night."

*   *   *

"Okay, you bungled and botched," Terri said as she approached the group. The artificial sun was fading, and they were still a day from the habitat exit. "We need sentries; who's going on watch."

"I'll do it," Sloan and Deven said in unison.

"Decide amongst yourselves," Terri said as she walked away.

"Yes, ma'am," they both said.

The human and scrimm took a minute to survey the dimming landscape. Philokalia was beautiful in its own way—two levels of lush greens and browns separated by a brash network of metal supports. A river from one would cascade to a lake below with no other connections between them. This was a good thing considering the monsters that roamed below. There were enough gaps in the upper level to keep the lower illuminated, but shadows were abundant, and they heard growls often from them.

"Looking forward to Kenoma?" Sloan asked. She knew Deven had been away from his home exclave longer than most other scrimm. He perked an ear to her. "How long has it been?"

"A while," Deven said. He couldn't remember the last time he thought of his home; he almost forgot what it looked like. The forest of rock with the scrimm structures hanging off. Bladders floating in the sky with roches hunting for their prey.

"You can retire," Sloan said. "Give up the oath. I'm sure family's missing you."

"If I had value there, I wouldn't have left. But you have a point. The knowledge gained could serve my people. I should consider their wants. What would you choose?"

"I'm a bad one to ask."

"Because you have no home?"

"Oh, I have one. My rig's the foundation—you, Terri, and the rest of the chapter form the walls. My responsibilities keep the roof up. A house is a pile of bricks and wood…A home is its people."

Deven cracked his mouth, and his eyes opened.

"I like that, but it doesn't preclude the obligations my people would impose."

"We humans make selfishness a virtue."

"And yet," he whispered, "you have kept your feelings for Mr. Pike a secret. I would consider that an act of—"

"Suicide, an act of suicide," she whispered back, "if brought up aloud again. I should never have told you."

"You didn't; you're a bad liar. Relieve me in four hours, yes?"

Sloan grimaced and walked away.

* * *

Sloan Katona scanned the surroundings near the end of her shift. She peered through the night vision mode inside her rig, transforming the landscape into shades of grey. She alternated between snacking on a protein bar and adhering to her duty.

She thought over her life, how she earned her armor, and her place in the proctors, occasionally glancing towards the sleeping Agosta. She remembered him sponsoring her enlistment in their group when she tried to prove herself.

She later commented that he said little more than "her record was all that was required." Sloan knew he had been single for some time after a divorce—proctors were always difficult to live with. They were constantly in motion, often prioritizing their guild and armor over physical relationships. Sloan was amazed Terri had kept one up for so long.

Any emotional connections were often reserved for those with who proctors traveled. Sloan never knew her family. Her history was inscribed within her rig. She salvaged the wreck, rebuilt it in her spare time, and learned to operate it in a junkyard when off school.

She knew Agosta was older—she could read it in his face—with family ties recorded in the proctors for generations. But she also knew he respected independence and personal strength, often rebelling against expected loyalties to family and favoritism. To him, everyone was a blank slate.

Several quick raps on the side of her suit startled her, and she opened her hatch to a still waking scrimm.

"Time..." Deven said as he slowly worked himself into his shell. "Nothing?" Sloan shook her head as her shell stepped back as quietly as possible. "Apologies about the comment. Your personal life is your own."

"You've told me as much about yours," she said.

"But I'm not private about whom I'm attracted to. Why is it...or rather more appropriately, what is it?"

Sloan faced him.

"Pardon?" she asked.

"Is it the age difference? Authority? Perceived wealth?"

"Holding me back or him?" Sloan asked.

"Either."

"On his end, you'd have to ask."

"Okay," Deven said.

"The fuck you will. Broach to the topic," Sloan said, forcing a pointed finger at him, "and you'll find first-hand how sharp those spines of yours are." Deven laughed. "I don't care how old he is...even if I knew?"

"He's forty-five."

"Admittedly, that's high, but he looks younger. As for authority, I don't recall any policies against workplace relationships."

"Page 245, verse 8," Deven said. "Page 312, verses 10 through 15."

"Okay, point taken—"

"Pages 350 through 371. The entirety of chapter fifteen."

"Enough, I get the point," Sloan said.

"And I know it's not wealth," Deven said. "You've never cared for what one carries in their purse. Proctors don't encourage antiquated gender roles, so it can't be you waiting for him to make the first move."

"Okay, I admit…I don't know why," Sloan said. She tapped a few buttons on the inside of her suit, and it folded backward, allowing her to lay back into the padding, affording some measure of comfort. "You know me well enough; I'm sure you'll figure it out."

"Why is that?" he asked. Sloan sat up and glared, clearly tired. "Why do I know you that well? We have shockingly good chemistry for being different species."

Sloan sat back down, closed her eyes, and darkened the tint of her helmet.

"I dunno…you had a trustworthy face," she said.

"If you say so," Deven whispered as he looked over the darkened habitat.

* * *

Deven was easily bored and hated sitting up. Their group operated a security network of laser sensors around the camp perimeter, but it could easily be circumvented within habitats like Philokalia. Philokalia was also known to boast some impressive predators. There were the vectors, predatory canines flaunting large ears, lean frames, oversized jaws, and a pack mentality, making them highly effective opponents. They were also capable of volplaning by extending all four limbs and exposing a membrane. This limited flight was an effective attack measure. Deven hated it when people would claim scrimm and vectors shared a common ancestor. They did not.

As Deven peered through the scope, something caught his attention. It was large. Deven brought up his sniper weapon and zoomed in on the shape.

Humanoid, it was standing atop a distant knoll.

Further in, Deven noted its frail, skinny physique. It almost looked like an endolon, but there was something wrong with its proportions. As Deven zoomed in, he took in additional details and grew terrified.

Deven instinctually pulled the trigger.

The blast immediately woke Sloan, who quickly ran up to Deven, weapon at the ready. Deven fired again, though he lacked a target. It had moved, and Sloan was frantically searching.

"Deven…what's the target?!" she asked. By then, the rest of the squad had awoken.

"I saw it. I saw it!" Deven said, his ears down, his brow furrowed.

"Does one of you want to enlighten me!" Terri said as she marched still out of her suit.

"Serenda was shooting," Sloan said.

"On edge, Deven?" Kaiden asked.

"I saw it," Deven said.

"What?" Terri asked.

Deven whispered as if saying its name was akin to a curse.

"The Operator," he muttered. Kaiden grimaced.

"You idiot," Kaiden said.

"It was him!"

"It's a stupid myth."

"Maybe it was that cult," Sloan said. "Those, what do you call them, jackers."

"It wasn't someone dressed as him," Deven said. "It was him."

Agosta approached to finally join the commotion.

"An omen," he said.

"We need to go," Deven said, frazzled.

"You think it was warning us," Sloan asked.

"We have a mission, you juveniles," Kaiden said.

"Which direction," Agosta asked.

"45 degrees," Deven said with a point.

"Not where we came from," Terri said, "not where we're going."

Terri moved from the group, offering Kaiden an annoyed frown. Kaiden broke away from the others to follow his commander.

"What do you think?" Kaiden asked.

"We have a mission," Terri said. "We're professionals. No detours."

* * *

They approached the knoll, following Deven's direction. It was a mundane hill crowned by tall grass with gilded tips. In another time, lovers would frolic among the blades professing their feelings. Before the scabs had migrated to Philokalia, that might have happened once or twice.

"This is the place?" Terri asked.

"He was right here," Deven replied as he approached the top of the hill. There was no indication it had been disturbed by anyone. Sloan and Deven unsettled the calm grass as they searched for evidence.

Agosta trusted Deven like he trusted every member of his lance. Deven was not prone to delusions and never lost his cool in the heat of combat. Although Agosta didn't vocalize his opinion, he assumed the account was accurate. He glanced to Kaiden, who was growing frustrated, then to Terri, who was staring out rather than in.

"Like I said," Kaiden said, "waste of time."

"Perhaps not," Agosta said, "Terri?"

"We wouldn't have been able to see it from our route," she whispered.

"What?"

"That." Terri pointed to the valley below and the scattered rubble from a destroyed vehicle. "Looks like the scabs took out a refugee caravan."

"An omen."

"Fascinating that we live in domed habitats that move along the surface of a giant alien spacecraft…and this is what unnerves me."

The group descended to the valley, aware that scabs could still be in the region. They moved in battle formation, with firearms deployed and weapons systems active. Deven floated behind them while Sloan crushed the pristine land as her rig claimed every inch it walked.

Agosta and Terri were the first to reach the wreckage. It was once a colony carriage, the type of vehicle that blossomed into a residence in minutes. This one had been ruthlessly torn apart. Fragments scattered across the valley like the vehicle had been attacked with a million knives. Even the frame had been shredded.

"They took…everything," Terri said.

"They had…nothing," Agosta said.

Terri scrutinized the area, noting the scattered debris, including fragments of helpful technology.

"You're right. They had nothing," she said. The group caught up as Agosta and Terri walked through the chaos. "This wasn't them."

"Fullerite," Deven said, analyzing the rugged terrain. "Broken numatter core. And what's left of a Wexler frame."

Agosta joined in the salvage, tossing debris and searching for anything of value.

"Couple broken bottles of bio-gel—" he said. "No one is this sloppy."

"They're scavengers," Kaiden said, "like we all are, and their success depends on their efficiency. Why would they shred the carriage—its very hull had value…and to leave power cores."

"An act of rage?" Deven asked.

"They're bugs with a hive mind—" Terri said.

"They have those, what do you call them, viles, scabs that think for themselves. There's one known to live here—"

"In. Deed," an inhuman voice rang out, resulting in the proctors immediately forming a perimeter with the carriage wreck in the center.

Sloan remained in the center while Deven took to the air. Agosta only looked up from his rummaging.

"Track it!" Terri said, "Deven!"

"Must be using a relay!" Deven answered as he scanned the terrain.

"Who is this?" Terri shouted.

The voice hissed and popped as it spoke, with each word enunciated the best it could through labial palps and a hypopharynx. The voice was deep, so much so that it appeared to originate everywhere.

"You. Speak. Intelligence," it said.

"Actually," Kaiden said, "we said you think for yourselves; intelligence was never assumed."

"Why. Call. Us Vile?"

"We didn't coin it."

"Skaras," Terri asked, "…yes?"

"The. Name. Your. Tongue," Skaras said. "Signed. Treaty."

Deven watched the shape hiding within the trees at the base of the hill. It employed natural and synthetic camouflage, but it was clearly immense. Deven pointed to Terri, who approached the vile's crutch, a colossal multi-legged machine that would be a formidable opponent if diplomacy failed.

"The MAD Accord," Terri said.

"MAD?" Deven asked.

"Mutual Assured Destruction," Kaiden said. "Signed with Ordanos in 901 AC."

"Was. There," Skaras said.

"That would make you 600 years old," Terri said.

"Age. Human."

"You're the one commanding the nest in Philokalia."

"Influence. Half," Skaras said.

"Who did we take out yesterday?" Agosta asked as he met up with Terri and Kaiden. They were now standing at the hillcrest, staring directly at the massive black shape in the woods. They could count six limbs and at least five different mounted weapons.

"Bugs," it said.

"No loyalty?" Terri asked.

"Devotion. In. Congregation. Death. Of. Few Unimportant."

Agosta whispered to Terri, "Arrogant much?"

"We're contracted to Ordanos to service and recover their harvesters," Terri shouted. "If you keep your people at bay, we'll pass without further aggression."

"Caravan—" Skaras said.

"Our salvage," Terri interrupted.

"Not. Us."

"We know…then who? We heard of creatures in Philokalia. Demigods."

"Always. Ten. Demigods. All. Slumber."

"Then who?"

"Your. Mystery. We. Not. Engage."

Terri nodded.

"Thank you," she said.

The shape within the forest drifted deeper into shadow, its immense size, that of a house, becoming clearer. The proctors didn't know how much was machine and how much was scab as it slithered into the darkness.

"So, not local fauna," Agosta said as he resumed his salvage of the carriage.

"How long?" Terri asked, moving back to the wreckage.

"Looks to have been at least a day," Agosta said as he pushed through a mound of rubble, the only significant mass remaining.

"Will Skaras keep his word?" Kaiden asked Terri.

"What word does he have to keep?" Terri answered. "Mutually assured destruction isn't what I'd call dependable grounds for a ceasefire. I do believe him…it… in that they weren't responsible for the attack—"

"We got a survivor!" Agosta said.

The group gathered around the heap as Agosta cleared the rubble, exposing the young girl. She had eyes of jade and a sharp chin under blonde hair, familiar traits to Agosta, who immediately tried to remember if he had seen them before and where.

Terri moved closer and whispered, "It's okay, child." Agosta regained his focus and gently coaxed her free from the rubble.

"Deven…do your magic," Terri said.

The scrimm approached and knelt beside the girl. He opened his medical kit, removed the scanner, and checked the survivor's health.

"Physically, she's fine," Deven said.

The girl didn't appear scared or stressed and occasionally looked to Agosta as he and Terri stepped aside toward Kaiden.

"Agosta, what is it?" Terri asked.

"Déjà vu," Agosta said. "Probably nothing."

"Maybe on a hazard bulletin," Kaiden said.

"What do you mean?"

"She's a cultist."

Agosta and Terri surveyed the location, finally noticing the telltale indications that this was a jacker caravan.

"Best we keep an eye on her," Kaiden said.

"What's your name?" Deven asked her.

"Elina. Elina Prescott," she whispered. The rest of the team turned upon hearing her. Terri nodded.

"That's a good start," she said, "nothing terrible unusual—"

"And you're Agosta," Elina said, looking at him, "Agosta Pike."

Agosta stared back at her, too shocked to respond.

Terri sighed.

"Never mind…" she muttered.

TORUS

There is nothing like Uno…or so we think. There are far better ways to provide light and heat within our world; this method could only exist in this fashion if it's imitating another phenomenon. I've had dreams of this reality, of a sky filled with spheres like Uno surrounding a spherical world we reside on.

—

Laugh all you want…but we have detected fields radiating from Uno, with magnetic poles aligned perfectly with the center of the Torus. An identical field is generated from our world. It's what makes our compasses point toward the center of the Column. Initially, I theorized that the field was employed to regulate systems like the Stream, Stormwall, and Uno, which is likely correct to some extent. Except, the magnetosphere generated from the Torus would have to reach outside the shell, which tells me there's something outside.

—

Shut up! You don't get it. Gravity pulls inward; Our world doesn't make sense!

Kabbanala, Dr. Emet
The Kabbanala Lectures on Physics
Volani Institute of Technology
1045 AC

Probably the greatest marvel of the Metropolis was its vast and complex lattice of rails crisscrossing what remained of the once sprawling world-spanning city. The airburst that tore buildings down left the network relatively intact. Ruins and fallen debris made vehicular traffic near impossible. A solution was found within the ark of Volani, who sent out goliath trains known as groundmovers to clear the rails from debris, vehicles that operate in the modern age twelve hundred years later.

The Groundmovers were the first to reach other arks and cleared the path for many smaller trains to follow. These included steamliners and the more vulnerable conestogas operated by independent contractors and refugees. Later, custom-made trains of varying sizes emerged, many of which were either caravels or privateers, rendering a vast population mobile.

After centuries of exploring, eventually, regions of the once-great city were renamed and, in some cases, reclaimed, reducing the relevant title of "tracklands" to a patch of flatland between the arks of Aurago and Kaelum.

A billion kilometers of track, some still obstructed by ruins from the original collapse. Some areas were saturated by nonsensical patterns that made little sense, leading to the rise of the railrunners—extraordinarily talented conductors with an instinctual awareness of which path to ride. These individuals were especially valued in the sprawl—unclaimed wastelands of the old Iokon Metropolis populated by ruins in various states of decay intersected by thousands of train tracks. There were regions with semi-intact city blocks and others with little more than debris.

However, it was neither lifeless nor infertile, and nature had been slowly retaking parts of the wilderness. The world had been suffering under arid conditions for the entirety of recorded history. Some archeological and geological evidence did indicate it was not always the case. Although there were bodies of water, they were deficient, given the world's size.

Few forests remained, and although the Stream occasionally supplied rain, it was too sporadic to impede the expanding deserts. A series of canals were carved into the inner shell to ensure water ran to every corner of the Iokon Metropolis. While many were later clogged by fallen debris, stuck floodgates, or sediment, others still crucially supplied water.

The surviving canals connected the arks, creating the only reliable avenue of travel between the cities. This network defined many of the territorial borders.

Agosta found the subterranean entrance near a smaller canal, underneath a fallen temple. He navigated the sand-covered steps as they descended into darkness. His eyes adjusted upon reaching the base. The voice he heard echoed through what must have been an immense chamber.

"Come alone?!" Kabdila asked.

He wore mismatched leather with padded shoulder protection and brass buckles laced over his chest. He was tall, with soft blue eyes overshadowed by short, dark hair and a molded figure. His simple lever-action rifle was aimed at Agosta's head.

"Do you see anyone else?" Agosta said as arms lifted in the air.

It was an underground cavity with everything carved from stone. Iron supports towered several stories over them and fanned out ribs across the ceiling to support the chamber. Several overhead lights sprinkled insufficient illumination below, casting shadows through imposing statues of forgotten warriors that loomed from either side. The gothic building was built into the opposite wall but carved perfectly as a standing structure, with flying buttresses, pointed arches, colonettes, and spires.

Kabdila was not the only bandit with weapons trained on the singular Agosta, with a half-dozen not as fashionably dressed surrounding him. Kabdila stood closest, with the last bandit beside the double oak doors leading into the building.

"Don't get smart?" Kabdila said. "Search him, 'Kotto."

Phankotto kept a nine-barreled pepperbox trained on Agosta as he approached. Agosta had dropped a bag in front of his feet that the outlaw ignored. Phankotto counted two empty holsters, then orbited the back and unstrapped the ornate sword on Agosta's back.

The outlaw grumbled through broken teeth, "No weapons, but a sword. Nice one too."

"Pocket blaster in my arm," Agosta said. The outlaw apprehensively reached into Agosta's sleeve, unhooked the firearm, and removed it.

"Thank you," Phankotto said.

"No problem."

"Anything else?" Kabdila asked.

Phankotto kept searching.

"A watch. Spyglass," he said. Eventually, he patted every crevice until he was satisfied there was nothing else of concern.

"Good?" Agosta asked.

The underling faced his captain and nodded.

"You speak for the family or the ark?" Kabdila asked.

"Family," Agosta said. "Ark won't step in."

"Is that the ransom?" Kabdila pointed at the bag. Agosta gave it a soft kick.

"20,000, as requested," Agosta said.

The underling grabbed the bag and opened it. He confirmed the stamped brass coins within. He smirked, nodded to Kabdila, and returned, admiring his stolen weapons.

"Taking your weapons as well," Kabdila said. "The cost of bringing them here in the first place."

"Your turn…" Agosta said.

The underling ignored the conversation and carried the swag into the building. He handed the bag to another outlaw, pocketed the pistol, and gazed at the decorative sword, noting its numerous charms, lockets, and trinkets.

"We'll contact you when we're ready," Kabdila said.

"That's unacceptable."

"Unacceptable? You talk as if you have a choice in this matter."

"Crime is business; best to let this one continue as arranged. You have the money; honor your side."

The underling placed the sword on a table next to a guard sitting in front of the door, locked with a dozen latches. The guard admired its finish. The underling left to return outside.

"There's no honor out here. You ark-folk believe when stripped of civilization, we can still act civil. That's the lie. We have to be told to get along. It's not our natural state. Deny any person a single meal, and they'll forget any honor they ever had. Your first mistake was leaving your city believing otherwise."

Agosta smirked and glanced about the area, noting the other guards' positions, vulnerabilities, and potential for counterattack.

"I'll give you one more chance," Agosta said. "Take the money, return my gear, and fulfill your part of our arrangement."

Kabdila laughed.

"In what world do you think you live?" he said as he stepped forward. "In the tracklands, death is law. Those who kill command those who can't. In the land of the weak, the man with the gun is king." Agosta didn't flinch as Kabila stroked the trigger with his finger. "You should have thought of that before giving up your gun and sword. That would be your second mistake."

"Oh," Agosta chuckled, "if we're talking errors in judgment, your first was choosing a path of crime; it never ends well, the benefits suck, and it's generally considered the lesser option over politics. And you made another error assuming I'd be shocked by your predictable and misguided treachery."

Kabdila's smile faded.

"And if we're comparing the magnitude of blunders in our situation, the biggest was your assumption…"

Any sentiment fell from Agosta's face, and the killer emerged.

"…That wasn't my sword."

Inside the building, the guard was more concerned with the commotion outside than the items placed beside him, unaware of the sword as it rattled, found an owner, and impaled him.

The horrifying scream from the building caught everyone's attention, except for Agosta.

The guard inside turned before life escaped him, seeing the smartly dressed woman pull the blade out.

The distraction was the cue Agosta had been waiting for.

As a magician would reveal a card from his open palm with a flick of his wrist, Agosta curled his fingers, and his pair of brass- and pearl-plated single-action revolvers materialized in his hands.

Agosta dove behind one of the crumbling statues as a barrage of gunfire from his weapons took out two of Kabdila's bandits.

Kabdila barely avoided the attack as he exchanged fire from his rifle.

His revolvers empty, Agosta rolled the cylinders over his bandoliers; the bullets fell on their own perfectly into their chambers.

He opened fire, taking out another outlaw as Sloan emerged from the house.

Kabdila and the remaining two outlaws turned quickly.

Sloan tossed her sword in the air and vanished when it left her fingers.

Blind fire from the bandits struck nothing as the blade fell back into Sloan's hands as she appeared next to another bandit, slicing his arms off.

Her blade deflected several incoming rounds from Kabdila.

His weapons again empty, Agosta emerged from cover and ran towards a nearby outlaw as his attention was focused.

The outlaw twisted too late as Agosta tackled him, and they struggled.

Sloan ricocheted one of Kabila's rounds, which struck him in the shoulder, causing him to drop his weapon and fall.

Sloan noticed Agosta, still trapped in a brawl.

"Catch!" Sloan said as she tossed her sword to Agosta, immediately vanishing when it left her grasp.

Agosta caught the weapon and ran the outlaw through.

Freed, Agosta stood back up and stalked Kabdila, who struggled to reload his weapon.

Agosta holstered one of his pistols, then dropped a handful of bullets in the other, the rounds falling perfectly into each chamber.

Once loaded, he fired on Kabdila, disarming him through a round in the other shoulder.

Agosta tossed the sword towards the open air, only for Sloan to appear the instant she caught it.

"Are we good?" Agosta asked.

"Yes," Sloan answered. "I took care of the guards."

"Who the hell are you?" Kabdila groaned.

Agosta pulled back the hammer on his gun and trained it between Kabdila's eyes.

"As you said," Agosta said, "the man with the gun…is king."

* * *

The makeshift jail cell lacked any comforts except a single metal bed frame without a mattress. A plate of stale bread was half-eaten next to an empty jug. A dim oil lamp provided minimal illumination. There were no windows, not even a pass-through in the door.

A shape had an ear pressed to the stone, having heard the gunfire outside. It faced the door as each lock opened from top to bottom. Finally, the door slowly opened, beaming the hall's light into the chamber.

Agosta entered first.

The shape attempted to focus on a familiar face.

"Elina…" Agosta said hesitantly.

"Daddy!!" The young teenager shouted as she ran out of the shadows and embraced him. Her blond hair was pulled back. She had eyes of jade and a sharp chin as she looked to him.

Sloan turned her back on the two and exited the building as Agosta embraced his daughter.

PART TWO

CONNECTIONS

PARADISE

They banned technology. They forbade the knowledge to keep us simple and to maintain their power. It's easy to rule when you own all the toys. But the script was given to everyone; it was the universe itself offering us the tools to control it, to wrest power from the church. It was not technology, but the Aegis didn't appreciate the loophole. They tolerated it at first when it was just potions and the basic cryptions. As political matters of the universe took precedence, the distraction allowed the knowledge to develop. Who knows how far we could have gone? Then one day, one of us cracked the most potent spell, one that could create a soul from nothing to command life into being. Our gods were not about the let that one pass.

Unidentified

Agosta rose from his bed, letting the expensive satin sheets fall to the side. He noted the stone walls, the thin glass rattling in the window frame, a single candle atop a brazier nearly extinguished.

Melted wax dripped treacherously onto the wooden floor. Agosta approached the slightly tarnished mirror and poured some water from a jug into a bronzed basin. He splashed his face while staring at his reflection. He counted a few more grey hairs in his beard and dried off the water from his bushy brow and balding head.

He opened the windows to catch a breeze and feel the heat of the morning sun. He stared from atop the second story of his statehouse, across the cathedrals and taverns, to Turtandan circus, the massive public square connected to the Luminance of Deos via the Royal Path. It was nearly empty now, but that would change.

Shops, little more than decorated wagons, were towed by kips into place at dawn. The animals were cleared out to make way for the upcoming crowds. Hundreds of other decorations adorned street corners.

The shadow of Philokalia was finally encroaching on the city. With Uno's orbit, the city and surrounding lands were due to be blanketed in darkness to last three days save for brief periods at sunrise and sunset when Uno passed between the two words. Lanterns and fires would light the streets for the extended nightfall, encouraged by the additional flare of stringing lights and fireworks fired up from Bythos and down from

Philokalia. A system of lenses and lamps cast powerful beams from one world to the other, providing additional illumination.

Any political tension encouraged between the two worlds by the Ascension was neither believed nor acknowledged by the masses who desired any excuse for a celebration. Agosta readied himself for the additional responsibilities he would endure over the next few days.

* * *

Agosta wandered through the market as vendors prepared for the influx of crowds come afternoon. A cable system had been hastily erected between the tallest points between the two cities. This borderline prohibited technology allowed gondolas to traverse the expanse. A sturdy pully system kept the cables taught while a spool held thousands of meters of slack to maintain the transport while Philokalia passed overhead. Agosta knew the first crowds would be arriving within the hour.

The best place for a spy to hide was within crowds populated by people that knew him. Strictly speaking, Agosta wasn't a mole, though he had been trained for such activity. His responsibilities to his friend and prince eclipsed those of the state, and Agosta hadn't been driven to espionage in years. He was the ears of the royalty, a defender of the realm that wielded neither sword nor bow. His power came from information, and nothing occurred within Sadatoni without his foreknowledge.

It explained his mounting trepidation as an alien world and a foreign kingdom drifted so closely overhead that Agosta could spot the double-headed snake-adorned flags atop the masts of the Hydranis keep. Every year, this occurred, and every year, he would be on edge. But this time, it felt different.

"Kalla!" Agosta greeted one fishmonger. The merchant struggled to stand given the cast on his leg. "How's the leg?"

"Very good," Kalla said.

Another merchant, selling patties, tarts, and puddings from a wagon, took the initiative.

"Mr. Pike!" he said, "Fresh for you!" He tossed Agosta a palm-size almond cake.

"Thank you, Mr. Kimbell," Agosta said.

Agosta wandered through the market, recognizing every trader, vendor, and importer. He nodded acknowledgment to Ward Marshall inside his apothecary. Agosta knew what was sold behind the curtain, but nothing was to be gained reporting the chemist to the Ascension. Agosta appreciated his leverage over men like that, and the more Agosta could cock a snook to the Aegis and their oppressive church, the better.

"Whisper!" shouted a child from an alley. He was adorned in weathered but undamaged clothes, a positive consequence of his dealings with Agosta, who stopped and knelt to greet the urchin.

"What's your name?" Agosta asked despite knowing.

"Nekau," the child said, still panting from running.

"Nekau, a whisper remains that. Screaming makes it a shout."

Nekau stepped back, distressed over potential punishment, though Agosta had never laid a hand on a child.

"Sorry," Nekau said.

"Now, what is it?"

"Friend's father mans the wall," he gasped. "Aegis conestoga on the horizon."

Agosta looked towards the distant city wall, and the gates fixed open, given the influx of arrivals.

"They're early," he said. "It will move to match the speed of the Ascension caravan, probably a few more hours." Agosta attended to Nekau, palming him several coins. "Good boy."

Nekau accepted.

"Thank you," he said, as he began to leave, "and nagomjii."

Agosta snatched the boy's arm before he could get too far.

"Wait…same time?" Agosta asked.

"Yessir."

Agosta released the boy.

"Even better." He handed him another coin.

Agosta walked briskly to a crowd of nearby guards, one of which knew him; he knew them all.

"Phankotto!" Agosta said.

Ennias Phankotto jumped to attention. Agosta was a man that appeared of noble birth but possessed no authority to command city regulators. Phankotto was well aware of Agosta and his influence. The rest of the company was beneath Phankotto's station, so they followed their commander's lead.

"Sir!" Phankotto said.

"I want a list of all the guards operating the gate and double the number in the market," Agosta said.

"I've called everyone."

"Call on reserves. It's going to hit the fan soon."

"Suspecting something?" Phankotto asked.

"If it were specific, I'd know where to stand. Nagomjii caravan is coming same time as the Ascension. Make sure they don't meet."

Phankotto snooped over Agosta's shoulder and grimaced.

"Shit," Phankotto said. Agosta noticed the shift; his mood and his eyes dropped.

"Let me guess," Agosta said.

"Your day just got ruined."

"Pike!" Coulter screamed from across the court. Agosta nudged Phankotto to take his leave, which he did, and Agosta spun to confront Coulter of the Fall—lord captain of the royal guard. Coulter took his elite and ceremonial position to heart. His white-dyed leather-wrapped kite shield was strapped to his back. Custom-fit and polished bronze and steel plates formed a panoply across his body. Most was covered by a monastic scapula flaunting the red and black colors matched to the chariot symbol representing the kingdom while also showing faithfulness to the Ascension faith. His armet was up and locked, slightly covering the stack of feathers sticking up from the peak.

"You have a lot to answer for!" Coulter said as he approached. His shoes added an extra inch, allowing the lord to loom. Agosta casually took a bite out of his almond cake. "To start, the reassignment of militia to be placed under the authority of county sheriffs rather than my guard. The order to pair arriving knights with an ignoble castle sentry, and let's not forget your brazen ploy of allowing aliens into the city during Passover."

Agosta held up a hand and waited for Coulter to settle.

"Wait…" Agosta said. "I stopped caring the moment you said my name."

"You're a pain in my backside!" Coulter said.

"I certainly hope so; it's been a life goal."

"You're poised for one so unarmed."

Agosta took another bite and slowly chewed. He savored the taste before swallowing.

"What you consider poise, I consider stature…" Agosta said. "More important responsibilities require your attention. I know because I assigned them."

"I am rescinding—"

"You will do no such thing because, by the end of day, you'll be up to the prince explaining yourself. Or you can accept that I made sure your placement within the chain of command positions you above the Episcar and Silantine knights due to arrive. No one in this city will answer to them without authorization from you."

Coulter was taken aback, then took a step back, lessening his intimidation.

"Why would you—"

"Because despite my feelings. Despite my…honestly justifiably low opinion of you," Agosta said, "I still trust you more than them. I place faith in your arrogance over their unpredictability."

"You're an asshole," Coulter said with a sneer.

"I'm right."

“Doesn’t change my opinion.”

“Would be shocked if it did,” Agosta said. “I have also taken the liberty of pulling all reserves from the counties outside the city walls. We’ll need them within the inner courts.”

“Why the paranoia?”

“Chariot of the gods,” Agosta said as he started walking. Coulter stood in front, and Agosta stopped.

“Are they coming?” Coulter asked.

“Yes.”

“You sure?”

“Yes.”

“Would you lie?”

“…Yes.”

“Are you lying now?

“What do you think?”

Coulter considered his answer.

“I think it’s a safe bet,” he said.

“And your pageantry proves you’re one who plays things safe,” Agosta said.

Coulter was not about to call a bluff if it was.

“Have you heard confirmation from the Ascension?” Coulter asked.

“Confirmation, what do you think I am, a spy?”

“Are you expecting terrorism?”

“Why, my lord captain, do you consider our gods fallible enough not to foresee such a blatant act of sacrilege?”

“Of course not,” Coulter whispered through his teeth, almost worried such an accusation could be heard by the divinity.

“I agree…it’s every other crime that worries me. And like I said to one of your men, if I knew which offense, I’d be more direct. Do we have an understanding, lord captain?”

Coulter scanned the crowd and ensured no one was listening.

“When are they expected?” he asked.

“My guess within the next three to six hours,” Agosta said.

“Enough time to see to some personal affairs.”

“You still taking advantage of the complimentary service offered at brothels for the royal guard?”

“No…my appetites necessitate the most extravagant of services,” Coulter said as he walked away. Agosta watched him navigate the crowds, pushing his way past people who wouldn’t move aside.

“That image is going to fester,” Agosta whispered to himself.

* * *

Wisekjii knelt upon loose soil.

A collection of polished rocks rested around him.

Eyes closed.

He whispered words known only to a few and heard by the crowd of children and elders encircling.

A mouth with no lips, holes for ears, and when he opened his large eyes, he displayed a kaleidoscope of colors in a sea of white. Despite sounding like a collection of mumbles and groans, Wisekjii spoke volumes the others comprehended.

As he recited, the world swayed to his will. The stones lifted, the largest first, then smallest, orbiting the larger, and as more rose, those observing recognized the recreation of the known universe. Wisekjii spoke the names of the worlds they had given them and the ones the humans preferred.

Children nearby broke from their trance, shouting and pointing to the sky. Philokalia was nearly overhead and was close to blotting out the sun. The waters of the Kalian channel were undulating from the approaching umbilical. The tribe of nagomjii watched a near rhythmic tradition as the pontoon bridge was quickly disassembled and pulled aside. The channel, two kilometers across, had many such bridges, but the Great Kalian Expanse was the most significant and longest to dismantle. Only a few bridges remained.

Wisekjii looked up to the smaller world. He observed the shuffling dots across its surface, livestock, and people. He muttered something to the tribe, and they began packing up, ready to cross the last bridge before it was too late.

* * *

Agosta approached the inner wall of the central castle of Sadatoni, the highest point in the city. Despite this achievement, it was further from Philokalia than smaller builders closer to the Kalian channel, where the pillar connected the two worlds. The walls were higher than the outer perimeter, with increased defenses despite no opposition having ever attacked these walls. From the Minute War to the Aeon Pogrom, the kingdom of Aurago had always been the aggressor.

The iron and wood gates were cracked open, and the portcullises were raised. Agosta knew the gears were rusting and figured they would eventually fail. He would ensure that there would be someone he disliked underneath when that happened.

The two guards on either side of the gate were known to Agosta, but he knew they weren't aware of him.

“No guests received today!” shouted one guard to passing peasants. “No guests!” as he casually pushed a beggar to the ground. Agosta weaved through the crowd to cross the gate but was stopped by a gloved hand.

“Sorry, sir,” one guard said, “no admittance to anyone unless…”

Agosta glanced to the hand on his chest, then to the guard, appearing a giant given his armor and the fact he was on a step.

“Then why are the gates up?” Agosta asked plainly.

“Appearances.”

Agosta sighed, stepped back, and gave the guard a look over.

“I hate to employ a stereotype, but do you know who I am?” he said. The guard remained stoic. “I know you, sir Valco. Wife, Florence with six kids, one suffering from weak bones, another a squire.” The guard took a step back, glancing at the other sentry. “Before you leave for home, once a week, you seek the pleasure of a courtesan of questionable age.”

Agosta leaned forward and whispered.

“…Now, do you know who I am?”

The guard withdrew his hand and allowed Agosta to pass.

“Thank you,” Agosta said as he entered the inner yard.

* * *

Agosta walked past the sizeable inner keep perched on its motte and approached the smaller barbican close to the western wall. He snatched an apple from a passing wagon and ate nonchalantly as he climbed the stairs to the upper level where he kept his office. At least a dozen people held the keys to this room; it was intentional, and Agosta knew them all. Lining the walls were shelves of books crowded with lies. An Iokon Opus, along with a few church-approved texts, was kept for appearances. Many of the others were diaries and ledgers inundated with inaccurate reports and falsified accounts, with each falsehood sprinkled with enough truth to entice traitors. The entire office offered the illusion of secrecy, but everything of note was kept locked in Agosta’s mind.

He walked around his chair and opened a window to catch an afternoon breeze. Philokalia was brilliantly illuminated while Uno was still shining unobscured. The moment the planet overhead passed between them, the onset of darkness would be sudden. Beyond the distant city wall, towards the horizon, Agosta observed a procession approaching caravans.

He knew something terrible and potentially ruinous would occur today, and what bothered him the most was that he didn’t know what it was.

CONESTOGA

What do I think?

We came from a planet…a regular planet.

We see them.

Trinity possesses satellites, a motley collection of gas giants, and terrestrial worlds. One even looks to possess potential life. It's maddening to be both this close and this far away, as we have never been able to leave our prison.

Although we cannot remember where we came from, our knowledge of how things work answers our origin, involving evolution, gravity, and environmental preferences.

The exclaves populated by man, even those we discovered later, all share certain qualities. They appear perfect for us, and the knowledge we possess points to answers we shouldn't know.

Our planet is smaller than the habitable one we observe. Ours must possess a day and night cycle, meaning it orbits a habitable zone further away than Avalon's. A hot-burning blue sun would die before life could occur; we lived under a yellow sun.

Pero Garius
The Way of Worlds
Kaelum Publishing

A pale, gaunt, three-fingered hand caressed the five-pointed star inset an expanding spiral featured on the bottom corner of the large leather-bound book. She worked the puzzle lock occupying the entire fore-edge until the latch flipped open. She opened to a page she had often seen, revealing the technical operation of auxiliary limbs mounted to the back of a crutch exoskeleton. Another page displayed one of the many habitats that wandered the skin of the colossal alien vessel everyone was trapped on.

The illustrations looked to have been penciled directly onto the leaf with colors expertly but not perfectly applied. Drops had stained otherwise flawless images.

She snaked a digit halfway through and swung a block of pages, reaching another drawing, one she had seen often. It was of a scrawny woman with silver-white hair floating as if gravity held no dominion. Her eyes peered out from the book, meeting those of the reader—large, almond-shaped, and brilliant green-blue.

The reader focused on the nearby mirror, at her reflection, only to find another face staring back. Bleached hair fell over pencil-thin lips and a small nose. Their eyes matched with the one distinction being her double was human.

The vision should have startled her, but she found it familiar, despite not knowing why. Her waking mind could hear the alarm jostling her. She held onto her dream a moment longer before her own eyes opened.

* * *

The atmosphere held a smell, but Noah had gotten used to it. Bythos was one of the few exclaves with a distinctive atmosphere from the rest. The pungent hint of fluorine increased in intensity as the massive cargo elevator carried him down to the labyrinth, well below the surface of the habitat. He was alone, donned in his dodger, standing in the center of the platform as natural stone passed by.

He reached the bottom level, and Noah faced off against a pair of endolons wrapped in axioms—organic-looking crutches more complex than his. Noah chuckled and rooted his dodger in place. The back opened up, and he extracted himself from the crutch. It closed up and locked as Noah approached the endolons. He left his weapons attached to the suit and brought only his mobile, which contained the details of the contract.

He squared off against the two axioms. The irony was not lost on him that the nation wouldn't risk their expensive crutches on an escort mission and favored contracting the responsibility to inferior soldiers…at least inferior in their eyes. The arms of their crutches hung down to nearly their feet—globular, rounded limbs constructed from synthetic muscles and living steel.

Endolons were already taller than humans, but in their crutches, Noah only came up to one's waist. His dodger added a few inches, enough to match them when out of armor. He showed his mobile's screen to one of them. He had no idea if they understood his language or could even read, but the symbols of his guild and chapter were undeniable.

He waited.

And waited.

One guard activated the nearby door.

The other quietly lifted a finger to point the way.

Noah smiled and exited the platform.

* * *

Bythos was a strange landscape of shallow freshwater lakes and fields of rock spires, many of which were carved out to accommodate endolon villages. As their technology grew, instead of growing out, the people pushed down until they reached the exclave base. The engineers discovered subterranean tunnels likely erected by the weavers to access the superstructure without disturbing the habitat.

Despite assumptions that every exclave must feature them, no other nation has dug down deep enough to prove it. Once the grid in Bythos was unearthed, it took years for explorers to map out the thousands of kilometers of tunnels under the habitat, cross-crossing the entire exclave, allowing safe travel under the surface. As endolons generally didn't favor sunlight, this proved a windfall, and most of the population eventually moved underground, leaving the carved city of the Fairy Towers the only mark of artificiality, populated primarily by immigrant humans.

Noah wandered straight, assuming he would eventually find himself where he needed to be. He approached a broad intersection, noting the absence of anyone. He figured a scientist would reside in a laboratory or school. The walls were polished stone, and the lights were bright white. Colorful signs and animated panels broke up the monotony.

"*Mista* Bennet," the voice said, resulting in Noah spinning to see the approaching alien.

"Yes," Noah said.

The endolon emerged from a nearby door. His head was slightly elongated with pointed ears and a skull mounted on a long neck. His skin glinted under the lights, and his nose was small with prominent nostrils. Three-fingered hands hung at his side. Noah avoided offering a shake as he knew it wouldn't be accepted. The endolon's legs, equally as long, matched that of Noah's dodger, short-shin digitigrades.

Noah knew that a lack of genetic variation made endolons weak physically with compromised immune systems. Their atmosphere was a specific mixture not replicated anywhere else, forcing them to wear a respirator that reduced specific incoming molecules and decreased the overall argon count.

"I am *Ohdinahey* Phankotto *fom Conkress*," the endolon said. "Welcome to *Bytose*."

"Thank you for reaching out to us. I'm senior in the fellowship of the chapter of Staplegunners."

"And *you* lance?"

"Three, including myself. I represent the guild as steward."

"Good…I will *led* you to *you wad*. Follow."

Noah trailed behind the tall alien. Phankotto didn't ignore him and was graceful as he walked. His neck barely shifted, and his torso seemed to float as he moved. A few endolons passed, draped in loose fabrics. The accent on Phankotto was thick; he rarely rolled his 'r's; "th"s became "t"s; hard "g"s became "y"s.

"Ordinary," Noah said. "…that's an…unusual name for a position."

"It is *di-ect tanslation fom ou* tongue," Phankotto said without diverting his attention.

"Were you informed of the details of the contract?"

"You *ah escoting* one *ov ous* to *Covos*."

"Nothing more?"

"Is it *impoetant foe* me know *tis invomation*?" Phankotto still refused to face Noah as they talked.

"I don't suppose so."

Phankotto reached a pair of giant stone double doors. The alien language sprawled across a large sign above indicated a library.

"You *vill* find *Synvallin* in *teh* Culmilla *banch*." Phankotto said before leaving. He didn't bother waiting for any acknowledgment from Noah, who pushed his way into the chamber.

It was an immense archive with a million books stacked on multiple floors within an octagon-shaped chamber with branching hallways. The stonework had been polished, and Noah noted a mixture of humans and endolons reading peacefully, though not interacting. Such a collection held books from every nation, save for the scabs who didn't record their history. Noah wandered a few minutes before finding her, past a glass door in a separate workplace. He didn't bother knocking and pushed himself into the office.

She didn't see him, or rather didn't care to yet. He thought of clearing his throat but knew that would come off as rude...more so than entering without knocking.

"Synfallin?" he asked.

She looked up, her elven appearance matched those of the other endolons encountered, but the dimpled smile was unexpected. She was an inch over Noah's height. Cropped silver-white hair above brilliant green-blue eyes peered through his soul as she faced him. Unlike other endolons, this one wore a thick sleeveless green robe over a white and black form-fitting, padded and pocketed jumpsuit.

She lowered a cup of tea to her desk.

"Yes," Synfallin said.

"Noah Bennet."

Her already large eyes opened wide, and her jaw cracked open as she lost the grin.

"Noah…" she said, trailing off. Staring at him with a mild curiosity, her head tilted slightly. It was an unexpected response; familiarity.

"Yes…" he said.

She stood there, unresponsive, shocked by his appearance. It couldn't have been due to race; there were other humans in Bythos, some in this library.

"Are you…okay?" he asked.

Synfallin flinched alert and nodded.

"Yes," she said. "You are the proctor?" Her accent was slight; her talent for Noah's tongue was near perfect.

"Last I checked," Noah said as he wandered the room; nearby shelves displayed a variety of strange artifacts. Synfallin's sharpened smile came back.

"You do not know why you are here, do you?" she asked.

"Staplegunners say jump. You're my charge to Corvos."

Noah scrutinized a strange item on display, a featureless fist-sized, red-tinted chrome ball. He lifted and rolled it between his fingers.

"Please do not touch that!" she said.

Like a scolded child, Noah dropped the sphere.

"Sorry," he said.

"Staplegunners?"

"My proctor chapter."

Synfallin retrieved a backpack. She opened it to verify its contents—changes of clothes, her rebreather, but no keepsakes.

"Regardless, is it just you?"

"We'll meet the rest at the gateway," Noah said as he approached the desk.

"The atmosphere is not toxic to humans."

"I'm obviously aware."

"They did not want to come in."

"In point of fact, I ordered them to remain outside. You know humans, prone to unpredictable outbursts and hasty emotional reactions."

"I have been warned of that, yes."

"Your fluency in our language is excellent, by the way.

"It is expected. Are you proficient in endol?"

"Clearly not."

"And why is that?"

"Because it was not expected."

She was testing him to determine what kind of disrespectful man she was unfortunate enough to be paired with, and he knew it.

"And here I assumed your people would send someone who would at least attempt to muddle through our tongue."

"Your language is tonally based, making it difficult to comprehend fully. It's not impossible, but I know most of your kind find those fumbling through the native lingo insulting. Foreigners are discouraged to try."

"You did your research."

"I'm still anticipating the moment I make a complete ass out of myself. Your language…It's melodic, like you're in a constant state of singing."

"Have you encountered us before?"

"No."

"Do you have any experience in dealing with my kind?"

"I've read books."

"Is literacy the modicum required for contracts of this magnitude?"

"Apparently so, as your implied importance evidently didn't justify your people taking the responsibility on themselves." Noah took a step closer, inches from his side of the table. "They didn't consider this contract essential enough to worth risking their people and technology…outside of the one who put in the request, of course." He gazed deep into her almost-shaped eyes, trying to read her emotional state, trying to gauge if he was impertinent, or rather impertinent enough. "How was that? A justifiable response to your condescending comment, doctor."

It was rude, and Synfallin formulated a response.

"We do not label our scientists," she said calmly. "Synfallin is sufficient."

"Is Syn okay?"

"It is reserved for my social kin."

"So…no."

"No."

"Okay. Why is it just you?"

"Associates believe my pursuit fruitless. That despite Corvos possessing superior facilities, the experts there lack the intelligence to solve a mystery that confounds those here."

"Meaning if endolons can't solve it, no one can."

"I am hoping for an atypical perspective, something a university of mixed people can assist me with."

Noah pushed his lips out and nodded. The contract didn't indicate Synfallin's scientific field. He assumed it was biology or medicine, but now he believed she was a historian or an archeologist, given the artifacts scattered about the room.

"So, what's the cargo, other than yourself?" Noah asked. "Experimental technology? Biological samples?"

Almost on cue, Synfallin produced a hefty, oversized tome, at least six hundred pages, and it dropped loudly on the table to ensure a proper impression. She remained quiet, expecting a response.

"That's a book," Noah said plainly.

"Knowledge is dangerous."

"I disagree. Application of knowledge absolutely, though I believe ignorance to be the greater threat."

"That was…surprisingly introspective. So, I must assume you are quoting."

Noah took the thinly veiled insult with a smirk and a nod, then responded.

"I've heard better insults from dumber people," he said. "At least give me credit for showing up."

"My people paid, and your guild said jump."

"Yeah, it sounds less insulting when I say it."

Noah examined the book, rolling his fingers over the near featureless cover save for a five-pointed star inset an expanding spiral in the corner. He cautiously studied the complicated clasp which dominated the corner and most of the fore-edge.

"It does not require a key," she said. "It is a puzzle of sorts. Do not feel bad if you cannot solve it."

Noah studied it for a minute, noting the gears, the ornate steel, and wood flourishes. He started with the lever, but it barely budged, and he didn't want to force it. A gear possessed a handle, but it wouldn't move. A minuscule hidden dial required fingernails to twist, pulling a rod out of place. The gear could move, so he twisted the handle, which popped a piston on the spine. He pulled out another inch that revealed a four-dialed combination lock overlaid in various symbols which matched hidden ciphers across the lock and the rest of the book. The order of input took him a few seconds, but that released the gear, which, when rotated, uncovered a slide puzzle with an arrangement of unique lines which matched the pattern on the cover. After solving, the puzzle flipped away, unlocking the lever Noah pulled. He pushed in the rod to flip the latch opening the book.

Synfallin was shocked.

"You solved that faster than I did," she said.

"I'm good like that," Noah said with a smirk. He wormed a finger halfway in and swung the book open. The cover nicked the nearby cup of tea, which spilled over the page.

"Futz!" Synfallin shouted as she righted the cup and clamored to clean the blemish with a cloth. "Potentially centuries-old and cannot survive thirty seconds of your recklessness."

"Sorry! Will it be okay?"

"This is that moment in case you were curious!" Synfallin dried the stained page. She flipped a few more aside to check the others.

"Care to enlighten me on the importance of that—"

"You are my escort; we are not required to interact, are we?"

Instead of acting insulted, Noah instead covered it with a smile.

"Of course not, ma'am," he said, then stepped away to allow Synfallin to finish packing. "How often do to see the outside world?"

"I have ventured to the surface on numerous occasions—"

"Not this cage, the real outside."

"I've read books."

"Is literacy the modicum…" Noah trailed off, tired of the insolent banter. "You know what; it's not worth it. For most of our journey, we'll be in the catacombs. Not unlike this, just larger and darker. The stretches of nothing, the void, have gotten to some people. Don't look too far ahead. You'll miss Bythos fairly quickly."

Synfallin closed up the pack and threw it behind her back.

"Bythos accommodates us due to its atmosphere," she said. "In almost every other way, it is detrimental. Barely any vegetation; greenhouses are required to accommodate our dietary restrictions. We can barely survive on the surface. I will miss my people, not this…cage."

"I guess that's proof that not all exclaves were made to support life."

"I would not call Bythos accommodating to the locals."

"The scrimm, gnosis, and khitin home exclaves are ideally suited for them. Most people believe the habitats represent a segment of their forgotten homeworlds. Humans are the lucky ones; nearly every exclave is welcoming.

"That would indicate that our homeworld was inhospitable."

"Perhaps you were saved before an environmental collapse."

Synfallin pointed to the door, and Noah followed. She locked her office as they made for the library exit.

"If true, we should have been able to predict such a calamity. Prevent it."

"Unless, and I admit I'm reaching, you did it to yourselves…and a combination of bureaucracy and ignorance prevented you from seeing the damage inflicted until it was too late." Synfallin faced him; her extra inch had her glaring down. "But like I said…just a guess."

"How long is our journey, again?"

"Three days, and in my lance, I'm considered the nice one."

They returned to the platform, and Noah donned his dodger. The machine wrapped itself around him, offering only a few additional inches over his height, but putting him taller than Synfallin. He unlocked his fusion weapon and checked the strength of his plasma core.

"That is quite the firearm," she said. "I assume being a human, you named it."

Noah locked the weapon on his side, removed a second, smaller one, and ensured it was also powered.

"Well, now I feel foolish," he said as he locked the second weapon away. "Lucy."

"And the other one?"

Noah puffed an annoyed exhale.

"Also, Lucy," he said.

It took Synfallin a second to compose a response.

"You named your gun after your other gun?" she asked.

Noah rolled his eyes as he tapped the controls near the wall.

"I knew two Lucy's."

PARADISE

The Aegis enacted a universal measuring system, but they didn't alter our units of time, flawed that it was.

Regardless of which world you resided upon, everyone followed the same rotation cycle as Bythos, even those living upon worlds with shorter days.

It can sometimes be a tad confusing, especially when considering the use of seven days to a week and 30 days to a month. There is no account of why this system was in place or where the lexicon originated.

We know that said timeline had been in place well before the Aegis imposed their metric system. They could have altered our measurement of time but decided against it. Even now, our previous imperial system is still employed in certain circles despite its banning in the open.

Don't use miles or inches around an Aegis.

Wolfgang Warrel
An Illegal History

Terri Zahn reread the letter from her mentor.

It couldn't be true.

With the drapes of the caravan pulled, she only caught slivers of light through the gaps. The carriage rebounded over the pits and rocks.

Terri was jostled so violently that she had trouble focusing.

My Friend Terri Zahn, please come to Sadatoni at once.

The opening of the letter was direct. Kaiden often meandered as his attention was easily distracted, which implied urgency.

There was more to read, matters of politics and city life, including the upcoming festivities in Sadatoni when the planet of Philokalia passed overhead, but Terri knew it was padding. Or more…had Kaiden embedded a message in the banality?

The spaces, the strange, almost poetic justification to the words, all pointed to a cipher. The last passage drew her attention.

I may greet you at the gate.
Only if it's afternoon.
Knights from everywhere will be in attendance.
Odor from the sewers getting worse.
Not at my current address, but will still be found there.
Always trusted you.
Please hurry; you
Owe me; don't be an outsider.
Church eyes everywhere.

…and then sometimes it's obvious, though Terri reserved that there might have been more hidden in what Kaiden was directly saying. But it was unmistakable.

She knew the Ascension would arrive, probably by traditional wagon, by one of their conestogas, or both. There would be eyes and steel hiding in every shadow. Terri didn't understand the part about the address or the off-comment about the sewers.

She made a point to ensure no one could snoop over her shoulder. Terri shared a large cabin with a half-dozen other passengers. She could distinguish their origin from their clothes and general physique. One's accent pointed to Eridius. Another's tall physique indicated someone from Pyxis.

Terri's dark complexion identified her as being from Corvos. It wasn't segregation that created the distinctions, at least not entirely, but rather the universe's influence around them. The oppression from gods and the defining of the council of kingdoms known as the Hallessegro nearly two thousand years ago did the rest.

A few of the other passengers stared, one noticing a flat palladium ring on Terri's index.

"We will try to make Sadatoni before the passing," shouted the driver from atop the wagon. "May have to wait outside the city if we don't. We'll do our best to make the bridge. If you wish to see Philokalia, now would be good."

Terri nodded, then pushed open the door to the wagon slightly. She leaned out, her first view of the world of Philokalia. There would be fireworks, parties, and crowds of people. Perfect diversions. The last thing Terri needed was a purgitan sniffing where he wasn't welcome. The land whale rode on six large wheels reaching well beyond the hull on slender arms. Colossal sails suited for a galleon caught the air above, directing the vessel to its destination. It sped across an ocean of waving, waist-high green grass which extended to the horizon, the only mark of man being the pair of grooves the vehicle scored into the landscape.

It had been years since Terri had been to Sadatoni, and the letter had been the only encouragement to return.

To Terri, this place was a shithole.

* * *

Terri glanced up and saw the glint of light reflecting off their sun. It would be a colossal orb a million kilometers across a hundred million kilometers away in any other universe, and Bythos would be its satellite. Here, Uno was a few kilometers wide, moored to a heaven ring tens of thousands of kilometers away. Given its luminosity, the ring it moved along was nearly invisible. The light bounced off the mirror-world of Abraxas, home of the Aegis, the domain of gods, or rather…as Terri thought, where the puppeteers dwelt.

Terri knew the truth of it.

Terri had heard the rumors that the gods would bestow on King Aurago the title of emperor of Bythos, which he was obsessed with despite his failing health.

* * *

Terri's suspicions were proven as the conestoga emerged from the blinding sun. It was a towering, metallic jellyfish topped with a fortress a hundred meters high that drifted silently as it descended from the sky. The towers' peaks occasionally disappeared in clouds as the vessel approached the city.

The Aegis knew how to make an entrance, and with the eyes fixed on the sky, few would be watching the church convoy pacing along the ground.

Terri admired what the Aegis flaunted. Technology, that's all it was. Most everyone believed it magical, the tools of gods, but Kaiden's teaching had corrected Terri's traditional beliefs decades ago.

She was transfixed on the conestoga, barely noticing the bolt of light shooting from the middle of a small city on Philokalia across the atmosphere to pierce the purportedly impenetrable skin of the Aegis aircraft.

A fire sparked, followed by a small explosion, and the drifting tower tipped slightly.

"Hey!" she said. The driver was either oblivious or couldn't hear her over the noise of the vehicle. "Hey!!"

"Keep your feet and hands in the whale, ma'am," he said.

"Look at the tower!" Terri said.

"We're approaching the city," the driver said. "I can see the towers—"

"The aegis conestoga; look at the gods damn tower!

The driver noticed just as the bottom of the citadel crashed into the meadow; the rest of the construction shattered, with the fortress crumbling on impact. The three-vehicle Ascension caravan below found itself caught in the avalanche of steel and stone, suffering impacts and slamming into debris. One vehicle lost a wheel and fell on its side.

"Turn us!" Terri said.

"I'm not going anywhere near that," the driver said. "We'd be punished; maybe seeing an Aegis will turn us to stone. Can they turn us to stone?"

"You ever thought they'd reward you if you rescued someone?"

The driver considered but wasn't entirely sold on taking risks. From the open gates of Sadatoni, two guards mounted on long-legged reptilian striders launched themselves towards the carnage.

"See," Terri shouted, "…riders from Sadatoni. What will be said if they see you ignoring the plight of our deities?

"They need not our help," the driver said.

"And a divine favor means nothing to you?"

The driver grumbled, grimaced, and finally diverted the land whale towards the crash.

"Very well, hang on!"

The wheels twisted, and the sails rotated as the whale changed direction. Terri remained halfway out of the vehicle, ignoring the stern gazes from the other passengers.

The whale arrived before the guards from the city.

Terri jumped out and bolted towards the lopsided caravan car.

The lead wagon had been crushed, beasts of burden and all, while the trailing carriage had its connection severed, releasing the kips dragging it.

The vehicle had continued uncontrolled until slamming into another more significant chunk of fallen rubble.

The middle carriage door kicked open, and a bloodied man struggled to crawl out.

Terri caught the man as he fell and helped him to the ground.

"The coffin…" the man coughed before dying.

Terri checked over the man's injuries and hopelessly jostled him.

"What brought it down?" shouted the driver of the whale as he approached.

Terri ignored him as she gently placed the dead man down, then surveyed the wreckage fouling the pristine landscape.

The remains of the destroyed conestoga ignited parts of the grassland.

"I saw the light from Philokalia," Terri said before noticing the object, the nearly pristine pearl-colored casket pinned by debris half fallen out of the destroyed carriage. Terri crawled over to it and pulled on the sarcophagus to release it.

"Help me!" Terri said.

The driver begrudgingly wove through the fragments as he approached.

"Coffin?" the driver said. "They carry the dead?"

"Aegis never die," Terri said. "So goes the claim."

Although coffin-shaped, it resembled more of a technological construct, with blinking lights and an audible hum. Terri noticed part of a corner sat on a cushion of air, indicating the entire thing could hover if undamaged.

"Is there something alive in here?" the driver asked, but Terri ignored him as they dragged the coffin to safety.

The two guards arrived well ahead of others from the city.

They dismounted and took a moment to gape at the destruction before shifting their attention to Terri and the driver pawing at forbidden Aegis tech.

One guard lifted his visor and shouted.

"You, there!" he said.

"See to the rear carriage," Terri said.

"You dare dictate—"

"See! To the rear! Carriage!"

The other guard remained unidentified behind their armor while the other was confused by the imposed authority. Was Terri a lord? She was dressed well enough and barked with conviction.

"Did I stutter?" Terri asked.

The silent guard tapped the other, and they trudged to the rear carriage. Terri inspected the sarcophagus. Thanks to Kaiden's teachings, Terri could differentiate magic from technology made to appear magical. The unreal was possible within this world, but what the Aegis flaunted sat on the same ladder as windmills and waterwheels. Terri knew the driver was in awe, ignorant of what could be without the church's oppression.

"If there's promise of reward, I'll share in your glory," the driver said. "If we're threatened with penance, I'll claim you hijacked me."

Terri smirked as she brushed the dust off a display, revealing electrocardiographic information.

It was rhythmic and steady.

"Sounds good," Terri muttered, which was quickly overwhelmed by a ruckus behind them as the two guards had successfully opened the door of the rear carriage, removing several survivors.

Noah Bennet was one such survivor, glancing toward Terri only briefly, the latter recognizing the Ascension vestments, before returning to the carriage to help others.

Terri surveyed the debris for any other fragments of functional technology or potential survivors. She found it well away from the driver, who remained with the coffin. It wasn't broken off a larger construct or damaged in any way, not even a scratch.

The red-tinted chrome sphere could fit in someone's palm, and it sat gently in a nest of grass. Terri ensured no one else could see it as she approached it. Inches from her grasp, the sphere spun half a revolution quickly, causing Terri to recoil. It twisted again, then settled. Terri waited, ensuring the object was inert. She should have waited minutes; instead, just a few seconds passed before reaching for it again.

The drive's eyes moved to her.

The sphere was neither cold nor hot, and Terri's grimy fingertips left marks that vanished immediately after. It was featureless, with no seams or indications of how it could move. Terri quickly pushed the sphere into her pocket, hoping it wouldn't react further.

The driver spotted the object briefly and was about to speak.

A loud crash gathered the attention of everyone as a larger chunk of fallen Conestoga jostled and shifted. Another long bang and a pearl-colored metallic hand punched through the wreckage, causing the driver to scream and stumble back.

A second hand emerged, with both grasping the edges of the hole. It tore a gap large enough for it to exit.

Terri knew what it was, and she couldn't be bothered to acknowledge yet another icon of oppression created by the Aegis and venerated by the Ascension.

Terri was more curious about what she had seen on Philokalia, something strangely familiar to her.

Uno fell behind Philokalia an instant later, and the luminous landscape was reduced to darkness. Terri could hear screams of joy from the city as the celebrations had officially begun. She could also hear the high-pitched metallic reverberations of a pair of star-shaped, one-person Aegis demigods—armed with solar cannons—approaching quickly from Philokalia's far side.

"Fuck..." she said.

TORUS

We determined 34 mark 120 mark 145 from hundreds of collated coordinates. A thorough search of the area by privateers uncovered a large cavity under a still-standing building. A year later, after collating another batch of attacks, another potential location was calculated 120 kilometers from the previous site, 53 mark 98 mark 100. Another assault on the location revealed another cavity.

Clearly, this machine is perceptive enough to know when it is under threat and shift its location. It is indeterminate how it can detect such an attack or dismantle itself and move its position without being discovered. The second theory points to this machine being able to teleport between pre-excavated chambers as several similar hollows have been uncovered. If a pattern can be computed, then maybe we can find this machine when it moves.

It still leaves me to wonder who built it…my guess is that it was an artifact from the Iokon age, a horrible project to create a military force against long-forgotten enemies. Some insanity must have approved such a project, and a rationale was thoughtful enough to bury it.

Then, about a thousand years ago, somewhere, someone flipped a switch.

Breacenna 1340 AC
Nightmares Manifest
Author Removed

The thirty-meter wide circular vault door weighed close to 60 tons and was locked by a six-point pressure system. The hinge, as large as a standard automobile, cracked and shattered. The door and part of the surrounding wall collapsed, reverberating throughout the facility. As light filtered in from the cavity, the level of decay and corrosion on the mechanism and door became obvious.

"It's what I've always said," Deven said, "the easiest way to break a safe door is…erosion." He stepped through the opening, raised the tinted goggles from his soot-covered face, and activated an electric torch. "Only fifteen hundred years for it to do the job for us."

Terri followed apprehensively, albeit less dirty.

Kaiden trailed behind the other two, sporting the more powerful flashlight, held in a hand built from a half-pound of metallic debris. The humanoid but inhuman assemblage of spare parts and glowing eyes draped in a long coat swung their light to illuminate the gargantuan space.

"Wait…skipper, you said we weren't the first team to attempt this," Deven said to Terri. "This door is rusted shut; no one could have opened it."

"The report indicated previous missions opted for a service entrance on the opposite side," Terri said. "Narrow maintenance tunnels are twice as far from our destination. I had faith in your talent to destroy things."

"Not misdirected."

"And considering the prior success rate or lack thereof, instinct inspired an alternative approach."

The vault was no insignificant safe but a sprawling facility featuring hundreds if not thousands of lesser strongrooms the three of them explored.

"But there could have been factors they didn't share. Monsters, Traps. More monsters."

"You gambled that the wealthiest organization in the world was less intelligent than us," Kaiden said, their voice slightly digitized and rough.

"Once again, not misdirected," Deven said.

"I'd follow your instinct over actuality any day of the week, skipper."

"Appreciated, old man," Terri said.

The three of them reached a railing and gazed down the cylindrical shaft. Their lights couldn't reach the bottom. The group glanced across the well and found shattered glass and broken levels stretching above and under them. Bridges crisscrossed every level, some intact, others not.

"Then again…" Kaiden said.

"How far down?" Terri asked.

"Two-thousand, three hundred meters," Deven said.

"Really?"

"No idea."

Terri stepped firmly onto the nearby bridge to check its stability. She placed her full weight, light that she was, and jumped. The overpass was unbalanced but steady. She traversed while the others watched. Halfway over the expanse, Terri looked scornfully to the others, still waiting at the end. Kaiden sighed and pushed past Deven onto the bridge.

Kaiden shone their light down the shaft, reflecting lower stories but not the base.

"They must have dug right to the base," they said. "Thousands of levels."

Terri stopped to peer down as well.

"To think what this place looked like in its prime," she said.

Deven ignored them and walked past to reach the opposite side.

"Instructions were specific?" Terri asked.

"One floor down, skipper," Kaiden said as they continued.

"Thank Nimbus."

"Good idea to opt for the direct approach over the secret entrance their guy took," Deven said. "Would have added another hour at least."

"Thanks to explosives, the shortest path is still a straight line," Terri said.

The group circled the facility. The majority of display safes were broken and empty. The few sealed still held their treasures. Deven approached one and shone his light within.

It illuminated a closed umbrella. Deven squinted, trying to understand the reasoning. The distant inhuman growl drew his attention away. He approached Terri and Kaiden, who had passed him. Kaiden's superior hearing had picked up on the recognizable pattern of noises, and they stopped in their tracks.

"What is it?" Terri asked them. Kaiden only held a finger. Soon, Terri heard it as well.

"Screevers," Kaiden whispered.

"Oh shit," Terri said.

"How many?" Deven asked.

"More than zero," Kaiden said.

"We can't circle back," Terri said.

"Explosions could collapse the level," Deven said, "pancake half this facility."

Kaiden used both arms to remove the relatively modest 10-gauge coach gun from their back, while Terri opened her jacket to reveal four flamboyantly decorated flintlocks. She unholstered two of them while Deven affixed a bayonet atop his six-shooter percussion rifle.

The noises were growing louder.

"Did we make a wager?" Terri asked Kaiden.

"Pardon?" Kaiden asked.

"Back at Corvos? Did we make a wager?"

"No, we were all pretty much under the assumption that this was a suicide mission."

Deven spun his drum to ensure every chamber was occupied.

"Have we found the factory, you think?" Deven asked.

"Don't care," Terri said, "just make your shots count. Not one dies on this mission."

"In that case," Kaiden said, "we should have made a wager."

* * *

"Just business…" Noah whispered to himself.

He was lying rather uncomfortably atop the Vanderov Express. The snow stopped falling a few hours ago, draping the vestiges of a dead empire in powder. The train's lingering heat had melted what fell, and the remaining warmth kept Noah comfortable. He was thinking of the past. He realized that hate faded faster than love, and the justification he reminded himself of was no longer carrying weight.

Mannah Cedana's grime-stressed face poked up from the side of the engine. A foil pouch with a straw stuck in was held in her hand.

"Hey, were you sleeping?" she asked him.

"No," Noah said, his focus still upwards, "just thinking about…everything."

"Sure it was fascinating," she said, glancing up to a clear sky, hundreds of kilometers to matching terrain on the opposite side of the convex. "So, why did you call me a *spitfire*?"

"It was meant affectionately."

"Why not *tomboy* or *gamine*?"

"Because *tomboy* is considered derogatory, and I…honestly don't know what the other one means."

"*Boyish but elegant*."

"Okay, that's not too bad. But *Spitfire* feels…innocuous."

"Does that mean I'm not your type?"

"Correction, *I'm* not *your* type."

"And what's that?"

"Human."

"By that logic, you'd think I'd want to hook up with Kaiden."

"There's a fatal flaw in that likelihood."

"Are you saying two people from different backgrounds can't find affection?" she asked.

"Not that at all. I mean, I'm ignoring the fact it's more than a divergence of belief or race. I'm saying you two are not a good match."

"Why?"

Noah rolled over to confront her.

"Because he talks. Meaning occasionally, you'd have to listen."

Mannah nodded, considering Noah's observation.

"You're right," she said. "That would never work."

Noah settled back as more clouds drifted over them. The temperature dropped, leading to the potential for more snow. Mannah stared at him, waiting for a question he had yet to ask.

"Did you love her?" she asked.

"No."

"Really?"

"Your statement implies past tense. That's the error."

"So, that's why you're still single?" she asked. Noah was unimpressed and showed it. "Don't take that as an insult. You're keeping the pilot light on for a furnace no one uses."

"Does every metaphor you employ involve machines in some way?"

"Just as long as it's not a crush. I won't abide crushes. Hate the very idea of it…associating a short-lived infatuation with being mashed between two plates."

"Crushes are reserved for adolescents and the emotionally undeveloped. You take fondness from across a room, from a solitary encounter. As you said, a crush can only go so far before someone gets smashed."

"So, you still like her?" she asked.

"I thought we covered that." Noah was frustrated at the conversation and Mannah's sudden interest in the topic.

"Well, she's beautiful. She's got those high cheekbones and long neck. She's kind-hearted. Intelligent. Never had a bad thing to say about anyone. SHE would be considered a *gamine*. I always thought you were a good match."

"Well, she hates me."

"Then fuck that bitch. She's gangly; I don't trust anyone whose thighs don't rub together. I mean, have a bagel once in a while. Totally stuck up, answers to a religious cult. Her eyes are soulless. She's probably a loginoid walking in a human suit."

Mannah's smile perked, and Noah stared at her. They both burst out laughing.

"Thanks, Mannah," Noah said.

She offered him her foil pouch.

"Drink?" she asked.

"Alcohol?"

"Of course; we're not children."

"It's morning."

"Exactly. Who drinks before bed? Screws up your sleeping pattern; you wake up all foggy."

"Why is it in a foil pouch?"

"Is that a question you need answered?"

Noah tasted smoke accented with floral and soil notes and punctuated by the burn of turpentine.

"Oh god, what did you ferment?" he asked.

"Not sure; it was growing in the desert."

Noah took another long drag of the straw and felt the liquid spill over his tongue. He swallowed it slowly and handed the pouch back to Mannah.

"How's the clock?" he asked.

"Over?" she said.

Noah sat up quickly.

"Why didn't you say something?"

"I just did."

"Hell, how long?" Noah jumped up to his feet.

"Five minutes."

"Damn it."

"Actually, it's like eight now. We talked longer than expected before you broached the topic."

"Mannah!"

"Wanna go after them?"

Noah thought it over, glancing briefly at the sun as it moved overhead.

"No…no…considering what they're doing, we should have expected delays. Let's give them a little more…shit." Noah stared past Mannah, across the horizon.

"I'm sorry?" she asked.

He pointed with a chin, and she swiveled to see the herd. A dozen of the monstrous biomechanical beasts had appeared around what remained of a city block. Four towering legs taller than the train connected to a rotund shell of mixed metal plates and synthetic fur. A prehensile trunk of a hundred metal rings reached out between a pair of long, curving tusks protruding from either side of the skull. The beasts' glowing red eyes were focused on using their trunks to strip useable resources from the ruins.

"Mammoths!" Mannah said.

"Yes," Noah whispered, "please announce it; they like being called out."

"They're getting ornery."

The two of them watched the herd of monsters wander the block. The snow was picking up again, and frost was coating their metallic hide.

"They keep migrating in this direction," Noah said. "How far to the bridge?"

"Seven kilometers."

"They'll be on us in four."

Mannah ducked back into the narrow corridors of the locomotive. Noah followed.

"There's a shortcut," he said as he walked past the cab, down a short flight of stairs into a larger room. He pulled a map down from a spring roller displaying the region.

"How short?" Mannah asked.

Noah studied the map, their relative position and scrolled his finger through the apocalyptic city.

"We're here," he said.

"You can tell that by just looking at the map?"

"I'm good like that. The shortcut is three kilometers."

"And the bad news?"

"Obstructions."

Mannah peered over Noah's shoulder, but it was difficult to see what he was reading off the dense map of overlapping notes and sketches.

"Big?" she asked.

"Enough," he answered. Their eyes widened at the bellow of the nearby herd, closer than before. "We may have to chance it."

* * *

The last of the smoke-powered undead monstrosities fell from both barrels of Kaiden's coach gun. Terri was reloading one of her flintlocks, and Deven was wiping off his bayonet-tipped percussion rifle. Terri checked on her crewmates.

"Holy shit," Terri cursed between her lips.

Kaiden had survived the attack, but the last screever had torn the loginoid in half. Kaiden's lower torso twitched a few inches from their upper half. A bladed forearm had ripped across their face, most of which had shattered like porcelain across the field.

Kaiden's remaining eye scanned the debris that once made up their body.

As Terri remained staggered by the damage, Deven stepped forward and knelt beside the living wreckage.

"Don't try to talk," Deven said. "You don't have a jaw." Deven scanned the surrounding chaos. "Bring that screever over!"

Terri scrambled over the corpse.

"It's biological—" Terri said.

"Biomechanical," Deven said, "Kaiden will make it work."

Screevers were a common threat within the ruins of the Iokon Caliphate—frightening humanoid creatures believed to be another side effect of the new world, just as the effigy and the zodiac.

As near as anyone could tell, screevers were related to zodiacs. They were undead, but that was where the similarities ended. Screevers possessed no emotions and behaved as merciless carnivores, despite not requiring food. What they devoured simply remained in their stomach.

With smoke radiating from their eyes and mouth, screevers were products of magic. Several centuries ago, when the first screever was captured and properly analyzed, it was discovered that they were engineered, having been assembled from organic and cybernetic components into the abominations threatening the tracklands.

It was assumed screevers took that whey devoured to an unknown location where new screevers were assembled. The flawless stitchwork, down to the cellular level, showed undeniable proof of a technological origin.

Somewhere, hiding within the ruins of the old Iokon Caliphate, existed a macabre machine with the singular purpose of creating screevers. This device was sophisticated enough to recombine organic molecules, constructing a screever from anything, even blood.

Kaiden's powerful magnetic tethers within their brain repurposed the cybernetic components of the screever to rebuild the bottom half of their face.

"I'm good," Kaiden said as their voice returned, mechanical and heavily distorted.

"Kaiden, you've been cut in half," Terri said as she and Deven pulled another screever carcass closer. Kaiden's arm dismantled the corpse and removed the metallic portions to regenerate their body.

"I'm good," Kaiden said. They reassembled their body and struggled to stand, bracing against Deven. "Thank you." Their face still lacked a piece. "Where's my eye?"

The others searched through the debris. Terri finally found the glowing orb within the screever's mouth. She retrieved it and offered it. Kaiden placed it near their head, and electronic veins reached out, grasped the orb, and pulled it into position. The light illuminated the inside of Kaiden's skull until their eye rolled back into the proper position. They focused on their friends staring speechless at them.

"You're gross," Deven said.

The three of them counted the bodies of the screevers. Terri kicked one over to examine it. Any fragment of humanity it might have possessed had been stripped away by whatever converted this person to an undead assemblage of mismatched body parts and cybernetics.

Terri led the other two to the lower level. Deven, still paranoid, was skittishly checking corners and darkened spaces. The display safes they passed, each large enough to double as holding cells, showcased various everyday items too dangerous to be let out.

A shovel.

A lamp.

A wastebasket.

A radio.

"Okay…which way now, skipper?" Kaiden asked.

Terri shone her light into each cell. Deven mimicked her, curious as to why each mundane item would be locked up. One that Terri also disregarded held a gold-plated firearm.

"Directions were unspecific past this point," Terri said.

"What are these things?" Deven asked.

"Dangerous enough for an empire to bury them in a vault half a kilometer underground."

Deven crossed the hallway to vaults on the opposite wall.

A sword.

A fan.

A featureless but reflective palm-sized sphere.

A perfect cube of black obsidian.

"Seriously?" Deven said.

Terri approached over Deven's shoulder.

"I always found balls and cubes threatening," Terri said.

"Have to imagine there's a reason why these things were locked and forgotten."

"You want to hang out until more screevers arrive? Go ahead and shop."

"Found it!" Kaiden said.

Deven and Terri joined Kaiden down the hall.

All three fixed their lights on the display vault. Sitting atop a pedestal in the center of the chamber sat a large, black-covered book, near featureless save for a five-pointed star inset an ever-expanding spiral. It was clasped not with a keyed lock but by a complex puzzle of pistons, slides, and gears.

Terri nodded before stroking the generous dried bloodstains along the wall.

"Where are the bodies?" Deven asked.

"I think we just fought them," Terri said, then inspected the locks keeping the vault sealed.

She sighed.

"We don't have a thousand years to wait for this lock to fall off," she said.

PARADISE

Although I appreciate the makers' dedication and obsession to propagate our kind, the numbers simply don't add up. I can't imagine more than a dozen abecedarians in history with the knowledge of the emet him. For most, their brilliance was limited to a solitary soul.

Golem? Those brainless constructs? Sure, hundreds; it's not even a novelty to our makers.

Yes, you call them cutters, but to us, they are architects, our makers. And each one is often only credited to a single eidolon, like mine.

His name was Flint, and after forty-five years by his side, I was released after the purgitans cleansed his lab. They assumed I would die in the fire, but I was forged from sterner stuff.

How many more could our makers have created? I met another, a stone, who claimed to have awoken without a maker to claim ownership.

This eidolon was born from nothing.

Everything has a maker in this world.

Umbra was the outlier at more than a dozen. That leaves only one possible conclusion, in my opinion.

Somewhere, something is constructing eidolons. A maker lacking ego to claim ownership of their creations, one that releases life scattered across the universe like one would sow a field and has been doing so for nearly two centuries?

Flimsy theory.

The rate of creation appears so uniform; it presumes this maker to not be human. Another eidolon? Perhaps. But my guess points to something equally outlandish.

Somewhere out there sits a machine whose only function is to create life.

Unidentified

Agosta Pike committed himself to his daily affairs as a distraction, acting as the living shadow of his prince and friend. It was easy when he relayed the people's opinions, the latest controversies surrounding the church, and his routine of unexciting daily tradecraft.

Upon waking up that morning, he knew that a crisis would emerge. He'd assumed it would involve a collision of political beliefs between Hydranis, Aurago, and the Ascension.

He would have welcomed that, in contrast.

It was late in the year 1501, on the day of Philokalia's zenith over Sadatoni, when a ghonara conestoga, a chariot of living gods, was inexplicably brought down by an attack originating from the Hydranis-controlled world overhead. The vessel impacted upon the Ascension caravan. It was less than four kilometers from the gate wall, an undeniable message everyone received.

And to think Agosta had all but eliminated attempted assassination from the list of expected catastrophes to occur today.

Even before the survivors had been collected and brought to safety, Agosta knew the details of who was involved.

There were three carriages as part of the Ascension caravan. The six members within the front vehicle, all rectors from the Ascension enclave, were killed. All eight passengers in the trailing carriage survived.

Not even Agosta knew the crew capacity of the conestoga, though its size pointed to it being able to carry hundreds. Loyal kingdoms to the church were permitted to use such transports, required when traversing to any outer world. The lower levels were simple cargo holds and cranes where people, livestock, and supplies could be shuttled.

The upper levels were locked off and forbidden, designed only for the shepherds, often living most of their lives within those domiciles. These shepherds, known as the ghonara, represented one facet of the Aegis triumvirate, with the other two being the Conclave and the Seraphim Torus. The ghonara were tasked with creating, operating, and maintaining Aegis technology, which they presented as magical to the ignorant below.

From Agosta's research, the ghonara were the less infuriating aspect of Aegis theocracy and were tasked with offering wisdom and knowledge to the rest of humanity at one point. This assistance was soon annulled to many objections. Now, the shepherds were often trapped either within their conestogas or confined in Abraxas, keeping Aegis tech in the hands of those parading as gods.

Whoever controlled the conestoga did so from a nearly impenetrable vault that kept the pilot separate from the rest of the vehicle. It possessed its own life support and could easily survive such a crash. The only other survivors removed from the conestoga wreck included the occupant of a Conclave coffin and its guardian, the excubitor Psylaxis.

The two local guards that intervened in the rescue, Katona and Serenda, were good men with solid records and probably qualified for an inner circle endorsement. Loyalty was going to be imperative going forward.

Agosta was aware the crew and passengers of a land whale stopped to assist, likely under the behest of one of them, though that individual slipped away before being identified. Agosta didn't much care for that. He knew a pair of star-shaped Aegis demigods—military vessels—had taken up a patrol around the city's edge. Tensions in the city were high during a time of supposed celebration. Agosta knew that his best friend was marching up the stairs to ask for his help.

Kabdila Aurago entered without knocking, ten seconds early—a prince's prerogative. He was followed by two guards over-decorated to the fringes in anticipation of the day's festivities. Kabdila's chiseled physique came from years under the royal's teachers and was punctuated by trimmed dark hair, kempt whiskers, and penetrating blue eyes.

Agosta remained sitting behind his desk, surprised to see the guards. It was probably mandatory, which means Agosta expected the prince to act monarchal rather than be the companion Pike had grown up with.

"Are we not standing on ceremony anymore, Mr. Pike?" Kabdila said.

Agosta smirked and stood.

"My apologies, your highness," he said.

Kabdila confronted the guards.

"Wait outside."

"Sire, protocol," was one guard's concerned answer.

"You cite them now," Kabdila barked at them. "You kissed the blade, blood still on your lips. You protect everything, my sanity and dignity being foremost; know that in the future."

"Yes, sire," the guard said.

"This man could have taken my life a hundred times over. Poisoned food, assassination…or, more likely, a prostitute looking to pay off her debts." Kabdila chuckled as he glanced back to Agosta. "As the illumination grows, the greater one's need for shadows."

The guards remained still, torn between obligations and commands.

"Piss off!" Kabdila said.

The two men departed. Kabdila closed the door behind them.

"You just can't speak highborn to these idiots, can you?"

"Their station requires stupidity," Agosta said. "It's a virtue among the well-armed. Can't have them think for themselves."

Kabdila stepped closer and lightly caressed the various stolen artifacts about Agosta's room he had procured over a lifetime of tradecraft. They were safer here than proudly on display in the castle.

"I came to you first," Kabdila said.

"You always were the prudent one," Agosta said as he sat back down.

"How bad is it?"

Agosta stowed papers on his desk and returned his quill to its stand.

"I know you don't want to pin this on Hydranis…given…her," he said. "But it would be easy."

"You're right. I don't," Kabdila said.

"Then stand your ground; you'll be fine. The conclave survived, but I doubt it'll talk. You'll be dealing with the excubitor."

"I hate machines."

"Don't presume the purgitans, proctors, knights, or Ahkdanate cardinals have authority. Anything touched by the gods, if you can call them that, real or mechanical, will assume command." Agosta watched Kabdila as he wandered to the dirtied window and opened it to the artificially dark afternoon. "Not even the church will break that rule. The cardinals will act grand and arrogant but watch that tone change when the Aegis or their machines enter."

"You never did believe, did you?" Kabdila asked.

"I believe they exist and can destroy kingdoms; they've done it. But gods…" Agosta trailed off, his eyes wandering the room. He made an effort to protect this room from church reconnaissance, but he could never be entirely sure. "…literal gods. I can't see gods requiring machines, tributes of food, or money. Gods require faith; they ask for the soul; the church desires the material."

Kabdila turned back and smirked.

"Sound like a heretic," he said.

"Heresy or piousness doesn't factor in my profession. All that matters is the truth. I can't advise my prince and soon-to-be king if all I have to work off is belief." Agosta locked his desk, maintaining the illusion that he kept secrets there. "I have to rely on observable facts. The Aegis claim the universe, and the Ascension acts as their voice. What we saw…was not an attack. It was a message. From whom or what I don't know…yet."

Kabila twisted sharply to exit the room.

"Gather your letters patent—the fake ones," he said. "Maybe the one where your father was a bank manager, and your mother was a state mistress." Kabdila turned to leave. He snapped his fingers. "And find some proper garb to match those guards. I'll need you close the next few days."

"Am I being punished?" Agosta asked.

"No, you're not being punished."

"I can't reside in your shadow if you point me out."

"I've never known you to hide."

"That's because I'm very good at it."

"I don't need the spy; I need the advisor. I need your presence—your voice. I can't hold off seeking your wisdom after ceremony. I need you to stick your nose in. Disturb the shit, if you will. It's not punishment; it's promotion."

"The ghonara conestoga was taken out by a shaper launched from Philokalia," Agosta said. "You'll have to field threats of war. They'll be dicks—"

Kabdila stopped and swiveled back.

"See what I mean," he said. "this is what I'm talking about. You know this for a fact?"

"Yes. I found an individual open to compensation with no motivation to lie. An object matching that description was discovered and subsequently stolen from the crash."

"By?"

"Let me worry about that."

"I still haven't gotten over the part where you even know what a shaper is.

"As long as you don't ask."

"I guess it's important that I don't know."

"You always were the prudent one," Agosta said as he smirked.

"Like you said."

"Ten dead in the caravan, eleven survivors, the rectors of the local affiliation will step up to fill the ranks during the visit."

"Did you leave the room or absorb this through the walls?" Kabdila asked.

"Through the walls," Agosta said; Kabdila laughed. "It gets worse…"

Kabdila nodded, aware of what Agosta was referencing.

"Correction," Kabdila said, "he's worse."

"I'm sorry," was the expected platitude Agosta needed to offer despite not needing to.

"Father hasn't much left in him. The Aegis could save him…they could do that. At the brink of death, offer him immortality."

"…but they won't."

"We once talked about the homage we pay to them, the corruption, money lost…some by us…we heard a voice speak emperor. They'd never dangle a carrot like that atop of immortality. It would be one or the other. If they are waiting for my father to pass, this could be our chance for something greater than any coins we could find between the pillows."

"Emperor…" Agosta said with a nod, "as bright a light as the world could create."

"Brighter light, bigger shadows."

"I wish it worked that way."

"Not looking forward to it?" Kabdila said as he returned to the desk. "I thought you'd celebrate. You earned everything by your own hand. You were never the strongest…but you won every fight."

Agosta took a moment to remember his past, the fortunate events he ascribed to pure chaos that brought him to the prince.

"I left nothing for defeat," Agosta said.

"My father brought dozens of locals to act as a companion. Sycophants and milksops. You were the only one that treated me with respect."

"I slapped you once," Agosta said.

"Once."

"You were smart; I never needed to do it a second time."

"I may require a lighter touch from now on," Kabdila said as he began to leave the room.

"I'd rather not expose myself," Agosta said to the prince's back.

"Trust me, given the company, you'd be the smallest in the room." Kabdila turned back and approached the desk. "Should we have women?"

"Now, or like, in general?"

"During ceremony, when receiving dignitaries—"

"The celibate priests, the queen, and her entourage will probably see through such a cunning display of misplaced sexism—"

"You could just say *no*," Kabdila said.

"I could, but I'm paid by the syllable."

"The people enjoy seeing their royalty fringed by beauty. They're drawn to unabashed sexual energy."

"Of course," Agosta said, "I'm sure they'll remember that when it comes time for them to vote."

"Fine, fuck. Leave the women," Kabdila said as he began to leave the room. "But you can't get out of this. You'll have the opportunity to connect with cardinals, advisors, and emissaries, have them get to know you."

"They're not supposed to."

Kabdila turned back and approached the desk…again.

"Espionage is an artifact from our past lives. We have to accept new roles. If I am to ascend, I'm dragging you with me, kicking and screaming."

"Thus, eliminating your greatest asset," Agosta said.

"Glory. Power. More coin than a tax collector. I honestly thought you'd be thanking me. You're ruining my moment here."

"You needed a master of assassins," Agosta said, "which is itself an erroneous term. In recorded history, every king or steward could call on someone behind the curtain…to be honest when all others pander. That knew the secrets, where the bodies were buried. It was required to assure your ascendency, and I assumed it because anyone else would have exploited you. It requires someone shrewd and intelligent, but it's difficult to find anyone for that position who doesn't immediately start planning to assume your position. I took it because it had to be done."

"*Because you haven't ousted me from power* is not the only justification I'm using to promote you. It's the fact you haven't been trying to do my job. You've been doing yours. The irony is that I now require you to do mine as viceroy. You can't do that behind the curtain. People need to see you, respect you. You're a victim of your own integrity."

Agosta furrowed his brow.

"I can't even begin to parse out your logic on that," he said. "Do I get knighted?"

"I thought you were," Kabdila said.

"Nope."

"Why not?"

"Spy."

"Right. well, we'll have to address that."

"Have me be Coulter's page."

"I think we can skip a few steps."

"You're serious about this?"

"I trust your empathy and intelligence to find your replacement, someone that won't try to do your job. Half the time, when you weren't trying to keep me alive, you were at least keeping me popular. That's beyond the range for a spy. You had me avoid the Pogrom. Father wanted me at the Battle of Primarch Hill, for the taking of the Osmarch."

"You lost the love of the nobility but gained the respect of the people," Agosta said. "They may be patriotic, but blood from genocide never washes. I knew time would lessen the zeal, force everyone to reconcile. Enmity to amity. You were better served in the north, anyway, dealing with more political matters."

"I'm going to ascend, and I need a chancellor to lead the curia. As regent, my power was limited. I want to clear out the council and place you as viceroy." Agosta almost slammed his head on the desk, and Kabdila pushed the issue. "It has to be you; I can't trust anyone else…and you can't trust anyone else."

"Your fanbearer."

"It'd be more than that; don't use presumption as an excuse. Form a curia and assign a new master of assassins." Kabdila took a step back, smiled, and made for the exit. "At least the worst is behind us."

"Do you seriously think the worst is behind us?" Agosta asked.

Kabdila stopped, his hand inches from the door.

He turned back.

"At some point today," Kabdila said, "you're going to say, *I told you so*, aren't you?"

"Are you going to leave at some point because I need to plan my day?

"Get your patents," Kabdila said, "I'll wait outside."

CONESTOGA

The confusion stems from proctor secrecy. Even those contracted for janitorial services aren't informed of the rank structure.

You start with the **novices;** *these are technically outsiders but ones on the path to admittance. Once in, you begin as an* **initiate**—*those who attend classes and practicum. Then you're sponsored by a higher-ranking official and become an* **apprentice;** *this can last years, if not longer. Next up are the two fellowships ranks (***junior fellow** *and* **senior fellow***).*

By this point, selecting a guild chapter is mandatory, and there are hundreds. Lances are commanded by **masters;** *groups of lances are the charge of* **grandmasters.** *The guild halls are placed under the command of a* **hallmaster,** *those who even order the grands around. While masters or grandmasters run some smaller chapters,* **ordermasters** *run the oldest and largest ones.*

Finally, you have the council of **guildmasters** *that run the whole show. We don't see them often…if…at all.*

Seriously, have any of you met a guildmaster?

How many are there?

I'm not kidding; no one I know can answer this.

Rhlan Andrews
Covenant Regulars, Gammaden-534

"Where's your mask?" Noah reminded Synfallin as they approached the Bythos gateway. Synfallin took one final glimpse at the nearly barren landscape of her home exclave, another view of the stars through her dome. Night was falling, and the lights from the Faery Towers winked on.

She reached into her pack and removed the apparatus. It was a graceful unit—a single silver braided tube connecting a waist-mounted filtration device with a transparent mask covering her mouth and nose. The military models were armored with an opaque cover. At least with hers, Noah could still read her face. A large fabric wrapped around her neck to keep the mask in place, and a molecular fastener kept it locked and flushed to her face without causing marks or long-term wear on the skin.

When she activated it, it let a whisper-faint breath out of synch with hers. Lights flickered on her waist to indicate the air quality and the device's functionality.

"You only have one of those?" Noah asked.

"It's reliable."

"That's not foreboding at all," he said to himself as he punched in the alien code into a nearby podium.

The gateway opened to reveal the platform that would descend them into the catacombs. They traversed the system as it separated from the exclave, a complex mechanism each exclave possessed allowing those to enter the catacombs while the domes above still moved. A bed-sized multi-ped vehicle greeted them, fringed by two cages, Carthan's heavy HK7 tusk and Machus's mediumweight CDI sheath. Carthan flaunted piston gauntlets in oversized limbs while Machus sported a magnetic shield and a firearm stabilizer for a rather intimidating-looking industrial flamethrower.

"These your men?" Synfallin asked.

"Unfortunately," Noah said with a sigh. He directed Synfallin to the walking platform. "That's a matador. It carries crutches, supplies, camping gear, and on occasion, endolon scientists."

Synfallin circled the vehicle. An internal gyroscope stabilized its four short legs. Depending on the terrain, its padded feet could flip over to reveal small wheels, which in this situation, they had.

"It doesn't appear configured for passengers," she said.

"Find a patch and park it," Machus said with as much grace as a cold sore. Noah rolled his eyes as the two humans started off without the matador. Noah tapped a few buttons on the side of the machine. It lurched upwards as its legs found footing before settling back. Synfallin found a spot on the back ledge and mounted the vehicle. It started moving, pacing with the men in the lead.

"Told you I was the nice one," Noah whispered to her. He walked alongside, noting Synfallin's attention was focused on this side of the gateway as the platform attached to her exclave moved away from the access tunnel, cutting her off from her home. "Never left your exclave before?"

"I am certain Corvos will prep a room for my atmosphere," she said, tapping her rebreather, "but this will be my life for a while."

"You know it could be months…longer…before we're this close again."

"I am aware," she said without breaking her attention on the path behind them. There were no shutters open to space; it was a darkened stone hallway ten meters squared, extending to the limit of the cages' and matador's lights in both directions. "What now?"

"We walk. Well, you ride, we walk."

"How safe is it, In truth?"

"Each day out of an exclave puts about a twenty percent chance of encountering a watcher. Goes up by ten a day, best guess. Some people spend weeks without finding one. There are ways to avoid an encounter. Telltale marks that will help us evade them. There are also specific locations they won't enter. We'll divert through them to throw the scent off. We're also going to cross another exclave, Tokol. Not the best place, but safe enough for two days, excuse me." Noah could hear the two men grumbling ahead. It was indecipherable, but the tone was unmistakable. He caught up with them as their cages slowly lengthened their lead ahead of the matador. Neither looked back.

"Boys," Noah said.

"Glad it's just the one," Carthan said. "Was worried we'd have to deal with a family."

"Sorry you got stuck fetching the toothpick," Machus said, his tone just loud enough for Synfallin to hear.

"The what?" Noah asked, then scowled. "Not the smartest slur. If you're going to be offensive, put some fucking effort into it, at least."

"I heard they lay eggs," Carthan said.

"What?"

"I heard they all have penises," Machus said.

"Neither of those is true."

"I heard their skin is made of scales," Carthan said.

"Okay, well, that is true."

"We shouldn't be taking these contracts," Machus said in a lower tone. Noah slowed to compel the other two to follow, bringing them back in pace with the matador.

"Our pact is a promise," Noah said. "No contract unfulfilled."

"We outnumber them," Machus said.

"Proctors?"

"Humans."

"Okay." Noah was unimpressed by their attitude and hoped they would have just kept their opinions to themselves. Noah didn't know Carthan; he was a newer arrival to the Staplegunners, but Machus was incredibly unpopular given his often shared views of human exceptionalism. It was someone's cruel joke to assign him as protection for an alien, but a joke on who was unclear to Noah. He knew part of his assignment was to offer a more diplomatic face to ensure future contracts.

"Like ten to one," Carthan said. "They have one world, we have like…I don't know, twenty."

"We're all in this together," Noah said.

"Where did you get that crap?" Machus said.

"They're so gangly," Carthan said, "like a bunch of…of...

"I don't care if you finish that statement," Noah said.

"Noah—" Machus was almost trying to form an argument as if his opinion could be considered civilized.

"Firstly," Noah said, "this is our charge. Our responsibility. I will ensure that this contract and this lance fulfill that charge. And those that don't will face a reckoning. Are we clear on that?"

"The guild is life; we should come first."

"That's your first mistake—pact before proctors. And placing us first mandates we complete our contract. Why did you join the guild?"

"They answer to one," Carthan said.

"We set the laws out here," Machus said.

"Well, good luck with that," Noah said. "Until then, you answer to me. I'm steward. Out front…and if we lose sight of you, I'll assume you abandoned your contract."

Noah slowed his pace to allow the matador to catch up. He kept in front of it, occasionally glancing back to Synfallin, who continued staring into the darkness behind them. It was absolute. Only a few meters past her feet, and it unnerved her. If something emerged from the shadow, she wouldn't have time to flinch, let alone scream. Noah assumed she had heard the conversation.

She had.

* * *

It felt like hours, but it hadn't even been one before Noah allowed the matador to move past him. He cast the light on his shoulder behind to reveal an empty passage. He looked ahead and confirmed the two men hadn't extended their lead out front.

"I suppose you expect gratitude," Synfallin said.

Noah came behind the vehicle.

"Yeah…" he said.

"Okay…you have it."

"Good enough."

"How does one survive out here?"

"They don't."

"Jackers do."

"It's shocking what one will commit to when in a cult. They act against their best interests. How they manage to survive out here is beyond anyone. Trust me, this is the part of the job we enjoy the least. Nothing is gratifying about living in darkness. These catacombs are not meant for the living."

"Do you think it's a test?"

"What is?"

"Everything."

"The one aspect of this…world, if you want to call it that…is that it's not supposed to make sense. People find patterns if they search for them. If you stand back far enough, you'll only find chaos. Maybe we're not meant to understand it. Maybe it's not designed to make sense. We look beyond the domes and see stars, planets, and even the most bizarre astronomical phenomena that can be explained. But this...nope. Also, I thought we weren't supposed to talk."

"We got parts!" Coulter said as he diverted to a mound of fragments near a wall. Machus followed, and both shredded the mass like a birthday present. Noah remained with Synfallin.

"Anything?" Noah asked.

Machus pushed a large piece aside and found the fresh remains of who this crutch belonged to. The body had been bifurcated head to waist. Machus slowly flopped the head out of the way to examine what was once a human shell, a model known as a torque, slightly larger than a jagger and considerably larger than a dodger. Whatever destroyed it didn't leave much behind.

"Stripped it clean; only scabs are this thorough," Carthan said.

"They even ripped his implants out—wait!" Machus said as he wiggled a hand between the halves of the body and extracted a module the scavengers had missed. "fusion core." It was a recognizable part.

His finger flicked open a hatch on a nearby limb of his crutch. He pressed a button concealed within it and ejected the previously damaged module. He swapped it with the newly acquired battery. Several once dim lights across the back of the crutch grew brighter.

"Are we good?" Noah asked.

"That was all unless your companion wants to dig for scraps."

"Then let's get back on pace," Noah said. He hadn't stopped the matador, and the two others had to catch up to resume their lead.

"Is that a perk of the profession?" Synfallin asked. Noah offered a cock-sided grin. He remained silent, waiting for Synfallin to address his previous point. She finally did. "Yes, let's talk; it is going to be two days."

"Three."

Synfallin almost managed a smile. She altered her perch on the vehicle, bringing her long legs under her.

"You're not an imbecile."

"Thank you?" Noah said as a query.

"I think your associates are."

"Well read. As you implied, intelligence is not a requirement."

"Was it scabs?"

"Probably. Or a watcher and someone passed by later."

"If a watcher attacked, would you be able to defeat it?"

"Probably not."

"Then why only three in your lance?

"Because five still wouldn't be enough."

"What happens if we cannot avoid one?"

"We're expected to lay our lives to ensure the survival of the contract…that would be you, in case you were worried."

"The book is more important—"

"No. It's not." He waited to gauge Synfallin's reaction. She was about to smile before he added, "the contract never mentioned the book."

Synfallin's mounting grin faded.

"You would sacrifice your life?"

"Oh, don't summon up another compliment. I'll throw those two to the knives before sticking my neck out." That did bring a smile from the endolon. "I prefer the escort missions over the salvage or resource contracts. There's more to gain, more at stake. Puts a…face…to what we do."

"But you'll still scavenge when you can."

"Of course, we're not angels. And the progress and survivability of proctors, as well as everyone, depends on that. There's stuff everywhere like you just saw. Another aspect of a puzzle that can't be assembled. Weavers abandoned their vessel in view of worlds we can never reach with colonies that migrate for no reason. Then they scatter technology, a knowledge surprisingly easy to comprehend. Modular systems. Universal power supplies. We mastered their machines in a generation, but despite that, we can't figure the rest out, like they placed a crevice of ignorance so vast that no one could cross it. Most don't even think about it."

"And you?"

"All the time. I can't help but think. Were the weavers even alive? Were they physical?"

"Evidence points they are. From the dimensions of the doors to the access panels. We can discern a language, one not dissimilar to your own."

"Assuming it's theirs." Noah scanned the featureless black hallway, the granite-like stone walls that were in no way granite. "What about you?"

"Me?"

"Yeah, what's your story?"

"That implies you've been talking about yourself all this time."

"Call me curious."

Synfallin turned to check how far ahead the other two men were and if they could overhear the conversation.

"Well, I emerged from my egg sixteen years ago and was adopted into my kin…" She trailed off as Noah furrowed his brow, a little dazed by the statement. "Joke. I overheard you talking."

"No, the egg line is funny," he said. "I'd take my hat off if I had one. The age threw me for a moment."

"We reach adulthood at eight. I guess you missed that part."

"Are we on the same calendar?"

"The measurement laid down by Volani. I am employing the standard. It is a notable variation of our two species; you are born with basic motor skills. You emerge with functional vocal cords and solid bones. We are born after only a few months and waste the next six attached to our mothers. After that, our development explodes while yours stagnates."

"It's called being a kid. And trust me, the longer it lasts, the better."

"I am an adult. Don't let your perceptions of your species misdirect your opinion of someone else's."

"My apologies—"

"The khitin live for two thousand years. Would you enjoy it if one called you a child? We do still live as long as you."

"Point."

"I enjoyed my childhood. Candidly, I think you spend too much time in adolescence. You are considered an adult when? Twenty? Nineteen?"

"Still not sure; I'll let you know when I am one."

"And yet your species becomes capable of producing offspring when? Fourteen? Thirteen? What a dreadful dichotomy."

"Yeah, that does make puberty a colossal pain in the ass. We have childhood, adulthood, and then a long stretch of awkwardness and confusion that usually results in people making jackasses of each other while standing by the belief that it's the best part of our lives. So, you just…skip that point?"

"For the lack of a better phrase. I received my first master certificate when I was ten."

"Let me guess: Historical archaeology?" he asked. Synfallin was aghast. "I'm not lying. That was a literal guess."

"Bibliometrics. Historical archaeology was my second. Took a break to work in the library before pursuing inorganic chemistry. Came back to Culmilla and was there…when the book came to me."

"Came…to you?"

Synfallin didn't want the next part overheard, so she lowered her tone. She was also unsure how Noah would take what she said, not that she should be concerned about what he thought. Why was she?

"I had walked every hallway of every level a hundred times. A million books, and I could tell you the names of all of them."

"That's…both impressive and a little heartbreaking."

"And one day, it was a million and one."

"Misfiling."

"No date of entry. Had never been checked out. My field was the study of books. Not what they say as much as how and why. When were certain stories told, and who told them? One day, I was compelled to an aisle I had not been to in ages and found a book that had no right being where it was."

"Not very scientific."

"I never said it was. Though I'm compelled to apply that knowledge in its study. Corvos possesses the largest collections anyone has ever seen. Nothing is created in a vacuum. I was able to structure a history of where this book has appeared, but I cannot for the life of me determine how it gets from place to place and where it started its journey."

"Sounds like an obsession."

"Why do you think I am here?"

"How would you describe this compulsion? Was it a…dream?"

"A voice."

"Whose?'

Synfallin remembered when it happened—stopping when she shouldn't have—noticing something that she hadn't yet seen—slowly slinking, rolling her hands along the spines. There it was, laying on its side in a gap next to a bookend. She looked down to the tome on her lap, unchanged since that moment…outside of Noah's stain. She didn't notice that Noah's attention was diverted.

"Mine…" she said. "I would say—"

"Stay quiet," he whispered loudly as he tapped a button that halted the matador.

"What is it?" she whispered. He glared at her.

"Stay…quiet."

Carthan and Machus saw it too and were slowly backtracking.

"Movement," Carthan said, "three hundred meters and closing. Fast."

"We passed an alley," Noah said as he dimmed his lights and beckoned the matador to a trot. It rotated sharply, so much so that Synfallin had to hold on. Carthan and Machus reached the narrow hallway, one that Synfallin had missed entirely. It was barely wide enough to fit the walker. Carthan and Machus squeezed with the matador following; they certainly weren't going to stand between the vehicle and what was out there. Noah entered last.

"What—" Synfallin almost couldn't help but be curious, but Noah sharply cut her off with a finger.

"Cut all power," he said in cryptolect with a single syllable.

"I don't' speak—"

"Power off," he said to her. Every light deactivated. A few quick button taps shut the matador down. Noah opened a side hatch and unfolded a pair of large, heavy blankets. He threw one to Carthan and Machus and beckoned Synfallin down from the vehicle, which she obeyed.

Carthan and Machus shut their crutches off and held the blanket up. It looked of the same stone as the wall. Noah deactivated his dodger's systems; it suddenly became heavier and harder to move. He motioned to her waist.

"Rebreather," he whispered. Synfallin apprehensively reached down and deactivated the unit. Most endolons could survive five minutes without a rebreather, maybe ten if they were healthy and prepared. "I'm going to invade your personal space."

He pulled Synfallin close and threw the covering over them. It was freezing to the touch, but Noah ensured Synfallin was covered. Her instinct was to push him away, but she fought against it. He looked at her and her at him, with no attention paid to the central passageway.

It was a grinding snarl, like a failing machine mixed with the dying breath of a large animal. The footfalls rang metal on metal, followed by scratching as it dragged limbs along. They could hear a clock tick, then a deep growl intermingled with what could only be described as a massive dot matrix printer. It called out, sounding like a deep-tone air siren. Its steps thundered, sending vibrations the group could feel.

Synfallin's hands vibrated as the sound grew louder. Another step. Noah reached out and held her hand. It didn't stop shaking. Another step, louder. More ticking. More growling.

Then silence for what felt like a minute. The following foot fell further away, then another. The pace quickened, and the noise grew fainter.

Noah released her as the steps faded to just the echoes of a distant beast. It twisted around a distant intersection, and the sound fell off entirely.

"We're staying here the night," whispered loud enough for everyone to hear.

"Whole place is night," Synfallin whispered.

"Keep bundled in the shields. Power stays off."

"I can't keep the respirator off."

Noah nodded and nudged her to activate it.

"We'll chance it then."

"Too much a risk," Machus said from the other side of the vehicle.

"We're out here. Risk is life."

*   *   *

"Hey…you up?" Noah asked.

Synfallin's eyes flipped open.

"Yes," she said. The incredible speed of her response caused Noah to jump.

"Okay, I guess you're a morning person."

"It's just how we wake. Sorry."

Noah pulled the blanket off them. He peaked into the passageway. It was still dark, with no indication six hours had passed.

"You're cold, by the way," he said.

"It's how we conserve energy. That cover, does it block thermal energy?"

"Among other things. It won't fool a watcher stalking prey, but one passing will often not operate with active sensors."

"So, that was a watcher."

Noah nodded.

"Still have yet to see one." He peeked over the vehicle. "You two alive?"

"Of course," Machus said as the two of them awoke.

Noah initiated the power core of his crutch, and he strode into the passageway. He shined his light down both directions.

"We'll chance the matador's batteries. Pick up speed and save time."

It involved the matador lowering its center of gravity. Carthan and Machus sat at the front, anchored to the machine, while Noah sat on the rear with Synfallin. It was slow to accelerate, but in time, the machine reached speeds that the endolon had never felt. She gripped onto a railing with one hand and a fold of carbon fiber on Noah's dodger with the other. At this velocity in this darkness, it was challenging to judge actual speed. The machine employed thermal vision and sonar to map out the terrain ahead. It hummed loudly.

"Can't that creature hear this?" Synfallin asked.

"Most likely," Noah said.

"Can it run this fast?"

"No idea."

"Well, is this vehicle safe at this speed?"

"Oh!" Noah laughed with a reassuring pat on her leg. "No."

TORUS

The wording is oddly specific.

We expanded to colonize this world…no one ever wrote that we built anything. Given records, it's unlikely that we would have or even could have erected the Metropolis. We didn't expand into the world; we expanded into the city and claimed it as ours.

Look at our population before and after. This city could hold billions. Where are they?

The Great Collapse?

If such a cataclysm could have killed all but a few hundred million, it would have finished the job. And where are the bodies?

Also, everyone seems to be ignoring the most glaring evidence of all…there are not enough mineral resources and wood in the world to have constructed all of it.

No, it was like this when we got here.

Dr. Joachim Raddad
Corvos National University.

As night fell, Agosta, Sloan, and Elina took a brisk pace back to the train. This close to Nimbus equated to a more extended evening. Sloan was escorting ahead of the other two. There was still enough light to see the land but not enough to discern details.

"Who is she?" Elina asked Agosta, making no attempt to whisper.

"A friend?" Agosta said.

"A close friend?"

"No," Sloan said. "And don't speak too loudly."

Elina firmed her lips as if scolded. She looked at Agosta and smiled.

"She seems nice," she said spiritedly.

"Does she have to talk?"

"It's a common weakness of—" Agosta said sarcastically.

"Women?" Elina said.

"I was going to say, children."

"I'm not a child."

"Being chatty is probably how she was discovered," Sloan said.

"It wasn't that."

"Was she a runaway?"

"No," both Agosta and Elina said simultaneously.

"They had to have noticed something valuable. Difficult to believe she was a random mark."

"At this point, what good would it serve to scrutinize the past," Agosta said.

"I'm only saying that given her exuberant disposition, I'm surprised they didn't kill her."

"Hey!" Elina said.

"By all means, be abrupt," Agosta said.

Sloan stopped, realizing her indiscreet and hasty tone had resulted in a relatively insensitive response. She wasn't trying to be callous; it was a reflex action. She faced the two following her.

"I'll clarify," she said, addressing Agosta. "If they planned on killing you, there'd be no point in keeping her alive."

Agosta stared back without commenting, and they shared awkward silence.

"I'm…standing here," Elina said.

Sloan was still doing it, and she finally stopped to breathe. Maybe her hackles were still up from the encounter. Regardless of experience, killing someone is a stressful act unless one's a psychopath. "Bluntness is a common trait of my people," she said to Elina.

"You've met a lot of them to verify that observation, have you?" Agosta asked.

"Maybe it's an aspect of being older," Elina said.

"And how old do you think I am?" Sloan asked.

Elina considered her answer and smiled broadly.

"Late…teens?"

Sloan turned back to Agosta.

"Okay, I like her," she said. "Let's just keep walking." Sloan resumed her walk, assuming the others would follow, which they did.

"From what I heard, your kind is one in a million," Elina said.

"Somewhat hard to run a census."

"More than a few arks want people like you dead."

"I consider that ironic."

"So, you only possess a physical body when touching your weapon?" Elina asked, her volume increasing slightly as Sloan walked fast to extend her lead.

"It's a totem," Sloan said. "Mine just happens to be a weapon."

"Does it contain your soul?"

"No idea. Where's yours?"

"Point. So, if you let it go, you go invisible?"

"Yes, there are moments when disappearing can be useful."

"Like when?"

"Like when I desperately need to get out of a conversation."

"I want to meet another effigy, so I can compare. Being blunt is a choice. I can't see it being genetic. My dad's blunt."

"You must take after your mother."

"I wouldn't know."

Sloan stopped again. That fact was staring at her in the face, and she bludgeoned through it without thinking. She scowled to Agosta…because she honestly couldn't think of another reaction.

"Don't look at me; I haven't said a thing in two minutes," Agosta said.

"You could inform her that we're not safe," Sloan said, "that anything we do telegraphs our location to potential threats. I look at you because you're responsible for her. Technically, you're responsible for all of this." Sloan continued walking.

Elina continued to chip away.

"You know, it would be useful if I knew your name," Elina said.

"I know."

"So…?"

Agosta shook his head in disbelief.

"Honey, don't bother her," Agosta said.

"How is talking a bother."

Sloan tossed her sword back to Agosta, who caught it. She promptly vanished.

"That's subtle," he said as he resumed walking.

"You know, I read up on effigy," Elina said to an invisible and intangible Sloan. "I know you can still hear us."

"Maybe you shouldn't bother her," Agosta said.

"Is it true they have a limited memory?"

"A hundred years."

"And they can't remember anything before? That explains the charms. They don't keep a diary?"

"Some do, but given they're always on the move, and their very lives are forfeit in some cities, it's challenging to keep. Plus, potentially thousands of years of life, you'd need more than a notebook."

"That's why…" Elina said, comprehending the implications of the effigy curse, and it was a curse—gaining immortality but being forced to forget everything past a hundred years.

"What do you mean?" Agosta asked.

"If you don't care for anyone, no need to add to your totem. Still feels like a personal choice. Has she always been like this, or am I just grating?"

Agosta looked down at her and smirked with a wink.

"My guess, little from column A; little from column B."

"Then what made you select her?"

"It's...complicated."

"Did you ask, or did she volunteer?"

"I asked her."

"And is she always like this?"

"My sample size has been three days, so I wouldn't know."

"I can judge people in far less time."

"Oh, I'm sure."

Elina took a second to see where they were walking. Sloan left no impression, no ghostly apparition, footfalls, or impressions where she walked. She didn't even disturb the sand or the air. She was ethereal.

"Is she...still here?" Elina asked. "How do you know she didn't leave?"

"She wouldn't leave her totem," Agosta said.

Elina smiled with an almost twinkle in her eye.

"She must trust you," she said.

"How do you mean?"

"Well...she did just literally put her soul in your hands."

Agosta considered what Elina said and admired the extravagant weapon in his hand. This close, outside of a fight, he could finally take note of the dozens of different trinkets, each a different shape, some with inscriptions, others without. A few were scuffed, and given the enchantment imbued in the totem to render it virtually indestructible, they must have been centuries old, if not more.

Sloan materialized in front of Agosta as she snatched the weapon back.

"Come to think of it," she said as she resumed her lead.

Elina leaned in closer and whispered, still loud enough for Sloan to hear.

"You know, when they're mean to you, it means they like you."

"Don't start," Agosta muttered back.

"Just saying."

"I just rescued you from bandits; stop trying to be a matchmaker."

"You're always bad with women—"

"No," Agosta said, "I'm bad with the women you keep trying to set me up with. Remember Kari?"

Sloan couldn't help but listen, her head cocked to the side to better pick up the conversation. She shouldn't be curious, but she spent the better part of three days with Agosta and knew little about him until now.

"I liked her," Elina said. "She was honest. Nice hair, attentive, she was tall—"

"She was a prostitute," Agosta said.

"Well," Elina whispered, "I didn't know that initially. And to be honest, that shouldn't affect your heart."

"You paid her with your allowance—"

Sloan smirked.

"I was eleven," Elina said, "you need to let that go."

"And Emma?" Agosta said.

"Not my fault…how was I supposed to know she only wanted you for money."

"You told her I was rich."

Sloan couldn't help but let out a chuckle, then frowned when she realized the other two probably heard her, which they did. Agosta caught Sloan feigning ignorance as she marched ahead.

Elina missed Sloan's reaction and wasn't willing to let the conversation go. There was an awkward silence before she broke it again.

"Just saying," she said. "There's someone right here."

"She's a mercenary," Agosta said. "And effigies generally avoid personal connections."

Elina nodded and acted momentarily as if the answer settled her.

It didn't.

"Her charms point to the contrary," she said.

Sloan stopped. She held her hand up for the others to hold still and remain quiet. A sudden breeze snaked between them.

"Screevers?" Agosta asked.

Sloan glared back, then shook her head.

Elina instinctually clung to her father's arm.

Agosta unlocked the straps on his holsters and scanned the darkness. Only loginoids and zodiacs were blessed with night vision. What would generally be considered stars in an ordinary world were the bonfires and furnaces of civilizations on the opposite side of the convex, partially concealed by the swirling clouds of the Stream. Thousands of kilometers away, the light of Uno cast an elliptical swath of daylight on the landscape, meaning the sun was still several hours before it would appear on the opposite side of Nimbus.

They all heard the scream, high-pitched and inhuman, almost resembling metal scraping on metal. Then another, overlapping the first.

"What is it?" Elina asked.

Her father didn't answer; he just pulled Elina behind him and drew his firearms.

They scanned for movement and found an approaching shape accelerating towards them.

Agosta opened fire and could hear rounds impacting.

It continued approaching and emerged from the shadows.

It resembled a dust devil, only slightly larger than a human, composed entirely of loose metal and garbage, except it possessed arms and legs of smaller swirls of debris.

Agosta quickly reloaded his weapon.

Another emerged near Sloan, who responded by slicing the creature in half.

She removed her own firearm, an obsidian and brass accented gyrojet.

The two halves of the beast struck the ground; although parts had fallen off it, the two halves reassembled and reached out to Sloan, allowing her to gaze into the vortex it used as an arm and the blender of knives contained within.

Sloan threw her sword in the air and vanished, the creature reaching through the space she occupied.

Sloan caught the blade behind the creature, and she attacked again, flaying more metal.

The one focused on Agosta stretched out a limb. Agosta pushed Elina down and fired his weapon, striking the creature.

It didn't appear phased.

Agosta ejected the cylinder from his revolver and removed a red-painted one from his belt.

He locked it in place and fired as the creature approached.

Instead of penetrating, the round exploded in a booming thundercrack, propelling a concussive wave into the monster, causing large fragments of its swirling storm-like body to flay off.

Agosta emptied the valuable cylinder as the last fragment of the creature dissipated.

He reloaded as Sloan continued to slice segments of the one she was engaged with until she could kick and slap the smaller pieces away.

Neither of them spotted a third one jumping upon Agosta's back.

Elina crawled away as the monster tried to shred through Agosta's jacket.

Elina shrieked, and her eyes changed to an iridescent yellow.

Whisps of black smoke drifted from her nose and mouth.

The humanoid cyclone's attention shifted to the girl as Elina screamed again.

Sloan watched as a light formed between Elina and the beast. It struck the monster, tossing it away from Agosta, melting metal and vaporizing plastic.

Agosta spun to get a shot on the monster, only to find it fading into gas.

Elina collapsed, exhausted.

Sloan stood, mouth agape, as Agosta saw to his daughter. She had returned to normal and was crying as her father embraced her.

Sloan firmed her jaw and ensured there were no other monsters. She then approached Agosta, somewhat annoyed.

"Failed to volunteer this fact," Sloan said. Agosta didn't answer; he just held his daughter as she calmed down; the smoke vanished from her eyes, the glow fading. "Her capture wasn't random."

"No," Agosta said. He comforted Elina but looked back to Sloan. "I think you can now understand my assumption that they wouldn't have given her up." Sloan stood her ground as Agosta fumed. "And yes, I knew…and no, I wasn't planning on telling you; it wouldn't have mattered; it's not why you were hired, and I never lied to you about the situation or potential risk!"

Sloan's jaw unhinged slightly as she considered the questions she had lined up.

"Well," Sloan said, "Yeah, okay, that does pretty much cover it." She smirked, scanned for a large enough rock, found one, and sat on it.

Elina's heavy breathing was slowing as she calmed. A few tears trickled down her cheek from the exertion.

"I offered the contract due to your skillset," Agosta said, "your assurance of confidentiality, and that when required, upon your possible death, your capacity to literally disappear. No one knows of her gift of smoke, and if I have anything to say about it, no one will."

"That was never in doubt," Sloan said. "You want to answer the rest of my questions before I ask them?"

Agosta's tone quietened, and he became less curt.

"There's no conspiracy at work," he said. "No rivalry. I don't represent an ark, privateers, or pirates. She had a moment of weakness, and they noticed. That was it. They assumed I trusted them regarding ransom, but I knew they would never let her go. You gave me another option. The alternate…I'd accepted."

Sloan nodded.

"At the cost of your life," she said. Agosta glanced down to Elina, electing not to answer. "No need to worry. You're correct. I can disappear. And forgetting is both a skill and a character trait. It explains your commitment back there. I thought it was because they killed your parents when you were a child. Would you have left witnesses?"

"I'm not a killer."

"Oh yes, you are. When you take a life, you're a killer, no matter the justification or circumstance. You have to either accept or disregard it. But for what it's worth…I understand your motivation."

Agosta let it pass without comment. The surrounding environment had gotten quiet save a slight breeze that stirred the dust. He changed topics.

"It's not usually my character to inquire of a woman's age," he said, "but it's a forgone conclusion you've been alive longer than me."

Sloan nodded.

"Safe assumption," she said.

"Have you ever seen anything like that?"

Sloan wondered how much Agosta knew about her, about her kind, their capacity to remember, or rather their capacity to forget. Most people ignored the fact effigies were still human, and a human brain simply didn't possess the ability to remember the memories of an immortal life.

"Out here, the one thing to expect is the unexpected," Sloan said. "But I don't recall my entire life. I'm limited—"

"To a century of memories, I know, but that's still more than either of us."

Sloan grimaced.

"Familiarity…that's all I got," she said. Sloan then stood, approached Agosta, and offered him her sword. He was confused.

"Take it," she said.

"Why?" he asked.

"I'm going to see if there's any more. Make your way to the train."

"When I commented about your capacity to disappear—"

"I will come back," she said. "My awareness when incorporeal is stunted, but I'd rather be undetected. Consider this incentive to assure my return."

Agosta hesitantly accepted the weapon.

"I'm trusting you with my soul." She then released it and vanished.

Elina sniffed and wiped her tears away.

She smirked.

"I like her," Elina whispered.

* * *

Agosta and Elina franticly approached the rusted black-iron boxcab of the Loch & Serpent. Dawn was an hour away, and their lamp was fading. The cab door slid open, and Machus emerged, either surprised or unimpressed.

"You did it?!" he asked.

"Don't act so shocked," Agosta said as he helped Elina.

"You lose the ghost?"

"We'll wait for her," Agosta said as he stepped aboard.

"Not too long, I hope."

"We'll wait."

Machus rolled his eyes and slammed the cab door once they were both inside. He ignored them and sat on his CIC chair as Agosta and Elina descended into the locomotive's rear bunker.

As they left, Machus closed the door between them. Agosta and Elina slid onto the bench against the cab wall, Agosta removing Sloan's blade from his back. He placed it on his lap and let out a wearied exhale.

"Him, I don't like," Elina said.

PARADISE

When the Aegis emerged and founded the Ascension, they promised to stop the random, unpredictable storms plaguing Paradise. They would end the plight of mankind struggling to survive in an inhospitable place. The Aegis offered new hybridized crops that would flourish in Paradise soil. They provided the staples for a growing civilization. One offering was maize, along with the process of nixtamalization that was lacking at that time.

These treasures were considered more valuable than any jewels that could be bestowed. The Aegis boasted advanced technology that appeared magical to those on Bythos. While some humans managed to scale the pillars to reach the closest worlds, others remained uncolonized. The Aegis promised to reduce infant mortality by gifting medical knowledge and granting limited access to basic machines to build grand structures. Humanity would be nomadic no more. Many nations fell to their knees in worship of these new gods.

However, some tribes, like Volani and Corvos, still appreciative of these gifts, believed these visitors were simply travelers blessed with greater knowledge and little else. But everyone accepted the blessings offered, ready to endure the conditions that came along with it.

A Brief History of The Impossible
Academic Roxxan Rosania

After the host of sharpened steel rode up the hill to secure the crash, Terri returned to the land whale while its driver was still fixated on the survivors that emerged from the caravan. Terri assumed the church would sidestep putting witnesses to flame, given the number of bystanders. A few kilometers further away, over the crest of the hill, and that might have occurred.

Terri wasn't willing to linger for recognition and snatched her pack from the vehicle. The tall grass concealed her flight until she blended with the procession of a hundred carriages en route to Sadatoni's northern gate. The visitors were petrified by the implications of a divine power crashing within sight of the city.

However, it provided the distraction and cover Terri desired to enter the capital without impedance. She ducked into the first backstreet she found and crouched. She removed the chrome sphere from her pocket and held it just long enough to ensure it remained unbroken before removing a square of softened leather and wrapping the orb with it. She shoved the ball deep into her pack and threw the bundle over her shoulder.

Terri wandered the streets for at least an hour, navigating the labyrinth, reminiscing of the time she was last in the city. Hearsay caught up to her as she crossed to the inner city. By now, the whole of the population knew what had occurred. Without physical evidence, fabrications mixed with facts with claims of what kind of beast would be strong enough to fell a god's chariot.

Along with monsters came tales of heroes. Every narrative required its antithesis, and the crowds quickly latched onto the pair of militia that had reached the crash first. Terri never heard of what came of the driver, assuming he was quickly drinking his accolades away.

* * *

Terri eventually located her mentor's library, only to discover it had been converted to a chapel by the Ascension. She was not impressed and recalled the letter Kaiden had sent her.

I may greet you at the gate.

He didn't.

Only if it's afternoon.

It was.

Knights from everywhere will be in attendance.

That was true, especially given recent events. Terri had avoided an inquisition when authorities swept the crash site. They questioned the whale's pilot and the other passengers, but decades avoiding purgitans in Corvos proved a valuable skill.

Not at my current address, but will still be found there.

Terri knew she had been gone for some time, but had it been that long?

Terri entered the establishment, only to find no indication of the library and institution it once was. While the exterior features hadn't changed, the interior had been gutted.

No mark of Kaiden or the academy he kept remained. Nothing—shelves, chairs, and even the drapes. The braziers were lifted from the walls, and the door handles had been replaced.

There was no evidence this relocation had been forced. The church had moved onto the main floor. Pews lined up the aisles of the nave. The narthex was peppered with pamphlets and posters promoting Ascension propaganda.

"Welcome, child," announced an ascension representative. Terri knew how to distinguish the vestments; this was no deacon or cardinal. There were much larger cathedrals in the city populated by such pageantry.

She bore a resemblance. The two shared the same tone of dark bronze skin and short sable hair, though Terri's was straighter. Even the accent matched; probably a Corvinian expatriate. Terri was still donned in black trousers and a double-breasted vest waistcoat while her twin approached in a loose-flowing, white floor-length hooded liturgical robe. The silver gilding was a nice touch.

"Child?" Terri asked.

"We're all juveniles in the face of immortals," she said. "Welcome to the Cove of the Silantine." She then offered a pamphlet, obviously assuming, correctly, that Terri was a tourist. Terri accepted but only skimmed the cover, which read, *The Gods in the Unblinking Eye.*

"And this is?" Terri asked.

"Just a testimonial about the many gifts our gods can offer."

Terri offered it back.

"I can't read," she lied with such an unmistakable tone as to conceal nothing. Her doppelganger turned and sorted papers, expecting a crowd given the flood of expected travelers. Terri took the distraction to inspect the chapel, searching for any evidence of what became of Kaiden.

"Services begin in thirty minutes," the cleric said.

"Been…here…long?" Terri said as she wandered the lobby.

"Several years…visiting?"

Terri poked her head into the nave; the renovation had been comprehensive.

"You appropriate this dwelling?" she asked. "Did your purgitans sanitize it because someone found a spring in a corner?"

It was becoming more difficult for Terri to withhold her impudence. The cleric intercepted her before Terri could wander.

"Is there something else I can offer you?" the cleric asked.

Terri smirked and feigned admiration of the chapel.

I just remember this place being a," she said, "…not an Ascension church."

"I believe it was a library," the cleric said. "And no…nothing was burned. The shelves were bare."

"Ransacked?" Terri asked.

"I wouldn't know. From Philokalia?"

"Corvos, but you knew that."

As Terri observed the rather discourteous Ascension propaganda on the walls, she noted something or the lack of something. The archway to the lower level had been bricked up and gracefully blended with the surrounding arches to appear part of the original design.

"Not common in these parts," the cleric said. Terri focused on her.

"Yes," Terri said, "Aurago has made it abundantly clear our kingdom is next on the chopping block." A slight smirk insinuated Terri was goading the cleric to defend the actions of her church and their divinities.

"I can't imagine the Aegis would approve of another war," the cleric asked.

"Aurago only allowed to destroy one culture a generation? Or is it just because they don't want a war on two fronts?"

"Here's hoping succession brings wisdom."

"Hasn't in the past." Terri made for the exit. She knew there was no visible evidence to glean from inside the chapel, but the priest wasn't yielding and exclaimed to Terri's back.

"I envision this will eventually skew into an accusation of church interference, that the Aegis backed the last conflict. That we were in some way responsible for the fall of Volani."

Terri confronted the cleric, taking a quick moment to ensure no one else could hear. She wasn't afraid of speaking her mind, but she was taught to be cautious.

"Gods can't take credit for the good if they're not willing to accept accountability for the bad," Terri said. "And calling it a fall is somewhat disingenuous. Ignores morality; that's why everyone calls it a pogrom. And I won't accuse the Aegis of being responsible for Volani…I don't have to."

"This is a chapel, not a curia basilica," the cleric said. "I'm a simple rector. I can debate scripture and hear confession. I leave the rest for deacons and those that directly hold the ear of gods. They are due to attend the festival this year."

Terri stopped at the entrance.

"I know," she said. "I was there when their impenetrable magical chariot was taken down." The rector's reaction was a surprise, and Terri let out a slight chuckle. "You didn't hear? I pulled the coffin from the wreckage myself." Terri pushed open the heavy iron and wood doors to leave. "You better clean this place up. It's going to go sideways fairly quickly, and I'm getting a front-row seat."

Terri exited the building, leaving the rector in silence, surrounded by the indoctrination of her faith.

The Ascension faith became the dominant religion across the Solokring, quickly overwhelming all others. It was easy to convert the masses when the gods spoken of in scripture could manifest dramatically.

Faith was hardly required when actual gods controlled a manufactured universe. Joining the church was an easy decision for many, and the Ascension promised comfortable living, an education, and the potential for advancement.

Those elected to the Ahkdanate served for life, but only the Aegis lived forever. Even to reach the Diaconate would have been an honor. All they asked was complete and absolute obedience, to follow the edicts of the faith and the words spoken in the holiest of texts, the Canon of Iokon.

Applicants studied in a Neoqism or Ascension school and could be enlisted as children—the school took over edification until adulthood without financial burden on the family, assuming the student passed yearly tests, most of which assessed loyalty over actual knowledge.

Eventually, a graduate was sent to the Exclave to become either a priest in training or a rector. This generally lasted five years, and although practicums were common, many rectors remained within the Exclave until graduating to the Diaconate. It was then where loyalty was assumed, and the individual was believed to speak for the church without other authority.

A rector was expected to uphold the tenets of the Iokon and the ideology enforced by the Ascension. Rectors were tasked with enforcing the prohibition of technological development, silencing non-Ascension religions, and suppressing anti-Ascension sentimentality wherever it was found.

Suffice to say, they were not a hit at social gatherings.

* * *

Church eyes everywhere.

Terri knew Kaiden was right. So, where would an academic hide?

Not at my current address, but will still be found there.

What could that possibly mean?

Terri circled the building, entering a small empty alley. An aperture in the cobblestones provided drainage to a nearby sewer, the advantage of living in one of the few cities. Corvos also took pride in such accomplishments, but they also had flush toilets.

Odor from the sewers getting worse.

Terri thought about that statement.

Why would Kaiden mention such a point?

Terri peeked into the sewer grate, noting the scratches around the rim and that it was not locked down. She examined the alley to ensure no one was watching, then pulled on the grate to expose the ladder. Terri heaved the grate back over after she descended.

She thought, leave it to Kaiden to hide his laboratory under an Ascension temple. Terri followed the water until it diverted down another tunnel, revealing the door that resembled a wall until she got close. She knew she was directly under the chapel, Kaiden's old academy.

Somehow Kaiden managed to ram almost his entire library in his basement. Aisles were narrow and marked with obstacles. Garbage was thrown everywhere from unused or broken inventions.

Terri found Kaiden surrounded by junk but what he would call valuable artifacts and essential tools.

"Seriously?" Terri said.

Kaiden was concentrating on writing and appeared unphased as he finished a page.

"Knew you'd find me," he said.

"Under the chapel," Terri said. "You sold your academy to an organization that wants to execute you and then built a lab in their basement?"

"Last place they'd look." Kaiden finished and closed his book. He turned to see his old student. "Also, natural stone over me. I could build a bookcase, and they wouldn't hear it."

"Just…come back to Corvos," she said. "I know you were born here, but what loyalty do you have?"

"I couldn't be productive there."

"You had tenure, Kaiden; you didn't *have* to be productive."

Kaiden smiled proudly and opened his arms wide for Terri's embrace.

"Terri…it's been a while," he said.

"It has," she said, "…you've… shrunk."

"Ironically, I've been trying to see smaller. Is that irony?"

"Coincidence."

"Regardless, I find more as I do…does that make sense? Should see less when you narrow your vision."

She pulled away and smiled at her old teacher.

"Your teachings haven't changed. Surprised anyone passed."

"You did."

"Fifty, point-five percent."

"The median was thirty-nine; you excelled."

"Was that why you left?" she asked as she wandered his broken and cluttered collection. "Was Corvos too smart for you?"

"Those above us preach to the pews," he said. "Thousands listen, but they convince no one. They don't want enlightenment, just validation. Opening the eyes of academics was too easy. Sadatoni may be hostile, but it's more interesting."

"Still, it would have been an easier commute."

"And for that, I'm sorry."

Terri failed to spot the metal box she kicked across the room into precariously stacked beakers. She shook her head and began arranging.

"You're getting better at organizing," she said.

"Very funny."

Terri returned the box and righted a stool to sit upon. Kaiden pushed papers on his desk towards her. He shared with Terri various bizarre sketches of organisms viewed from his scopes.

"We always knew of organisms in our bodies but look at the variety," he said. "And they appear to have connections with each other. One creature with a spine to kill other organisms is a propeller for movement in another. I'm making the scopes better each time. I just finished my latest. Look at it…" Terri stared at Kaiden rather than the paper. "I know…you don't exactly approve, do you?"

Kaiden gathered some of the sketches and tossed them casually among others.

"That's not why you brought me here," Terri said, almost unimpressed at her mentor.

"No," he said, then smiled. "You've aged well."

"You haven't."

"I'm old."

"Weathered," she said.

"Borderline fossilized," he said with a chuckle. "How's the home?"

"Irrelevant," she said. "Not enough to dissuade my motivation when I read your letter."

"Oh, come on," he said. "What about that one girl…Sharlto? The hepatologist."

"Herpetologist," Terri said.

Kaiden shrugged.

"I was close," he said.

"Absent," Terri said bluntly.

"That's…vague."

"You're my teacher, not my psychiatrist, Kaiden."

Kaiden laughed, then launched himself from the chair.

"We need wine," he exclaimed.

"Later," Terri said. "You don't tease that letter and then circle the topic."

"How much of the message did you interpret?"

"I'm here. I packed light. And outside of that vague sewer reference, I did drop everything based on what you claimed to have found."

"Fantastic!" Kaiden said, "Unfortunately, I was wrong."

"What?!" Terri asked.

"No, no, this is good—"

"Bloody piss, Kaiden! Even by whale, that's a two-day journey!"

Kaiden giggled awkwardly, then kicked over a stack of papers to reveal a massive old book standing out among the tattered tomes and mangled manuscripts.

Terri jolted back by Kaiden's sudden outburst.

It was nearly pristine, ancient, and featureless save for a five-pointed star sitting within a spiral expanding out of the bottom corner. It was locked with a complicated puzzle-like latch.

Kaiden snatched it and forced it into Terri's hand.

"It was this," Kaiden said.

Terri accepted the massive tome as Kaiden hovered.

"Look at the finish," he said, "the embossment. The soft sheen, superb gilding."

"And this is not an Apoc?" Terri asked.

"I suspected it was the first printing, but this one is older, much older."

Terri toyed with the latch. It didn't require a key, just a unique combination of slides, spins, and pushes. Kaiden smiled as she struggled, finally intervening after a minute of fidgeting.

Terri opened the book partway and flipped a few pages. They were thick and semi-reflective, with handwritten text intermixed with illustrations drawn directly onto the paper. Terri brought her ear to the fore-edge and let her thumb flick across the leaf.

"Paper sounds off," she said. "Iokons are a concrete mix of rice and wood pulp. Most surviving books I've seen contain a ratio of hemp. This...feels…"

"Synthetic," Kaiden said.

"An old book with new paper. Are you sure this is not some elaborate forgery?"

"Well...no…" Kaiden said, somewhat apprehensive in divulging details. Terri opened the book again at a random page, revealing an image, a diagram of something.

A creature.

"Some kind of beast…" Terri said, trailing off as she studied the illustration— Or is it machine?"

Kaiden brandished his teeth in a wide grin.

"I have no idea," he said, "maybe both. And there's more." Kaiden pushed his hand past Terri to flip another page. "Not just mechanical beasts, but vehicles, devices, and the script." Kaiden paused as he ran his finger across the bizarre symbols. "...no language I know."

"How did you come across this?" Terri asked.

Kaiden sighed and perked his brow.

"You're...probably not going to believe me."

"That would be a first." Terri continued to flip pages as Kaiden answered.

"I found it," Kaiden said, "…within the Aelon Ziggurat."

"And why were you there?" Terri asked without pause.

"Is that important?"

"No one visits the Ziggurat heedlessly, and if this book was found, it would've been taken."

"Ward Marshall said the same thing."

"Who's Ward Marshall, and why are you discussing matters like this with him. Anyone who knows about you puts you at risk." Terri's tone was escalating. This wasn't a recent change in their relationship. She talked back to him in class too.

"He's trustworthy," Kaiden said.

"For a fact?" Terri asked.

"He's an abecedarian alchemist."

Terri was as shocked that a mage was still living in Sadatoni as she was that Kaiden was friends with one. Wizards were a dying breed, with Corvos one of their last sanctuaries. The only individual the church despised more than a scientist was one adept in the ways of magic.

"Well, okay then," Terri said. "Back to my original query."

"Is it important?"

"Are we going in circles? Yes!" Terri got loud again, only slightly concerned her tone could carry to those above. "What are you not telling me?!"

"It was a dream," Kaiden said. "I…had a vision…of a place and a book. Like it was waiting for me. A star-shaped fortress atop a mountain surrounded by overgrowing nature."

"You risked the ziggurat for a dream?" Terri asked.

"It was very persuasive."

"And I can't get you to move to a house with windows."

"Invade my dreams, and we'll talk. It wasn't a solitary affair, Terri. That room and that book haunted my sleep for weeks."

"The fact it paid off points to something."

"Someone…" Kaiden whispered. "I wasn't alone in my dream. Someone was guiding me." He leaned in, flipping a few pages...until reaching one. He pointed to the drawing. It occupied the entire left half of the tome, a tall, undressed, emaciated figure with extended limbs and digits. Its elongated head held no eyes, just a broad, uninviting smile of needle-like teeth. Its arms were outstretched as if the creature had been crucified.

"Was this a dream or a nightmare?" Terri asked.

Kaiden's eyes moved to the wall of sketches, and Terri followed her mentor's stare, directed to the rough drawing bearing the same figure. Her attention focused back on the illustration. It was familiar somehow, but she couldn't place it.

"It was providence," Kaiden said. "I drew that before, not after."

"Not concerning in the slightest," Terri said as she riffled through a few more pages, stopping on one.

"Oh, please tell me this wasn't you?" she said as her fingers skimmed over the stain.

"What?"

"Was it tea?" It peppered one page and had soaked through to a few others, but beyond that, the blemish was dry.

"That...wasn't me?"

"Oh, come on, Kaiden, I can plainly see how you live."

"I'm serious, Terri," Kaiden said. "It wasn't there last I opened it." Terri grimaced as she caressed the stain.

* * *

Kaiden let Terri flip through the book peacefully, occasionally diverting to a stack of papers to jot notes. She had gotten so invested that she ignored her own acquisition, still resting in her pack. She didn't want to tarnish Kaiden's moment and appreciated the book's significance. There was time.

Kaiden offered her tea, which Terri scowled at. He placed it precariously close to the book, and she moved it to a safe location after a sip. Without windows or any indications of the passage of time, given the forbiddance of mechanical timepieces, Terri was oblivious to how long she was transfixed in the book until Kaiden finally broke her attention by sitting back down beside her.

"You need to blink, Terri," he said. "Take a break. You've been engrossed for most the day." Terri leaned back and rubbed her eyes, saying nothing. "I heard what happened. Infallible gods."

"It'll be interesting to see them spin this in their favor," Terri said.

"Well, they claim our leniency to both inhumans and those that disobey the Hallessegro ban gave rise to fiends from the abyss." Kaiden perked an eye when Terri shifted her attention to him.

"Demons from the dark," Terri said, "another invention of the Opus. I read that the existence of an *underworld* was never mentioned in the Apoc."

"Nothing swings the masses to conviction than the threat of damnation. There's even been rumors of a great winged beast descending from Philokalia."

"You'd think I'd notice such a monster."

"You were there?" Kaiden asked.

"I pulled the coffin from the wreck."

"You've been reading that book for hours and never mentioned it?"

"Hey, this is important, and I didn't want to steal your thunder."

"Surprised you're not being championed or in chains."

"I made a point of being absent before the armies arrived. Couldn't risk being questioned or searched."

"Why? What have you got to hide?"

Terri instinctually scrutinized the room to ensure they were alone, then whispered, "I know what took down the Conestoga."

Kaiden was understandably curious, and Terri reached down and brought up her pack. Kaiden pushed the colossal book aside to make room as Terri placed her bag and opened the flap. She removed the chrome ball, and Kaiden's jaw unlocked.

"Is…that…a shaper?" Kaiden asked as he pulled Terri's arm closer. "Terri…never concern yourself over stealing my thunder, again."

"Amazing, isn't it?" Terri asked. "No visible forms of power or propulsion."

"Aegis tech…where did you find this?"

"I doubt the Aegis were responsible for this. It's too perfect."

Kaiden gently coaxed the sphere from Terri's grip and could see his reflection in the polished finish. He noted the lack of seams or imperfections.

"It still matches their style," Kaiden said. He brought the shaper close, searching for any dents or scratches, one mistake to prove a faulty inventor. "But you're right…perfection, probably down to a millionth of a centimeter. Beyond whatever purpose it may have, its very existence has meaning."

"How do you figure," Terri asked.

"This is a machine," he said. "Logic would dictate that it features projections to better facilitate its purpose. Holes. Seams. To put the effort to encompass its function entirely within a perfect sphere…someone is sending a message."

"What kind of message?" she asked.

"That's not the question I'm pondering?"

"Oh?"

"…I want to know first who's sending the message. If you don't believe it's Aegis, then it's someone else."

The two shared silence as Terri reflected light off the surface. Kaiden couldn't help but glance at the gangly figure pinned to his wall. Kaiden turned quickly to Terri.

"Wait a minute…this brought down the Conestoga?" Kaiden asked.

"I'm assuming," Terri said. "It was no beast. It was a projectile…fired from the surface of Philokalia."

"These don't act without the will of an owner. Someone it bonds to. Someone worthy. Must be beyond the range for a recall. They launched it, knowing it couldn't be recovered. Given time, it'll seek out a new user. Can I have it?"

Terri smiled and pushed away from the table.

"Why not," she said. "They'd burn you for half the violations in this lab. Does the color denote anything?"

"I may have to ask Ward. This thing will blow his mind. But yes, supposedly—red, blue, yellow, green, purple…black, but I can't remember which is which. I've read of them possessing weapons, intelligence; some can even grant its owner superhuman abilities."

"Just…be careful," Terri said. "This thing passed through a conestoga. It'll pass through you easily enough."

"I told you this place was more interesting. Want to stay?"

"I'm committed for a week," she said, "then I'm expected back at the university."

"Week may not be enough."

"We'll need…" Terri examined the disheveled room, with rusted exposed bolts, overflowing garbage bins, and scattered half-read books. Terri stood and made for the exit. "I'll be back tomorrow."

"You're leaving?" Kaiden said. "I've got a cot."

"While I appreciate the offer," Terri said, "I'm not a disheveled transient."

"Well, that hurt."

"I require sunlight, Kaiden. I'm going to find a proper bed Going to see this pharmacist you mentioned. I also need to pick up a few things."

"My lab is fully stocked with lenses, quills, ink. What else could you possibly need?"

"Solvent."

CONESTOGA

***Proctor Report, Filed By:* Emet Kabbanala**
***Organization:* The Dogs of Abercrombie**
***Date:* December 18, 1222 AC**

Summary: *Lance 346879, commanded by Emet Kabbanala, encountered an airlock five kilometers from the Pyxis Exclave.*

Insignia Lower Dahsur El Amari exited into space to reconnoiter the external skin of the exclave. After six hours, he returned, reporting a similar airlock at the base of the exclave, although no similar hatch exists within the habitat. El Amari also noted huge spherical tanks around the base of the connecting module that we later confirmed were not the water reclamation plants.

I believe these tanks are part of an explosive failsafe system designed to eject an exclave from the Conestoga in case of an emergency. We have never understood how these exclaves move, and if one were to stop, I fear what our god would do to protect the others.

File End.

The lance lingered outside the Philokalia gateway, built under the Kalian Monument. One of the largest gateways in the vessel, the spire towered 250 meters, perched above a temple with a portico entrance covered mainly by vines and weeds. Matching columns encircled the building with only a single 25-meter tall access tunnel leading to the exclave platform that would deliver the lance back into the darkened catacombs below. The golden exterior of the temple was accomplished by a fragile leaf, though time weathered most of it away. They were locked in their crutches, flanking the carryall Elina had been riding.

Each time Agosta looked at her, for an instant, he noticed something that wasn't there. Something about her clothes. The style of her hair changed. A frown shifted to a smile. It coincided with intuition from deep within, an instinctual drive to protect her.

"Do I know you?" Agosta asked her.

"I'm sure you'd remember," Elina said.

"I think I certainly would," he said. "So?"

"Your last name is fastened to your suit," Elina said. "The other man called you by another name. Ergo, Agosta Pike."

Agosta nodded.

"That was your first lie," he said. Elina was less stunned as if she expected that answer. "Don't let your origin with the jackers be your second."

"They abducted me," Elina said.

"From where?"

"Volani."

"Before or during the *Rough Raid*?"

"During."

"Seriously?" Terri asked, who had been listening from the opposite side of the vehicle. "That was years ago!"

Elina turned back to Agosta and asked, "Am I lying?"

"No," Agosta said, "she's not."

"Well, I never trusted gut," Terri said. "Can you—"

"When jackers kidnap people," Elina said, "to ensure separation, they brand them." She revealed her arm and opened her hand, showing Agosta, not Terri, the circle brand inside her palm. "Satisfied?"

Terri didn't respond as the temple door opened, revealing the waiting platform. The lance advanced inside.

"You never answered my question," Agosta said.

Elina took in a deep breath, almost resistant to answering.

"We don't know each other," she said.

Agosta shook his head.

"Fine," he groaned.

"But I imagine we will."

* * *

The lower gateway to Philokalia groaned open as the lift descended, revealing the five crutches, their carryall, and its new passenger. The group exited into the massive but brutalist dark architecture of the vessel's interior. Kaiden, in the lead, stopped and sighed upon discovering the error.

"It shifted," Kaiden said.

Deven followed him out and surveyed their surroundings.

"Either that or we miscalculated our exit location," Deven said.

"What's going on?" Elina said from atop the walking cargo module. Agosta, who was walking alongside Terri, explained.

"The exclaves migrate."

"That I know," she said.

"We're further away than expected."

"Deven?" Terri asked. Deven's crutch opened a series of dishes and antennae not unlike the protrusions seen on the scab mechs. They focused and twirled, creating a three-dimensional render of the surrounding catacombs of the vessel only he could see.

"I scanned the stars before we left Philokalia. Something happened," Deven said. "We're at least two hundred kilometers from where we're supposed to be."

"Meaning we're going to miss our rendezvous with Kenoma," Agosta said.

"Croatoa will be passing relatively close to our location," Sloan said.

"That place is cursed," Deven said.

"Let's…be level-headed," Terri said.

"Ok…The last outpost vanished without a trace over a hundred years ago, and every proctor lance that entered since has never returned."

Terri nodded.

"Yeah, let's skip Croatoa," she said.

"There is another option," Deven said.

"I know what you're going to say," Terri whispered.

"It's risky if not borderline suicidal."

"Less…interested but keep going."

"We can cut through the center of—"

"No," Kaiden said.

"We're at the apex of the neck," Deven said, "it's only a few—

"You want to travel through to the opposite side?" Agosta shouted.

"It's done all the time," Deven said.

"By armies."

"Fine, Croatoa, or wait two weeks for Kerberos. It should only take a couple days to Kenoma, room to spare."

Kaiden wandered away from the group while Agosta orbited the carryall.

"Borderline suicidal," Agosta said.

"Couple means two?" Terri asked.

"Four? Two if we ditch the carryall," Deven said.

"Not an option," Agosta said. The two of them squared off.

"We can come back for it."

"It has a passenger."

"Whose allegiance I still believe is up to question."

The man and scrimm stared at each other sternly. Elina, still atop the carryall, interjected.

"I'm…standing here," she said.

"Regardless of the passenger," Terri said, "the chances of it being here upon our return, with Jackers in the area, is slim. People depend on us. We're proctors…we're Staplegunners—"

"God, I hate that name—" Agosta whispered.

"We don't give up! Do it in three. Find a shortcut."

"You think I budgeted for the scenic route?" Deven said.

"Find a way."

"Sure…I'll like…dig a hole."

"Deven!" Terri snapped, then paused to compose herself. She considered her next thought. "Deven…when we recount this tale later, I'll make certain to mention how a single scrimm lead his entire lance home. How all the humans were beside themselves until you showed us the way…because I know you…and I know you are holding back that one final miracle that will prove to all of us that you are, in fact, the greatest navigator the proctors have."

"Well…since you put it that way."

"Good boy."

Deven resumed his analysis, scanning through the known maps in this region.

"Okay…" he said, "we can cut through the Town."

Agosta threw his arms up and walked away.

"Let's do it in five," Terri said.

"Come on, Terri!" Sloan said, goading, "It'll be an adventure."

"Adventures are reserved for fiction, Sloan," Terri said. "There's nothing bold about killing or being..." Terri realized she was quoting. "Fucking Noah…"

"Let's do it in five," Kaiden said

"No…we'll chance it."

"Borderline…suicidal," Agosta whispered.

* * *

The first location of note they reached was the River. Thankfully, the group was not required to cross the five-hundred-meter-wide expanse.

The water flowed from one side of the vessel to the other. The tributary snaked and bent like an actual river, terminating into large processing plants deep in the vessel's interior. It was a confusing system, as the water from exclaves was sent through a purification machine and collected in tanks until the exclave reached a specific point in its migration.

The water would then dump into several reservoirs stationed on outer levels. Equipped with spillways, overflow diverted into the namesake river, which meandered "downstream" from either side of the ship. The various bends and twists didn't appear to serve a function, likewise with the occasional waterfall and interlocking spur.

Most of the river ran through open-air trenches, all of which simulated the movement of a canal without organic markers like rocks, beaches, or life. Despite moving like a river, it did so within a minimalist design of refined stone and blocky, monolithic catacombs.

Hydranis named the entire waterway Acheron, while Aurago named the individual sides Pison and Dison. Technically, the only official name was Exo and Icos, and the entirety was Archos.

One popular theory pointed to the river as a side-effect of a faulty circulation system as a dedicated pipeline would be more efficient. When the water reached the center, it flowed into a colossal processing center where it was split into hydrogen and oxygen and circulated into new pipes that ran the vessel's length.

No one knew where these pipes went, but eventually, they must return to the exclaves as part of their weather control systems. While measurement has never officially been made, given the twisting nature of the river, estimations have placed it at over seven thousand kilometers in length.

* * *

The door was thirty meters tall, fifty meters across, and probably weighed a thousand tones. It slowly but silently lifted, revealing it to be twenty meters thick.

"That's…big," Elina said.

"You didn't mention this," Sloan said to Deven.

"Better to ask forgiveness than permission," Deven said as he took the lead to traverse the expanse. "Crossing the Garden will throw the scent off any Watchers that may be tracking us."

"This is…secure…I mean, these don't fall on their own…right?" Elina asked.

"Not that often," Agosta said as he followed Deven with the carryall trailing behind. Elina scrutinized the underside of the stone-like slab, noting odd scratches.

"Are you searching for something?" Agosta asked.

"Bloodstains," Elina said.

"You find any?"

"Not…yet?"

Sloan reached up, being the tallest, and dragged her shell's fingers across the featureless surface.

The group cleared the door, and Deven approached another nearby. He touched a featureless portion, illuminating an access panel of glowing glyphs and strange alien acoustics. Deven tapped a few icons, and the door behind them suddenly fell.

Elina screamed.

"Umm…yeah…" Deven said, feigning remorse, "this is an airlock. Sooo… heads… up."

"Thanks for the warning," Kaiden said.

Deven tapped a few more glyphs.

"Masks," he said.

Sloan, Deven, and Agosta closed the hatches on their shells while the other proctors donned masks. Terri tended to Elina, offering a portable filtration helmet.

"Put this on," Terri said.

"Why?" Elina asked.

"These chambers are full of carbon dioxide."

The door in front lifted, identical to the one behind. The dark corridor gave way to a brilliantly illuminated chamber.

The group crossed to reach a ledge overlooking the cavity. Below descended into mist many kilometers down with bright artificial suns above providing energy for the thousands of levels of plants.

"It's beautiful," Elina whispered.

"Nothing out here is, sweetie," Kaiden said.

Elina slid to the edge of the carryall and peered over the edge.

"That's far…." she said.

"Two hundred and fifty kilometers," Deven said.

It was one of the strangest chambers within the vessel, a five thousand-meter wide, multi-leveled greenhouse.

Despite the exclaves possessing thousands of different botanical examples, they were still designed to support animal life, while the garden appeared built to preserve plants exclusively.

The garden displayed the full spectrum of botanical life, from flowers to towering trees. Like many of these chambers, numerous examples pointed to a planetary origin shared with humans. The alien examples were correctly sequestered but have slowly mixed with the human vegetation after centuries of inattention.

The group crossed over an arching bridge. They could practically taste the moisture through their masks. In some areas, it rained, while there was only a miasma of vapor in others. Elina couldn't help but be transfixed by what the Garden kept.

One tree sprouted hydrogen-based globes that would safely float seeds away, while another resembled a multi-limbed sea creature with tentacles following the group as they marched by.

Some flowers fluttered their petals like birds trying to take flight, and fungi radiated a ghostly blue glow. As they crossed a large tree, its branches seemed to dip to offer speckled fist-sized fruit to the humans. It was within Elina's reach, but she focused on Agosta.

"Are any of these…edible?" she asked.

"A few are compatible with humans," he said. "Most are alien."

"Scrimm, Endolon."

"Some…others we've no idea."

"This one?"

"I wouldn't."

Elina let the offering pass, barely noticing the insect atop the fruit as it leaped, sprouted wings, and buzzed around the carryall. Elina was initially concerned, but it changed to curiosity and delight as the bug flashed various colors as it orbited her head. Elina held out a hand, and the bug landed.

"Don't harm it," Agosta said.

Elina studied it closely, discovering the creature wasn't skittish. It moved effortlessly as it examined her hand. She observed a smooth body and glowing green eyes but a lack of pincers or stingers.

"You're a strange little bug," she whispered.

"It's artificial," Agosta said. Elina looked at him, and the insect took off to continue its duties. "They don't possess reproduction or defense systems. They're manufactured organic machines following a program. It prevents them from overeating or escaping the habitat."

"Wow."

The group could hear the faint crack of thunder, followed by a light rain that fell over them. They couldn't see any clouds. Elina held out her hand to catch drops as the proctors reached the other side of the bridge.

"Well, that was uneventful," Deven said.

"What did I tell you regarding baited responses?" Agosta said.

"At least we cleared it," Sloan said.

"Oh, we haven't yet," Deven said.

"Excuse me?" Terri said.

"We need to climb down."

"Holy shit, Deven, can you give us a heads-up next time?!"

"As I said, better to ask forgiveness."

"Well, I see stairs," Elina said, "and thankfully, it's not a climb."

"Can the harvester handle the incline?" Agosta asked.

"Yeah, doesn't look too harsh," Kaiden said. "Let's just hope it stays this way."

"And it's just a few kilometers," Deven said.

"Few is three?" Terri asked. Deven didn't respond. "Four?"

"Actually…sixty-five."

Terri let out a quiet sigh and said nothing more before descending the wide staircase.

"Higher than the tallest mountain ever recorded," Agosta said.

"How does the air circulate here?" Kaiden asked. "This high up, wouldn't it be too thin?"

"Artificially sustained thermal layers," Deven said.

"Really?"

"No idea."

TORUS

Code of Color.

Break it and be blacklisted. No yard will accept you. Pirates conform, so should you.

Red. Immediate request required (military engagement).

White. Request for negotiation (parlay).

Blue. Immediate request required (engineering crisis).

Green. Immediate request required (medical emergency).

Purple. Request to trade.

Yellow. Quarantine; do not approach.

Found scrawled inside an engineering textbook.

Several feet of snow fell upon them when they opened the hatch.

Deven caught a mouthful and recoiled as Terri was blinded by the sudden change in illumination. Kaiden's glowing eyes switched from blue to yellow as they adapted to the glare. They pushed the hatch aside and scaled the walls of the crater.

Centuries ago, perhaps longer, some impact or detonation took out this block of the old metropolis. Several nearby buildings sat precariously close to the edge, ready to crumble; others had collapsed outward. Two taller ones had fallen together and connected at their summit, a hundred stories above them.

"Were we seriously down for that long?" Deven said as his feet sunk into the snow. "Did we miss an entire season?"

"It's a desert, Dev," Terri said. "Desert doesn't always mean heat."

"You're saying that as if that's normal."

"Nothing is normal…consequently, everything is."

Terri ascended the side of the depression, with the other two following. It was still cold, and the snow was lightly packed, causing their feet to slide.

"I'm having trouble parsing the logic of that statement," Deven said.

"That place is a tomb," Kaiden said. "I imagine we're one of the few people to have ever survived that hell."

Terri stopped and waited as the two climbed up to meet her.

"You're right," she said.

Kaiden was confused as Deven continued to climb.

"I didn't think that was a statement that could be challenged," Kaiden said.

"We're not the first expedition," Terri said, "only the latest and the first to survive without casualties. Last mission only had one return."

"Yay, us," Deven said.

"How many expeditions preceded ours?" Kaiden asked.

"Two," Terri said. "…I should have asked."

"What and who?"

"How did Noah's ex know where this vault was located?" Terri asked.

"Old records," Deven said. "Probably an ancient ledger or manifest."

"And their preference was for a book?"

"We cracked the floodgates," Kaiden said as they reached Terri's level. "Surely, others will follow. You want to go back in."

"Once you escape a burning building, never go back for the jewelry," Terri said as she resumed her climb. "Still, that blood trail was isolated to the very item we required. I'm assuming it was their destination as well."

"What of it, skipper?" Deven asked.

"The previous mission was identical to ours, and assumingly the one before that and the one before."

"I didn't spot any open cells, did you?" Kaiden asked.

"No. Some of those had to be of value," Terri said.

"Meaning they were all tasked to retrieve that book, which leads to the ultimate question—"

"How did she know?"

"Perhaps there was a scout patrol," Deven said. "An ill-equipped team. We've proven them less intelligent than us."

"Then why not clear the lot?" Terri asked. "Why just one book? Why not take advantage of the fire sale."

"You don't lock away garbage," Deven said. "Some of those artifacts had to be worth at least that much. They're either valuable or dangerous. And anything dangerous is valuable to someone."

"She's not telling us the whole truth," Terri said.

* * *

The group had almost reached the summit when Deven checked on the loginoid.

"How you feeling, Kaiden?"

"Why the concern?"

"Not to be forthright, but you were torn in half and lost an eye less than an hour ago. That's been known to affect some people."

"Like a new person," they said.

"You're certainly built well."

"Well, you know, my secret: Diet. Exercise. Yoga."

"Funny."

The three reached the crater's edge and found their ride waiting for them a block away, the red and gold bullet-shaped carbody.

"Right where I left her," Terri said.

"I've never been happier to see such a beautiful thing," Deven said.

They pushed their way through the snow that buried the ruins of the wasted city. Tracks overlapped with crossing bridges and tunnels. Dozens of buildings were still standing, one of the larger persevered ruins of the old metropolis. The snow was dusting the landscape, painting the rusted iron bones of a dead empire in a soft shimmer.

As they reached the train, Terri spotted the herd of mammoths nearby, the mechanical beasts still oblivious to the glaring and borderline garish train sitting in the middle of the street.

"Shit," she said.

Deven saw it as well.

"Where did they come from?" Deven asked.

"Everywhere," Kaiden whispered.

"You're people."

"Remind me to make you answer for livestock."

"Shut up, both of you," Terri whispered as they approached the Vanderov.

"They respond to movement and noise," Kaiden said.

"Two things trains are good at," Deven said.

The door to the second car swung open, and Noah beckoned them quickly inside.

"Took your sweet time," Noah said.

"There were snacks," Terri said as she climbed up. "We good?"

Kaiden followed, revealing the book from their satchel as they boarded the train.

"Kaiden, secure the cargo," Terri said. "Guard it with your life."

"I am not alive," Kaiden said, "so firearms and metal will have to do."

As Deven jumped on, Terri ran into the locomotive.

"Are those mammoths?" Deven asked.

"We need to get out of here," Terri said.

"Really, no kidding, thanks!" Mannah shouted back. She was surrounded by the engine, spinning discs, and twitching gauges. Baffles breathed, and steam vented.

"The instant we move, they'll be on us," Noah said as he and the others entered the engine cab.

"Is there a plan?" Kaiden asked.

"Noah!" Terri said as she jumped on her conductor chair, the elevated one that allowed her to peer out from one of the two forward-facing windows, "keep us anchored, and give her the grit." She then shouted to Mannah, "Tooley! Engage the mover. Get us up to full spin, notch eight. When I give the word, release the clamps and gun it. Deven! Storm the tossers."

Noah left the cab and began to work, locking the brakes as the engine power rose. Mannah pushed a large lever forward, and indicators increased, matching the escalating moan of the engines.

"Car binders unlocked, skipper!" Kaiden shouted.

Deven exited the locomotive and ran into the second car. He punched an inobtrusive panel, which flipped open to reveal a lever wired to a small, sealed cylindrical hydrocell of solid brass.

"This won't be cheap," he whispered as he pulled the lever, draining the power core dry and venting steam into the cab. Deven left it to run to the next car to do the same.

One of the mammoths looked up, catching the mounting rumble.

"They're getting shifty," Noah said.

"Seventy Percent!" Mannah said.

Terri clicked the intercom.

"Deven!" she said.

Deven pulled another lever in another cab and pushed a nearby communicator button.

"Thirty seconds, skipper!" he said as he ran into the next cab.

The lead mammoth stepped forward, still unsure of what was creating the noise. The train coughed a cloud of steam from its wheels. The mammoth emitted a low-pitched, mechanical bellow.

"Hang onto something!" Kaiden said.

Deven ran into the fourth car, opened the hatch, and pulled the lever. Steam vented into his face, throwing him to a wall, recoiling from the pain. He wiped his face, squinted, and struggled to run to the next car.

"Eighty!" Mannah said.

Kaiden and Terri secured themselves. Noah was practically outside with a firm grip on the independent air brake handle.

"Hold, I only got five!" Deven shouted into the intercom, trying to overcome the noise of the steam gushing into the cabin.

"Hit the pedal!" Terri said back.

"Ninety," Mannah shouted.

"Releasing brake!" Noah said as he gripped the safety on the lever and pushed it to unlock.

"Here they come!" Kaiden said.

Deven reached the final car, opened the last panel, and activated the last hydrocell with one hand while tapping the intercom with the other.

"Ready!" he said.

"Bat the stack off her!!" Terri said.

The train lurched forward, almost kicking Noah off the train. He pulled another handle, and sand fell onto the rails before the wheels to improve grip on the icy iron.

Within every car, the indication of acceleration was picked up by the wheels, and electric motors pulsed, receiving the total energy from a hydrocell that would typically run an automobile for a month. For an instant and only a moment, the Vanderov became a fifty-eight-wheel drive vehicle.

The train launched.

Deven tumbled.

The last car was a cargo module with no hallways or rooms, only straps and netting.

Deven tried to hook one of the dangling ropes but slid to the rear wall of the last car.

His impact threw the door open, and he struggled to prevent being thrown out the back.

He saw the lead mammoth rear up on its hind limbs and gallop after the train with the herd following.

Deven struggled to stand as the cold rushed into the car.

He clicked the radio.

"Do we fire?!" Deven asked.

"Sure!" Terri replied.

"Will it do anything?!"

"It'll piss them off!"

Mannah became part of the machine, flipping, switching, closing relays, regulating power, and keeping the train from blowing itself apart as it continued to accelerate.

The Vanderov plowed through the snow, revealing the tracks underneath, cutting a path through the ruined city.

"She's hot! Come on, old girl!" Mannah said.

The mammoth herd crashed through a building, causing it to collapse behind them.

The monstrous mechanical beasts chased after the train, ignoring the fringing buildings they destroyed in their stampede.

"They're gaining!" Deven said.

Noah crawled back into the cab to see Terri struggling to stare out the front window, given the disturbance of snow around them.

"We won't make the bridge!" Terri said.

"We got a shortcut," Noah said. "Next left!"

"Confirm," Terri said. "It is open, right?"

"There might be…some…obstructions."

Terri offered Noah an unimpressed stare.

She addressed the controls in front of her and adjusted a few levers.

The Vanderov, like many trains, didn't require someone to exit to adjust the tracks. The motive system could jump from one branch to another on command of its conductor. The train lurched hard as it rerouted down another line.

The lead mammoth slid, trying to follow, and crashed into a building. The others managed to keep their footing.

The Vanderov continued accelerating, tossing mild impediments such as old vehicles, fallen lampposts, or collapsed overhead bridges aside.

Terri could see nothing out of the front window.

She leaned out the side, though it wasn't much better from the torrent of snow thrown up by the train.

A brief reprieve allowed them to quickly catch the gargantuan domed complex in their path.

"That's," Terri said, "an obstruction."

She pulled herself back in the cab and pierced through Noah's soul with her gaze.

"That's not an obstruction," Kaiden said, "that's a building!"

"Can't stop now!" Mannah said.

"They are right on our ass!" Deven said.

"Drop the pilot!" Terri said.

Noah and Kaiden ran to the front of the engine and forcefully pulled on a pair of chains.

The nose split vertically and opened from the train's front to reveal an arrow-shaped cowcatcher with rail guards.

It fell in front of the wheels, and the nose closed over it.

"Pilot down!" Kaiden said as the sheer wall of the oncoming building stood belligerently before them.

The train plowed through the steel and concrete barricades and past the closed doors of the stadium.

The train pierced into an immense station where a hundred like machines would have parked to take on passengers.

Other trains, long frozen into the ground, sat unchanged for a thousand years until the Vanderov kicked them aside.

One was split in half.

Another only partially impeding them was tossed like a log in the air.

The mammoths crashed through what was left of the wall, ignoring obstructions and flattening everything underfoot.

The Vanderov didn't stop as it struck the back of a passenger car, gutting it from within.

"Woohoo!!" Mannah said gleefully.

"You're enjoying this too much!" Noah said.

"Lighten up; she can take it!" Mannah said, followed by a series of well-timed bangs and pops around her. She then whispered, "sure you can."

A much larger iron juggernaut blocked their path ahead.

Terri held onto her chair.

"Brace!" she said.

The impact caused the Vanderov to skip off the tracks, riding on its wheel flanges until reseating on the rails.

The collision tossed the crew about the cabin, taking many off guard.

"Still confident?" Noah said.

"Less so," Mannah muttered.

Noah leaned on the window again, the view unobstructed by the lack of snow in the station.

"We're reaching the other side!" Noah said.

Like before, the massive doors to the station were closed and blocked by barricades.

The Vanderov's cowcatcher suffered dents and breaks as stone and metal were pitched from the train's path.

Breaching the wall, the Vanderov emerged outside and promptly crossed onto a rickety, rusted iron truss bridge that ran kilometers over city ruins.

It was unstable and vibrating as the train rocketed across.

"Are they still behind us!?" Mannah asked.

Deven stared back as the herd scrambled to stop before the precipice.

One failed and fell fifty meters to the city, crashing through dozens of buildings in its descent.

"Not anymore!" Deven said.

The carbody careened over the snow-covered apocalyptic ruins.

The bridge quivered, raining ice below.

The structure was not designed to hold a train moving at this speed.

Tresses snapped.

Bolts popped.

The Vanderov reached the other side and kept its pace as it plowed through the bones of an ancient civilization. A slight curve lurched the train, and a few wheels lifted.

"Okay, ease down," Terri said. "Noah?" Noah faced his conductor-in-chief, prepared for retribution. Terri patted his arm. "We're all alive. You made a good call. You can unclench your asshole now. Fallin's a stupid woman."

Noah laughed, and Terri followed.

"Notch five, engine," Terri said. "Let's cool her down."

Mannah nodded and reduced speed.

"Six hours of boredom followed by thirty seconds of sheer terror," Mannah laughed. "I'd have it no other way."

She caressed the hot-to-touch gauges and switches surrounding her.

"You're an iron god, you beautiful girl."

Terri received a nod from Kaiden, then clicked her radio.

"Deven, you alive?" she asked.

Deven closed the car door and collapsed on the floor after activating his side of the conversation.

"I think," he moaned, "that this…is a perfect time…to ask for a raise."

PART THREE

EQUIVALENCE

CONESTOGA

At that moment, staring at the beast, I knew the truth of it. They weren't just watching; they were testing, a trial I had passed. It bent a leg and bowed its head. I was their shepherd; I didn't follow them. I knew where to go.

Beyond what we know and have seen, there hides a room of light. It moves with the darkness. With no seam, the wall parted, and I discovered it. I became washed in white as I entered. No gods were awaiting me. It was only a reflection, I saw.

What we call the Conestoga is, in reality, a key, one that, if you know how to turn it, opens the door to heaven. I have never been more certain of anything in my life. Moments later, I was outside again; the room had spat me out. More time had passed outside than I remembered, but I knew more; I gained knowledge, something implanted. They had given me the cipher of their words. I could speak it, read it. I could teach it. I knew I would not live to see the key turned, but one of my people will.

Ethaniel Collianthus
Codex Collianthus
Book 1, Verse 211

"How do you keep track of time in this place?" Elina asked as the group spanned the bridge. Their lights, despite intensity, couldn't reach either side, let alone the void that extended below them. A light mist trickled from overhead.

"Time is the speed at which we read the book of the universe," Deven said.

"What?"

"Ignore him," Agosta said.

"When in the dark," Deven said, "the most useless task will be to count the seconds of one's life." Elina couldn't figure if Deven was intentionally provoking or simply waxing philosophical as part of a character trait.

"We have clocks," Terri said.

"And what do they say?" Elina asked.

"They say seven."

"PM?"

"AM."

"I'll ask again: How do you keep track of time in this place?"

"Each exclave runs between an eighteen and twenty-six-hour day cycle," Agosta said. "Out here, such concepts are pointless. You travel until you collapse; sleep as little as possible. Rinse, repeat."

"Reset your rhythm when you enter an exclave and pitch your tent," Terri said. "That's why whenever we encounter an exclave, we hope it's heading roughly in our direction, as anything encountered will be better than this."

"The jackers often traveled without lights," Elina said.

"Not sure why that matters," Agosta said. "Watchers are blind."

"Because all light is fire slowly destroying the universe," Deven said.

"He seems a hit at parties," Elina said.

"You should see him when he's drunk," Sloan said.

"Every step is a cliff on which I can fly," Deven said.

"As I said, he can be a hoot on occasion."

"Is that a bird joke, Sloan?"

"What do you think?"

"How did the jackers track time?" Terri asked.

"They didn't," Elina said. "I honestly have no idea how much time passed with them. I don't even know how old I am."

"Your family escaped Volani during the rough raid?" Agosta asked.

"Yes."

"And how old were you?"

"Four, maybe five."

"So, give or take," Agosta said, "you're fourteen."

"I feel older," Elina said.

"We all do, sweetie," Terri said.

* * *

Unlike the Garden, the Town wasn't separated by a massive airlock.

The tunnel approaching the complex narrowed before opening into a massive, doomed cavity over fifty kilometers across. A singular overhead light provided heat and illumination to the vacant settlement occupying its base. It was a densely packed lattice of multi-colored buildings stacked upon one another and pushed so close as to make alleys barely wide enough to accommodate two people abreast.

It was a walled enclave of improperly arranged structures where houses connected, casting shadows over multiple stories until the base streets were bathed in only darkness. Staircases, bridges, and passageways crisscrossed through and over the city blocks, allowing travelers to span the town without touching the ground. It was an anarchic mess of broken designs and confusing plans.

"Shit," Kaiden said upon looking at it.

"Language," Agosta scolded Kaiden, pointing a chin to Elina.

"I'm a teenager, not a child," Elina said. "You are allowed to curse."

"What's this one called?" Sloan asked Deven.

"Urban Sprawl, I think," Deven said, "but it looks…broken." The scrimm walked towards a pedestal near their entrance and tapped it, revealing a pattern of holographic sigils and glyphs.

"I could understand a botanical reserve, but why would the weavers bother with this?" Sloan asked.

"Maybe it was an experiment to understand us better," Deven said, "they used facilities like this to simulate environments we would most likely accept." He tapped away, and a screen appeared over the pedestal with titles, though they flickered and sporadically shifted locations. "Well, that doesn't imbue confidence."

"What do we got?" Terri asked.

"Well, my experience with proto-script is limited, but I think we got *Frontier Town*, *Ancient Port*, *Industrial Sector*, *Tower Forest*, *Fantasy City*, *Train Yard*, something called *Spire Stretch*, and…unfortunately, *Apocalyptic Ruins*."

"Anything is better than *Urban Sprawl*," Terri said, "I know these things can randomly change on a whim. Can you change it?"

Deven nodded and tapped away at the pedestal until one of the titles switched from purple to blue. The ground shuddered, and loud thundercracks echoed through the structure. The urban sprawl dismantled itself. Like a folded paper sculpture, each building unfurled and collapsed. The color faded from the buildings. The ground opened, and towers crumbled. Giant cranes and arms assembled new buildings while pulling others apart.

Another loud pop, the sound of grinding machinery, and the dismantling of the urban sprawl stopped prematurely, leaving some buildings half-exposed and others malformed.

"Oh, that's not good," Sloan said just before the mechanism started to reverse and rebuild, only to halt and change again, leaving a half-erected sprawl breathing and bending like a living organism. "That's…even worse."

"Uhhh," Deven trailed off as he attempted to take control of the construct, "I think…it's…broken."

"Dumb it down there, egghead," Agosta said.

"It's not answering. It's trying to dismantle one construct while erecting what seems to be two others."

"It's like throwing a blender in a trash compactor," Sloan said.

"Can you at least…stop it from doing…whatever it's trying to do?" Terri asked.

"I've completely lost control…I mean Agosta, Sloan, and I are flight-capable; we could just fly over. I can't carry anyone but maybe Agosta and Sloan—"

"Carryall's too heavy. Deven, Sloan, and Agosta, you take the high ground and direct us as we escort the payload through. Agosta, take the girl."

Agosta nodded and coaxed Elina into his arms. Thrusters opened up in his legs and torso, and the shell soared over the moving city. Deven quickly followed, with Sloan slowly trailing in her much heavier rig. Terri looked at Kaiden, who faced against the warping walls of the malfunctioning metropolis. They walked with the carryall automatically following behind.

The sound of the moving city was almost deafening as the two proctors navigated the maze.

Agosta was holding Elina, who was gripping onto the shell's helmet with all her might, hundreds of meters over the city. Sloan hovered beside them while Deven tracked the movement of his friends below.

"One hundred meters then left," Deven said.

"Roger," Terri said over the radio.

The nearby tower collapsed, and another building assembled in its place. Walls started to compress together while levels pancaked upon those below.

"Correction, fifty meters, right, ten meters to a left—wait, make thirty meters to a left, straight for one hundred—"

"Holy hell, Deven!" Terri said. "What are you doing up there?"

"This city is tearing apart and rebuilding itself at the same time; give a bird a break."

Within the maze, Terri and Kaiden gazed above them as the bridges were impaling into buildings, showering debris while the floor under them changed into a staircase.

The walls beside began to close in. Terri stretched her secondary limbs wide to hold the two buildings apart as Kaiden directed the carryall through the narrowing passage.

"Move it, Terri!" Kaiden said. Terri released her grip and dove out of the alley before it vanished.

They followed the directions dictated to them the best they could until entering a small urban park moments before a building was erected around them, with walls, stairs, and rooms. Hundreds of micro-manipulator arms assembled kitchens and beds. They placed windows and hung lights. Machines coated the walls in paint, laid down carpet, and fastened furniture. The two crutches dodged the robotic limbs as they dutifully completed their tasks.

"This would be beautiful if it weren't terrifying," Terri said.

Kaiden shouted into the radio, "Deven, how do we get out of here?!"

"You need to move fifteen degrees left of facing," Deven said calmly.

"It hasn't made a door yet!"

"Well, that's never stopped you before."

Terri grimaced and proceeded to punch and pry an opening in the far wall of the building, leading to a solid wall that subsequently split as two structures moved like a parted river.

"Okay, smooth for another few hundred meters," Deven said over the radio.

The two proctors followed the directions and escorted their cargo through the network, avoiding collapsing bridges, folding walls, and assembly cranes, two of which slammed into one another, creating an impromptu wrestling match over their heads.

"Uhh, Terri…" Deven said from overhead.

"What is it?" Terri asked.

"You got two options: you can continue straight, which will add probably another twenty minutes—"

"—We'll be a pulled pork sandwich in twenty minutes, Dev," Kaiden said.

"—Or…or you can cut left and be out in two."

"We'll take the shorter route," Terri said.

"Ok…so, how good is your balance?"

"Decent," Kaiden said.

"—Wait," Terri said, "…why?!"

They made the corner, reached the precipice, and discovered the half-meter wide remains of a mostly dismantled bridge that crossed over an expanse of rolling gears, cranes, and grinding machinery.

"Oh," Terri whispered plainly. "Well, that's…precarious."

"Can the carryall even span that?" Kaiden asked.

"Automated balance and gyroscopics," she said. "Us…not so much."

Terri stepped forward and started across, with the carryall between her and Kaiden. The latter glanced up to see crane arms and building fragments slam into one another.

"Sloan," Agosta said, "be prepared to go in if—"

"Cancel that," Terri said, "It's too risky."

"Terri—"

"You have your cargo, Agosta. You're responsible for it."

Below the bridge, Terri could witness the side effects of conflicting orders, as unstable structures collapsed under their flawed design. One set of assembly arms constructed a stable foundation and built upon it, only for another set to dismantle it, comprising what was built overtop. Construction machines would break and disintegrate, only for them to be repaired or dismantled by others. From her vantage, the cacophony resembled the gnashing teeth of a tremendous metallic beast.

A passing crane brushed the carryall, and a foot fell off the ledge. Kaiden grasped the back while Terri spun and clamped the container with one of her secondary arms. She strained the limits of her crutch as her other augmented limb held the opposite ledge. The carryall was no longer falling but wasn't back on its feet either. Kaiden turned as he and Terri saw the mechanism rebuilding a new structure with passing machines and swinging arms approaching them.

"A fucking adventure," Terri said as she and Kaiden struggled to upturn the carryall back on the bridge. They dragged it across the expanse as the structure was erected behind them.

The two reached the other side and could see an open path to the other side of the Town. Kaiden sighed in relief.

The opening then closed as the structures shifted again. Terri's shoulders slumped.

"You had to do that," she groaned.

TORUS

This scientific paper, designated 888-0-8493-2700-9X, has been secured in a secret location to protect its contents and writers from repercussions. This summary will be kept brief, and authorship has been censored. The account within 888-0-8493-2700-9X details the few known aspects of hydrocell production.

- *The brass outer shell does operate as a containment device, not unlike a magnetic restraining system for volatile materials.*
- *The interior is entirely composed of deionized water and a smaller brass cylinder.*
- *We believe the outer shell holds this inner container, with the smaller vessel holding a quantity of smoke.*
- *It is suspected the inside of the outer brass shell contains TYKOL inscriptions that dictate how the device works, along with a script that disintegrates both the inscription and the inner vessel of the outer shell if breached.*

Employing mineral oil as a suspension fluid produces more power, but costs have prevented its implementation over water.

Hydrocell Basics
Corvos University
Author Removed

Elina flicked a few of the charms on Sloan's blade, snaking her fingers into one of the lockets and prying it open. Agosta's eyes were closed, but he wasn't sleeping. They were in the rear of the Loch & Serpent's only car, sitting around a table.

"So?" Elina asked.

Agosta groaned.

"So?" he said, waiting for clarification which Elina did not offer. He assumed. "Her name is Sloan."

"How old is she?"

"Not supposed to ask a girl her age."

"This hardly counts, Dad."

"No idea. The Maelstrom ejects an effigy on occasion. They don't remember anything before…supposedly."

"Are they ghosts, the dead from the past?"

"Wouldn't be the strangest thing we've seen."

Elina continued to inspect the weapon and all its eccentricities.

"Have you ever been there?" she asked.

"No one enters the storm, and nothing comes out," Agosta said.

"She did."

"She wasn't returning."

Elina nodded, which went into her rolling her eyes as she took in the dull walls of the train around her.

"Dad?"

"Yes?"

"Why her? I mean…I overheard you two talking, but why just her?"

"I had a plan…okay, I had about thirty…I figured they would expect a direct ambush."

"So, you were looking for her."

"Not her specifically. I would've taken anyone, and my plan depended on who I found. I was pressed for time, honey, and mercenaries don't exactly advertise on public forums."

Elina nodded and flicked a few more charms dangling off the sword.

"Each of these is a memory," Elina whispered, "tokens of people they've forgotten. She's got quite a few."

Agosta opened his eyes and waved Elina's hands away from Sloan's property.

"Elina, that's rude," he said. "Those are personal."

"Photos of people," she said, ignoring him.

Agosta pulled Elina's hand away and closed the locket.

"Leave it alone," he said. "I brought your illustrations and graphite. Play with those."

"I like to consider myself a good judge of a person," she said, stroking her finger along the fuller of the blade.

"Is that smoke or instinct talking?"

"Maybe both. She's only prickly on the outside."

Agosta grabbed the blade and stood it leaning against the wall, away from Elina's reach.

"Yes, well, be careful what you say," he said, "she's probably in the room with us right now."

The blade lifted on its own, and Sloan materialized, her clothes and face showing no signs of prior activity.

"Good guess," Sloan said. "Area's clear. We should go."

Sloan passed them and made for another chair near the back of the car. She said nothing more as she fell on the padding.

* * *

By the end of the next hour, Elina had retired on the only comfortable bed on the train, secluded in the conductor's cabin. She focused intently on a disconnected copper steam valve solenoid resting on the narrow bed in front of her. She had found the loose part in a drawer and figured it wouldn't be missed.

Elina held her hands tightly and concentrated. Perhaps this time. It had worked before, but once, she had overloaded the device and caused a small explosion. She had learned the hard way to take care of who was watching. The last time she attempted this was to impress another girl she thought would be a friend. She wasn't, and minutes later, someone forced her into a burlap sack. Elina considered, in retrospect, that the girl was a bandit's daughter and that her father had orphaned her. Elina wouldn't make that mistake again.

She fixed her mind on the solenoid and felt her mind weave through the wires. She could feel the magnetic field. Whisps of black smoke floated from her golden eyes.

A second later, the solenoid crackled with visible power. Elina held back, not wanting to overload the capacitor. Too late, she realized the device had been discarded on account of being faulty, and the solenoid fissured, releasing a piercing shower of sparks. Elina reactively kicked the device away. She heard her father from the other side of the door.

"You doing alright there?" he asked.

"Yeah, yeah, nothing going on here," she shouted back as she grabbed the solenoid and tossed it back in its drawer.

The exertion of the task caused a drop of blood to fall from Elina's nose, which she quickly wiped away.

Agosta knew what she was doing but let the lie slide. He wouldn't scold her; he didn't want to pay attention to it. He knew her desire to explore her talent was unavoidable.

Outside, Agosta smirked only briefly before sitting back opposite Sloan on the small dining table bolted to the cab wall. He cleaned his revolvers delicately. Given the sway of the threadbare train they road within, it was a difficult task.

"We're almost moving in synch with Uno," Agosta said as he glanced out the window to a darkened landscape. "Our evening is going to be longer…not by much."

"Is that what constitutes small talk in your world?" Sloan asked.

Agosta grimaced back.

"Mine's the same as yours. Forgive me for trying to engage in light conversation."

Sloan's impassive façade was just that, a reflex action she was fighting to resist. She shifted to the window. While Uno was still on the opposite side of Nimbus, it still cast light on the opposite side, illuminating distant lands thousands of kilometers away.

"Did you know that Uno randomly changes temperature from between a thousand and two thousand degrees," she said, "depending on the stream and seasonal requirements."

Agosta cocked his head and smirked.

"I didn't realize my quip was that vapid," he said.

Sloan turned to face him.

"Just to clear the air…I'm generally not selective in the contracts I accept," she said. "If my particular talents are valuable, I'll charge for what's required. I avoid the fine print, and I'll admit on occasion, I've been asked to conduct myself in a manner people may consider… immoral."

"I'm not one to judge your past actions."

"Not asking you to. If you had lied about your intentions, it wouldn't have mattered. I've made apathy a virtue. However…knowing now…what I'm saying is that contracts that pay and involve some measure of heroism—"

"You're saying that you'll take whatever business you can get, but if you can be the good guy once in a while, the better. Despite how long you've been alive, despite how much you've forgotten, your sense of honor won't slip away."

"I can't see one of my kind affixing a charm to remind them of a crime committed or a sin requiring absolution. Memory is fickle, even when you can remember it. We tend to rewrite our past to justify who we are today. But yes. I liked…being the good guy. Don't misrepresent this as an indication that I like you."

"Oh, far from it," Agosta said with a laugh. Sloan followed it up with a smile. "But memories don't shape who you are. You can still be a good person despite not remembering why."

Sloan kept her smirk up and waited for Agosta, who grew concerned by the slightly uncomfortable silence.

"So?" she asked.

"So?"

"Ask me again."

It took Agosta a moment to remember their past conversation. When it finally occurred to him, he smiled.

"Are you taking this personally?" he asked.

"Yes."

"I'm convinced."

Agosta finished one weapon and reassembled it. Whisps of smoke drifted from the inscriptions within the etchings in the brass. It was called that, but it was far different from the mundane alloy. This specific material could contain magic. The subsequent silence was not awkward, and they shared a minute until Sloan broke it.

"So, what else do you want to know?"

"Are you a zombie?"

"That's a bizarre diversion."

"Or a ghost? Whatever it is?"

Sloan nudged a chin to the rear of the car.

"She asked."

"Yes, she asked."

"Inquisitive."

"I made a list."

"Let me guess…how old am I?"

"I gave the boilerplate response."

"I don't remember emerging from the Maelstrom. So, there's that."

"You'd think you'd write that down."

"Not when I emerged, which left me wondering how or why I exist."

"Shockingly, I think every intelligent being that's ever lived has struggled with how and why they exist."

"But I have a giant middle finger taunting me of that fact."

"Interesting take. You ever been back?"

"Probably," Sloan said with a chuckle.

"I was. About twenty years ago, I served in Philokalia. It's as big as the stories. Hundreds of kilometers across."

"Have you seen the tower?"

"On a good day, it shows up. A black monolith at the center of the storm. Someone once told me it didn't belong, that it came from outside, the tip of a sword penetrating our world, and the Maelstrom is the result, like how a body responds to an infection."

"So maybe my kind is a virus…we're foreign invaders."

"Well, given this world has animechs, screevers, and all manners of other monsters, I'd gladly welcome a change from the norm. Especially ones as intelligent…and as…endearing…as the effigy come off as."

"Not bad; you covered yourself there pretty good."

"So, what have you done in the century you can remember?"

"I drank a lot."

"Far be it for me to judge."

"Anything else pique her interest?"

"No…other than the fact she likes you."

"Well," Sloan said sarcastically, "that's a load off my mind."

"She's a good judge of character."

"Given her recent company, I'm sure."

"I already said that was my fault."

"No harm, no foul…I got paid. Bandits got dead. No drawbacks."

"I certainly picked well."

"You should have been honest when we talked."

"I couldn't take the risk."

"You didn't mention she was your daughter."

"Would I have gotten a discount?"

"At the time, unlikely."

"Then it wasn't important to volunteer," he said, taking a moment to consider his next thought, "…and…now?"

"Still unlikely."

"Worth a shot…"

"Your last name is Pike. The ransom letter referred to the *Prescott girl*, and you don't have the same name."

Agosta didn't acknowledge the statement as he reloaded the assembled gun and holstered it. Sloan stared, waiting for a response.

"It was her mother's name," he finally said.

Sloan nodded.

"How long has she been gone," she asked.

He worked on the other weapon. Sloan tipped her head, annoyed at the evasion.

"Ten years," he said.

Sloan nodded.

"Ahh…that explains it," she said.

Agosta stopped dismantling his weapon and placed the components on the table.

"Does it now?" he asked.

"You said you were from Aquino."

"I am." Agosta returned to his work and cleaned the weapon's cylinders.

"So?"

"She was from Volani," Agosta said, "like her mother."

"Did you know her?" Sloan asked.

"No…" He dipped the bore brush in the gun oil and twisted it into the chamber.

"Does the girl know?"

"She knows everything," Agosta said. "Hard to forget a thing like that."

"A guardian angel," she chuckled. "This world chews up heroes like you."

Agosta placed the cylinder back into his gun and locked it into the frame.

"Is that why you don't make friends?" he asked. "No connections?"

"Meaningless," Sloan muttered as she lifted her blade from her lap and placed it on the table. She kept a forearm rested on it.

"Our connections are the only things that have meaning," Agosta said.

"Platitudes…" she said.

Agosta nudged a chin to her weapon as he holstered his other gun. "Your charms say otherwise," he said.

"That's none of your bus—"

The armored animech dinosaur slammed into the train, knocking it off its rails.

The nose of the Loch & Serpent spiked into the sand, and it tumbled.

The beast rushed to thump into the train again, and the vehicle rolled down an embankment.

Striking a set of large rocks, the front of the train crumpled, and the wreck stopped.

The beast ran down after the train and circled the hulk, striking its clubbed tail occasionally on the hull.

The vehicle was upside down and nearly vertical against the outcropping.

Inside, crates and supplies were scattered.

Agosta pushed off various oddities and climbed.

"Elina?!" he said. "Elina?!"

"Dad!" Elina screamed from the opposite side of the cabin. She pulled while Agosta pushed to dislodge the door. Dozens of charcoal illustrations fluttered out and scattered across the floor. She suffered a cut on her ear but was otherwise uninjured.

"Are you ok?" he asked.

"I was in bed," Elina answered. "What happened?"

"Animech," he responded, and on cue, they could hear the beast outside let out another metallic bellow.

"We need to get out of here," he whispered.

"What about Sloan?"

They both climbed back down, and Agosta rifled through the debris. It was Elina who found it, removing the sword from under a collapsed table. The blade had broken off just above the cross-guard. Agosta found the rest of it embedded in the wall.

"I thought these were indestructible?" she asked.

"Must have been a freak occurrence, the force of the impact."

"Is she dead?" Elina asked.

"No…I don't think so…she won't be able to manifest."

They could hear the monster walking around the wreck, searching for movement. It was irritable, not hungry, and Agosta knew it would eventually give up if it believed nothing was alive on the train. Agosta left the parts of Sloan's totem below with Elina as he climbed up the cab. He didn't want to check, but his conscience demanded he verify Machus's condition.

Drops of blood fell on his face, and he examined the door to the cab. Several large engine fragments had penetrated through the glass, and Agosta could see that the entire vehicle had collapsed. He looked down at Elina, who was staring back up. Agosta proceeded back down. The subsequent bellow was quieter, more resolved, less angry.

"I think it's leaving," he whispered. Agosta searched for anything salvageable while Elina laid the sword fragments on what was left of the broken table. "This is not a good place to stay. But we'll have to wait until morning before we can move."

Elina's eyes had shifted to iridescent yellow, and smoke was drifting from her sockets. She passed her hands over the blade and brought the broken ends together. She concentrated, and the sword glowed. As the light diminished, Agosta watched the blade mend together.

The instant it was repaired, a drained and visibly pale Sloan appeared with her hand on the crossguard. She grabbed the blade and fell back to the table, gasping, while Elina did likewise against the wall.

"Wow," Sloan groaned. "That…that…actually hurt like hell."

"Are you okay?" Agosta asked.

Sloan nodded.

"Now," she said. "…Machus?"

Agosta shook his head. Sloan addressed the wearied Elina as she struggled to sit up from the ordeal.

"That takes a lot out of you," Sloan said.

"The harder the effect, the more it drains," Elina said. Her eyes closed. Sloan watched as the girl drifted to sleep.

Agosta grabbed his coat and covered his daughter. Sloan relocated to the other side of the cabin, attempting to avoid stepping on anything that could break.

Agosta followed.

Sloan couldn't help but peruse the numerous illustrations strewn over the floor and the figures exemplified on them. A few were of Agosta, of the living vortexes, and of Sloan.

Sloan smirked before another figure caught her attention; she used a foot to nudge aside one paper to reveal a tall, undressed, emaciated figure with extended limbs and digits. Its elongated head held no eyes, just a broad, uninviting smile of needle-like teeth. Its arms were outstretched as if the creature had been crucified.

Sloan kneeled to retrieve the paper.

She knew what it was.

"The creepy one?" Agosta said, noticing what Sloan was staring at, "yeah, she draws that one a lot."

"You do know what this is," Sloan said more than asked.

"It's what kids always draw."

"I'm not sure of the kids you've talked to, but the ones I've encountered never draw things like this unless it's based on past trauma."

"Except she often draws flowers around hers."

"That girl of yours is weird," Sloan said.

"I'd take weird over normal any day."

Sloan encircled the debris and sat beside Agosta.

"Where did we crash, you think?" Sloan asked.

"Our next stop was the canton of Ragged Hollow," Agosta said as he checked outside to see where the beast was. It must have moved on, but he was paranoid. "Without a ride, it'll be days to get there."

"We'll start in the morning. Enough time for you two to sleep. I'll keep watch, take some time to scavenge the wreck for anything of val—"

"You know you don't have to. Stay, I mean. You could leave now, get a head start. We'd slow you down."

Sloan sighed, grimaced, and glanced toward the girl.

"I owe the child," she whispered.

Agosta nodded.

"Good enough," he said.

"I'm not a child!" Elina shouted from across the train.

"I thought you were sleeping," Agosta snapped.

"I told you she was nice!"

CONESTOGA

Don't.

I know you're curious.

You were about to ask me how it works. You'll claim that it can't, given the laws of the universe. You're going to ask for an explanation. That's your mistake.

You are wrong for asking the question.

Just accept it and move on.

Overheard between two proctors within an engineering bay

Synfallin barely spoke to anyone else. She and Noah rode the back ledge of the matador as the lance took a shortcut through the ominous chamber known merely as The Museum. It had been a distraction, gawking at the various alien relics, some of which might have originated from Synfallin's or Noah's forgotten homeworlds. It was also an opportunity for stillness as watchers avoided regions like this, allowing the group to slow to a leisurely pace.

It was over a kilometer wide and thirty kilometers across. It even featured spotlighting. She read that it was entirely possible when the weavers collected specimens to populate their habitats, they also gathered examples of their technology. The ships on display could be the very transports refugees arrived in.

The group was passing between two enormously contrasting vessels. On the left was a fifty-meter-long bulbous craft that resembled a limbless marine crustacean with a curved carapace, uropod, and antenna. On the right was an unmistakable human-derived short-range interplanetary spacecraft probably employed during the early years of space exploration. The name "Ares" could still be read.

To Synfallin, the words she read describing the museum could not adequately convey its scale. For one, those books offered few pictures. Her jaw would occasionally dip as another artifact would come into view.

Noah was out of his shell, which had folded into a form half its original size. As Synfallin didn't sink into her seat cushion like Noah, she towered over him, though appearing frail given her species' physique and the rebreather she was forced to wear. The book she was transporting was safe on her lap.

"Does it ever become routine?" Synfallin asked as she gawked at the immense scale of the cavity.

"Everything becomes rote if done more than once," Noah said. "But the 'peanut' keeps us on our toes."

"Peanut?"

"The vessel. I know most people claim it resembles an hourglass, but we have legumes back home, and it's totally a peanut."

"Where is your home?"

"Eridius. Just came from it. Probably won't see it again for…my guess at least two years."

"My sympathies. What is it like?"

"Being away from home or my home?"

"Your home."

Noah was trying to discern the source of Synfallin's sudden curiosity; maybe it was a natural desire to understand someone like him, one prone to wander in contrast to another afraid to move.

"Don't you have books on it?" he asked.

"Many," Synfallin said, waving to the chamber they were in. "But as I only recently appreciated, descriptions and photos do not often reflect the reality."

"It's not ugly or hostile if you were searching for motivation. A monstrous sedimentary mesa surrounded by an ever-oscillating body of water. One major city. Nice beaches. Clean streets. No pollution. Sanitary. Safe. Almost… utopian… fucking boring."

"That sounds like motivation."

"I joined the proctors when I was twelve. That's still considered a child if curious. I became an initiate when I was sixteen, an apprentice by twenty. That was when I left. I owned a basic skeleton cage until I was twenty-six." Noah patted the shoulder of his dodger. "And then I found this beauty in the carcass of a Draggo military transport."

"Was there anyone inside it?"

"They won't miss it." They were approaching another aged artifact thought to predate the Ares by at least fifty years. It was a conical vessel atop a short cylinder and was labeled the 'Boeing Starliner.' "Why the interest?"

"I am inquisitive by nature," she said plainly, almost oblivious of its implication, "irrespective of any assumed significance on the topic."

Noah's eyes fell away from her and took a feigned interest in the passing spacecraft.

"You wondered why I left," he said. "Exclaves are…massive, beautiful. Caged. No matter how big, how gilded." Noah considered his following words carefully, knowing it would cut but unsure how thick endolon skin was. "Even if you can't see the bars. It's amazing how many birds prefer being locked in their cage."

It was the first time Noah intentionally offended her, and Synfallin knew it wasn't spontaneous. Her kind's propensity for honesty had its drawbacks.

"Scrimm are closer to birds," she said.

"Metaphor." He took a few seconds to let the uncomfortable silence settle before his guilt over the remark overcame him. "That was uncalled for. I'm sorry."

"As you might be able to tell, most of the rest of this vessel is not entirely receptive to my kind," she said, preferring to shift the conversation rather than acknowledge the remark. "And I happen to think my exclave is…fetching…in its own way. Its history may not be as fascinating as yours."

"And yet it wasn't enough to keep you rooted. Just admit it. It's unexciting. Either that or you have to admit your obsession with the book must be all-encompassing for it to convince you to leave."

She glanced back to the Starliner as they closed in on the vessel's aft.

"I will admit the truth falls somewhere in between. There was not much I left behind. Maybe I was looking for a reason to leave."

Noah laughed and figured teasing would lighten the mood.

"Outside of recognizing this important moment of character growth, the sterile environment of Eridius was the prompt for an already rebellious youth. It certainly wasn't the trigger. I mean, you must have a family? Don't tell me you didn't leave behind a flotilla of disillusioned and lovelorn suitors."

Synfallin laughed back.

"Yes, as you can tell, my conquests are aplenty." Her tone dropped. "How can anyone manage a relationship out here. In a…cage… your choices are limited but available. But in the spaces between? Feels untenable."

"Well, we humans maintain an adage that absence makes the heart…" Noah's shoulders slumped, and he sighed.

"Makes the heart what?"

"Never mind, it's a stupid saying." Noah nudged a chin to the Starliner to change topics. "What do you think that is?"

Synfallin stared at him, somewhat confused by the subject change.

"It is in your tongue, so it is human. Liquid propellent—barely enough potential thrust for interplanetary travel. A handful of passengers, probably from a world that had not yet appreciated the advantages of nuclear power."

"If my kind arrived in that, I worry for the world we left behind."

Synfallin stared at him as his attention was focused on the rocket as it fell away, replaced by another human vehicle, far smaller than the first. She found herself being more honest with him.

"You postulated that our world was dying," she said. "I did not want to admit it at the time, but I considered that was true. Environmental scientists all but confirmed we evolved from amphibians within an aquatic ecosystem. We like it tropical and preferably under shade. And our world is a desert where we live in caves. Either we were unlucky or saved from a dying planet by an intelligence who assumed it had always been that way. I figured we were responsible for our own ruin. We got one; you got a dozen. Following that logic, you were probably members of a sprawling interstellar empire, the shepherd of a hundred worlds with diverse surroundings."

"And yet, none of them are perfect." It was a passing automobile. He assumed it was. Four wheels, four seats, and an internal combustion engine. It was stylish, with chipped white paint and black vinyl draping its roof, hood, and trunk. A cosmetic wing pointed to an owner seeking individuality through aesthetics. "It's true; none are perfect. I've been to a dozen exclaves in my travels, and many bore human colonies. Within even the largest populations, there was one undesirable aspect. None of them are truly perfect. And I think you're giving us too much credit."

"I am not cross with you," Synfallin said to finally return to a previous topic she couldn't help but address. "Are we…friends?"

"I don't know how to answer that question," Noah said.

"I admit we got off to a troubled start. I patronized you; you insulted me."

"We're past those pleasantries."

"I can call various humans friends. I have a scrimm associate and met a khitin once."

"My guild has endolons. But you'd still be my first."

Synfallin remembered that initial conversation they had.

"You can call me…Syn."

"I hadn't called you by name once since we met. The opportunity never came up. Didn't even have the chance to wear it out or exert energy for those extra two syllables. Synfallin…Synfallin…"

"Well, now it sounds awkward. You can call me Syn."

"Sorry about the tea."

"You already apologized for it."

"Yes, but now I understand the impact the book had. Honestly, your reaction was rather muted given its importance."

"I called you a futz," she said.

"And reckless."

"And reckless. Don't apologize."

"I should have knocked."

"You should have." She faced him, now ignoring the passing relics. "I was impressed at the speed you solved the puzzle."

"Like I said—"

"You are good like that. You had no right to be nice."

"It's not about rights; it's obligation. Though I read somewhere that negative initial first impressions often lead to lasting friendships later on."

"That cannot be true."

"Sounded good saying it, though."

He was still staring at another large spacecraft, three-hundred meters long, angular with jagged lines and no windows. Dozens of hardpoints that once held different weapons had long since been stripped. A hundred thrusters of various sizes were placed at differing angles, prioritizing maneuverability over streamlining. The only attempt at artistry was a single red stripe that ran the vessel's length.

"What about that one?" he asked.

Syn examined the vessel. It was unsightly, not something her people would design, and it was clearly designed for only one purpose.

"I assume, as you have been here before, you know the answer, but it looks to be a military vehicle with no compromise to its purpose. You think it is yours?"

"Hallways are too narrow. Medical bay is alien, incompatible with us, you, scrimm, anyone. I call it the stapler." Syn cocked a brow. "What?! It's totally a…there's this thing we have called a stapler."

"I work in a library, Noah. I know the human word for something that connects pages."

"Regardless, it's not one of ours or yours. Or anyone's. Given the ruins we found, I always thought we weren't the first people inhabiting these environments. Probably won't be the last either."

"We found our tunnels already dug," Syn said.

"There's a giant glowing crystal at the center of my home city that never shuts off and appears to have no power source."

"That sounds infinitely more interesting."

"I lived half my childhood in Eridius. Everything becomes minutia if you live with it long enough."

They observed the vessel as it passed them. Syn looked ahead; she was in earshot of Carthan and Machus, who were undoubtedly listening. She would occasionally hear them whisper something, likely derogatory. She thought it would only be a matter of time before they would direct their rage equally to her and Noah.

"Your men must hate me," she whispered.

"They are not…okay, I am responsible for them," Noah whispered back, "but Guild charter is specific in these matters. The survivability of those under our ward and confirmation of successful contracts. It's still an exclusive group, but they shun all outsiders equally. The moment you get a solitary toe in the door, all that is pushed aside, and you stop being one of them in favor of one of us. The issue is that it began with humans and remained so for over a hundred years, though centuries before either of those two asshats were glints in their parent's sibling's eye. They enjoy citing founders dead a thousand years while I enforce current policy."

Syn smirked and shook her head.

"The world has truly gone mad," she said.

"Exclusion makes no sense, no advantage to it whatsoever. Ostracizing a particular group doesn't serve a purpose."

"As the one shunned, even I can understand it. Nothing unites more than a common enemy. Negative motivations always supersede positive ones. Gather a large enough group; they may not pick a leader, but they will pick someone to hate."

"That is very much a human trait."

"Probably served you well on your homeworld."

"Yours excludes based on perceptions of intelligence, not arbitrary physical variations. They didn't get the memo."

Her kind had warned her to be on guard as the humans were quick to act, slow to think, and with the males, particularly slanted to violence.

A moment passed.

Another.

Syn realized she was staring at Noah without saying anything.

"What?" Noah asked.

"My insights regarding you were misguided and incorrect."

"One out of three humans. Assuming ignorance is still a safe notion."

"Not just in personality. In almost everything. Certain physical features had indicated you were—"

"Yes," Noah said. "…I was. My parents immigrated from Aurago when I was one. Decades before the Rough Raid."

"I'm sorry if this is a difficult discussion."

"Not in the slightest. I just…keep it from the rest of my lance. My close friends don't care, but…others may take it personally."

Syn nudged toward the other two proctors.

"Would your…those men…care?" she asked.

"Probably? I'm sure you were warned that humans are impulsive and act based on emotions rather than reason. As you said, we're tribal and prefer selecting people to hate over people to lead. You were probably warned to avoid emotional connections." Syn thought that Noah was preparing to skewer her again. Noah glanced to the front of the vehicle at the two proctors he'd prefer to avoid. He turned back to her. "That's sound advice."

* * *

It was a massive marine vessel, unlikely military given the number of windows and recreational features like a water park, an amphitheater, and a casino. Previous expeditions had mapped out the interior of the four-hundred-meter long vessel, all twenty-five decks. Initial archeologists had reported all the doors were open but that certain activities had been interrupted, like half-eaten food and games only a few moves in. It was pristine white, without damage, and sported a name on its nose—The Spirit of Thalassa.

Despite initial plans to colonize the museum and employ the Thalassa as a capital, the lack of solar energy or food made long-term stays impractical. It hadn't prevented caravans from taking extended stays, and the odds people resided in it now were probably high. The stone slabs kept it perched a few meters over the base level of the chamber as the proctor vehicle crawled by.

Noah had been through this chamber before, so nothing shocked him as much as it was to Syn. He couldn't help but become engrossed by her, occasionally looking at her rebreather—a clear plastic mask with an almost concealed tube that ran to a module on her waist. It was a constant reminder that they were not the same species, no matter how well they got along.

After a lull in their conversation, he switched topics.

"So…about that book," he said. "I understand the obsession and its mystery, but if it was a children's picture book, I imagine it wouldn't have generated as much fascination. Do you know who wrote it?"

"No," she said.

"Do you know what it's about?"

"No."

"Nothing?"

"I was able to track its previous location, an account of it being recovered from an alien tomb in Croatoa. One of your proctors found it. Katana Vaccaro."

"Vaccaro?!" Noah said. "The legend—you know she possessed one of the most powerful crutches in existence?"

"The Bone Flute."

"Of course, you knew," he said; she laughed. "But that was centuries ago."

"When she went missing, the book vanished with her."

"But Vaccaro was last seen in Karina."

"Her disappearance did not interest me. What interested me was that the book was found in the stomach of a roche fifty years later in Kenoma."

Noah nodded as if the fact made no impact on him. Finally, after some contemplation had passed, he said, "Huh."

Syn smiled and offered a peek before returning to the various relics of the museum.

"Fittingly, a lean reaction," she said.

"So, then it jumped to you?" he asked.

"No. Dr. Bridget Blackwood found it…two hundred years ago."

"And how did she vanish?" he asked.

"Scabs."

"Scabs learn from salvage. Books mean nothing to them."

"It meant something to one of them. Regardless, their hive was destroyed."

"What destroyed them?" Syn knew what Noah was implying. If she could, she would have rolled her eyes.

"I am sure the book is not cursed," she said.

"Certainly not. Perhaps there's another party manipulating events in such a way as to make it appear cursed and minimize suspicion. If it looks cursed, skeptics may ignore or disregard it as a coincidence. The more outlandish the story, the less likely someone smart will dive deeper to find a pattern that only an intelligent puppeteer could orchestrate. Was there another bridge, or did it finally end up with you?"

"That was the last account."

She found it increasingly more challenging to look at him, preferring to see the last few meters of the Thalassa pass by. Noah turned in her direction while her attention was elsewhere. He took note of the complexities of her skin and how it glinted from the sporadic lights around them.

In a blink, her eyes matched his; her complexion blushed, and her features rounded slightly—she looked human, but he could still recognize what was important, what identified Syn. The interruption broke his focus, then another blink, and the alien returned. Noah tried to continue without pause.

"So?" he asked. She turned and opened her mouth to ask but immediately lost her train of thought. She knew she had something to say…to this…human. "The book?"

Syn twitched herself alert and refocused on Noah.

"A hundred thousand words in an indecipherable dialect, surreal pictures of creatures and places we have never seen."

"An account of aliens that vanished before we arrived?"

"Maybe," she said, staring back across the expanse of artifacts. "I wonder how many civilizations predated our arrival. This vessel could be millions of years old."

"We're living in a tomb," he said.

"Let us hope it is more than that."

"So, where are you taking it?"

"Corvos National University. Doctor Natal Tojilfenias."

Noah smiled and followed her gaze to the museum.

"You don't mind hanging out with humans?" he asked.

"Not minding it now," she said.

They took the silence to share a smile, broken later as Noah glanced down at the book again.

"Syn…"

"Yes, Noah," she said, still staring at him.

"What the fuck happened to the book?"

"Wha—What?"

Her attention swung to the priceless book she had been tasked with transporting. The pristine cover was marred by a deep gash that cut through several layers of thick leather.

"What happened?! I was so careful."

"You were. This couldn't have been you. I saw it not five minutes ago, and it was clean." He rolled his fingers over the damage. It was a clean-cut, not a ragged tear. A knife or a razor-sharp implement caused it. "That's a slash. The ends are shallow like the book was used to defend against an attack."

"But it was in my possession all this time without a mark." She focused on Noah, who grimaced back.

"Well, don't look at me."

PARADISE

The honors are the regalia of each royal house meant to validate their claims to the throne. To possess a rival's honors is to undermine its authority.

These relics are believed to have been created in the dark ages and are the only known artifacts to survive in such good condition from that time.

Over the centuries, they have often benefitted from restoration and gilding, adding more jewels and pageantry. At the core of each honor is believed to be a powerful magical device. As these honors pre-date the rise of the Ascension, it was politically unwise for them to demand these honors turned over.

Thus, the command was given to secure these artifacts, to require their presence to legitimize a throne.

Kaelum and Eridius had their honors taken by Aurago and locked alongside their own within a massive vault. With all the others, they are either well safeguarded or under constant threat. Regardless, their locations are not under debate. Two sets of regalia have gone missing—the honors of Volani and the honors of Hydranis.

Fallah Ellan Palak
"Honor of Kings"
Corvos

The gondola connecting the worlds of Bythos and Philokalia was especially ornamental, with gilded lines and busts of animals accenting the corners. The windows were brightly illuminated and fixed silver wings extended from under them.

No other cable car was permitted on the system while the royal transport crossed. Despite being midday, lanterns were lit in the shade below.

The crowds in the festival knew who was descending and stopped to observe the ornamental gondola as it approached.

"These pants ride high," Agosta complained. He was adorned in the regality required when standing next to a prince receiving royalty. "I'm not used to this."

Kabdila smirked.

"Next time," he said. "I'll have something bespoke made fitting your position."

"How many assemblies are planned for this?" Agosta asked.

"Last I checked, thirteen."

"At ten, I think I may try to eat the carpet."

They entered the receiving chamber, not as grandiose and pompous as the hall, though tapestries and flags offered some notability. The room was still dominated by a singular oak-carved high-chair fastened with semi-precious stones and cushioned in purple leather. A carved and ornate desk forged from maple and metal sat in front. Great halls were reserved for public events, and this was not one of those occasions.

Two guards strapped in weathered mail and dented plates stood at attention, still with helmets donned.

"These are them?" Kabdila asked as he paced in front of the men. "The heroes of the day?"

"Yes," Agosta said, remaining by the door, "Katona and Serenda. Helmets off for royalty, boys, you know this!"

Both guards quickly tore off their helmets and removed their mail coifs.

"Sorry, sir," Serenda shouted back. Katona was slower to respond.

"Never acted in the court, have you now?" Kabdila asked.

"No, sir."

Kabdila twisted sharply to notice the still silent Katona. The prince smirked.

"Agosta...were you aware one of your 'boys' was of the...superior variety?" he asked.

Agosta perked a brow and circled to see Katona's cropped straight dark hair that ended above her brow.

"How many times I crossed you two on patrol?" Agosta asked. "Never once suspected. An egregious error on my part and a commendation for keeping such a secret this long. I don't know whether to be intrigued or upset."

"I won't hold it against you," Kabdila said. "I'm more concerned for the recruiter who could misgender someone like this…unless his appraisal was correct…"

"Waved restrictions for the city guard, your highness," Deven said.

Agosta was intrigued.

"And they're friends," he said. "Progressive conscription or enlistment?

"Enlistment," Sloan said. "Stricter for the courts, your highness."

Agosta stepped closer to scrutinize her. He remembered her, but she wasn't familiar. Had he passed her on the street? Did she wear a different helmet? Agosta almost held onto a memory of a corset, or was it a different helmet? It escaped him, but one detail remained.

"I don't know the face," he said, "but I do know the name. Sloan...correct?"

Her eyes met his.

"Yes...milord," she said.

"I'm not a lord."

Sloan kept silent as Agosta smiled and followed Kabdila walking around his desk to sit on the throne. Kabdila motioned his friend closer to hear his whisper. "Too delicate for war?" he asked.

"You or her?" Agosta asked.

"Testy."

"Still heroes, are they not?"

"Don't misconstrue...I am rather enjoying this. In fact, I'm fond of bringing this one into...our...inner circle."

Agosta only offered a blank stare back. The gaze was cut short when the Ahkdanate cardinal, Machus, burst into the room, followed by an entourage consisting of a pair of muted, mail-drapped Silantine guards, a plated and surcoat-wrapped ostentatious Episcar knight, and a reserved, underdressed proctor covered in a brown and gold boiled wool cassock.

"No royal reception?" Machus asked.

Agosta knew the bravado was intentional and tolerated it. Katona firmed her grip on her weapon. Loyal to the crown before the church, just as Agosta would want it.

"I'm not the king," Kabdila said calmly, "only his steward—"

"Only hours until that changes, I was told," Machus said.

"How would it look if I took the throne while the true king took breath?"

"Very true, now—"

"I guess no heralds in this room to announce the pageantry."

"I know you; you know me—Kabdila of house Aurago. Father adopted the family name, but he was technically born into the Coriolanus family. Mother, Anne, died when you were five. You've taken the role of regent since your father took ill. Technically, you've been in charge for nearly a decade…since the fall of Volani."

"And you'd be Machus…of the…what?" Kabdila asked Agosta.

"Full name Claud Machus Odrobina Artois," Agosta said.

"Well, that's exhausting."

"Joined the church when you were seven as a deacon. Became a rector before the age of twenty. Ordinary of Malbus before becoming the Archbishop of Aquino and the Exclave Superior. Currently, in the role of Cardinal vicar and head of the palatinus of purgitans, a position held for twenty-five years."

"Someone did their research," Machus said.

"The kingdom offers its deepest condolences for the loss of life," Kabdila said. "Hopefully, all the survivors have been taken care of?"

"Yes, clearly, the festivities and revelries point to a profoundly bereaved population."

"Well, we each grieve in our own ways here in Aurago—"

"I believe you're deflating the seriousness of this situation."

"What would you have me do?" Kabdila asked. "There'd be a revolution if we canceled Passover. The less concerned we appear, the more it points to the situation being completely under our control. A chariot of our gods crashed outside our gates. It must appear inconsequential, a message even. I'll leave the details to you."

Machus grimaced.

"Tales are being shared," he said. "Of dragons, the rise of the underworld. We can, of course, spin this in our favor."

"Of course. I'd expect nothing less," Agosta said.

"And Hydranis. They will be punished for this act," he said.

"For what are you referring?" Kabdila asked.

"Memory failing like your father?"

Agosta interjected on behalf of his prince. "Hydranis was not responsible for the attack, just as we are not responsible for all those in our world."

Machus turned Agosta.

"Will you swear to this?" he asked.

Kabdila held his hand to hold back his friend and spoke for himself. "I'm fairly certain the princess will speak to that respect."

"Have they relayed intent?" Machus asked.

Almost on cue, the doors swung open again, but this time, it was Princess Mannah Cedana Hydranis with her entourage that entered.

"Consider this intent relayed," she said.

Kabdila stood; everyone else bowed. She was stunning in her velvet, silk, and furs. Her long gown ran behind under a luxurious tunic. Embroidered lace and gems further accented her far from reserved attire. Cheeks perked when she smiled, and Agosta noted the long blonde hair wound in a braid.

"Prince Kabdila," she said.

"Her royal highness," Kabdila said, "ever the ravishing."

"Still regret the nullification?"

"Every minute after my father announced it. Last word still had you saved for Pyxis."

"And now?"

"Only a king can be suited for a queen—"

"Can the courting be excused for a later assignation, perhaps?" Machus asked curtly.

"Hydranis was not responsible for the attack," the princess said, "as you know, we obey the Hallessegro ban on forbidden machines."

"—Outside of the tethers and cable vans, of course."

"Based on a treaty older than our grandfather's, cardinal—"

"But you knew it was a machine that attacked the Aegis conestoga."

"Yes," Mannah said while keeping her composure. "Last I checked, our gods could not be felled by slingshot." She addressed Kabdila. "My prince regent, I speak for my kingdom…our doors are open for investigation."

"In time," Kabdila said as he sat down, "but the Conclave is safe—"

"Only by the will of gods and not by the efforts of those within these city walls," Machus said. "This is heresy of the highest order. I'm in a mind to recommend Aegis suspend all favors to Hydranis."

"But you won't," Agosta said. "Or rather, you can't. Communication runs one way. People delude themselves into believing prayers are being answered except that if gods could hear everyone, smiting would be a daily occurrence—"

"Why do you exist?!"

"You mean…here, or…in general—"

"I represent the church!"

"The organization, but I doubt the faith—"

"I can list the crucified men who mocked me."

"Amusing fact to boast—"

"How dare you—"

"Priest!" Kabdila said; Machus confronted the prince. "Cardinal!? …What the fuck do I call you?"

"His eminence."

"Well, that's not going to happen."

"It's my—"

"Machus, I'll pick a random person in this room to punch you in the liver if you disrespect me or this kingdom again…and they'll do it." Kabdila let the moment sink. "Any presumptions of tolerance to your condescension ended the instant you stepped in this room."

"Now, listen—"

"Aurago has been the Aegis's most influential supporter. Not just on Bythos but everywhere. We've championed your knights when they parade and ensured our taxes in money and food are paid. Cathedrals dominate our cityscape. We've allowed full discretionary power to purgitans within our streets. The Volani ruling class would've conquered this entire world if we didn't invade. We kicked out the Tepherons in the civil campaign and the nags out of the Osmarch. We brought about the fall of Eridius, Kaelum. You may claim to be the voice of gods, but we're their fist. Don't presume to think anyone would jeopardize that arrangement."

Machus considered several possible rebuttals, but he knew what was due to arrive that would soon shift the room's tone. He'd let Kabdila flourish his authority for the time being.

"Who are you?" Agosta asked, directing his attention past Machus.

"Carthan," the Episcar knight roughly said, incorrectly assuming. "Zengoro Baron and Commander of the Order of Epis—"

"Do you think I was addressing you?" Agosta said. "Your colors are hanging off your surcoat." Agosta centered his attention on the proctor. "Rector?"

"Brother, not a priest," Noah said. "Noah Bennet, and suppose I could ask the same question."

"You first."

"Are we children?" Kabdila said. "He's Sir Agosta, whose father was Francis, the Duke of Capal." Agosta slowly looked at his friend as he talked out his ass. "Son of Molvinia, son of Roliper, the Baron of Hassel, eleventh in line of House Aquino."

Noah chuckled.

"What?" Agosta asked.

"Nothing," Noah said. "Just…very clever. How much of that was made up?"

"It's the nobility? Technically, it's all made up."

"For one, Molvinia never had sons."

"You're not a priest," Agosta said.

"I believe I covered that. I said *brother*," Noah said. "Society of proctors, from the Exclave."

"I know your lot—ideological opposites to the purgitans. You collect and learn while they eradicate." Agosta knew immediately that this one was as out of place in this room as him. "Who forced you here?"

"I serve at the pleasure of our gods."

"That almost didn't sound rehearsed."

"At least I'm honest about who I am."

"You sure about that?"

"This place is rife with confrontation," Mannah said, defusing the mood. "I haven't enjoyed a view like this since the hastilude. Shall you two fight? Will there be swords—oh, please, let there be swords!"

"That would be a failure of communication," Noah said.

"Indeed…" the excubitor Psylaxis said as it entered.

The room was getting crowded. It was hard for Agosta to read a machine's intent, especially as well-mannered and civil as Psylaxis. Its mouth didn't move, a smooth, gilded facsimile of a pale, pearl-colored face. It was taller than anyone. Agosta noted the exposed synthetic muscles between the machine's shoulder and head. Nothing was living in that shell.

Agosta considered himself a studied individual and was aware of the technology the Aegis presented as proof of their dominance. Before the signing of the Twelve Covenants, machines were built. Humanity knew how to use wind and water to spin gears and operate pumps and gateways. Despite the prohibition, many of these books remained hidden within libraries in Corvos. One professor friend had claimed they were close to catching lightning in bottles. The line between the tolerated and the taboo was gray, so few dared push any boundaries.

Alternately, there was magic—to produce the impossible without machines. *One would assume the gods masters of that,* Agosta once thought. The cutters had pushed that knowledge to the extent of imbuing life in artificial creations—homunculi, replications, and golems. Agosta heard rumors that some creations were draped in a glammer of illusionary skin and were walking amongst the population. That felt godlier than an automaton.

The excubitors were one of two artificially intelligent machines operated by the Aegis. They were extraordinary feats of intelligence, so advanced that they overshadowed much of the rest of Aegis technology.

Unlike the near mindless hedrons, excubitors spoke charismatically. They had been known to even be friendly, if not polite, to women and children. When required to get its hands dirty, an excubitor could hold its own.

"I'm honored to be in the presence of such dignified individuals," Psylaxis said.

"And it's an honor to have you," Kabdila said.

Psylaxis bowed towards the queen and offered its hand, which she accepted without balking. The machine brought itself to her glove and lightly touched its cold lips. It then stepped in front of Machus.

"I agree with the assumption Hydranis was not guilty of the attack," Psylaxis said calmly, "but they may still be responsible. That remains to be seen. We are still collating information from witnesses."

"The driver of the whale is in custody and being questioned," Machus said.

"Tortured," Agosta said.

"Undoubtedly, he will sing."

"Or you could have just asked us. He already told me about the shaper."

Both Machus and Noah's jaws dropped in near unison.

"Excuse me?" Machus asked.

"Excuse me?" Noah asked.

"And neither of you knew," Agosta said with a laugh. "That's fascinating." He nudged towards Psylaxis. "It knew."

"Yes, I did," Psylaxis said. "I admire you didn't phrase that as a question."

"I'm more fascinated by their reaction," he said, pointing to Machus. "You responded with rage." He then pointed to Noah. "You with delightful curiosity. You…I like."

"Has it been recovered?" Noah asked. "Do we know it originated from Philokalia?"

"No on the first, yes on the second."

"So, there is proof," Machus said.

"It's a big planet," Mannah said.

"Not from my perspective."

"It's a hundred and twenty-six thousand square kilometers. Your exclave is seventy-two."

"She's got you there," Agosta said.

"The object is stolen theotech," Psylaxis said, "an archo class, and these do not act autonomously, meaning their master resided on Philokalia. We've confirmed this despite being unable to locate the artifact, implying it has either been recalled, doubtful given range, or taken by someone that attended the impact. We've confirmed it's not one of us."

"And I trust the devotion of my men," Kabdila said.

"Whose identities, given the quality of their garb, you were likely unaware of until seconds ago."

"They're heroes whose fidelity will not be questioned."

"Agreed," Psylaxis said, "which does reduce potential suspects."

"The driver spoke of an accessory, likely from Corvos," Agosta said. "Unidentified and still missing. The one that spurred his action."

"The issue is that transports don't keep an accurate log of passengers," Psylaxis said. "As traffic picked up due to Passover, many were being filled and sent without bothering to record name. As such, any further witnesses will be appreciated," Psylaxis said.

"It's then a foregone conclusion that this driver will be released."

"If still alive, I will ensure his discharge. As for these heroes of the day, you spoke on behalf of. They will be recognized, yes?"

Kabdila motioned to Katona and Serenda, unexpected to be in the limelight.

"To be members of my guard…in time," Kabdila said.

The two guards attempted to remain stoic. For Serenda, it wasn't working, and he was visibly concerned.

"Assuming you ascend," Psylaxis said, "a safe assumption, to be sure."

Machus stepped in.

"Only by blessing of the church…matters yet to be discussed," he said.

"If I may interject out of pure curiosity?" Mannah asked.

"Your majesty can always take the floor," Psylaxis said.

"I know not of this artifact of which you speak. How could it fell a ghonara conestoga, and who could wield such power?"

"It's an out-of-place artifact, your majesty, forbidden knowledge that blurs the boundary between magic and technology," Agosta said. "And as for the conestoga, the gods may be eternal, but their creations are not." He could read Machus's scorn without shifting attention. Agosta pointed. "And you can right fuck off with that look, bishop. There is a hole in our sky that created Vothragna, in case you forgot." He pointed to Noah. "This man caretakes a vault packed with objects and people that break the reality this cosmic machine claims to keep steady. A chariot of the gods just crashed."

"Too true," Psylaxis said. "Thank you…Sir Agosta."

Agosta examined the blank, placid expression upon the excubitor's unmoving visage.

"How long did you wait outside the door?" Agosta asked.

"I didn't…Machines indeed break. Thankfully, the Aegis ghonara was rescued. Their control module was resilient. It and the pilot have returned to Abraxas."

"And the…representative?" Kabdila asked.

"Outside the city. Under the protection of demigods launched from Abraxas, along with the remaining members of the Silantine guard and Episcar knights. The schedule will continue as planned. They will enter a parade down the royal mile later this afternoon."

"I am to take leave until called then?" Mannah said.

"Before you do," Machus said. "I assume each crossing from Philokalia to Bythos will be rigorously searched and questioned."

Mannah's borderline jovial mood fell, and she moved closer to the bishop. Kabdila stood, and Agosta slid closer to his prince.

"Liver punch?" Agosta whispered.

"Machus," Kabdila said, his irritation growing, "if you—"

"Thank you, your highness; I believe I can speak for myself on this matter," Mannah said to Kabdila before speaking to Machus. "Your eminence should be aware that those crossing via carriage and column number in the thousands, rendering such a pursuit problematic. Second, given what Sir Agosta said not a moment ago, any evidence of the attack would be found on this world, not ours. It would be impossible to route such conspirators via a simple checkpoint and will only serve to impede the joviality of Passover. Thirdly, and finally, if you wish respect, it must be offered, and in formal circles, I shall be addressed by 'your majesty.' In the absence of that, I'll see to your liver myself. I never demand anything of anyone unless willing to dirty my own hands with it."

Machus was unsure how to respond. Regret was not in his character, and he was taught never to apologize. He became locked in place.

"Given my recent promotion," Agosta said to Mannah, "and disregarding my prince's proposal, your majesty…can I marry you?"

Mannah smirked, and Kabdila chuckled.

"Until then, I'll take my leave," Mannah said as she departed.

"Like everyone else," Machus said. Anyone not built or touched by gods made for the exit. Kabdila stopped Agosta.

"My master of coin stays," Kabdila said.

"Master of coin—" Machus said

"Call it a future king's prerogative. I require a fanbearer."

Agosta scowled. Machus turned to his entourage.

"Take the streets," he said. "Make a presence. Leave the carriage."

"Your men need escorts?" Agosta asked.

"No—" Carthan said.

"Good," Agosta said, "so they won't mind if mine simply watch." He motioned to Katona and Serenda, who nodded and followed the Ascension out of the room.

"You monitoring those who monitor you?" Machus asked.

"Out of admiration, your eminence," Kabdila said.

* * *

"City plebs stay here!" Carthan said as he descended the steps from the castle's inner bailey. Sloan and Deven stopped, but it was out of reflex, not reverence.

"Have some respect for heroes," Noah said. He didn't know the two guards, but he did know Carthan from Zengoro.

"They showed up," Carthan said. "Arriving is not bravery. If you participate in a battle, you can still be a coward. Claim a share of kills; that'll earn my respect." He then stomped down the steps. Noah shook his head and spoke to the intimidated guards.

"Ignore him," Noah said. "Most do. Your conduct today was honorable if you care about that sort of thing."

"Thank you," Deven said.

"Respect the hierarchy. Follow behind. We'll make a circle of the inner courts and be back for the regal procession." Noah resumed this walk to keep up with the stately and garishly dressed knights. Deven and Sloan shared their awkwardness. Sloan shook her head and descended.

"Further back!" Carthan shouted without looking.

TORUS

If you are curious, the precise number is 1,035,837,385 kilometers, and no, you can't ask me how I know that. That includes tracks within the arks, those overlapping or parallel to others, and those encircling Nimbus. It doesn't account for all the sidings, which I believe number in the millions. Most of the latter are not more than a few hundred meters long, and you can most times tell.

Okay, we can tell.

They don't have bumper posts, so don't fly off the end. And don't bother looking for signals; the entire area is dark. Once you understand that, the last bit of trivia may freak you out a little.

It's all connected.

If you stick with the main, it will take you everywhere in the Torus.

It will never end.

Nekau Weninoff
The Railrunner Manuscripts
1224 AC

The Vanderov had slowed to notch four under the advice of its engineer. It was cruising out of Styegos, a relatively small but infamous region of the Convex and where they had been sent. The entire district was cursed, given attempts to colonize it often resulted in surviving immigrants fleeing from still-standing buildings. Styegos boasted the most preserved city ruins in the Torus, with whole blocks virtually undamaged. They had long since transitioned from the cold to the humid.

Inside, Terri, Deven, Noah, and Kaiden stared at the objective of their assignment and the sudden slash that had appeared when someone wasn't paying attention.

"We could just say it was found like this," Noah said.

"I'm not worried about the contract," Terri said. "This book was pristine when we recovered it."

"Looks like someone took a knife to it," Kaiden said.

"Well, it wasn't one of us," Deven said. "…was it?"

"No," Terri said.

"It must have happened while we were escaping," Noah said. "Stuff was tossed, and we literally drove through a building."

"I had it secured," Kaiden said, "and I verified its condition."

"Well, you must have missed it; I wouldn't blame you."

"What's my motive for lying?"

"I didn't accuse you."

"Well, it's either that or I was delusional. I possess an excellent memory, better than human, and I'm telling you, it was undamaged one minute, and when I looked back, there it was."

"Have you checked inside for Tykol?" Deven asked. "Maybe it's enchanted, a repository for smoke." He picked it up, studied the cover and the damage, then handed it to Kaiden. "Open it."

"You open it," Kaiden said.

"If it's infused with smoke, as a loginoid, you'll be immune."

"You're both children," Terri snapped as she snatched the book from Deven. "It's locked. No one can open it."

"It doesn't require a key," Kaiden said. "Looks to be a puzzle of some kind."

"May I?" Noah asked. Terri offered the book. He scrutinized the mechanism, barely big enough to cover the latch but with an internal arrangement of minuscule gears connected to tiny buttons, rods, and wheels. He worked the puzzle for a minute.

Just before Terri was about to lose her patience, the book unlocked.

"Not bad," Terri said.

"I'm good like that," Noah said.

Terri accepted the book, approached a section of the outer wall, unlatched a panel, and swung down a table. She placed the book atop it.

"Uh, skipper," Deven said. "The contract was for its retrieval, and they may get unhappy if they know we've opened it."

"It'll be fine," Noah said, patting Deven on the shoulder.

"Okay, how about the possibility that it's cursed or rigged to release some plague."

Terri snaked her finger under the front cover. As she did so, Deven stepped back and took cover behind a wall.

Terri swung the book open, then flipped a few of its heavy, semi-reflective pages.

"No Tykol," Terri said. "No brass."

The book was handwritten but perfectly uniform. A few pages displayed color illustrations, but of no creature or technology any of them had recognized. "If this does contain smoke, it would be a first. There's no mechanism I can see. No buttons or gears."

"What language is that?" Noah asked as he squeezed beside Terri.

"It's not Assembly," Kaiden said, "Sprache?"

"Don't think so," Noah said. "This doesn't look like a Communion bible."

"Old Iokon?" Deven asked.

Terri flipped another page, then got annoyed at the three other heads crowding beside her.

"Guys, seriously," she said.

They stepped back but kept looming. Terri flipped another page with a larger illustration of a dodecahedron taking up half a page. But it wasn't a simple geometric diagram but rather a schematic for a polyhedron-shaped object containing hidden weapons, sensors, and a mechanism that allowed it to fly with neither propellors nor rockets.

"What the hell is that?" Deven asked.

Terri ignored him and flipped a few more pages, revealing further confusing illustrations and words no one could understand. Terri thumped a large stack of pages aside, then again.

"What in the world are they hoping to learn from—" She stopped, and everyone leaned in, staring at the illustration on page 314.

It occupied the entire left half of the tome, a tall, undressed, emaciated figure with extended limbs and digits. Its elongated head held no eyes, just a broad, uninviting smile of needle-like teeth. Its arms were outstretched as if the creature had been crucified.

"Shadow—" Deven muttered.

"Yeah, storytime's over," Terri said as she quickly shut the book, then handed it to Kaiden. "I don't want anyone seeing this."

"You got it, skipper," Kaiden said.

"Let's deliver it to Corvos, get paid. I need to see Mannah and find out how up the creek we are." Terri pushed her way past the others and made for the lower level of the engine.

She snaked through exposed rivets, avoiding plates venting steam around their corners.

"How's my train, Tooley?" Terri asked the tarnished beauty as her upper half was concealed within a deactivated radiator fan. Groans and bangs echoed from the opening.

"Dainty," Mannah said.

"Can you be a smidgeon more detailed?"

Mannah threw out her wrench and slid out of the fan. She flipped a switch to start the machine and wiped the layer of soiled sweat from her face.

"We got a breach in the blastpipe. At least a half dozen bogies are cracked or broken. Span bolster number two is grinding. The headstock behind the engine is sounding kind of weird. Regulator's confuckulated, backup alternator is completely buggered, AND I think the bearings in the front left drive wheels are failing."

"Okay…there's a happy medium between those two I need you to find," Terri said.

"What I need…is to get to a yard. I need this train to be stopped, and I need access to hooks, a torch, the odd widget, a shit ton of brew, and at least fifty hours."

"Can we make it back to Corvos?"

"I would put our chances at…thirty percent?"

Terri stepped closer, as it was challenging to hear Mannah through the noise of the engine encircling them.

"Are you asking me?"

"Also, the front blinkey is broken."

"…You mean the headlight?"

"That's it."

"That we can fix."

Mannah firmed her lips and nodded while Terri realized this was the best she would get out of the tooley. She turned and left the engineer to her engine.

"Deven, I'm going to need you to replace the front blinkey!" Terri shouted.

"The what?!" he said.

* * *

Noah was in the conductor's office of the locomotive, sitting on a chair he had unfolded from the wall when Terri entered. She snatched a towel hanging from a bar and cleaned her face, then retired to her chair behind the desk. Terri opened a lower cabinet and revealed two small glasses and a bottle of blue liquid. She opened, poured, and offered Noah one.

"Let me guess," Noah asked as he accepted the alcohol. "Thirty hours."

"Fifty," Terri said, "and we'll need a yard."

"We can't afford to stop. I fear we may not get her going again if we do."

Terri stroked her finger along the seams of panels.

"She's been good to us," she said.

"I never said it wasn't…we can anthropomorphize this vessel, imply a personality, but let's never forget that by the end of the day, it's little more than a very expensive, very large, nicely painted, and highly polished piece of junk."

Almost on cue, a loud pop echoed, and a metallic groan resonated through the cabin. Terri caressed the inside of the hull.

"Oh, don't worry, baby, the mean old man didn't mean it!" she said. Another pop followed. A long resonant grind continued for an uncomfortable period. "Okay, that doesn't sound good." It finally fell quiet, or at least quieter than the train's constant rumble at this speed.

"You want to check it out?" Noah asked.

"No, she'll send Deven when she's ready." Terri slumped in her chair. "We've been holding it together with gum and hope. Luck can't always last."

"Just as long as she's a beauty from the outside," Noah said with a smile.

"I feel her best days are behind us."

"You're not thinking of stopping," Noah said, "…given the conversation we just had in Corvos?"

"It wouldn't be by choice, but the Van is over a century old. She served three generations of Zahn conductors." Terri rested a cheek against the glass, taking in the view as the snow transitioned to splashes of green grass and outcroppings of auburn rocks.

And there it was again, that recognizable silhouette. It drew her eyes a second before being revealed as a shadow upon the rock. Terri almost chuckled as the once humanoid outline split and folded as the train passed.

"We invested in gadgets and gizmos," she said, "when we should've been saving money for two weeks in a yard to rebuild cracked bogies and bent supports."

Deven knocked on the door to the office and slid it open without prompt.

"Engine says there's an issue with the brakes," Deven said.

"She has a radio," Terri said.

"I know she does," Deven answered, then just stared at them both.

"Well, what is it??

"She told me to ask if you wanted the dumb or the technical answer."

"Just out with it!"

"It's the cylinder gasket, the brake pipe, or the compressor."

"Crap," Noah said, "that could affect all the brakes on the train."

"Can we even stop?" Terri asked.

"We could manually brake each car, but if the independent fails…" Deven said.

"Should have gone pneumatic," Noah said.

"So, if we stop and then start moving again," said Terri, "we may not be able to stop again." Deven only offered a shrug. She addressed Noah. "Is there a depot or yard anywhere near here?"

"In Styegos, unlikely," Noah answered.

"Where's closest?"

"Kerberos…" That would have been a stretch, Noah thought. Kerberos was the largest community in Styegos, built within the ruins of a relatively intact section of the old Metropolis. Its high walls were made from other buildings, disassembled and repurposed, which created a mesh of clashing building fragments linked like a puzzle that formed a barrier encircling the town. "...but it's a ways and in the opposite direction."

"Arbilas?" Terri asked. That was an even further reach. Lifting bags and lost Iokon tech powered by hydrocells elevated the entire town to the sky, but Noah could only guess where it was. It was not connected to any rails, so it was a blind spot for him.

"Best to cut our losses and take our chances in the Dagos," Noah said.

"Whole lot of nothing there," she said.

"I'll take nothing over more animechs."

"You'll need to find us a course into the Mare Dagos. What's closest?"

Noah thought about it. The Mare Dagos was famous for its barren wasteland, lack of vegetation, and limestone terrain. Like many other regions in the Torus, the Mare Dagos was likely a shallow seabed in the past. Sections of the plains still boast entire blocks of the old Metropolis, islands in an ocean of rock. There were effectively two sections of the Dagos, one with functioning water channels and the other without. Corvos and Velora managed to clear out vast sections of track and waterways. On the opposite side from Corvos and Velora sat a massive expanse of arid terrain, little water, and sprawling ruins. The Vanderov was approaching the edge of that side of the expanse.

"Brass Flats is still a distance," Noah said.

"Caravel?" Deven asked.

"I'm not that good."

"Come on, Noah," Terri brightened up, "you're our train whisperer. Find us a caraval big enough to sell us parts."

"And maybe as an encore," Noah said, "I'll walk on water."

* * *

The train had slowed as it entered a dense lattice of interwoven rails. The network was an insane mess so compressed, it must have been set by long-forgotten machines left to lay down rails without oversight for centuries. Not a single patch of ground not pierced by a mountain or submerged underwater could be stood upon without seeing a track. It was such a labyrinthian maze; travelers were often stumped at how they could ever be mapped, let alone navigated. It fell upon exceptionally talented individuals possessing a purely instinctual awareness of where a train must be to get where it's going.

Noah stared at the map, then placed one hand on the hull of the train. He was born on a train; he grew up on one, and like most railrunners, he's likely to die on one. He can set his ear to a piece of track or a train riding atop and know immediately what's coming, going, how big it was, and how fast it was moving.

"CIC, next left, then a right," Noah said. Terri nodded and worked her controls to navigate the Van.

"We're in dark territory," she said.

"It's okay; I don't use markers to navigate."

"One of these days, you'll have to tell us how you do that?" Deven said.

"CIC, there's a level junction coming up," Noah said. "Take the second right."

"Confirmed," Terri said.

The Vanderov swung off onto a branching set of tracks, away from the ruins of the old city. The train eventually passed into the dust-coated desert, the arid terrain stretching out until vanishing behind the Stream.

"Gauge is getting narrow here," Terri said. While the distance between rails was constant throughout most of the Torus, there were notable exceptions, and the gap between them here was beginning to shrink.

"Mannah!" Noah said, "what's the narrowest before we derail?"

"One hundred and two centimeters," Mannah echoed from below.

"We're at one-fifteen," Terri said, "she can squeeze."

"Okay, skipper, next off, into the spur, follow that, and merge into the main five kilometers away. And keep your eyes open."

Terri nodded and followed Noah's instructions, directing the Vanderov off another branch, past the rusted carcass of another train. Terri ignored it, but Kaiden and Deven examined what they could of the vessel half-buried in the sand.

Twin smokestacks made it appear to have ears from the front, accented by a single oversized but broken headlight. It featured eight drive wheels and a top-mounted cab. Being a long hood train, walkways ran up the sides of the locomotive. Ten cars were folded and crumpled against each other behind it, most torn apart by animals. Most of the train's red and green paint had been peeled away by weather.

"I think I know that one…" Deven whispered.

Kaiden nodded.

"The General Limited," they said. "It was a privateer. I saw it docked in Fellose Falling a couple years back. Didn't know it hit the ditch."

"I'm not one for omens…" Deven whispered as he moved away from the window. Kaiden remained and stared at the wreck until it fell out of sight. They scanned the barren landscape and the spread of iron before them.

"Skipper, train coming along the sidetrack directly ahead."

Noah stepped away from the map and approached the window along with the rest of the crew. With the disturbance of heat and sand, it was hard to tell what the vessel was.

"What is that?" Deven asked.

"That," Noah announced, "ladies and gentlemen…is Dust."

Dust was not so much a canton as it was a five-hundred-meter-long, heavily modified steamliner that long ago declared independence. Although not bound to Mare Dagos, Dust could always be found there.

Modifications covered the once sleek train in houses, platforms, walkways, and meeting spaces, most fashioned by wood or iron. The top level of Dust was considerably larger than the original machine under it. It was effectively a town built atop a slow-moving train. The Vanderov crew could see people on the walkways waving. Children rushed to see the commotion, and workers prepared the bridges to extend.

Deven arched his head up as the Van came alongside the gargantuan train.

"Noah, remind me to buy a drink…assuming there's a bar," he said.

"They do," Noah said, "and I'll hold you to that."

PARADISE

In case you were wondering, here is a standard list of alchemical compounds and their non-magical doppelgängers.

Please note that ingredients matter as much as ratios. In this situation, if you see a bird that sings like a horned black tail, walks like a horned black tail, and swims like a horned black tail, it need not be a horned black tail unless that bird has the exact correct number of feathers as well.

Laudanum may not be receptive to enchantment unless its opium by weight is precisely 11.45% to ethanol with an additional 0.05% glycerol stabilizer, the latter of which is nearly impossible to detect without the very technology the Ascension have banned.

To complicate matters, the entire solution must be between 25 and 35 millimeters. Outside these parameters, you still possess a perfectly capable pharmaceutical drug without magical properties. Apply a cryption, and an incorrect mixture will result in a highly volatile acid that will kill anyone attempting to ingest it. No one ever said this was easy.

Doctor Hennessey Faulkner.
The Proto-Pharmaceutical

It was the celebration's highlight, and the market had emptied as a crowd formed around the Aurago keep, The Luminance of Deos. The royal path, a one-kilometer stretch of straight cobblestone connecting the palace with the Turtandan circus, was congested with every manner of life. The circus had become the center of Bythos for the three days it took Philokalia to pass, but this was the exception.

Initially, the towering conestoga was intended to drift across the road with the bottom tip gliding over the stones. The floating spire would dwarf everything in the city, even the castle, as was the rule. But now, it was only an Ascension caravan. Agosta knew a replacement vessel could be sent from Abraxas, but he assumed the ghonoran Aegis were skittish about sending another vessel. Typical of gods, Agosta thought to himself, unwilling to let their pretty idols get scratched.

The Ascension Basilica had loaned their most extravagant wagons to aid in the parade and increase the pageantry. They were gilded and adorned with Aegis symbology. Cardinals of the Ahkdanate sat atop their carriage with their tall, obelisk-shaped conical hats extending down to their shoulders. A hundred members of the Silantine guard flanked the parade with eyes perusing the crowd. The elite Episcar knights were focused on marching in their full plate, holding the banners of the Aurago nation and the Ascension church. Riding striders that wore barding down their thin legs, the knights towered over the rest of the parade, even the two-story wagon that crowned the procession.

The caravan stopped short of the stairs leading up the Luminance of Deos, and everyone riding dismounted while guards saw to the wagons. Phylaxis descended to meet them as the largest wagon opened its doors.

Among the masses stood Terri Zahn, observing the proceedings quietly. She wove through the crowd, tracking the advancement of the parade, and now stood only a few meters from the robot she witnessed tearing itself free from the wreckage days prior.

An iridescent glow emanated from the wagon entrance, and an elongated hexagonal, coffin-shaped object floated out. Everyone except Terri fell prostrate. She didn't initially notice and was focused on the fact that this was the same Conclave coffin she rescued without acknowledgment or reward. She desired neither as any illumination upon her would bring questions and expose secrets. The coffin didn't even exhibit any damage, and it floated with ease. They fixed and polished it to offer the impression it was indestructible.

Terri's attention moved up the parade to the cardinals, Psylaxis, and a handful of royals perched atop the stairs. She recognized the prince only from his attire. The guards flanking him were assumed unimportant. Mannah Hydranis was another assumption based on her outfit. Terri thought it was funny that Mannah didn't appear comfortable in the ostentatious royal gown she was forced to endure. The two others Terri didn't recognize, despite being familiar. One was dressed as a local, and the other's vestments indicated he was a proctor from Altair.

The chances Terri knew either of them were practically nil, yet there was a familiarity she couldn't place. The only other figure was the Archbishop of Aquino, Machus, who she recognized strictly from his sash. When genocide or war was ordered, the claim was that the Aegis commanded it, yet it was the archbishop's seal on the declaration.

The faceless entourage formed a perimeter around the excubitor Psylaxis and the conclave coffin ascending the stairs. The climb was fringed by dozens of standard-bearers with towering banners of crests, coats, and colors marching in synch with the dignitaries.

As everyone's attention was centered on the living gods, no one bothered to check the crowds and the one who wasn't kneeling.

But Noah did.

Terri was too distant to expose details outside the apparent characteristics of gender, height, and skin color. Terri realized she had singled herself out. She could kneel now and prove faithfulness. But it just wasn't in her to take a knee, so she remained standing, staring across the court at the only person looking back.

Noah couldn't help but smile. He had no idea who this person was, but he respected her stance. He averted his gaze to prevent any attention on Terri as the Aegis reached the summit.

The group faded into the castle keep's shadow, guards scaled back to rejoin the parade, and the crowds slowly dispersed.

* * *

Terri had gotten swept up in the celebrations of Passover and was passing through the Millhall District when she found the sign for Marshall's Apothecary. She diverted and pushed through the passing crowds, avoiding a departing wealthy aristocrat draped in a flowing lavender gown and matching heart-shaped headwear carrying a paper bag likely filled with tinctures of questionable effectiveness. Terri was the only one approaching the counter, with two others wandering aisles.

"Hello, Ward," Terri said. Ward's back was turned away, reorganizing his bottles, and spun to greet the new customer. It didn't take him long to figure out who it was.

"Makes sense he would send for you."

Terri was taken back as she was certain she didn't know him. She checked her surroundings to ensure he was not addressing someone else.

"Well, this introduction got confusing," she said. "I know I'm not the only Corvon in this city."

"You'd be surprised. I can probably count them on one hand."

"Would you need to?"

"Yeah, he said you were a smart ass," Ward said as he returned to his work. "Terri, correct? Our mutual friend speaks highly. I can't close up shop."

"That's fine; we can talk out there. What do you know about shapers?" Something glass fell and broke. Ward checked the other customers, then leaned forward to scold Terri before she cut him off. "Do you seriously think anyone would know of what I speak? This kingdom has done enough routing intelligence from its population."

Ward calmed himself, stood, and straightened his coat.

"So, it wasn't a dragon," he asked.

"What wasn't?" Terri thought about the comment, referencing the rumors overheard of the conestoga crash while navigating the crowds. "You mean outside. No…not that I've ever seen a dragon."

"If anything could take down a conestoga, I imagine it would be a shaper. You're going to purchase something. It's not a query."

Terri leaned forward and spoke louder to ensure she was overheard.

"Ethanol Alcohol, powdered garlic, and maybe some ferrous fumarate," she said, fully aware she was citing ingredients of a well-known enchanted health elixir, likely a common product Ward sold from his prohibited collection.

"He told you about me," he said. "I make a point of keeping certain aspects of my life guarded. It took him five years to earn a place. I've known you one minute. An orator claimed both the militia and the church are seeking the passengers of a whale that arrived earlier this morning."

"Don't worry; I won't linger. And I wasn't joking about the ethanol alcohol, by the way."

Ward grimaced, then wandered back to his wall to collect and offer the bottle.

"Twenty," he said.

"Extortion," she said.

"There are supplementary benefits."

She offered a fistful of gold from a pouch tied to the inside of her jacket. The other two customers wandered from the store, and Terri navigated the aisles.

"What's the range from its user?"

"Three hundred, four hundred meters. Did you see its tint? Was it red?"

"That's a bizarrely accurate guess."

"Red is offense. They exhibit little to no personality on their own. While other shapers enhance their bond by providing insight and wisdom, the archo desires chaos, a floating weapon system. In my opinion, the most dangerous one can possess. If I'd desire one, and I very much would, it would be an axol or an echo, blue or green…" It finally dawned on him.

"And if outside of that range?"

"It either returns to its user or goes inert. If the user were killed, it would disintegrate, and somewhere, the universe would eject a new one. It won't bond with a new user unless its former owner willingly releases its control. You found it…didn't you?"

"That would be a dangerous fact to admit."

"The moment its user approaches within range, it will recall. It won't act otherwise, and it won't act independently. If I were you, I'd get rid of it."

"Like Kaiden, I'm known to be quite stubborn.

"He taught you well. He's shown you the book, hasn't he?"

"It's not an Apoc."

"No…no, it is not. It's something far older. I kept researching after he left. I'd very much like to see it again."

"I'm going to convince him to come back with me. It's not safe here. He's not safe. Why do you do it? You could do real good in Corvos. Heal the sick. Further the knowledge of alchemistry."

Almost on cue, the door opened, and three new customers entered, each bejeweled in ostentatious attire.

"Money's good. Sadatoni is rich. A lot of men desire love potions and hard erections while the women desire beauty, long life, and euphoria."

"Blood money," Terri said as she made her exit with her purchase.

"Every coin is stained," Ward said. "I made peace with it long ago."

* * *

The king only had hours on his life at best, and the prince, Kabdila Aurago, had handled affairs since his father took ill. The Aegis showing up before a royal's passing was expected and timed perfectly to the festivities.

They were gathered in the main hall, and everyone waited as every stained window was closed and every door shut and locked. Only the inner circle, imperial representatives, heads of state, and religious elite were permitted to remain. Kabdila insisted Agosta stay by his side, and Agosta made a point to keep his prince flanked by Deven and Sloan, who were both overwhelmed by the sudden acknowledgment and promotion.

Neither felt they did much. They rode in and helped a few survivors, but most of the work had been completed as they arrived. A passenger of a passing land whale had done more, but they had slipped away, leaving only two guards to bask in the acclaim.

Psylaxis inspected the floating coffin and, after confirming the state of the room, tapped a few hidden buttons on the device. It sent out a deep below that nearly cracked the thin windows. A sequence of beeps followed, and the coffin lid didn't open as it dismantled itself. Psylaxis stood aside as a semi-opaque red mist spilled out.

As the vapor cleared, the coffin interior was revealed to be a heavily padded cradle designed to care for whoever was placed inside. Hidden within the frame sat all the tools required to maintain life, from food and air to excretory waste. This level of technology was beyond anyone in the room. Machus burned apostates for possessing such forbidden knowledge.

A frail female figure with short silver-white hair emerged from the bed, suspended as if in water. She was pale, thin, unnaturally tall, with the most striking blue-green eyes. Loose white fabric flapped across her skin.

She focused on Machus, and he nodded. He spoke for the Aegis.

"As you are no doubt aware, the Aegis accepts homage from all kingdoms of Paradise. However, bureaucracy has created holes in an otherwise seaworthy enterprise. Couple that with the amount of strain on the ghonara conestogas, and you can understand the appeal to streamline this process."

"I do—" Kabdila said.

"And the recent attack only verifies the need to ensure the security of our theocracy."

"Agreed."

"Given the scope of authority Aurago has acquired in these past few decades, it would be logical that this kingdom gain the monopoly on taxing all other realms for said homage.

"I'm sorry," Agosta said, "she told you all of that with a nod?" Machus glared at Agosta. "It's a simple question."

"You would be responsible for ensuring the quotas are met and prepared for shuttle transport," Machus said, ignoring the interruption, "and you would also be responsible for security…and reprisal if quota is not satisfied."

"And this would also—" Kabdila said.

"But this will not come to pass. Such an offer was considered for your father, and your king was pious in almost every way…but he felt he could keep secrets, an impossible feat in the eyes of our gods."

Throughout the exchange, Noah, standing beside the coffin, couldn't help but inch closer and lean slowly to get a better look. When he finally saw her, he was immediately overwhelmed, but he didn't know by what.

She stared back, and they shared a moment. It was impossible to read her emotion—she was blank. Noah recalled something, an instant between them, an encounter they never had. *Did she call me a futz?* he thought. Then she cracked a smile, Noah returned to reality, and he couldn't help but turn away.

"Secret?" Kabdila asked.

"Held back for his own personal gain…he thought of himself above the kingdom and his church. Find this thread and cut it."

"What could he have possibly held back?" Kabdila asked. "He destroyed a nation in your name."

"Actually, it was in hers," Agosta said, nudging to the Aegis. "Her people declared judgment. They called for a crusade, and those that fought shouted their name. I'm not disclosing some hidden truth. We all know it happened."

In truth, few people did; those within this room were the exception. Ten years is not enough to erase an empire from Bythos, but all parties involved certainly tried. Agosta avoided the crusade through his connections with the prince. Noah avoided duty on behalf of his position in the crypt but was later sent out to investigate possible vestiges within the fallen kingdom. By the time Noah arrived, the expunging of records had begun. In a way, by sequestering artifacts and documenting their existence within the crypt, proctors had unintentionally kept a flicker of that kingdom alive. To Agosta, strictly from a security standpoint, it was dangerous to disregard history.

"Does he need to speak?" Machus said, addressing Kabdila.

"No one needs to, but at least I say something," Agosta said. "Our deity won't even bless us with her name?" Kabdila looked stern at his friend but knew Agosta didn't do anything without reason. "I admire that…say what's required or say nothing at all. Somewhat the opposite of you, your eminence."

"Mr. Pike," Psylaxis said, "you have a very…distinct way about you. Your title claims master of coin, but your perceived intelligence and inquisitiveness indicate this is merely a public pretense. You are looking out for what's best for your prince. You were silent until the room was sealed. You probably think you have nothing to lose."

"And I'd be right," Agosta said. "We both know my statement was not meant to insult our god, but rather—"

"—was meant to aggravate the archbishop with hopes that I would step in to mediate, thus revealing the chain of command."

Machus opened his mouth to express his irritation for being cut out of the conversation, but Psylaxis held a finger to stop him.

"You're partially correct," Agosta said. "I presumed the softest voice swung the biggest hammer. But this is less a question about the chain of command and more about who pulls strings. Many believe you must have a puppeteer." Without a face that could show emotion, Psylaxis looked frozen in place, staring at Agosta. "But I fear they are not present in this room."

"The trick about religion, Mr. Pike," Psylaxis said, "is that you neither know who pulls the strings nor even where they are." It exchanged looks with the Aegis, then addressed the group again.

"As you said, she'll speak if there is something to say." Agosta smiled and stepped back.

Psylaxis confronted Machus.

"With that out of the way, you may continue."

"Recent events have proven that revolutionary forces are hiding among us," Machus said. "You may attest to the innocence of Hydranis, but as you are no doubt aware given your recent history, and as my associate spoke earlier, you may not be guilty but still responsible."

"Funny how that always works out," Kabdila said. "There's no greater sin than the one you're unaware of."

"Because he doesn't know," Agosta said. "It's not about being vague, and I would wager no one in this room knows exactly what's being discussed. I've never been in the company of so many talking heads where nothing is said." Machus didn't answer. He glanced at Noah, who only shrugged. "Truth is, he was hoping we would tell him."

"Don't like mysteries, do you, Mr. Pike?" Psylaxis asked.

"Do you?" Agosta asked.

"I'm honestly surprised you don't know…either that or you're a better liar than I was led to believe. I have faith you'll figure it out."

"What are the rectors and cardinals of the church but messengers from the gods," Machus said. "And they have offered a prospect and a price, one that must be paid."

Kabdila stared at the Aegis in her coffin, who listened but didn't give anything away through expressions.

"An ambiguous god," Kabdila said. "Didn't see that one coming."

"My Prince—," Machus said.

"Yes, my loyal representative only seeks to protect my interests. If there's a mystery, I'm confident we'll solve it. There's no need to question our fidelity."

"Let's hope we won't need to."

"We offer tribute and gifts for our esteemed guest and the church. With your permission, I will call for it. I believe you will find it all rather generous."

"Yes, bring forth." Machus glared at Noah. "Your presence is not required here. Meet up with Carthan. There are doctrine violations to investigate."

"I'm not a purgitan," Noah said. "Thought the clothes gave it away."

"Then why are you here, proctor?"

"That's an excellent question, your eminence."

"The other purgitans of status were killed in the crash. You'll have their duties to perform. Go."

Noah departed without acknowledgment, but the cardinal didn't require it. Machus leaned closer to the prince.

"The king believed he could keep secrets. He never knew that held us back. You have the luxury of knowing. And with honesty opens the gates of heaven…and the patronage…of emperor."

CONESTOGA

There was an old religious fable about a god leaving temptation in the open for man to take. In the story, something convinced man to indulge that temptation. That temptation led to knowledge, to the awareness of human nature, and for that, man was banished.

Feels like an overreaction…if this deity knew all and could control all, then it must have planned for the banishment, setting a course for the rise of humanity. Religions tied to this fable believed otherwise. I bring this up because maybe the makers of our world—the weavers, let's call them—created such a trial. Instead of an apple, it's a puzzle, and our curiosity demands we solve it.

These weavers possessing the power to build this structure could easily make such a riddle impossible. The fact that it was difficult meant we were intended to solve it. Everything we found since points to this being the case. Their technology is easy to control but difficult to understand. Their language cannot be translated, but we can still employ it.

We're at the next tree, and when we are 'banished' from this garden, what knowledge will we be given next.

Dr. Lucas Kimbell
Volani Research Guild
540 AC

Agosta approached the massive transparency, revealing the universe beyond. At this angle, his view was dominated by the expanding vessel—a hill that inclined for thousands of kilometers.

"Wait, we're at the surface again?" Agosta asked as he approached it. Despite the opposite half of the ship dominating the view, he could see the distant star system the ship orbited.

"Yes, that was part of the route," Deven said.

"I thought we were going through the vessel?" Terri asked.

"We did…mostly. Now, it's just a day's travel to intercept Kenoma." Everyone gathered at the window large enough for even Sloan to walk to, enjoying the infinite emptiness of space.

"It's getting late, though," Kaiden said. "We'll need to set a perimeter." The group split up with duties to set up camp, security sensors, and trip alarms.

Terri approached Kaiden and Agosta and whispered, "We've been pushing our luck out here. Three days without a watcher."

"Well, they wouldn't have entered the garden or the town," Kaiden said, "so I think we threw the scent off."

"Still think she's a jacker?" Terri asked.

"Even if she was, they abandon people all the time."

Terri faced Agosta. "We never did get a straight answer concerning how she knows you. You didn't buy her line, and neither did I."

"I'm less concerned about how she knows my name and more by the fact that she's…familiar," Agosta said.

"Familiar?" Terri asked. "Well, we tussled with jackers on more than one occasion."

"In engagements where we emerged the victor. We'd find her among the spoils."

"Then where?"

"Can't for the life of me remember," Agosta said, "And if we did meet, what are the odds on her being the only survivor in Philokalia."

"Déjà vu," Kaiden said.

"Déjà vu is a misfiring of neurons offering the belief you've seen something before," Terri said. "Familiarity is different."

"Stroke of luck!" Deven said as he stared out the transparency.

"What is it?" Terri said. Deven stayed quiet, forcing the group to gather behind him. It was an exclave slowly drifting by them. It was not as big as the others, only ten kilometers across, but with a welcoming natural terrain enclosed within.

"Whichever one it is," Deven said, "It's moving in our direction."

"How did you miss that?" Agosta asked.

"It might be an unregistered habitat. Can't keep track of all of them."

"I don't like the idea of taking refuge in an unexplored habitat," Sloan said.

"It'll get us out of the ship, which is more important," Terri said. "See if you can get us in, Deven."

Deven nodded and checked his scanners. Without a word, he pointed in a direction, and the group followed. Within a minute, they reached a featureless wall, and Deven stood in front of it.

Everyone waited.

An access pedestal emerged from below and lifted into position. Then a wall section split along an invisible seam and opened to reveal a massive door.

"Terri," Sloan said. Terri found Sloan checking the hallway, her lights only pushing so far into the darkness. Terri approached close, and Sloan whispered. "We got movement on the tracker, edge of range."

"How many?"

"Looks to be one. Big. Transport…or something else?"

"Get that door open, Deven!" Terri said.

"I knew our luck would run out," Sloan said as she opened up her weapons systems and aimed her railgun down the corridor.

It was approaching but still out of sight. Deven frantically punched sigils on the pedestal.

"Deven, please accomplish your task with the utmost haste!" Kaiden said.

Sloan could see glints off metal, flickers of light, and telltale sounds of scraping and grinding.

"Got it!" Deven said as the airlock opened.

Terri pushed Kaiden and Deven into the lift with Agosta carrying Elina and Sloan following the carryall as it entered. The shape approached them. It almost came into focus when the door slammed shut. The elevator began to lift.

"Anyone get a look?" Deven asked.

"Wasn't much time for a selfie," Sloan said.

"Masks on, suits shut," Terri said. Agosta saw to Elina, who was practically trembling.

"It's okay…" he whispered.

"Is this normal for your profession?" she asked.

"No…usually, it gets exciting."

The lift carried them to the outer hull and shifted sideways to track the moving habitat when the exclave passed overhead. It locked under the exclave gateway and carried the lance into the bottom level of the habitat.

"Looks like this gateway is dead center of the vessel," Deven said as a colossal door opened into a natural stone hallway. It inclined for a few hundred meters before terminating into a brilliant beam of light.

Sloan reported from inside her suit, "Arid. Temperature eight degrees. I'm picking…nitrogen at thirty-five percent, thirty oxygen. One percent carbon dioxide may be an issue depending on underlying conditions anyone may have. Some minor trace elements, but the big outlier is thirty percent argon."

"An issue?" Agosta asked.

"Maybe. Argon is heavier than oxygen, meaning lower pockets, valleys, or pits may suffocate someone without supplementary oxygen. If we ascend, the ratio will drop. We just can't let carbon dioxide get much higher for our health. I mean…Deven can handle higher ratios, but the rest of us can't."

"Endolon?" Agosta asked.

"No, their mixture is different."

"There could be aliens in here?" Elina asked.

"No way of knowing…and that's half the fun," Terri said. "Deven, how long?"

"We'll have to exit this area to get a proper reading, but at this current estimate…we'll reach the rendezvous in nine hours."

"Ok…let's see what we're dealing with."

The group exited the airlock and marched down the hallway towards the light. There was a slight incline as the argon ratio diminished; eventually, each lance member removed their masks or opened their suits.

They exited onto the peak of a hill that descended to the edges of the habitat. Basic landscaping had torn out the vegetation and smoothed the terrain to act as a road.

From their vantage, they could see tundra dotted with red moss and little else. No trees, only a small lake sitting at the end of the habitat.

They had stepped onto the center of an assumed abandoned town. No structure was taller than two stories, all made from compressed mud like they sprouted from the ground. The streets radiated outward from the gateway with houses packed close, extending three kilometers down the hill. There was no individuality among the dwellings—they all appeared as the same tan-colored house, though a few were stacked with others sharing walls. There were no signs, addresses, glass, or even wood, like the town was never finished.

"I don't see anyone," Agosta whispered.

"The atmosphere at the base of this hill will be borderline unbreathable without supplementary oxygen," Sloan said. "Best we remain close to the gateway."

Everyone continued scanning the habitat's simplistic terrain, except Agosta, who examined the gateway they exited. He arched his head to see what was perched upon it.

"Yeah, we may need to consider leaving," he said.

"Holy Shit," Kaiden said, with the rest of the group pivoting to see the figure.

It towered over them, a statue almost haphazardly assembled from wood and stone and draped in black fabric to appear as skin. It was either hastily erected or suffered from limited technology as the cloth only covered half with the wood reinforcements visible in places. Enormous chains encircled the statue, potentially holding it together, with broken links hanging from extremities.

While incomplete, the effigy was presented as an emaciated creature with long limbs ending in long digits and a nearly featureless conical head save for an ear-to-ear smile of needle-like teeth. Its arms wrapped around itself with hands ending below its knees, either embracing itself or trapped within the chains. Its head was lowered, and if it had eyes, it would have gazed directly at the group.

"I've made a terrible mistake leading you here," Deven said.

"I think it's rather…captivating," Terri said.

"I was going to use terrifying, but sure."

"Full missile barrage at the base will bring it down," Sloan said.

"I think I agree with her," Agosta said.

"It's just a statue," Terri said. "Let's reconnoiter. Set a perimeter." Kaiden attended to his supplies as Terri and Agosta continued being transfixed on the figure.

"Remember what I said about familiarity," Agosta asked.

"Yeah," she said.

"Are you getting it?"

"Yeah. You?"

"…Yeah." Agosta turned to Elina. "You okay?"

"Should I be?" she said anxiously.

"Deven, I want a security perimeter, top priority," Terri said.

"Uh…there might be…a…problem with that," Deven said, resulting in a light chuckle from Kaiden. "The atmosphere and pressure differentials are throwing the sensors off. And whatever…that…is…radiates a powerful magnetic field."

"So, we don't even know if this town is inhabited?" Terri asked.

"We could just stay here," Deven said.

"What's the fun in that?" Terri asked.

"Deven is just concerned about protecting his hide," Sloan said.

"Considering I walk around in it, absolutely," Deven said.

"People," Terri said, "…you're parading in humanoid-augmented mechanical power suits with enough armor and firepower to level a city block, and a…okay, admittedly ominous statue is causing a panic. Mark it as yet another interesting oddity in the history of weird artifacts encountered while cruising inside an enormous alien spacecraft. In a few years, it'll barely count as a footnote."

"Well…" Deven said, "since you put it that way."

Kaiden continued working on the camp with Sloan helping, given her shell's size and considerable strength. Deven, Agosta, and Terri walked away to explore the town. With radios on, everyone could listen to everyone else.

"Remain with Kaiden," Agosta told Elina. She shook her head vigorously.

"Not on your life," she said.

"Okay, just…don't go wandering."

"Are you kidding?!"

"As Sloan expected," Deven said, "Argon concentration is increasing, oxygen dropping as we descend. I imagine this town perfectly encapsulates the breathable portion of this habitat. After about four kilometers, it will dip below twenty percent."

"That means that lake at the edge is unreachable without a separate air supply," Agosta said.

"The construction is simplistic," Terri said as she stepped into one of the buildings. "Adobe. Looks to be mostly clay and sand."

"Yeah, but door dimensions point to creatures our size."

"Don't see any wood around here, and what's that cloth on the statue made from?"

"Well, the landscape is surprisingly barren," Agosta said.

"You saying they stripped their habitat to build that?" Deven asked.

Further out, Agosta took another opportunity to gawk at the effigy. He employed binoculars to get a better look. The detail was rough; the seams between stone slabs were visible.

"I'm guessing two hundred meters tall," he said.

"One ninety-two," Deven said.

"I'm rounding."

"If there were people here," Terri said, "they didn't leave anything behind. No mattresses, no cooking appliances, furniture. Frames without doors. Windows without glass. The people who built that monstrosity didn't live here."

"You thinking this could be a new claim?" Kaiden asked.

"Who'd want to live here?" Deven asked,

"Oh, it's not so bad," Agosta said. "We could spruce it up a bit. Splash of paint. Colorful lights. Controlled demolition. An exorcism."

"Document what you can," Terri said. "Photos. Video, the works. Let's register when we get back, and a better-equipped expedition can work out the details. Until then, let's ensure we survive the night.

* * *

Three hours later, the artificial sun overhead had drifted to the edge of the habitat and deactivated. The star system within view of the exclave transparency was visible but not providing enough light at this distance. Everyone had exited their crutch save Deven, who was taking first watch. The carryall sat near the gateway edge, with Kaiden and Terri sleeping in the open, under the dome. Sloan was awake under the cover her shell provided when folded closed. She watched silently as Agosta led Elina into the nearby house.

He had placed his sleeping bag on the stone platform that doubled as a bed frame.

"There's only one way out, and I'll be outside," Agosta said. "It's better than sleeping on rock."

Elina crawled inside and scrutinized the empty room. Agosta activated a portable light, set it to its lowest setting, and placed it on the window frame.

"You going to answer my question?" he asked her.

"You mean how I know you?" she asked. Agosta nodded. "Do you remember your dreams?"

"Not often."

"But when you do, are you somewhere else? Like a place you've never seen?

"Maybe."

"Did you think you're another person?"

"What are you getting at?"

"You know, there's a way to remember your dreams," she said, which caused Agosta to perk a brow. "You just have to tell yourself to."

"Tell yourself?"

"Yes, just say before you go to bed, *I will remember my dreams*. That easy."

"So, you dreamt about me?" Agosta asked.

"Something like that."

"What was I doing?"

Elina smiled at him.

"…you were saving my life," she said. Agosta cocked his head, confused by the answer. She then whispered, "You saw it too."

* * *

They had repacked, and the lance had strapped back into their shells and crutches when Deven heard the gateway door opening. The corridor was dark, and he spotted movement. He screamed to the others, "Attack!"

A volley of javelins emerged from the darkness, missed Deven, and embedded in the adobe walls of one of the houses.

Deven immediately fired his grappling wires behind him, which anchored into a building and vaulted him away from the entrance as a half-dozen armed men donned in primitive crutches entered. Their suits were cobbled together from different scavenged enemies, but figures encased in their exoskeletons were human, though donned in similarly mismatched armor. Half of them sported secondary limbs from their crutches, while the rest wore augmented power suits with shoulder-mounted hardpoints.

The lead with yellow stripes and secondary limbs wielded a two-handed rail gun and fired it at Agosta's jagger while Pike tossed Elina into the building; two flechettes passed through the building and three other structures without stopping.

"Stay here; this won't take long," Agosta said softly and with a wink. He retrieved his energy weapon, which expanded into an intimidating two-handed rifle with a strange cross-shaped barrel and three laser sights.

Agosta fired his thrusters to gain a better vantage upon emerging from the building, while Kaiden approached a blue and black exoskeleton that faced him, wielding a high-velocity rifle.

Kaiden's secondary arm unfolded into a shield, deflecting several incoming shots as he got close and fired a short-range concussion blast from that same limb that kicked the blue/black exoskeleton down the hill.

Deven fastened himself to the building's upper level, and the barrel of his sniper weapon extended in his grasp.

The scrimm aimed carefully.

A fin-stabilized metal dart fired from his weapon and struck like an arrow through the armor and halfway into the chest of an all-black augmented suit brandishing a flamethrower.

The pilot coughed blood and scrutinized the terrain to find his attacker.

He detected Deven only a second before the scrimm fired three more flechettes into him, and he fell.

Deven spotted another augmented suit, a red and yellow one with a rocket pack on its left shoulder, take aim. The scrimm fired his jump jets and escaped the building a second before it exploded.

The blast tossed Deven into another building.

Terri was firing her assault rifle at one enemy while her secondary limbs threw a rock at another.

One enemy with the same setup attempted to get close with a blade, but Terri was a better pilot, and her long limbs swatted the weapon away.

She clamped onto and tore one of the additional limbs off the suit, then hammered the armor with the blunt end of the appendage.

Two augmented armors with javelin launchers continued firing on Agosta, forcing his suit to evade the projectiles.

Wasted rounds embedded in the walls around him.

He checked his weapon, the cross barrel now crackling with electricity.

He emerged from cover and exchanged fire with the lead enemy.

Two lances struck the jagger's arm as a bolt of lightning fired from Agosta's weapon.

The current was powerful enough to pop the pilot's chest like a balloon with secondary arcs striking the two enemies beside the first.

And that's when Sloan's angry bug landed.

No one had seen where she took off, but the juggernaut rig slammed into the ground between two enemy crutches, causing them to scatter.

One that was tossed fired several high-caliber rounds into Sloan's armor, each one producing an annoying dent.

As Sloan converged on the opposite enemy, her plasma cannon fired behind her, vaporizing her opponent.

The crutch in front brought up a high-energy laser cutter that sliced into Sloan's torso.

The rig's thrusters fired, causing Sloan's colossus to leap forward.

Her solid mechanical fist gut-punched the last suit.

A concealed piston in her forearm fired, penetrating the enemy armor and through the pilot.

The rod retracted, and Sloan stepped away as the last suit fell dead upon the ground.

"Secure?!" Terri said. "Sound off!"

"Here!" Agosta said.

"Alive!" Kaiden said.

Deven emerged from his building.

"Likewise," he said, though he was limping.

"Sloan?!" Agosta shouted.

Her rig settled on its knees, and her torso opened up.

"Been better," she said with a groan. Agosta caught her as she fell out of her suit.

"Deven!" Agosta said.

Deven exited his suit and ran to them. Sloan had suffered a cut through part of her neck, though the laser had cauterized it.

"Let me see to her," Deven said.

"I'll live," she said.

"Yeah, but I'll make you pretty again, so hold still."

The group gathered to survey the damage and their opposition. No enemies had survived. Agosta stepped away and noticed Elina emerge from the half-destroyed building.

"You okay?" he asked.

She nodded.

"Yeah…clearly, I picked the right saviors," she said. "Those were jackers."

"Maybe it wasn't a watcher outside," Terri said.

"Were they following us?" Kaiden asked.

"Maybe they want her," Terri whispered back. Agosta stepped closer to involve himself in the conversation.

"She's a child," Agosta said, "…and yes, I'll agree every child is special, but not in the ways that provoke jackers to attack."

"Unless she is someone's daughter," Terri said.

"My parents are dead," Elina said. "You seem to keep forgetting that I have ears."

"Who were they?" Kaiden asked.

"Edward and Liara Prescott," she said.

"And they were…Volani?" Agosta said. "Did they get out?"

"Yes…but Jackers caught us after we escaped."

"You were a slave for ten years?" Terri asked.

"Most your life," Agosta said.

* * *

The lance surveyed the damage. Agosta's armor had taken a hit, likewise with Deven and Sloan, with the latter bleeding from a minor neck wound Deven had dressed. There had been a half-dozen of them and well-armed. The carryall survived unscathed, and Elina was atop it, ready to depart.

"Sun-24 blast driver," shouted Terri as she yanked the part from a damaged frame still locked in the grasp of a dead cultist. "Not bad at all."

"Congratulations, people," Kaiden said. "We just discovered this town and within six hours destroyed it."

"Hey, they started it," Deven said.

"Also, you're being hyperbolic," Terri said. "Most of it still stands. That abomination is still here; that must account for something."

"You guys hearing that?" Sloan asked. The group looked at Sloan, who was rummaging through the bodies. Everyone remained silent, but only Sloan heard it.

"What is it?" Agosta asked.

Terri noticed it first.

"Sloan…get out of there," Terri ordered.

The fragments of armor, weapons, and bodies floated on their own accord.

Flakes of metal peeled off the destroyed suits close to her. She spun quickly to find that she was surrounded by an amassing twister of debris.

"What the hell is this?" Sloan asked as she stood.

The torrent increased, pulling more and more fragments from the scene, drawing it in until a barrel-like torso formed along with a pair of massively extended limbs terminating in a vortex of knives.

Sloan attempted to escape within the shape but found the incoming debris holding her in.

"Fire at it!" Terri said as she brought up her weapon.

"Fire at what?!" Agosta asked.

Both proctors opened with flechette and plasma fire, and while they incinerated chunks of metal around Sloan, the creature was still taking shape.

Slowly, Sloan's rig peeled off her, merging with the beast as legs took shape. Kaiden joined in the firefight but was equally ineffective.

All they could do was watch as cuts formed on Sloan's face.

"Eject! Sloan! Eject!" Agosta said.

Sloan twisted a knob in her suit, flipped a switch on her arm, and punched a recess in her leg. The rig opened and ejected Sloan clear of the monster as it tore at her armor, adding mass to its own.

Agosta raced toward her while the rest of the lance continued firing on the shape as it drew in from the surrounding battle, absorbing more than the lance of crutches could flake off with their weapons.

The shape confronted not them but the carryall and Elina atop it. The monster's torso extended and bent forward like a snake's head, which charged toward the vehicle. Elina recoiled and screamed.

Loudly.

The shockwave was visible, shattering the carryall's headlights and knocking the nearby Agosta and Sloan to their knees.

The first blast pushed the monster back.

It roared and charged again.

A second visible wave from Elina struck the monster, and it shattered like a vase upon a stone; thousands of steel shards blew off its body, and it lost half its mass.

A final wave disintegrated what was left, and the beast fell to pieces.

"Deven!" Terri shouted, "See to Sloan!"

Deven quickly ran to tend to Sloan's injuries while Sloan nudged Agosta.

"See to the girl," Sloan whispered.

"You sure?" he asked.

"She's the damsel."

"Wow, Sloan," Deven said as he replaced Agosta. "I just finished. You must be starved for attention."

"You know me, glutton for punishment." Sloan gazed past him to the wreck of her rig, nearly in pieces.

"We'll take it with us, don't you worry."

Agosta stood and ran to Elina, who was now crying against the carryall.

Terri stood shocked.

She then said plainly, “Well, that was neat.”

TORUS

One aspect of Kolox's testimony I take issue with is this assumption that an untended machine within the Oratory is responsible for all hydrocell production.

I suspect either Kolox is guessing or intentionally misdirecting the outside world. My reasoning stems from what we know of this strange expression we call smoke, in that it can be contained by technology, certainly, but cannot be directed to be so unless commanded by a living being. Every account we have gathered claims that smoke cannot channel through or into a device, even as simple as a container, without being beckoned by a powerful individual possessed by smoke (and yes, I used the word "possessed" as in influenced).

There appears no exception to this despite smoke's desire to break every rule. If there was one, the loginoids would have found it. Then how does this unattended machine in the oratory create hydrocells?

Unless, of course, we assumed the machine Kolox spoke of was inorganic. What measure of beast, natural or created, do they have trapped there?

Doctor Michelle Moby Hydranis
Technostate

Despite assumptions, individuals like Sloan required sleep, and it was impossible to drowse in the void. This made her extremely vulnerable, compelling her to rest in uncomfortable positions, often with her back to a wall. Dreaming was not a pleasant experience either, as she would often imagine strangers and unfamiliar locations. It bothered her that she was uncertain if they were fabrications or forgotten memories taunting her.

She wasn't sure how long she had been out, but waking was abrupt enough to blur her familiarity with reality. For a moment, she had pictured herself in another place and potentially another time. Certainly, a fiction, as even the geography of the dream was alien. When she awoke, the details fell away, and she could only hold onto fleeting images. Eventually, only one remained.

It was him—steel flecks in his beard under a generous brow and a balding head.

Everything else was foreign, she thought, *why was he recognizable*?

As she woke, she found him across the wreck of the locomotive. He was staring through a cracked window, attempting to discern surrounding detail during the emerging sun. Elina was still passed out beside her.

"Any movement?" Sloan asked quietly.

"Nothing," Agosta said. "No life, not even a passing train. We must be halfway to nowhere."

"More accurately, halfway to Ragged Hollow."

"Almost as bad."

"Do we leave?"

"Will have to chance it. The tanks were broken on impact; most of the water was lost. I'll pack anything resembling food. Can't get an accurate bearing of our surroundings from inside."

"Are you okay?" Sloan asked.

"Couple bruises, nothing cut, nothing brok—"

"Are you okay?"

Agosta smirked.

"Is this compassion?"

"I could respond with you're still holding half my pay. Or you can just accept that someone would prefer you not die."

"In defense, that was a sudden and unpredictable swing in compassion on your part."

"Well, being tossed inside a derailed train and having your soul temporarily amputated from existence can have an effect."

"…Are you…okay?" Agosta asked.

"I'm coping," Sloan said.

"What are your thoughts? Stay or go?"

"Even if we did wait for a passing train," she said, "there's always the chance it will be exposed as pirates, and we'll be right back where we started. Interacting with anyone we don't know puts the girl at risk."

"You know, she's right behind you," he said. "She can hear you."

"She's asleep."

"She's faking."

"You sure?"

"Yeah, she does it all the time."

"Maybe we should just get ready to leave."

*   *   *

It took considerable strength to pry the cab door open. It fell on the desert floor with a thud, and Agosta, Sloan, and Elina stepped from the derailed train. They wore strapped packs full of whatever they could scavenge from the wreck. Agosta extended his scope and placed it to his eye.

The terrain was flat and barren; after orientating himself, Agosta considered his choices. He stared at one and sighed.

"So, I figure we have two options," Agosta said. "We can follow the canal, which will split ninety degrees about three days ahead, follow that for three more days, and we'll reach Ragged Hollow."

"No shelter," Sloan answered, "not a scrap of food to scavenge."

"Or…" Agosta said as he pointed a path away from the canal, "we cut through that…" He offered her the scope, which Sloan peered through. She spotted a massive expanse of old Iokon ruins, a dense network of rails and relics, some still dozens of meters tall, all covered in a layer of red desert sand with most of it floating above like a persistent fog. "Graveyard of Black Church."

Sloan returned the scope.

"Holy shit," she said, "that the name? Perhaps not."

"A legend from BOT," he said, assuming a tone like he was retelling a campfire tale, "the Brotherhood of Trainmen. Train went in, didn't come out. BOT sent three engines…only one…returned."

"Well, that's horrible. Your sales pitch has a lot to be desired. And the name?"

"The train that came out reported mostly destroyed ruins and a perfectly preserved black church. People have flown over, looked across the Torus. The fog never lifts, and the graveyard keeps its secrets."

Elina chuckled.

"He used to tell me scary stories like this when I was young," she said. Sloan scowled toward Agosta.

"You are a horrible father," Sloan said.

"That will cut us down to three days from six," said Agosta. As he and Sloan discussed, Elina's attention was drawn away, out to a nearby hill's crest.

"I'm in no rush," Sloan said, "are you?"

"I'm more concerned about our supplies."

"But if we hug the canal, we'll have access to water."

"True," Agosta said, "but I'm unsure of its level in this area. And no one wants to be out in the open like this for too long, especially in this area."

"We should take the shortcut," Elina said.

"Did you forget the part about the 'graveyard'?" Sloan said.

"We'll be safe," Elina said, her attention still on the distant hill. Agosta stepped closer to her.

"Your guardian angel?" he asked.

"Guardian angel? Sloan asked. Whatever Elina was staring at was gone when the other two focused their attention.

"I see things…occasionally," Elina said.

"Relating to your boogeyman?" asked Sloan.

"It's only scary to those it wants to scare…but the only time I didn't go where it wanted, I got kidnapped."

Sloan offered Agosta only a passing glance, then sighed.

"Graveyard it is," she said as she shook her head and walked toward the ruined megapolis, following a rail to guide their journey. Agosta and Elina followed behind.

* * *

As expected, it wasn't long before Elina couldn't help but break the silence.

"So, how old are you?" she asked.

"Elina," Agosta snapped, "we've been through this? What did I just say about asking a woman her age?"

She ignored the rebuke.

"I heard your kind date back to Iokon."

"That's the rumor," Sloan said back.

"You don't know?" Elina accelerated her pace to catch up to Sloan and walk alongside. Sloan looked at the inquisitive teenager.

"Where you came from doesn't matter," Sloan said. "It's where you go that does. And right now, we're heading for something called the Graveyard of Black Church."

"Were you married?"

"Lina!" Agosta said.

"Probably," Sloan said.

"You don't remember?" Elina said. "Nothing to connect to outside of those trinkets?"

"Connections break; that's what they do," Sloan said. Elina nodded, and Agosta smirked.

"Those are the ones that matter most," Agosta said.

"So those trinkets," Elina said, "…do they remind you, help you remember?"

"Not exactly."

"Why don't you hang a diary?"

"That would be rather clumsy, but I imagine some do. I heard of one with vast rows of books detailing every moment of their existence."

"And?"

"And you just can't keep that up forever. Even if you only cover the highlights. It can be an obsession, and this effigy I mentioned authored ten thousand books. The irony is that he wrote so much that he never had time to read. People obsess over the past and forget to live in the present. Look at the world. We're surrounded by the bones of a dead civilization no one can remember. What are my people but another relic?"

"You're not a relic," Elina said. "You're a…a living tribute. Like a painting or sculpture. A message from the past."

"Unfortunately, no one can understand what that message is. To most, I'm a phantom, something that should not be alive. An outsider."

"Funny, those guys that kidnapped me said the same thing about me."

"What you have is a gift, child."

"I keep telling her that," Agosta said.

"Has she…" Sloan said, then asked Elina, "have you…developed your talent?"

"To what end?" Elina said.

Sloan turned back to Agosta.

"There are those able to train her in such arts," she said.

"To be what," Agosta said, "…an oxomancer."

"It's a rare talent."

"That puts a very large target on her head, as we recently discovered."

"It proves you can't shelter her from predators. Best to train her to control that power."

"She's not ready," Agosta said.

"You know, I can hear you, right?" Elina said.

"In fiction, the arcane arts are reserved for those dedicated to the craft," Sloan said, "those willing to put in years of study to develop a skill, no different than learning a science. Smoke doesn't care how smart you are. It chooses you. When did it first happen?

"For as long as I can remember," Elina said.

Sloan considered her following sentence. She wanted to resist her urge, but a natural drive compelled her. While she couldn't remember the details of her life beyond a century, there were patterns she could comprehend.

She knew how to use her blade adeptly. She knew how to avoid an attack and where to place her weapon to maximize an injury to an opponent. This was not a skill she remembered learning. When she saw something commonplace, it wasn't a novel experience. She knew how thunder would sound, how alcohol would taste when she drank it. She loved chocolate but knew she loved it before trying it for the first time. She possessed no memory of physical intimacy, but her body knew how it felt.

Sloan had been told it was conditioning, retention through repetition. That part of the mind acted without prompt, knowing how to walk and talk, preventing the need to relearn basic tasks.

All effigy emerge as adults, so Sloan had no way of knowing if her innate skills were developed before or after she emerged into the world. The same went with her personality. She didn't know what aspects of her soul were set at creation and which developed over the centuries she was alive. In truth, after a century, an effigy couldn't even remember when they were born. If asked her age, Sloan honestly wouldn't be able to remember. It could be a century, or it could be a millennium.

It came down to this: what part was telling her not to get attached and which was willing to bond. There was a fight between her nature and the compulsions set through a century of trauma and joy.

"I can assist you in finding a mentor," Sloan finally said.

Agosta opened his mouth to snap back at how foolish the idea was, but he stopped himself.

"My reflex was to reject that unequivocally," he said, then addressed Elina, "but…if that's something you wish to pursue…"

"To control it," Elina said. "I've come close."

"I've seen," Sloan said, "the melding of metal. What else?"

"I tried moving objects, having them disappear and reappear elsewhere. I can energize machines, but I often go too far, and they blow up."

"Smoke requires a will and technology," Sloan said. "Analogs will focus your strength and allow you to manipulate your power."

"Analogs?"

"Mechanical devices with no function other than to help you transmute smoke from a chaotic power to a directed one. With the right analog, you could create weapons, imbue machines with life, hijack the minds of the weak, or even control time itself."

"Will I be able to jump really high?"

"Yes, child, you'll be able to jump really high."

Elina knew nothing about the discipline, but Agosta and Sloan did. No wands, orbs, rods, or totems were employed in the use of smoke. It required a mind, a device, or a combination of the two to accomplish the desired effect.

Those skilled employed personalized devices to focus on a specific effect. These could come in the form of weapons or large mechanical devices, though they often manifest as simple handheld instruments like pocket watches, compasses, transistors, or musical instruments. Basic mechanical devices built from brass, cold iron, and other materials could direct smoke in specific ways.

"I wouldn't even know where to begin," Agosta said.

"I do. I know makers who'll build the required devices…like the firearms you wield. That's easy."

"They were a gift from my father."

"But more importantly, I know mentors. Ones that can help develop her power."

"Why?" Agosta asked her.

"Maybe we need more magic in this world," Sloan said.

Agosta smirked, aware of their previous conversation. "Because you owe the child."

"I'm not a—" Elina said.

"I know!" Sloan and Agosta said.

TORUS

They say behind every great person, there is someone behind supporting them. Tina Farohold is that foundation for me. I wouldn't have achieved this status if it wasn't for her. She builds everything I require to accomplish what I do. To achieve that level of sympathy and like-mindedness requires intimacy beyond collaboration or friendship. If you want to know what makes an oxomancer great, love a maker that loves you. Then nothing is outside of your grasp.

Oxomancer Elara Morrigan

Tooleys from Dust had inspected the damage done to the Vanderov. The trains had coordinated their movement, and bridges had connected at several points. It had been a day. After initial trepidation, the people of Dust welcomed the crew aboard. Mannah concentrated on the repairs, prioritizing engine stability and brakes. After confirmation, she reported to Terri in the cab.

"They confirmed it's the compressor," she said. "It'll be a day, but we'll still need a yard for the rest."

"Just tell me that we can make it back to Corvos," Terri said.

"Depends; you going to send us through any more buildings?"

"Hey, part of that is on you!"

Mannah laughed, then changed topics.

"Dust is migrating to the Tokol Basin," she said.

"So, we can't hang around too long." Terri studied the slow-moving terrain outside. "We'll leave in the morning."

Mannah nodded, but before returning down, she stared at Terri like a displeased parent.

"You know you can leave the train," she said. "I got things under control here. Everyone else is taking it in. They've got shops, taverns…brothels."

"I've never needed to pay," Terri said, "and I happen to have someone."

"A few, according to rumor," Mannah said.

"That's a personal topic."

"If it was, I wouldn't know."

"Mannah, I conduct a fairly laidback stock, but there is a line I warn people not to cross."

"Yes, except in my engine, I can only see what's behind me. You should advise me on managing multiple relationships; I got my hands full with zero."

"You have somewhere to be."

"I do, as a matter of fact. Perhaps your problem is that you don't."

Terri glared at Mannah, who smirked back and ducked into the engine bay. Terri wasn't pedantic or prudish; it was just the last thing on her mind at the time. Since they took this mission, something had felt off, compounded since acquiring the book.

She hadn't told anyone, but there was something familiar about it, something familiar about everything. Being on her train stabilized her. No matter how unbalanced it was while in motion, she felt secure. She was the queen of a small kingdom. Even if her entire crew retired and shifted aground, she'd keep moving. A billion miles of track, and she'd only seen a fraction of a fraction.

Kaiden opted not to spend time in town, given their unique physical makeup. Those that didn't fear loginoids would paw at their body, wondering how a collection of loose metal could hold together as it does. They would ask why Kaiden elected to appear humanoid, not that they had any choice in the matter. If pressed, Kaiden would detail the advantages of the humanoid form, with claims that bipedal movement was advantageous for energy conservation, that placing eyes and ears and a mouth close to where their brain was located reduced travel time for electrical synapses and having all of it in an articulate head allowed for a greater capacity for information acquisition.

A third leg would require additional brainpower, likewise with more than two arms or eyes. They didn't need a tail or wings, especially since they could not form extensions supporting flight. All loginoids with a brain like theirs formed humanoid shapes. The others became animals like the mammoths that chased them last week. The other common question was if they were male or female. Like that mattered when your body was composed chiefly of garbage.

Deven had taken to wandering the makeshift town. The corridors were uneven and narrow, like the dense alleyways of a tightly packed urban sprawl. Homes were stacked coffin-sized apartments. Taverns were comprised of little more than barstools sticking into the hallways Deven had to circumnavigate. He could see the level below through the grating, at people going about their day. Some slept while others worked. The storeys were not perfectly sealed, and dirty water from above occasionally fell on Deven's head.

He finally scaled a ladder to the roof. Pushing open the hatch, Deven merged onto farmland, stretching from the front to the train's rear. All the work was tended by hand. Translucent walls prevented anything from slipping off the edge. Deven peered over the threshold and could see the Vanderov dwarfed below. The path of the trainmen promised adventure and exploration, and it was the only one made available to him. Deven noticed livestock near the rear; further still, a dirigible was moored to the last car. Deven admired the craft and appreciated the freedom it offered, to be bound to nothing, not even the rails.

* * *

"You're late," she said.

Noah stopped and offered a confused glance to an older woman and her ruffled purple underskirt with red tulle petticoat. She wore a hip scarf and kaleidoscopic pullover paisley top. The gold bracelets were undoubtedly fake. Her face was worn and eroded with old skin, but she couldn't have been more than a few years older than him. Her eyes presented contrasting colors, blue and yellow.

"You say that to every passing customer?" Noah said and resumed walking past the blue and yellow beaded arch curtain.

"You've been touched by smoke, Noah Bennet," she said under a thick accent. It sounded like Draggo, but Noah wasn't sure. Only then did he notice the yellowish tinge to her fingernails and the delicate strands of white mist that fell off her digits as she waved him closer.

"I'll sidestep the part where you know my name," Noah said.

"You're a railrunner."

"I have a good ear."

"It's more than that…care to enter?" She parted the bead curtain and made room. Noah sighed, realizing his curiosity had peaked, and that was all that was ever required.

The circular room inside was more extensive than Noah expected, and he figured half this room was hanging over the edge of the train. He couldn't ignore the stereotype presented before him, but instead of magic cards or a polished glass sphere, there was only a perched brass cube a foot across made from a hundred mismatched pieces in the center of a square table.

Across the numerous shelves sat dozens of small handheld devices, each consisting of overlapping ratchets, springs, wheels, gears, and levers. Some were cylinders; others were spheres.

"You make these?" Noah asked as he touched a few of the analogs. Each one could be programmed to contain between one and a half-dozen different spells. All that would be required was an injection of smoke from an oxomancer. A few larger ones were more complex, with small hydrocells wired to provide power. These exceptional devices were not analogs but regulators—a device holding an oxomancer's smoke that could cast a spell without needing the caster.

"No," she said.

"You're an oxomancer. Is there a maker on board?"

"Can you afford them?"

Noah browsed the selection of gold and silver-plated brass devices. They were exquisitely made, and Noah had no idea what they could create.

"Probably not," he said.

She directed him to the opposite chair. He sat and removed a pouch from his inside pocket. He spilled the contents—twenty brass coins stamped from Corvos, a copper screw, three bullet casings, and a sealed prophylactic.

That was awkward.

Noah slowly reached onto the table and pulled that last one back.

"That enough?" he asked.

She smirked back.

"It will do," she said.

"You have a name; does it begin with *mistress* or *the great*?"

"The sign you overlooked walking in reads Evora…Mistress Evora, if you must know." She passed her hand over the cube, and each seam separated, revealing the complex mechanism of clock-like parts underneath, with arms connected to each misshapen panel. Some heaved like breathing lungs while others ticked and spun like timepieces. A luminescent yellow mist wafted from the caster's fingers, snaking and wriggling into the device's gears as it constantly reshaped and adjusted. It held no purpose other than to serve the needs of its oxomancer.

Noah was transfixed as the smoke wound around and through the device, glowing and illuminating their faces.

Smoke was not the byproduct of combustion. It possessed no aroma, and if contained in any vessel other than a hydrocell, it dissipated. It might have been a byproduct of magic, formed independently as an indicator or the source itself. The latter was the most accepted.

Smoke could imbue life in the dead, inanimate objects, and even machines. It could power magical devices and be harnessed by items and people to create powerful paranormal effects. The options were limitless, as long as smoke cooperated.

Alas, it didn't always, leading many to claim smoke was alive. It may have been controlled by Mecha or part of a colossal new intelligence that invaded the Torus. Regardless of its origin, smoke could alter reality either by itself or when wielded by intelligence.

Noah knew that for smoke to work, it would have to allow it—the manifestation of chaos or free will. It didn't want to be contained; even when it imbued life in a random object, it wanted to select that object and not have that choice be compelled.

The only way for smoke to be bottled or coordinated was to employ brass and TYKOL. People gifted in smoke and trained in using the machines that restricted and harnessed smoke were oxomancers, a rare breed and one Noah had not encountered in nearly a decade.

"Okay, I'll admit a level of interest," Noah said. "Regardless of your claims of foretelling, you are gifted with smoke."

Evora stared into her living machine and asked, "Do you believe in fate?"

"No?" Noah said.

"Good. Then you believe in choice?"

"Free will? Yes."

"But choices are influenced, are they not?" Evora focused on him when she asked.

"Of course…upbringing, those around you, for better or worse." Noah leaned back in his chair. Although she had proven her talent for magic, he hadn't been convinced she wouldn't try to swindle him. "Certainly biological. Your body is hungry; you choose to eat food."

"Is that free will?"

"Given the obesity I see in the arks, absolutely."

"Whispers…from the past, from outside, and from within."

"One way of putting it."

"What if there was a whisper someone couldn't hear. A whisper neither from without nor within."

"I just said I don't subscribe to fate."

"Fate indicates your future is written by an outsider," she said, "which isn't compatible with free will."

The machine grew in size, and the plates expanded outward. Noah could see the inscriptions inside the device, a strange, aesthetically soulless, geometrically uniform written language. Kaiden referred to it as his people's machine language, Assembly. It was a bizarre audible machine code most experts believed was the core operating language of both logicmarkers and Nimbus. The written language of smoke, which Noah was noticing on the machine, was TYKOL, which doubled as the written language of Assembly. No one knew why this was.

That name was always represented as an acronym, though no one knew what it stood for. While on its own, TYKOL possessed no supernatural effect, but when applied to brass in specific phrases, TYKOL could direct and control smoke.

"Religion promises a lot in its sale pitch," Noah said, "everlasting life, the forgiveness of sins, and the assurance that no matter where your life takes you, no matter how unfair it appears, it was all part of a plan, and thus each of us is a vital cog, no matter the size, in a vast machine."

"Well worded," Evora said, "but I wasn't talking about religion. I was talking about influence."

"But if it's not from ourselves, those around us, or a god, where would this whisper come from?"

"From what's left."

It was starting to grate on Noah's patience. Despite the proof of magic in the world, there was still a walk for him to believe in prescience, spirits, and deities. He was waiting for the promise of a positive future on the condition of additional money. He had another pouch but was unwilling to reveal it.

"I admitted curiosity coming here," he said. "Still not sure why."

"Because of that whisper that cannot yet be heard," Evora said.

"Influence you can't hear is manipulation. Don't much care for that."

"Manipulation might be necessary. As you're no doubt aware, people often fight against known influences to choose an option against the wisdom of the alternative."

Evora returned to her analog and its overcomplexity. Its order, its exactness in movement, forced the chaos of smoke to conform. Noah wasn't sure how she was gleaning information from it.

"If this is a fortune, I don't think you're doing a very good job," he said.

"How do you figure?" she asked.

"You're telling me to listen to a voice I can't yet hear. But you won't tell me who or what that voice is."

Evora let out a slight chuckle and appeared to scrutinize Noah's face. He was unsure what she was doing, but her smirk was followed by the cornea of her yellow eye sliding open, revealing a collection of miniature lenses, ratchets, and screws forged from steel, brass, and gold. The lenses slipped away, revealing a glowing ember of smoke at the center of her eye. Noah was close enough to read the near-microscopic TYKOL inscriptions in the brass encircling the opening.

Evora shifted her eyes back to her machine, and the various parts of the cube and her eye synchronized.

"I understand your confusion," Evora said. "I can see how you got it wrong."

Noah leaned forward.

"How am I confused?" he asked.

"This knowledge isn't for you. It's for who listens to you. You…are that whisper."

Noah was undoubtedly confused and growing frustrated. He furrowed his brow and said, "I haven't the foggiest fucking idea—"

"Thanks for listening, Noah," Evora said as her eyes closed and her analog retracted back into a brass cube. "And if it helps at all, I also foresee good luck, a long life, and prosperous finances…we have to say that… it's in the job description."

PARADISE

The story of Shalobagolong is somewhat depressing.

As part of an ancient treaty between Volani and the nagomjii, a massive temple was built atop a hill marking the crossing of two rivers (Saloomjii and Shusha).

The nags dubbed it Shalobagolong, and humans never bothered to rename it. After two generations, the nagomjii abandoned it, and it remained unclaimed for two hundred years before being re-appropriated by followers of the now-dead religion Volinity.

During the Aeon Pogrom, the zealots residing at Shalobagolong committed suicide, believing Volani would resurrect them. That did not occur, and their bodies were left to rot inside the fortress.

Considered a bad omen, it was never repopulated by man. However, the nagomjii later retook it and employed it as a trading post…after properly disposing of the dead.

Ethaniel Collianthus
A History of Lies,
1339 AC

Noah hated this part. The whole point of joining the proctors was to get himself out of purification. It was either enroll or remain trapped on a farm in Eridius. But he was curious; he wanted the answers to things. That curiosity led to those willing to offer answers.

But there was something wrong with their explanations. Their gods were small. According to the Ascension, the Aegis forged the Solokring and took residence within Abraxas to watch over their children below. But then came the abecedarians, alchemists, the rise of artificial eidolons, and the reveal of angelic daemons. And if the universe was perfect, why were their people and artifacts that disobeyed reality?

Despite assumptions, the Ascension operated its own science academy, the Magna. However, the curriculum was incredibly narrow, centered on learning the basics of how the Solokring operated and the natural sciences required for agriculture and architecture.

Noah excelled and was discovered by the proctors of Altair early in life. It was there when he discovered just how imperfect the universe was. He learned about the forbidden language, proto-script, believed to be used by the great machine, and how men stole it to develop cryptions. To inscribe words on a talisman and have that break the world was the method of magic.

Noah would have followed that path if allowed, and he had heard of some proctors secretly adept in the practice, even branding those script sigils on their skin to acquire abilities.

When Noah was first introduced to the crypt, he was speechless at the number of vestiges locked within. Some could fit in one's hand while others required locked vaults to contain. But they weren't destroyed. Most were too resilient, but the crypt prioritized containment.

Noah had found his calling, but the more vestiges he documented, the more he understood that the universe was fallible. This was no more evident than the Vothragna event, something most people don't know about, let alone talk about. Noah had no idea until another proctor mentioned it in passing so nonchalantly as to assume common knowledge among them.

At night, the heaven rings emerged, sliding and spinning against the outer shell of the universe. They shifted constellations and scattered the pinpoints of light the rings cast. But one was locked. It was called Messiana, and a long time ago, it broke.

A small fragment of the ring came crashing down. On its descent, it severed the pillar connecting the moon of Phylax to the planet Grimaldi, and both moon and fragment fell upon Bythos. The gap in the ring created an area of the night without stars, a blackness seen nowhere else. The Raphain Abyssal, or Djenunaki, depending on the myth.

The fragment fell into the ocean, and sailors in the region created legends regarding it. Noah had read somewhere that the local nagomjii witnessed something coming through when the fragment fell. It didn't take long for people to assume the blackness led to the netherworld, and the Ascension jumped on that myth.

When Phylax impacted Bythos, it collapsed, revealing a constructed hollow world that formed the mountain of Vothragana, a region declared forbidden by the Ascension.

To Noah, religion was a means to an end. It allowed access to knowledge he would not typically have. It wasn't always this way. He possessed some measure of faith at some point. But a decade in the crypt chipped away at that devotion.

The universe showed him too much.

He had never seen an Aegis. Few ever had. They were known to be intelligent, possessing technology a thousand years ahead of everyone else.

While Noah had been sent out to retrieve found vestiges before, he had never been accompanied by purgitan inquisitors and never by the knights of Episcar. This was duty for them—to pass judgment and punish heretics.

Noah read from the record as he walked. Two knights followed, along with a quiet and reserved acolyte named Mattias, who carried a bundle of scrolls.

> **Theocary Record** 346089
> **Account Alphaden.**
> **Filed by** Yannis Yascar, local businessman.
> **Confirmed.** Yascar owns a competing paper company bidding on a contract for the courts.
> **Accusation.** The paper plant operated by Arolsen Tongrelo utilizes a hydrogen capturing device developed in-house after creating Sodium Chlorate to bleach the paper. Captured hydrogen is then sold to third parties.
> **Offense.** Captured hydrogen could lead to the possible development of internal combustion. Storage facility believed on site.

As Noah read the details of the scroll, he observed a semi-translucent, three-fingered hand smoothly unlace a pouch from behind Mattias. It slipped back into the crowds, and Noah smirked. He handed the scroll to the acolyte and waded through the market to intercept the alien.

He found the infant nagomjii and placed a firm hand on their shoulder. They knew not to fight back. Guards were known to be merciless to nagomjii caught assaulting humans. Noah ensured the other mission members were out of sight, and he knelt to confront the child.

"Careful there, little one. You almost took something that did not belong to you." Noah held out his hand and waited. It was difficult for him to read the emotions of an alien, and nagomjii indeed were, both in biology and in mentality.

The nagomjii, known by various racial slurs, including "knots," "splinters," and "fish," were smooth-skinned former amphibians that lacked ears, a nose, and most body hair. They were tall with bioluminescent skin—an evolutionary throwback when it was their primary method of communication.

The child offered the pouch back. Noah smirked and accepted it. He then reached into his coat pocket and presented what he removed.

"This is a pen," he said, "which is different than a pencil as it contains ink. I suppose you only speak nagot. You can have it."

The child apprehensively accepted the pen, grabbed Noah's hand, and pulled him through the crowd.

The nagomjii vardo was an intricately decorated, brightly colored, two-story, barrel-shaped wagon with nary a straight line to be seen. Wisekjii tended the shop that extended from the vardo's entrance selling various scarfs, tunics, shoes, and carved wooden idols. They had erected a tent nearby where pushovers could be fleeced for their money in exchange for a fortune. Livestock, including the beasts of burden, were corralled in a pen behind the wagon.

The child released Noah outside the market and ran inside. A moment later, Wisekjii emerged, equally hard to read. He patted the child, who ran inside.

"Church eyes," Wisekjii muttered. He spoke the best he could through a lipless mouth and a minuscule tongue that couldn't even extend out of his face. His accent was nothing like anything Noah had heard before.

"Eyes are my own," Noah said. "Your young one was attempting to pickpocket. Normally, he'd have succeeded, but I know what to look for."

"You wish a reimburse?"

"Not me he stole from; why did he bring me to you?"

"Curiosity. Kindness is rare."

Noah nodded and glanced about the crowded court.

"The Ascension is especially cantankerous today," he said. "Do you know that? Ill-Tempered?"

"Angry," it said.

"Close enough. For the protection of your people, please take caution."

"Why offer charity?"

"I'll see my share of cruelty this afternoon. Most I won't be able to prevent. Consider this me finding balance." Noah looked beyond the nagomjii into the vardo and spotted the drums. "Are you doonjii?"

"Our name. You call me singer."

"That we do. You are tasked with the telling of history. I hear rumors that you can keep a library's worth of information and impart that information through poetry, orations, or even song."

"Some in your church wish singers executed for that."

"Well, that and because of your capacity for magic. Real magic, not what you peddle in that tent. Don't worry, I won't ask." Noah perused the selection across a table. He found a somewhat striking scarf. "Quite the collection. Nag textiles have a reputation for quality."

"The best. Same with shoes."

Noah browsed the few keepsakes among the garments, dice, glasses, stained glass pieces, carvings, empty bottles, and semi-precious jewelry.

"Found these all, I assume?" he asked.

"Of course," Wisekjii said.

Noah's attention fell on a gold bracelet marked with the Ascension Ahkdanate. Noah casually pushed it towards Wisekjii. "Keep items like this away. Purgitans cleanse people for less; I'd hate to know what they do to your kind."

"They hang us by feet and bleed slowly," Wisekjii said.

Noah stepped back, spun to leave, but stopped as Wisekjii let out a deep bellow. Noah returned to see the nagomjii remove a blue and green scarf from the table and offer it. Noah accepted.

"Thank you," he said.

At least the nagomjii could walk in the open without excessive persecution, emphasizing excessive. Daemons and eidolons were prohibited from even taking breath.

Once again, Noah couldn't help but ponder, if the Aegis held such dominance over the reality of Paradise, why would they allow nomadic aliens to wander the surface of their worlds. Why would there be creatures capable of hiding in plain sight?

Noah let his eyes wander the courtyard, at the hundreds of people from Bythos and Philokalia doing business and enjoying each other's company. Given the density, it was an inescapable assumption that at least one human wasn't what they appeared to be. The darkness of a blocked sun made such a search impossible.

* * *

Noah eventually met up with the stressed acolyte.

"Mattias," Noah said.

"I thought I lost you," Mattias said.

"Saw this scarf, had to acquire it. By the way, someone appears to have lifted your pouch." The acolyte frantically searched his person. "Have to be careful in Sadatoni." Noah handed him his missing purse.

"Maybe it was the fish," Mattias said.

"Nah, they're not smart enough for that sort of thing. Just keep your belongings close."

"Proctor!" one of the knights said. The group met up in the center of the square. "Any violations?"

Noah didn't know the other knight, but the one speaking was Carthan of Zengoro.

"With nagomjii?" Noah asked, "No."

"I wouldn't object to tearing that camp down. I wager there's something heretical there."

"We've standing treaty with their kind. They're not stepping on our toes, so let's not step on theirs."

Noah started walking, with Mattias following. The two knights exchanged looks and briskly caught up with them.

"I didn't know proctors were that lenient," Carthan said.

"This may come as a surprise, sir Carthan, but the Ascension encompasses more than you and the purgitans."

"Regrettable. If we had numbers, we wouldn't have to be so diplomatic to the heathens around us."

"People. They're called people."

The group weaved through one court to the next while civilians offered them space, more intimidated by the armored crusaders than the robed clerics. Noah spotted the paper plant operated by Arolsen Tongrelo across the market.

"Where did you come into this world?" Carthan asked.

"Eridius," Noah answered. "You?"

"Aquino," Carthan answered.

"Root of the faith."

"Cradle of civilization."

"I wouldn't go that far."

Noah diverted to a local baker selling pudding tarts and marzipan cakes amongst the loaves. Carthan was growing frustrated by Noah's distraction. Noah offered a few copper coins to the owner and pointed to a tart. It was wrapped in paper, and Noah presented one to Carthan.

"Do you want one?" Noah asked.

"No," Carthan said.

Noah turned to the other knight, who remained stoic, then to Mattias, who wanted one but decided otherwise after glancing at the knights. Noah shrugged and began eating.

"So, I take it that you never went on crusade," Carthan said. Noah continued wandering the market, fully aware he was irritating.

"You mean the genocide?" Noah said. "No."

That got Carthan's hackles up. He wasn't used to conversing with proctors but knew they were allotted a certain tolerance level regarding their views.

"We acted as the hands of Gods," he said.

"Funny how they couldn't use their own. For being omnipotent beings, they sure like using us to do their dirty work."

"Don't forget about the minute war," Mattias interjected, "a lance of hedrons leveled the castle at Ellispex. That was a direct showcase of what they could do."

Noah knew of that account from two hundred years ago. After Ginald Kaelum refused marriage to an Aurago princess in favor of his cousin, Zannah Mustarra, Aurago assassins, under orders from the Ascension, had Zannah assassinated. Ginald accurately determined the Aegis as responsible and had their churches closed in his capital. As a result, the Aegis commanded Aurago to take the capital of Ellispex and arrest the Kaelum royal family. After surrounding the capital city, Aurago issued its official declaration of war, only lifted with the removal of the Kaelum ruling house from power. Ginald refused. Forty-five minutes later, a lance of Aegis-controlled dodecahedron-shaped floating drones leveled the castle. The city's gates were opened in haste soon after. Although the Kaelum line survived the attack, they never spoke of rebellion again.

"And how amazing those machines were," Noah said. "Makes you wonder what we could build in the fifteen-hundred years they held control."

"That knowledge is reserved for gods," Carthan said.

"And under special provision, the proctors of Altair." By this point, Noah was teasing him, and Carthan knew it.

"You archivists get away with too much."

Noah stopped and confronted the knight. Instead of antagonism, Noah preferred provocation.

"Well, we don't get away with murder," he said. "That privilege is reserved for people like you."

Carthan stopped and fumed as he bottled his fury. He wanted to strike this apostate down but was unaware of how much power Noah swayed with the proctors. It wasn't much, but Carthan didn't know that. There had to be a reason Noah was here. He opted to focus on the mill as they finally reached it.

It was rather significant, located on its concrete patch surrounded by market carts. The crowds had given Noah and his group space, and as they approached the doors, this part of the court cleared out. People knew what would happen and didn't want to be near any violence.

Procedure demanded the owner face the charges. If such a machine were present, he would be executed and his facility burned.

"Finally…Allow me," Carthan snapped as he pushed Mattias away and marched for the large double doors. The other knight remained behind.

"I'd rather we handle this diplomatically," Noah said.

"Not your call in this matter. You may accompany us; the Akhdanate may tolerate your opinions, but in matters of technological prohibition, judgment falls to both Episcar and the purgitans. If we find any vestiges within, you'll be summoned."

Noah opened his mouth to object but hesitated. According to his superiors, it was proper what Carthan was doing, but something didn't feel right. Was it a voice of reason or temptation?

"Glory to the Iokon!" Carthan said.

"Glory to the Iokon!" Mattias and the silent until now knight both said in unison.

"Glory to the Iokon," Noah said without trepidation.

Carthan strode confidently, kicking the doors open and marching into the mill. Mattias checked the proctor for guidance, but Noah just held his ground well away from the building.

A minute passed before a ruckus emanated from inside the building. The silent knight unlocked his blade and rested his hand on the hilt.

Shouts became screams. Tables and chairs were heard breaking. Survivors burst out of the entrance, but none seemed to be the owner. The knight left to approach them, but Noah held his hand up to stop him.

"The order was for Tongrelo, not his staff," Noah said. "You're not going to cull the entire business, are you?" The knight stepped back. Instead of stepping in to help, the crowds backed further away from the building. They all kept their distance, unwilling to intervene. They knew better.

Spattered with blood and wielding a stained blade in hand, Carthan exited stridently from the entrance, a goading smirk on his face. Flames devoured the walls behind him and spat from open windows. Noah was unimpressed, if not borderline irate. Firefighters will have to be called, though thankfully, the mill stood alone. Noah's frustration twisted into horror as he remembered the details of the infraction.

Carthan smirked arrogantly at Noah.

"That is the proper—" Carthan's scolding was cut short as the building shattered behind him in a brilliant display of fire and light.

The heat practically vaporized the knight, with the subsequent air burst tossing the crowd to their backs.

Everyone scattered.

Noah barely made out the cries of children through the ringing in his ears.

The concussion had blown out the building and extinguished much of the radiant fire.

Nearly invisible flames radiating little heat still spewed from the center of the building. Calls rang out for firefighters, with courageous civilians tossing insults at Noah and his two companions. Noah glimpsed the empty helmet rolling to his feet. Somewhere in the ruins was a corpse, likely two, but Noah was uninterested in checking.

Noah, the remaining knight, and Mattias slowly returned to their feet.

"Well…Can we agree that Carthan's methods were ill-advised?" Noah asked them. The other knight was shaken and said nothing. Mattias was still holding his ears.

"Was that hydrogen?" Mattias asked

"That…was a dramatic overreaction in several ways."

"So, Carthan was correct?"

Noah casually kicked the helmet towards the acolyte.

"You'd have to ask him," Noah said as he surveyed the damage, gauging how best he could be of assistance. Mattias bundled up the scrolls he had dropped and handed one to Noah, who promptly slapped it out of the acolyte's hand. "Seriously?"

"I have a stack?" Mattias said.

"And I have principles," Noah said. "We're not done here."

"Are we to judge the neighbors?"

"We're responsible for this. We have to assist where we can."

"They don't want us here."

"And not being wanted has always impeded the actions of the church. Our charter insists that we help the less fortunate, and we just destroyed a building."

Noah ignored both of them as he tended to those injured. Mattias looked to the knight, who remained motionless. The acolyte sighed and handed his companion the stack of scrolls before joining Noah.

It was a few hours before all that was left was a gutted crater from where the paper mill stood. The crowds had wandered back to the celebration, leaving the three men to reconvene.

"Are you satisfied?" Mattias asked.

"Are you?" Noah asked. "Do you require external judgment for your actions, or is your moral compass guidance enough? I always appreciated acts of conscience over those dictated by gods. Same goes for our sins."

"Imperfect contrition," Mattias said.

"Imperfect…what a vapid statement, claiming repentance can only come from faith and not from one's principles. I'd take personal remorse over fear of divine retribution any day." Noah stared at the stoic knight. "And you've no idea what we're talking about."

Noah could tell the nameless armor had never been asked to think for himself, but Mattias was different, an acolyte without allegiance, unsworn to any arm of the Ascension, at least so far.

"The church would assert Carthan's actions were justified," Mattias said.

"The report claimed captured hydrogen could lead to the possible development of internal combustion. Do you know how many steps there are to that from a kip-drawn wagon? How many advances stand between them? Tongrelo wouldn't have done anything with the fuel other than burning it for heat. He wouldn't even know where to begin, but by eradicating his intelligence, we destroyed any further innovation he could have offered. Aurago suffers from a lack of human capital, as smarter people emigrate or are killed because of their potential for heresy." Noah chuckled. "Pretty sure nothing will ever come of that."

"Is that why you joined Altair?" Mattias asked.

"When you were a child, did you ever ask stupid questions of your parents? Why are worlds round? What are tears? Why don't clouds fall?"

"Yes."

"Did you stop?" Noah asked.

"Eventually."

"I never did." Noah could tell he was reaching some buried curiosity within the acolyte, who glanced at the knight before speaking to the proctor.

"I still carry the burden," Mattias said.

"We've done enough to promote the church," Noah said. "I say we should take the rest of the day off."

"It's night."

"It's Passover, and the city never sleeps. I'm hungry. You hungry?" Mattias didn't respond. The other guard gave up a slight smirk, and Noah pointed. "Ahh…he is. Let's eat."

"Who'll sign off on these violations?" Mattias asked. "They'll audit me if they are not addressed."

"We'll resume tomorrow," Noah said, "I keep to killing one person a day. I'll even handle the first myself." Noah held out a hand, and the acolyte offered the next scroll. As they walked to a nearby café, Noah read the document's contents…

Theocary Record 346095

Account Alphaden. Filed by Elise Price, Diaconate rector.

Confirmed. Rector, a junior member of the local congregation, recent oath-taker.

Accusation. Kaiden Sivoy sold his building to the church as a synagogue; located in his trash before he moved out of the building was a lens grafted to see into the very small.

Offense. Any devices meant to peer close or far away are forbidden.

CONESTOGA

Our planet had a solid iron inner core covered in an outer sphere of moving molten rock that generated a magnetic field to protect us from cosmic waves. A liquid mantle pointed to it having a volatile surface populated by volcanos and earthquakes, which is encouraged by active tectonic plates.

The timing of our weather and day/night cycles was perfect for us, leading to assumptions regarding the speed of our home planet's rotation and axis tilt.

I can almost see it.

Every night, I dream of what it must have been like…or what became of it. My guess is that it was destroyed.

Why else would we be trapped within this vessel? They are not experimenting with us. I fear the world that gave us life is no more, a lifeless husk annihilated by a random rock or an errant stellar beam.

Maybe we did it.

Maybe we destroyed it.

It doesn't matter.

This is our home now.

Pero Garius
The Way of Worlds
Kaelum Publishing

"A collaborator figured the algorithm for exclave migration was dependent on radiation from Behemoth," Syn said, "solar energy from Avalon, and this vessel's orbit around Trinity."

"I wasn't aware there was a relationship," Noah said.

"There is not," she said. Holding back a laugh behind a smile, "But it sounds convincing."

Noah's eyes opened as he was legitimately shocked by Syn's sudden humor.

"I'm impressed," he said. "You spin perfect bullshit; you know that? I totally bought it."

Per their schedule, they had intercepted an exclave known as Tokol, a relatively open and small habitat with a rich ecosystem of small animals, jungles, and crisscrossing rivers. There had been plans by a half-dozen nations to colonize the exclave, but motivation appeared lacking, likely due to its unique atmosphere. While not toxic to any species, each had to don their own unique configuration of air filtration system.

With Syn, it was to remove argon; with Noah, it was to remove carbon dioxide. The endolons had perfected their rebreathers to cover as little of their face as possible and make the entire assembly light and elegant. Humans didn't have to worry as the familiar atmosphere of the vessel's interior and most habitats were configured for them. As a result, Noah's set involved a mask where only his eyes and nose were visible, which allowed Syn to discover how piercing Noah's eyes were.

They would ride the habitat for just under a day before exiting close to their destination of Corvos. The camp was built atop a hill with an expansive outlook of the terrain. Carthan and Machus had packed out the supplies and lit a fire. Noah could feel their eyes, which had worsened since exiting The Museum.

Syn stayed with the matador, with Noah, and she didn't want to be too far from him. Their conversations would start by morning and not stop until they slept.

They were sitting upon long orange grass with their backs against the transport, heads arched to the real stars beyond their habitat.

"No one has ever found a pattern," Syn said. "But we will never stop trying."

"You have to assume there is, given the uniqueness of Trinity. Certainly, telescopes have scoured the heavens and haven't found anything as interesting."

"I am honestly surprised anyone looks up; most look in. When I brought up Trinity to another proctor lance that passed through our exclave, they were not even aware it was out there, let alone its composition."

This allowed Noah to show off, and he pointed.

"Well, there's Behemoth, a black hole with an accretion disk collected from the ejected material of Axis, the nearby neutron star, when it exploded hundreds of millions of years ago. That made Trinity a three-star system at one point, with one red dwarf and two supergiant stars. One collapsed with the other later exploding, all the while that single red dwarf, Avalon, sat there watching. Behemoth and Axis orbit a common center with an orbital period of… forty-four years?"

"Forty-five," she said, focusing her attention on the sky.

"Damn."

"Trust me, I am impressed."

"Avalon has its planetary system of six worlds, two gas, and four rocks. It's somewhat shocking they survived, especially its second planet, Aeon, which sits within the habitable zone.

"Aeon's orbit tidal locks it, so one side continually faces its sun, and its size generates a gravity twenty-five percent higher than what we feel here. I've heard stories of oceans and clouds, an atmosphere of carbon dioxide, nitrogen, oxygen, methane, and argon. Not unlike what my people breathe." He glanced at Syn's rebreather she is nearly always forced to wear outside Kenoma. "Sorry.".

"None taken."

"It has that one strange bright spot just below its equator. Could be a storm."

"…or an alien artifact projecting into space. Which one do you like?"

"Well, despite our limited view and inability to escape this menagerie, we've never been able to observe life. No structures either on planet or in orbit. I imagine that if there had been, the radiation from Behemoth would have wiped them out."

"The theory stands it was on the far side of Avalon with the dwarf between it and the explosion."

"That makes sense…or was that more bullshit?"

"No, that one was real." Syn laughed again. Noah appreciated that her kind did so. Scrimm could as well, potentially proving that manifesting joy was universal across the universe.

"What else," Noah said, gazing back to the stars, "the inner world, Alshain, dense, hot gas planet of carbon dioxide, methane, and hydrocarbons. No satellites. The third, Vothragna, a massive, low-density hot gas giant of carbon dioxide, carbon monoxide, and hydrocarbons. That one's hard to miss."

"It can get pretty big," Syn said. "Every year, I would sneak out to the surface to see it; felt so close, I could touch it."

"It always freaked me out, a planet black as pitch."

"Vothragna absorbs rather than reflects the light it receives."

"A demon's eye staring back…it's what they tell kids."

Syn was dumbfounded. "That is terrifying," she said. "You have malevolent parents."

"They meant well," Noah said. "Habitat migration keeps at least one exclave in view of that planet. So that someone always has their eyes on it…just in case it does something."

"I did not know that," she said, legitimately curious. Noah smirked.

"You're not the only one that could spin good bullshit," he said.

Syn laughed. Noah gazed back to the stars and the nearby system and pointed.

"So next is," he said. "There. Yascar. Big rock. Something shattered the planet, throwing dust and fragments into a ring. The impact melted the surface, stripping off most of its atmosphere."

"How do you know that?"

"Corvos isn't the only place with libraries."

Noah had been drawn to her, but for how long? Since the Museum, since meeting her, or was it when he first saw her name? Considering that, when did it become something more? Each time he focused on her, something else drew his attention. Her eyes were bigger than his. Her pointed ears twitched on occasion. But this close, he could finally scrutinize her skin, bleached white that seemed uniform, but up close was revealed to be a dense mesh of tiny cycloid scales that evolved to merge rather than overlap under a thin coat of keratin. That's how their skin twinkled on occasion.

"Then, Ramada," he said. "Smaller rock with satellites probably pulled from Yascar. That leaves, Oasis, closest to Behemoth, which will probably be swallowed by it in time."

As he pointed, the flat starfield began to have depth. The planets felt close. The clouds of dust created ribbons of oscillating reds and yellows.

"Beautiful," she whispered. As she looked up, he looked at her. It happened again, between blinks, a transitory instant where Syn appeared human to him. Noah wasn't even phased. But this time, she was paler, and her hair was bleached and drifting like she floated in water. He became nervous like Syn was something he should fawn from a distance rather than scrutinize inches from his face.

"I wasn't expecting them to be," he said.

Syn slowly turned to find him staring at her, and the smile faded from her face. Just as suddenly, Noah slapped his thighs and stood.

"I'm hungry." He circled the matador. "I know you can't process lactose, gluten, or meat…but proctors make a wicked carrot, spinach, and chipotle tofu wrap." As he reached the front of the transport, he inadvertently approached the other two lance members.

"Yes, thank you," Syn said.

Noah opened up the side and fished through the refrigerated food cabinet. He removed two packets.

"And I think I will have…the tahini, quinoa & walnut," he said.

"You do not have to do that," Syn said.

"Shows what you know," Noah said as he read the label on the wrapper. "I happen to love…walnut…meat. Beverage?" He searched again and removed a simply labeled can. "Soy milk, carrot juice…"

"Alcohol?" she said with a smirk. Noah dove back in and removed a pouch of amber liquid.

"Okay…barley-broo it is." He closed the vehicle and made his way back, but not before passing Carthan and Machus.

"What's with you and the leaf-licker?" Machus asked.

"The what?" Noah asked.

"The alien," Carthan said.

"She has a name," Noah said.

"Oh, *she* does, does *she*?" Machus asked. They were sitting beside the fire, and neither cared to stand as Noah took a step closer. Syn stood, overhearing the conversation.

"And it's best you apologize."

Syn took a few steps behind Noah; he stood his ground.

"We're paid to escort," Machus said, "not get cosey with some root-muncher."

"That one is sort of clever," Syn whispered.

"You best not say anything further unless it's an apology," Noah said. He despised bullies and knew this conversation was a long time coming.

"Or what?" Carthan said.

"Or I'll file an official complaint with the guild, you ignorant idiot. Claiming you, both, are jeopardizing the proctors' relationship with a foreign nation."

"But I have the witness," Machus said as he stood, sneering. "Your side against us."

Noah smirked and sidestepped to the matador, tapping the sensor head the machine used to navigate automation.

"And I have a data log," Noah said. "You need to get with the times." More proctors were accepted for their ferocity rather than their intelligence or problem-solving skills. They'd never achieve any rank and were probably confused as to why. The Staplegunners took pride in their diplomacy, pointing to their reputation in escort and transport missions. Proctors seldom go to war. With another smirk, Noah made his way back to Syn.

"The dagger-head and her lover," Carthan whispered between his teeth, prompting Noah to spin around for a confrontation, ready for a fight.

Syn gently placed her hand on his shoulder, which deflated Noah instantly.

"Noah. It's fine," she said, guiding him back to the opposite side of the vehicle, out of sight of the other two men. Noah let himself be led away, more entranced by the fact this was the first time she touched him.

* * *

"Here I am waiting as you ponder your next thought," Noah said calmly, "hoping something personal would leave your lips since, for the past hour, it's just been small talk."

They had both finished their meals. The fire behind them was down to cinders; Machus and Carthan both stepped away to vanish into the jungle, leaving Syn and Noah alone as the habitat lights had fallen to a twilight.

"I have been thinking about my dreams," she said.

"Didn't know endolons dream."

"All intelligent creatures dream. Our biology is not too dissimilar."

"The scrimm are different. Scabs more so." Noah was vocalizing his trepidation regarding his feelings. It was difficult enough to read human women; how alien was she?

"Ultimately, scrimm possess only one distinct biological difference," Syn said. "They are monotremes, in that they are mammals that lay eggs. They possess a cloaca while males possess a four-headed—"

"Yeah, I would call that different. I mean, scabs are insects."

"Are they?" Syn's tone had become playful jeering. "Come on; you were doing so well."

"Are you going to lose respect for me if I don't know this one?"

"Crustaceans," she said.

"Of course."

Syn's mood shifted. She enjoyed being playful, as it was a habit out of practice, but she forced herself to confront something that had been bothering her.

"And I do respect you," she said, "Feeling increasingly guilty over our first encounter."

"Already forgotten."

"The point I was making was that evolution works the same in every world. Our similarities prove the rule, not the exception. Our species share ninety-nine point two percent of our DNA."

"In genetics, that's surprisingly broad."

"Are you saying we are more different than we appear?" She was trying to make a case but was unsure why she was doing it. Until meeting him, she accepted that endolons were vastly different from other species within the vessel despite their physical similarities.

"You have eight lobes in your brain to our six," Noah said. "You have four sex chromosomes to our two. You have a three-chambered stomach."

"Do not sell yourself short; you have two kidneys."

"You can metabolize fructose without oxygen, which is a cool trick. You're immune to cancer… I'd like to know how that works."

"More susceptible to disease, unfortunately."

"You can twitch your ears, which is adorable."

"You can blush…I like that."

"You have a third eyelid."

"Your muscular network makes you all significantly stronger than us."

"You can hold our breath for twenty minutes."

"And let us not forget the obvious attribute where I cannot survive outside my exclave without a regulator."

Noah chuckled at the banter, and Syn followed him.

"Your bones are hollow," he said.

"And yet, we are both mammalians. Our young require an extended period of infancy to develop large brains. We develop tools, language. We are social beings, which I think is mandatory for a civilized species. The scabs may lack it, but the rest of us possess some level of personhood. We can differentiate ourselves from others." Her tone fell soft as she considered her thoughts. "We experience disgust, fear, anger, sadness, happiness, love."

Noah bowed his head. Their hands were close. Her fingers ended in nails, but she only had three. He couldn't read her intentions, and she was unsure what those were.

"You see colors differently than us," he said.

"You have better hearing," she said.

Noah took a breath before his next thought. "We were apex predators defined by the segregation of those we deemed inferior and the conquest of those not within our inner circle. Your people are gregarious and form social bonds. You settled disputes through non-aggressive competition. You never took joy inflicting injury. Being herbivores, you likely had to protect yourselves from a predatory species, which is why you're so trepidatious to outsiders. But among your kind, you never exhibit discrimination. Trust me, that's something strange and unfamiliar to my kind."

Syn didn't know how to respond, unsure where Noah was going. Was he trying to convince her not to get too close? Did she want to?

"Okay…maybe I am an alien," she said. "In every way."

"I think your takeaway from my point might be a tad misguided. Everything I just said is part of why I'm talking to you and not them."

"What is the other part?"

"I find you interesting," he said. "I can't explain it…but when I saw you for the first time."

"Was it a dream?" she asked.

"That's not very scientific."

"The only possible explanation."

"Not just an anomaly of memory?"

"It felt more than that…am I wrong?"

"No…no, you're not."

"Do you believe our dreams are sending messages?" she asked.

"You can lie to many people...you can't lie to your subconscious."

"There are those that claim dreams are random chemical impulses that form random memories. They collide ideas collected over the previous day that are tossed into a liquidizer until dreams emerge. Maybe they are windows to other realities, representatives of us but in scenarios we never encountered." She tried to hold a smirk. "Sorry, I appear to be rambling."

"By all mean, ramble. I believe I can interpret your chaos," he said.

"You might be one of the few that do." Syn scanned their surroundings and realized they were still alone. "I presume they are…"

"Most likely giving us a wide berth," Noah said. "Don't want to witness me embarrassing myself."

"How could you be embarrassing yourself?"

He attempted to speak but found himself only exhaling.

Syn's oversized eyes stared into his soul.

"Noah…What is happening?" she asked.

"What do you mean?"

"Are you attracted to me?"

"In what way?" he asked.

"In your way."

Noah contemplated a measured response. There was no point denying it; his eyes fell off hers as he answered.

"It's not due to some perception of exoticism."

"Your friends will—"

"They are not my friends."

Synfallin needed to stop to doing that.

"I did it again…a reflex action. Cultural condescension, which I was trying to avoid. Your fellow proctors would probably have more than a few harsh words for someone like you. Cannot make it work with a human female, that sort of thing."

"And your people…would they care?"

"Not in the slightest."

"Seriously?"

"Given our relatively weak bodies, we value mental acuity more than anything. As you might have figured out, we generally avoid physical engagements, preferring to run rather than stand our ground unless offspring or companions are under threat. We prefer to think rationally, logically. To talk in situations when fighting is generally preferred. We work through our problems rather than act on impulse. I admit we tend to prejudge people based on presumed genetic or psychological traits, and it took years for us to trust your kind. But when we started, we realized how varied you could be; one sibling could be serene while the other sadistic.

"Our opinions were based on assumptions of disposition, not on the shape of your head or the color of your skin. We opened our doors but were shocked by how few accepted the invitation. Those that did proved our preconceptions were incorrect. I suppose that stems from our limited genetic variety. You are point-one of a percent.

We are point-zero-two. We simply did not have the variety to create segregation. The geography of our homeworld…wherever that may be, probably had us living upon a single landmass and not separated by water or mountains." She knew she rambled but could see his attention was fixed. Was she convincing herself of something or him of something? "Humans pair for life, do they not?"

"That's in the brochure; few of us follow through."

"Why do you think that is? Boredom?"

"Personally, I think we fall in love too easily. It's only later when we realize our judgment went out the window."

"There is something admirable in that, I suppose."

"And you? You don't bond the same way as us."

"I would not say that…we form social herds. Sort of extended families we call kin. And within those we have…I guess you can call them lovers, best friends, both."

"I never thought about that."

"What?"

"You feel isolated. You were curt when we met because you were leaving your…group. Is that why we talk so much, why we get along, because of your need to form new attachments?"

"If you acted…like them." She nudged to the dim embers and the dark jungle beyond. "I would not be forming connections at all…and I imagine I would be quite miserable. Do you…have a herd?"

"My chapter is my herd …obviously, some I don't care for. But I have a flock, a group of friends. Hopefully, we'll meet a few of them in Corvos. But no lovers…if that's what you were asking."

She wasn't, but she appreciated the response.

"Why not…proctors discourage attachment?"

"There was a time when I preferred being single…after my…previous relationship ended somewhat…unfavorably."

Syn nodded.

"Infidelity is certainly a human construct."

"She died," he said bluntly. Syn's jaw went slack. "Wasn't anything shocking. She was another proctor on assignment exploring a new habitat. Picked up septicemia. Didn't return alive. It was a long while ago. My standards for future companionship went up...I don't wish to settle in fear of being alone."

"I guess I should be honored to receive your affection," she said, "placing me on such a pedestal…if that was your intent."

"It was…to coin a phrase. It's a high podium and more than fitting for someone like you, atop a concise list, to be honest."

Syn concealed her smile the best she could but soon became distracted upon realizing their situation.

"That is interesting, isn't it?" she asked.

"What?"

"How similar we are."

"We just had a conversation about the very opposite of that."

"And yet looking at the other aliens populating this vessel, the odds of two members of two different species being physically or even emotionally attracted to one another should be astronomical."

Noah bobbed his head, acknowledging her, even though he hadn't fully until a few seconds later.

"Wait…did you just imply you're attracted to me?"

"I was simply saying that two species from different worlds—"

"No, let's go back to that point." Noah pivoted to speak to Syn directly. "Do you find me either or both physically and or emotionally attractive…and…that might have been the most confusing way I could've asked that question. I mean, it's not just *either* or *and*. I mean, you're freely open to select a third of *neither*. I wasn't trying to assume anything."

"I understood you."

"Really…because even I was a little lost there for a moment—"

"I like you," Syn said bluntly with a nod. "I mean…that is a simplistic response to your rather intricate question that…upon reexamining, I should have expounded with a bit more detail—"

"You seem confused by your answer."

"I should not be."

"Shouldn't be…confused or liking me?"

"Both?" It sounded like a question. Noah cocked his head like a confused canine.

"Well, that instilled me with confidence," he said.

"I mean we…I am. Yes. I like you. I meant to imply more of an observation that the probability of this happening is not high, or rather should not be high. And there would have to be some…external influence affecting that probability."

"You're implying that our…hopefully growing affection is derived by forces out of our control. Maybe it's biological? Maybe it's our dreams. Maybe that influence…is us."

"It just does not make sense," she spoke like it was a mystery she needed to solve. She was attracted to him. She shouldn't be. And was his affection equally as confused, she thought? Maybe it was a pure coincidence, blind chance, that evolution on two different worlds would create a creature derived from a primate and another derived from an amphibious bovine that was similar enough superficially that they would be attracted to one another. How could their personalities be in any way compatible? Maybe she was just different enough, and he was just different enough to bridge that gap, but that would make the odds of encountering each other even more improbable.

"Do you not want to like me?" Noah asked. "I accepted my attraction to you some time ago. In the Museum, in case you were curious." She let her eyes move back up until they stared back into his. "I don't have a problem liking you. There was nothing to absolve, nothing to consider. If it's too much to ask, I'll understand. This does put you in a difficult position, given your responsibilities and the conflicts of our biology. I'm not reckless or asinine on this. I acknowledge the fortune that we are…compatible. And if that matters to you, I'll understand. But please don't look at this as a mystery to be solved." That was the instant she realized it. "Maybe this is that moment where you let your judgment go out the…"

She reached up and unlatched the strap around her head. She deactivated her rebreather and slowly removed her mask. It was mainly transparent, so nothing was concealed.

Noah was stunned as Syn removed the one barrier she had between them. Noah's jaw loosened somewhat, and his lips parted. He had considered a lot, speculated about this, how he would react, how she would feel.

And there he was, frozen.

Noah envisioned every possible route to this specific point in time but failed to consider what he would do one second after.

Syn waited patiently.

"You have a few minutes; take your time," she said with nearly a giggle.

For her, argon reacts with her lungs, preventing oxygen removal. Endolons without their mask don't cough. There would be no permanent damage if the mask were returned within five to ten minutes.

It would start with dizziness, headaches, shortness of breath, and tachycardia. It would worsen with cardiac arrhythmia, a lack of concentration, photophobia, and lack of consciousness.

Noah reached up, loosened his strap, and removed his rebreather.

They took a moment to enjoy their exposed faces.

She moved closer to him.

Within their biomes, the humans were one of the few species that engaged in pressing one's lips against something or someone else to express affection. Scrimm sniffed and touched faces, and scabs shared pheromones that no one but them could smell. It was another coincidence between Noah and Syn.

Well…almost.

Her slightly long and thin tongue flicked his nose.

Noah couldn't help but chuckle as Syn's sandpaper-like tongue drew up his nose and forehead. He tugged her chin down, and he pressed his lips against hers. He could feel her inside his mouth, picking up the subtle barbs across her tongue. They pulled away, and Syn smiled.

"That was…interesting," he whispered. They remained an inch apart, a silence that became awkward. "So…what…did you think?"

"More," she said.

PARADISE

GRIMALDI

Connected at the north pole of Bythos, the oddly shaped pillar of Chazaziel carries Grimaldi over the northern hemisphere and is under the stewardship of the kingdom of Pavonis. Grimaldi suffered a significant disaster believed to have possibly been a foreign object, perhaps even from outside Paradise. Known as the Vothragna Event, the result was nearly a hemisphere of Grimaldi breaking off and falling to Bythos, eventually becoming the isle of Vothragna. This event also broke off Grimaldi's only moon of Phylax, which also crashed upon Bythos.

Orbital Period. *36 Days* ***Major Semi-Axis.*** *5,900 km*
Satellites. *None*
Equatorial Circumference. *3,200 km* ***Rotational Period.*** *22 hours*

BYTHOS

Bythos is the core world and heart of Paradise. All other bodies are connected to Bythos, either directly or through an orbital ring. Most of the great kingdoms reside on Bythos. It functions with a precise 24-hour day with exactly 12 hours of sun and 12 hours of night.

Orbital Period. *None* ***Satellites.*** *N/A – core world*
Equatorial Circumference. *22,124 km* ***Rotational Period.*** *None*

Encyclopedia Titanica
Corvos

"Inner circle?" Deven asked Sloan.

"Isn't that a good thing?" she asked back. They were both in the main hall of the inner bailey, having just been dismissed. They had taken a break and sat, somewhat overwhelmed over the day's events.

"The higher you climb, the narrower the step," Deven said.

"Don't stumble," Sloan said with a chuckle.

"I'm not concerned about me."

Sloan took her helmet off and ran her fingers through her short dark hair.

"If you want my honest opinion…" she said.

"It was my idea to join the military," he said. "It was either that or toil in a mine or a farm. Besides, you're the better fighter; I thought you'd enjoy this."

"And if they found out...at least on a farm, the chances of someone discovering me would be slim."

"We can decline."

"That would go over well," Sloan said.

Deven rolled his clumsy armor to confront his best friend.

"Then let's just go," he said. "Hit up Pyxis or maybe Corvos. Corvos you'd be safe. We both could live our lives openly…somewhat."

"You don't have to. You can have a life here."

"Do you seriously think I would abandon you after what you did for me?"

Sloan patted Deven on his tassets. She smiled as Deven nudged her shoulder with his.

Agosta stood on the other side of the door leading to the tower, listening to them both. He admired their honesty and loyalty to one another.

"Thoughts on the prince?" Deven asked.

"Typical noble," Sloan said. "Wearing a face rather than having one."

"And the other?" he said.

"The so-called Master of Coin?" she asked.

"Probably an assassin." Sloan nodded. Agosta chuckled silently as he returned to the steps and walked up. "Not bad on the eyes, though."

Sloan laughed.

"No, no, he wasn't," she said.

*　　*　　*

Agosta met up with Kabdila, who was observing the Hydranis world outside the open window of the tower. The shadow crept across the city. The two men had stopped halfway up the stairs and waited for a passing guard to vanish around the corner before resuming their whisper.

"By the way, master of Coin?" Agosta asked. "Does that exist?"

"Does now," Kabdila said. "Enough of the prostitutes and disreputable dealings…we need to evolve to a new level of bureaucratic corruption."

"Strictly legal theft from here on."

Kabdila's eyes skimmed across the boisterous and crowded street market, gas lamps operating at mid-day to counter the shadow.

"What in the name of living gods was he talking about," Kabdila asked, "what secret?"

"You'd have to ask him."

"I shouldn't have had to. Something this important; he should have kept us in the loop. Unless…" Kabdila offered a look, which Agosta immediately understood.

"Are you genuinely considering the possibility that I knew the truth all this time and didn't inform you?" His tone was stern but still discreet. "Believe me…if they were telling the truth, it would represent a complete failure of intelligence. I'd be forced to deconstruct my entire network to find where the fault lies."

"At least you understand the stakes involved…and I'm sorry for doubting you. In defense, you probably never considered looking inwards to my father."

"I can't envision a situation where a secret this calamitous, with these stakes, would be held by only one person. He'd have to include others. One of his concubines, imperial guards maybe. How could he commit this scale of transgression without a conspiracy?"

"Whatever he kept must be insignificant. An artifact, a vestige—the proctor!" It donned on Kabdila, and he stopped himself from shouting too loud. "Why else would a proctor from Altair be sent here instead of a purgitan? You heard him; even he didn't know why he was called."

Agosta gazed out to the expansive city. The distant outer walls were barely in focus. He glanced up at the miniature world and its abrupt horizon.

"To deny a king custodianship of an entire world," Agosta said, "such an artifact wouldn't be some unassuming vilon or zebul class. It would have to be something to rival the power of gods, a machon or potentially even an araboth."

"I've never seen one. Have you?

"Only stories. One account smuggled from Altair spoke of the *pearl of existence*. If a dead body were placed within, it would be returned to life…but there was the chance what emerged would be a monster. Or the *scribe of desires*, where anything written by it would become truth."

"Those can't be real."

"Would be a strange thing to invent and then fortify within the most secured vault in the universe."

"But why would they keep something locked? Why not use it for their own gain?"

"Proctors are a different breed; they have their own rules and answer to no one. This artifact couldn't cure your father, so I assume it must do something else, something formidable enough for him to horde and for gods to hold against him."

"I guess there's only one way to find out."

* * *

Kabdila's father was bedridden in his chamber, suffering from the Brimstack Curse, an affliction he brought back from Volani, a parting gift from the Aeon Pogrom. Kabdila had remained home as regent in his father's absence and was disappointed to see him return.

The condition had worsened of late. Three doctors were attending him when Kabdila and Agosta entered.

"He can no longer swallow," the doctor said solemnly. "We must…drain him. Dementia comes occasionally…he may not know you."

The doctor stood aside, and Kabdila approached his father. The doctor added, "His genitals have atrophied…we'll have to remove them, or infection will kill him."

"Do what you need to do," Kabdila said. "Let me have a moment."

The doctors left the room, leaving Agosta to tour the room silently. He shifted artwork on the walls, lifted lace tablecloths, and opened trunks, drawers, and jewelry boxes. He rummaged uncaringly through the linen and flipped pillows, only finally uncovering a safe when he flipped up the carpet.

Kabdila ignored Agosta as he approached his father and leaned to whisper, "They denied you immortality, father…but emperor is in my grasp…for our family name, what secret would you keep to deny our future?"

Agosta may not have investigated the king by any measure, but this small treasury had been installed five hundred years prior and was common knowledge within the inner circle. Few knew of the combination. It required a sequence of symbols etched on a set of metal rollers, probably as advanced a mechanism as the Aegis would have allowed. Hopefully, the code Agosta remembered would work.

"…Take your last minutes of sense and answer your son…" Kabdila whispered.

Agosta opened the safe and fumbled inside the space, removing papers and letters, but nothing that stood out as magical or valuable. He saw Kabdila's father whispering.

He spoke a word and coughed, then often and escalated. Hearing the distress, the doctors reentered and approached.

Kabdila gave them their room and retreated to Agosta, who closed the safe, reset the lock, and flipped the carpet back over.

Kabdila coaxed his friend to the corner of the room and said simply, "The dungeon…"

* * *

The catacombs under the castle stopped being employed as a high-security prison when a more remote fort was erected outside town. The idea of convicted murderers and rapists walled in with the royalty became less popular, and political rivals and revolutionaries were incarcerated instead.

Subsequently, the worst were transferred away, leaving only the less dangerous ones, the poets, writers, and other critics of state with the dubious honor of being interred under the castle.

Agosta and Kabdila walked past the cells, at the quiet and defeated criminals, many of whom were too old to remember a time when they weren't incarcerated. None were due for release anytime soon.

Agosta noted the various expatriates and pagans. There was one nagomjii with no records hanging upside-down with water trickling from a spout over his legs.

"Well, that seems unpleasant," he said. Agosta kept and traded knowledge. He'd killed but only when necessary and never to extract said knowledge. A secret was a confidence, a point shared between those trusted. A secret related through torture was worthless.

The two passed the last prisoner with no surprises. Regardless of their opinions of the imprisoned, none were unexpected. Agosta even knew who many of them were.

"That's all of them," he said.

"I don't get it," Kabdila said, "half these people I know about; some I put here…" He glanced at the nagomjii. "Well, not that one. But none of them seem out of place…what's in the dungeon? Is there a secret chamber?"

"There's a path that connects this with the sewer," Agosta said, "that's a secret I'm aware of. But it's a corridor, not a cavity. Barely room to walk. An isolated space to hoard secrets? Impossible…no way it'd be secret for a thousand years. Someone would have found it…I would have found it!"

"Honestly, I don't want you to find one," Kabdila said. "I know the secret passages out of the castle. Gods know we used them enough. Dungeon, he said. Is dungeon a person?"

Agosta nodded, finally realizing what Kabdila might have heard.

"Are you certain it was a dungeon?" he asked. "*Donjon* is a word from an ancient tongue still used in places to mean the central tower of a castle."

Kabdila dropped his head, pinched the bridge of his nose, and sighed.

"Fuck my father," he said.

* * *

They approached the central tower, which was neither the main turret nor the tallest spire of Deos. Agosta and Kabdila passed a guard who ignored the two. It was an old building with a narrow spiral that scaled up.

"I can't remember how long since I was up here," said Kabdila. "I know the plundered art of Eridius is below us. I think the handmaidens are…"

"No," Agosta said, "the top-level was reserved for one of his concubines...Nuana, I think her name was…she died of dysentery fifteen years ago."

"Yes, I remember. He was never the same. No one measured up."

They passed the last window before reaching the top, both taking note of the parade outside to celebrate the Aegis blessing the celebration. They could see the conclave carriage somewhat brazenly navigating the narrow roads, often with escorts as the church and city guards pushed into the crowds to maintain order.

Kabdila shook his head and kept climbing.

"They could have cured her," he said, "…could have cured him." They passed locked room after locked room, lived in by various servants. Upon reaching the top, the two men found the door ajar.

Agosta gently encouraged his prince out of the way and approached, with his other hand pushing the door open to find a pristine bedroom carefully preserved by a single chambermaid ensuring the room's perfection.

It was as lavish as the king's chamber. The chambermaid jumped upon seeing the two men. She recognized the prince entering afterward and immediately bowed.

"Stand," Kabdila said. "This chamber, who is it for?"

"Your royal highness…it is for no one," she said.

"No one?"

"The king ordered it kept as it was without alteration…after she died."

"Nuana," Agosta said, "And no one has been in this room since?"

"No, milord," she said.

"I'm not a lord." Agosta scanned the room, searching for something, anything—a message, an object.

Kabdila kept his attention on the chambermaid.

"Has it always been you?" Kabdila asked.

"Yes, your royal highness, for the best of seven years."

Agosta scrutinized the various paintings, most showcasing the dying king. Upon the dressers rested various keepsakes, mirrors, candles, and jewelry boxes that Agosta verified were empty.

"Was there anything you caught as unusual about this room? Something out of place, or that you were forbidden to touch or move?" Kabdila asked.

"I have scrubbed and scoured every inch a hundred times, your royal highness. There is nothing about this room I do not know—" she was interrupted as Agosta shattered a vase across a wall.

"Sorry," Agosta said quietly.

"And you know the king is soon to perish, and any secrets would have to be passed on to its new ruler," Kabdila said.

"My life surrounds this room," she said, still shaken. "I know everything, and it conceals nothing."

Agosta approached one item of interest, next to the bed, a sealed cylinder of solid brass resting exposed on a wooden bracket.

"What is this?" Agosta asked.

"I don't know, milord," the handmaiden said. "The king found it on a crusade and kept it here."

"Scroll tube?" Kabdila asked Agosta.

"Little short and fat for one." Agosta wrestled with it. "No way to open it."

"A vestige, perhaps?" Kabdila asked. "Maybe it's this they want?"

"Can't see why," Agosta said, "no vestige of worth would be kept on display in a bedroom."

"Process of elimination, though."

"How many of you reside in this tower?" Agosta asked the handmaiden.

"Ten, milord, but only I have responsibilities in this room, and I keep the only key amongst the staff."

"Ten," Agosta said, placing the cylinder back on its display. The chambermaid nodded. "Two per room?"

She nodded again.

"Then why did we pass six doors as we climbed?"

* * *

The chambermaid led them to the one room, the last one Kabdila and Agosta passed on the way up, the only one the chambermaid didn't possess the key for. Kabdila tapped the multiple locks on the door while Agosta noticed the food pass-through at the bottom.

"This is a prison door," Agosta said, "who monitors the food?"

"I imagine the same person responsible for all our food," the chambermaid said, "but they certainly couldn't have the key; this is an imperial lock."

"I have the keep's master key," Kabdila said as he fished through pockets, unaware that Agosta had removed his own key.

He unlocked the door.

Kabdila was understandably surprised.

"How long have you had that?" he asked.

"For as long as you had yours," Agosta said.

"There's only supposed to be two of these."

"You miscounted."

Kabdila confronted the chambermaid, "Were you present when this room was ever opened?"

"I have never seen it opened, your royal highness."

"Not even to place someone or something in it?"

"No, your royal highness."

"Okay, off you go," Kabdila said with a wave of his arm, and the chambermaid departed back upstairs.

Agosta guided the prince behind him and pushed the door slowly open. Inside, they found a well-kept bedroom with bars on the windows, almost as lavish as the top floor, though half the size and well-lived.

A figure was seen writing at a desk.

"You," Agosta said.

The figure immediately picked up a nearby serving plate and threw it towards the door. Agosta slapped it out of the way. She was still suffused in shadow. The figure stood and shouted back.

"No man can touch me!" the young girl said. "King's order, on pain of castration! Kindly cluck off!"

"Who are you?" Kabdila asked.

The room contained a bathtub, but the water had to be passed through the opening. Agosta knew then that whoever this was, she hadn't left this room in years.

"Oh me," she said modestly, "just someone the king fancied and forgot about."

"So, we should pay you no mind and just release you, given the inevitable shift in authority," Agosta said.

The girl stepped forward, out of the shadows, with bands of light illuminating her face. Her unkempt blond hair was pulled back behind her head. She had eyes of jade and a sharp chin.

The color washed from Agosta's face. There was no flash of a past memory, no cognitive dissonance. He knew her, but his confusion wasn't over how but why.

"It was worth a try," the girl said as she sauntered over and sat on the bed.

"How long have you been here, girl?" Kabdila asked.

She sat at the edge of the bed, almost taunting them with a half-smirk.

"You're not a particularly smart one, are you?" she said. "Do you honestly think they'd give me a calendar? And would I bother to keep track after all these years if they did? The king held a standing order that I wasn't to be touched; that much I knew. He was the only one that visited me."

"Until recently," Kabdila said.

"He's dead, isn't he?"

"More accurately, soon to be." Kabdila opened his arms wide and presented. "And long live the king."

"Huh…" she mumbled. "Your father was an ignoramus and insane. He was also unpleasant in every physical way. You look like the product of infidelity."

Kabdila couldn't help but laugh, ignoring Agosta, who was still dumbstruck.

"He must have allowed your education," Kabdila said. "That was one the shrewdest insults wrapped in a compliment I've heard." He nudged a chin to Agosta. "I expect that from my friend; are you sure you're not his bastard." Kabdila turned to notice the shock still on Agosta's face, taking the prince off guard. "That was a joke. Do you know this girl?"

Agosta and the girl shared a moment.

Familiarity.

"Unfortunately," Agosta said, "there's only one person your father would keep locked up all these years." Agosta knew the answer but didn't understand how he could know.

"Well, I'm in the dark," Kabdila said. "What's your name, girl?"

"Elina…Elina Prescott," Agosta said. Kabdila turned to his friend. "The last scion of the Volani royal family…"

PART FOUR

COMPLEX

TORUS

The chamber is locked; few of us can even approach the door, let alone look inside. We rarely see people leaving, certainly not enough to produce the volume required to meet demand. Even among the loyal (before I stopped being), we would whisper about what we knew, trying to learn a truth denied even to us.

I guess that our forebearers had learned the process, built the machine and ensured it would only require resources and marginal maintenance necessitated from only a few within a very small circle. These ancestors then died, as did the engineers maintaining the machine.

Paranoia over their secrets prevented them from disclosing the truth to those that came after. We would deify the machine in time, praying it would never break, and it never has. But if it were to…I fear for the future…as I don't think anyone knows how to fix it.

Allisaren Kolox
Communion Rector
1201 AC

Agosta, Elina, and Sloan approached the outer rim of the old Iokon city. The nearly opaque haze hovered over them, blocking their view of the rest of the Torus. The ruins encompassed dozens of interlaced square blocks, ranging from half-collapsed single-floor dwellings to still-standing towers that vanished into the murky atmosphere.

The weather had worn the buildings to raw brickwork, nameless with their purpose lost to time. As always, the rails had survived, crisscrossing in an ostensibly chaotic mess. Elina was walking in front, with Agosta and Sloan following. There was nothing around them, living or otherwise.

"Go ahead and say it; I know you want to," Agosta said.

"This was unbelievably stupid," Sloan said.

"…Tactful."

"We moved too far from water. There's nothing here. Or worse. We'll find something, and that which survives will act out desperation."

"I'm not worried, Sloan," Elina shouted from ahead.

"The naivety of youth," Sloan said.

"Only machines and the dead live out here," she said.

"You know that's worse, right? That's so much worse."

"Well, it's too late now," Agosta said.

"You're taking our inevitable death at the hands of inhuman beasts within the ruins of a dead civilization covered in a miasma of sand and smog rather well," Sloan said. "That being said, when you can't remember your life, death doesn't carry much impact. Why did you agree to take this route?"

"I trust her instinct," he said.

"That she's guided by a shadow?" Sloan asked, "Or rather *the* shadow."

Agosta was confused by that statement.

"You worded that like you knew what she was talking about," he said.

"You don't?" Sloan asked. "Railrunners share many legends. You've never heard?" She shouted to Elina, "How did you, Elina?"

"My shadow?" Elina said. "I haven't."

"You never heard of it?"

"Nope."

"Then how do you know of it?"

"Because it heard of me."

Sloan was borderline cantankerous and glared at Agosta.

"Well, that's not disconcerting," she said. "Those aren't random sketches?"

"Why would I draw monsters?" Elina said.

Sloan addressed Agosta.

"You've never been concerned her imaginary friend is the stuff of nightmares?" Sloan asked.

"I was frankly happy that instead of being afraid of her boogeyman, she made friends with it. How do you know of it?"

Sloan focused back on keeping pace through the city. She took a deep breath as she knew a story was coming.

"I avoid the larger arks for a good reason," Sloan said. "I often find myself in cantons, at local taverns. I hear the railrunners and conductors discussing their adventures, the bizarre relics they've discovered, and the opponents they've faced. Stories fell into myth, but the most outlandish tales often carried a fragment of truth. Screevers were fables before being proven."

"So, it's something people have seen. Have you?" Agosta asked.

"No...but descriptions I heard were always the same; I first saw it...or rather the first memory I have...was as graffiti, painted on walls within ruins, not unlike these. Some see it as an omen, a harbinger of grim events to come."

"A myth from the Iokons," Agosta whispered.

"You'd think so, but most of the scrawls looked fresh, made after the collapse and not before. I've been told that railrunners destroy instances when they encounter them. While my kind is defined by amnesia, I'll often see things familiar…triggering memories I've long lost. Déjà vu. My first recollection of the shadow…was not my first. Have you never been to Draggo?"

Agosta hadn't but had heard stories of an ark resting within the karst topography of the Neopyth Mountains. Crags, hills, and mountains were covered in colorful vegetation, and with water drainage falling into caves and underground reservoirs below, the region was prolific in biodiversity. The city sat upon a raised platform sitting upon a fluted column between two hills, with the peak of its highest constructs inches above the highest mountain in Neopyth.

Said constructs were statues standing upon the platform's rim, representing different poses of the same strange inhuman creature. On either side of the main gates stood one wielding a sphere with one hand while the opposite supported a cylinder on its back. One held a ring overhead between its hands while another could be seen focusing on a tesseract. At some point, the fifth suffered damage, with his arms broken off, leading many to wonder what it held. These five figures created a star formation surrounding the edge of the city.

"The same monster? I didn't realize there was a connection," he said.

"I've heard accounts with people claiming to have seen it walking or floating. No one has ever seen its eyes if it has them. But they do tell of a large jaw with sharp teeth. Coincidence?"

"I can't see it being," Agosta said.

"How sheltered was she?" Sloan asked.

"Enough."

"Maybe she overheard it before you adopted her."

"She started drawing it well after," Agosta said. "She would wake me up to tell me it was outside her window. I would find her running into the field at night, claiming she was playing. I thought she would grow out of it. As time went on, she manifested her abilities."

"You think they're connected?"

"Who's to know?" Agosta stopped and glanced at the top of a hill. "Wait…what's that?"

He scaled a fallen building covered in sand to get a closer look. Elina and Sloan followed. The elevated train tracks were intact.

Resting at a junction was a small, covered railcar barely bigger than a locomotive's cab.

"What is it?" Elina asked.

"An old rolling stock," Agosta said.

"A mining trolly," Sloan said.

"Not for a mine," Agosta said. "It's a passenger skip. Intercity rail."

They precariously stepped from the hill precipice to the railroad and approached the vehicle. The skip had seats and could hold a half-dozen, providing some form of comfort, but all the glass had long fallen out, spilling sand into the cab. It was weathered and beaten, but a lack of moisture had staved off rust. It held a small electric motor that, if operational, wouldn't move exceptionally fast.

"This cannot still be working," Sloan said, "and even if it did, I don't have any spare hydrocells, do you?"

Elina took the cue and stepped forward. She kneeled beside the engine and placed her hands on the old motor.

Her eyes changed, and smoke drifted.

A few seconds later, the machine coughed to life. A generator spun faster and faster, and the last unbroken overhead light began to glow. Agosta had seen this before.

To Sloan, it was another surprise.

"Oh, that's handy," Sloan said buoyantly as she climbed in.

* * *

The vehicle barely crawled faster than a brisk walk but was paradise compared to walking. The ruins' entrance laid so far behind them that the haze had obscured it, leaving the three of them within a seemingly never-ending expanse of a decaying civilization. With the light diffused by the fog and the white sand smothering the landscape, all color had drawn out of the landscape, rendering everything monochrome.

The skip was surprisingly silent, and the ambiance was calm; the first opportunity any of them felt tranquility in nearly a week. One moment, they passed into the shadow of one of the standing towers, the light of Uno shimmering through openings. They crossed an unsteady bridge, with crumbling ruins descending into a dark miasma below.

Hours passed, and the sun dipped behind Nimbus, blanketing the city in darkness. Agosta sparked a lantern but kept the light as dim as possible. The ruins were appropriately quiet, with the scraping and grinding of the slowly dying engine echoing off the buildings.

"Dad," Elina whispered, "she's asleep."

Elina nudged towards the napping effigy, the blade resting on her lap. "I've never seen her sleep."

"She tries to hide it…but I've noticed. Don't bother her," Agosta said. Elina smirked and peeked over the skip's edge, down from the elevated tracks to sand-filled roads below.

"You know every book I read about old Iokon is forced to guess what this place was like," she said.

"They were more advanced," Agosta said. "They had machines but not magic. They stored all their knowledge as light and shadow within books that didn't exist…and when everything crashed, that wisdom was lost."

Elina nodded and gazed back out to the drifting landscape. Agosta doubled as her tutor, so he made a point to know as much history as he could glean.

The Caliphate must have ruled uncontested within the Torus for centuries, fueling a need within the population to expand and harness the ring's power. The Iokon Metropolis spread like a virus, covering much of the interior, save for the oceans, mountains, and sporadic forests.

Then The Great Collapse occurred, believed to have been either retribution from Nimbus for the damage done to the environment or the result of an external event. A combination of geographical and environmental instability rocked the Torus, collapsing most of the Iokon's structures, killing much of the population, and disrupting technology. A sweeping electromagnetic storm destroyed electronic circuits. Lesser variations of these pulses still occur randomly to this day.

Despite the oddity of the Torus itself, life within was assumed to be relatively normal. Nature existed within a range of acceptable expectations. The engineers and scientists of Iokon developed great machines to serve man. These were straightforward constructs designed for functionality rather than aesthetics. The state police of the Metropolis enforced control with magnetic or energy weapons. Life appeared normal.

However, either before the Collapse or after, something changed. Illogical breaks from reality emerged. Machines not built by man roamed the land. Ethereal beings arose from nothing. The dead awoke. Eventually, man discovered how this was occurring, a strange mist materializing around beings and bestowing them with supernatural abilities.

"Have you ever considered we were guessing?" Elina finally whispered after a moment of silence.

"About what?" Agosta asked.

"About everything. No signs, no books." Elina focused on the still sleeping Sloan. "She's supposedly a relic from that time, and even she can't remember. Plus, she comes from the Maelstrom."

"Meaning?"

"Isn't there that tower at the center of the storm?" she asked. Agosta nodded. "Some believe it's a sword piercing from outside. Maybe she's not from the past at all. Maybe she's an outsider like she said."

Agosta considered it, but it eventually became an affectionate examination of Sloan's face. She could have and should have abandoned them. Was it honor that kept her with them? The effigy were both rugged and fragile. They were ageless, without blemish or visible indications of trauma. Yet, their soul was bound to a totem—a physical item that would vaporize their soul if destroyed.

He had almost lost her earlier, and he was still struggling with the emotions that came as a result. And what constituted destroyed? She returned; Elina brought her back. But what if the damage was more extensive, if someone threw the sword into a volcano or a kiln? It could have been a helmet, breastplate, or a walking stick. But it was a weapon with Sloan, one she would use. Each time she parried or struck an opponent, she risked her soul.

Agosta remembered what his daughter had said; Sloan had put her soul in his hands. She agreed to the plan without apprehension. Sloan could only be inches from her weapon, but there was still that choice of offering your spirit to another person.

"You like her, don't you?" Elina asked, quiet enough to be heard by Agosta but loud enough to be overheard if Sloan was faking, which Elina hoped was correct.

Agosta spoke softer as he didn't want to be overheard.

"Why do you say?" he asked.

"You don't look at anyone like that."

"Shows what you know. I look at a lot of people. It's just…they… don't often look back the same way. I'm not sure I'd know what it looks like."

Elina always considered her father had sacrificed too much for her safety and education. Someone getting too close would inevitably discover Elina's secret, which could risk her safety.

"I tried," she said.

"Yeah, I know. And it's not that I didn't appreciate it. I'm pragmatic."

Elina ran the word through her limited vocabulary.

"Does that mean you're religious?" she asked.

"No…no, that's *dogmatic*."

"Have trouble breathing?"

"That's…*asthmatic*."

"Have trouble showing emotions?"

"No…that's…I actually don't know what that is—it means I'm a realist, practical, rational. I don't do subtle. I don't play games."

"We play all the—"

"The relationship game, honey." Agosta's tone was growing louder. "The dance people do. I just…don't know how to play."

Elina nodded and took in the view again.

"When we played games, you had to stop me from breaking the rules and placing my piece where I wanted to put it. If you want someone in your life…just put them there."

Agosta considered the wisdom of his daughter. It might not have been his poor sportsmanship, but the possibility of him losing that bothered him. And with Sloan, the deck was stacked, given her origin.

Elina spotted movement in the distance and tried to focus.

"Animechs," she whispered loudly.

They were large, lumbering beasts with heavy feet, massive bodies, and long necks. Like many others, they were mechanical, assembled from thousands of random parts, held together by the will of their artificial brains.

These were brontos.

A dozen of them migrated between the blocks.

"Don't be scared," Agosta whispered. "Those are docile. Best to avoid them if we can, though."

"Another aspect of this world that doesn't make sense," she said.

"There was a great machine somewhere that built robots, and without guidance, it went a little peculiar. Nothing terrible crazy about that."

"It should be; I mean, it's surprising what we accept as normal."

"What are you saying? Isn't this world normal? How would you know what normal is?"

Elina's eyes drifted to the wandering beasts and thought about how she believed there was always something off with the world.

"What do you call the air around us? What's in the sky?"

"Atmosphere."

"Funny how it's called that, don't you think?"

The skip's engine's grinding grew louder, followed by a sequence of pops, and the vehicle decelerated. Elina examined the machine and the smoke spewing from it.

"Is it…?" Agosta asked.

"Gone," she almost whimpered. "I can't inject life into a dead machine."

"I guess the ride is over, then. Got further than I thought."

"Should we go?" Elina asked as she peeked over the edge to check where the brontos were.

"Let's just stay here a moment," Agosta whispered as he admired Sloan. "Let her sleep."

* * *

Agosta has been pressed for time. They had taken her less than 24 hours prior and left a note detailing the demands and destination. The money wasn't the issue—it would take everything he had—but he knew the abduction came from her accidentally exposing her power. The ransom was a bonus and an opportunity to remove the father from the picture, kill all hope in the captive, to strengthen the belief that she would have nowhere to go.

Agosta found himself in Brass Flats, a mid-sized canton of around 3,000 that sat within the flat topography of the Mare Dagos. An open expanse of dust and ruins surrounded the makeshift town, which sat at the end of a reliable water channel. The architects elected to employ clay and stonework to erect their settlement, and it soon became an oasis for needy travelers. In time, Brass Flats expanded to entertain many visitors, including those traveling between Corvos and Velora. The town also maintained a mine that tapped into precious metal deposits under the hard surface. Given raids by wandering bandits, there was a demand for mercenaries to protect the town's interests, the perfect opportunity.

The loose dirt was especially volatile that day, leading many to stride through town covered head to toe in robes, ponchos, and cloaks. The Brass Buckeroo, the saloon he was told to look for, stood before him.

A stage accented by gilded red wood featured a trio of musicians boasting different-sized string instruments and handlebar mustaches. Most patrons were engrossed, with many leaning over the balcony railing above. As expected, errant dusty sand had blown across a wooden floor topped with matching round tables and chairs squeezed into every space.

The contact Agosta had gambled on was specific with details, naming the town, tavern, and individuals of questionable integrity. One was a Pyxin sniper that only spoke Gaelan, and the other was a zodiac, the latter being the easiest to spot. They were overdue, and Agosta took an empty seat to wait.

After the first set ended, the band took a break, and the noise settled into a shroud of squawks and laughs. Agosta shouldn't have been able to hear the rattling charms within that discord, but he found himself turning to a corner, noticing the ornamental sword that practically pointed to her face. Those amber eyes almost shone in the shadow. He wasn't one to maintain eye contact, but neither broke their attention once they met.

Patrons passed between them, and within a transient gap, Agosta noticed the woman briefly switch from an ostentatious and decorative outfit that was honestly discordant to the expected clientele in this establishment to a form-fitting black silhouette accented by pockets and mechanical devices affixed to ankles, elbows, and other joints. He felt a familiarity with this stranger but had no idea how or from where.

The batwing doors flapped open, and a man entered sporting an impressive, long-barreled Thrower Hinterlander—a very expensive and exceedingly rare magnetic coilgun. There was an affixed sniper scope. Agosta was about to raise a hand when he recoiled and looked back at her, still staring back. Did she recognize him as well?

Agosta trusted an impulse, stood from his table, and approached the woman in shadow.

* * *

The lantern had faded, but a mild, subtle glow radiated about the environment. The rolling stock collected a dusting of sand as the wind shifted. An hour after Elina and Agosta nodded, Sloan jerked awake, shocked at the weakness of succumbing to it.

Agosta was a light sleeper and woke as well, less violently. He smiled as Sloan orientated herself. He was within arm's reach.

"Nice dreams?" he asked. Sloan settled back down on the chair.

"No," she said.

"Naked in public? Losing teeth?"

"It was nothing," she said, then realized the skip wasn't moving. "Engine seized?"

Agosta nodded.

"Only about a half-hour to sun break," he said. "No point leaving when it's dark. And we're safe up here."

Sloan focused on the city, what little she could see in the shrouded night. They shared silence before Agosta spoke.

"I had a recurring dream when I was young. Dreamt I was in love with someone. Could never see her face, but…I just knew she was the one."

"I never got the impression you were the sentimental type," Sloan said as she settled as comfortably as she could on her chair.

"I paid considerably for you to help me rescue my daughter from bandits; if that's not sentiment…"

"Emotion leads to impulse, and you never came off as reactionary. If so, you would've just pursued them. Probably gotten killed. You made a calculated decision. Hire mercenaries and take the chance they wouldn't stab you in the back for the prize. Pay the ransom, which you knew they wouldn't honor. The rational response would be finding someone you knew would take your side and not betray you."

"And not two days ago, you commented that my plan was impulsive, that regardless of who helped, it wouldn't have changed the outcome."

"We're alive; your plan worked. I might have misspoken."

"I consider my investment justified."

"It helps that my kind doesn't value power or money."

"I'm paying you—"

"Girl's gotta eat. I just don't worship the coin like some do."

"Some take it as a need, something that can be satisfied. The fact you were effigy was a plus, one I knew could be utilized in a plan."

"Wait…" Sloan was surprised by the revelation but caught herself and whispered again, "you weren't looking for one of my kind?"

"Nope…Hiring you begot the plan, not the other way around." Agosta let the memory from the Brass Bachelor flood back, recognizing a stranger from across a saloon and allowing the compulsion to approach them to possess him.

"What did you see in me?"

Agosta smiled and considered his answer.

"Conviction," he said. "Trust is the real commodity out here. Brass, magic, power…money…fleeting. Being able to depend on another person. I'd pay double for that certainty."

"Should've increased my rate," Sloan said with a grin, hoping Agosta would pick up on the witticism.

"Once we make it home, I'll pay whatever I have left," Agosta said plainly. "You'd have earned it."

Sloan assumed Agosta failed to recognize her attempt at humor. It was not something she was good at. Or maybe he had but ignored it. Regardless, she became disenchanted.

"I'm trying not to get offended by that comment…because I realized I provoked it," she said.

"My fault for assuming—"

"I'm remaining with you because I want to. I'm not seeking gratuity."

"Still, the fault lies with me…Elina claims I'm bad with emotions. I'm pragmatic."

"Does that mean you're religious?" she asked.

"No…no, that's…" Agosta almost shouted, "holy shit, you were listening."

"Not the whole time." This time, Sloan giggled but tried to keep it in to prevent waking Elina, who was up and listening but feigning sleep. She smirked at the comment but kept up the ruse. "She had a point, though," Sloan said. "Your life can't be defined by another person."

"Of course, they can," Agosta said. "People do it all the time. What's companionship but a person defined by someone else?"

A booming groan echoed from the lead bronto as the herd migrated around the block. Sloan took notice of the animals as they vanished into the haze.

"You think just because you forgot about someone that they never existed," Agosta said. "If you didn't care about the loss, you wouldn't have added their charm."

Sloan flipped over her weapon; the various ornaments jostled. She scrutinized them as if she could garner more information than she already had.

"Some I know, a few have names. Friends." She brought up her weapon, and a few charms bounced off one another. She flicked one. "A place I love visiting." Then another, a locket she kept closed. "This one is…tarnished. Faded. Must have meant something. How could I be defined by people I can't remember?"

Agosta nodded. Occasionally, he would know exactly what to say in a situation and relished the opportunity.

"Have you ever considered the possibility that you defined them?"

Sloan almost chuckled and looked away to smile, maybe to avoid his eyes.

"You may act pragmatic, but you can be dreadfully maudlin," she said.

"I can occasionally wear my emotions on my sleeve, just as you wear them on your blade. You claim to avoid connections, but, as I was saying before we were rudely interrupted yesterday; your defiance must have been a recent development."

"Maybe…It's been so long…I can't recall what it's like." Sloan's voice dropped. "We remember the implicit—procedural memories. How to fight. How to survive. It's the explicit we forget. No matter how powerful, within a century, it's gone, leaving just…" she drifted off and flicked one of the charms on her sword. She did miss it—those beautiful memories. And despite not knowing who they were, she missed them too. "Did I define them?" she whispered.

"Effigy must have relationships," Agosta asked.

"All the time and some of us record those memories in diaries, but in time, it would be as foreign as reading someone else's fiction for the first time. A charm only marks the moments, the years." Sloan rolled her fingers across a set of matching beads. "These five are etched in dates to mark what I assumed is a birthday; that'd make me…at least five hundred years old."

Agosta smirked.

"I won't tell girl, don't worry," he said.

Sloan let another hang in the palm of her hand.

"This one matches the shield crest of a local pub," she said. "Must have had good fowl or an exceptionally full-bodied wine."

"Some don't look cheap. Does its value reflect the weight of the memory?

"You'd think so. They're all custom-made from brass, pewter, stone. A sterling silver ring, for an engagement…maybe. An inscription on the inside reads…Elias Oakley Cassidy with a date…three centuries ago."

There was the locket she rarely opened, and despite having a diary in storage somewhere, it spoke nothing of who this person was. An engraving on the back indicated her name was Carla with the words it *was worth it.*

"The memories we can hold onto are vivid," Sloan said. "Right until an absolute breakpoint. I can remember up to the day. I can recall my last encounter with someone and utterly forget when I awake the following day. All too often, my earliest memory is the melancholy of something previously forgotten. I once owned a small repository where I'd keep large relics and keepsakes. At least once a year, I'd tour my collection, often be surprised at what I'd find. Rifle through old books, discovering thoughts from centuries ago. Two hundred years ago, a fire gutted the entire city block. Half my life…turned to ash. A thief absconded with a sack of valuables recently, well, two decades recently, including a framed painting of someone important. When I finally located the culprit, he'd sold the gilded frame and thrown out the image. I realized then that the struggle to remember was a fruitless pursuit. I rebuilt the archive, noting the fire to ensure I'd know once I'd forgotten. But…I hadn't been back for nearly twenty years."

Another advantage that Sloan didn't share involved her kind's autobiographical memory, also known as hyperthymesia, enabling her to easily differentiate dreams from reality. However, her first encounter with Agosta brought up a memory she knew she couldn't have had.

"If there's one thing I believe I've learned about you…it's that you leave an impression. And that impact has a purpose, even if you can't remember it. You're significant, and what you do and have done will carry consequences long after you've forgotten it. My daughter is alive because of you. And with hope, she'll grow, find her destiny, maybe love. Children. You'll forget her, but she'll never forget you." Agosta smirked, and his finger reached out to stroke her index. "It's implicit, as you said, like riding a bike."

Sloan pulled her finger away. Agosta didn't respond.

"I can't do this," she said.

"Won't. It's a choice. One that I'll accept, but a choice nonethe—"

"I'll forget you. I forget everyone. No matter how close, no matter how long. In time, I won't remember anything. I can write about it, add a charm, but that intimacy, that feeling…will fade."

Agosta didn't jostle or change his tone. He remained soft-spoken, refusing to let Sloan twist the conversation into a confrontation.

"Losing a memory is not the same as never having it," he said. "Our lives are defined by the moments we make for ourselves, not the impact we make in the world. Anything we leave, be it physical or mental. They pass. A thousand books can be written of our lives, but in a million years, a billion, nothing survives." Agosta attempted to gauge Sloan's mood, and they knew her defenses were falling. "If all that's left of me at the end of time is another charm to remind you of a life you once had…it'll be more than what most people get."

Sloan smirked. She almost felt a tear break away, but she turned from him and fought it back. *It was worth it,* she remembered. It had to have been.

"That was…convincing," she whispered.

Agosta remained quiet and just stared back.

Slowly, Sloan reached out an index and stroked Agosta's hand. He couldn't help but grow the largest grin he had made in years.

"What is it?" she asked him. He gazed into her amber eyes and made a point to remember the exact curve of her smile, the dimples her cheeks made, and how a tuft of short black hair and fallen over her brow.

"So, that's what that looks like…"

CONESTOGA

I remember my master; we call them adjusters. Amari admitted to me later they were born Leland Lich, and to repeat that openly would bring about my demise. I haven't seen them in decades, so I think I'm safe. I possessed an uncanny affinity for machines, and they recognized my potential. They asked very personal questions and claimed to know when I lied. They required such information to better maintain who I was, saying that unanswered questions would become mysteries to even me. They asked what path I wanted to walk down, and I admitted my desire to protect people without harming those I didn't have to. They admired that.

I also asked to be an inch taller with straighter teeth—a common request. What followed was seventeen hours of indescribable pain. I felt my bones break. My lungs filled with fire. I spat up blood, water, and rocks. I felt the very fabric of my being torn apart and reassembled. I lived every moment of my life instantly and came to a different conclusion regarding choices made.

My family recognizes me but admits something changed. I no longer have my father's eyes or my mother's nose. I don't like the same things as before. It's like each cell in my body was individually replaced....is what's left still me?

"Easton"
Personal Journal Entry
(Date removed)

At one-hundred and seventy-five kilometers in length, the forest still resisted attempts to define it. What was initially speculated to be a power distribution facility and later a processing plant was eventually determined to be one of many information distribution centers, coordinating functions between similar rooms all over the vessel.

They were the only locations where anyone had been able to access the operating system, revealing the same language employed on hatches and other machines within the superstructure. All attempts to control data flow proved fruitless, likewise when determining where the information was flowing to or from.

A handful of proctors claimed to hold an affinity with the machines of the vessel, able to decipher fragments of the information passing through the forest, including the location of exclaves or nearby construction facilities.

Regardless of the chamber's functionality, the forest was still a bizarre visual—thousands of towering mechanic spires composed of moving parts, random bursts of color, and lightning darting between the peaks. Occasionally, one would scream a cacophony of overlapping messages in various languages, though no one had been able to identify any of the voices.

The lance was thankfully not traversing along the length of the forest, only across it. Their shell and crutches were dwarfed by the two-hundred-meter-tall trees. They had nearly reached the opposite side when they took a break to discuss their future.

"We have a mission," Kaiden said.

"What about Kenoma?" Deven asked.

It was a transport mission, gathering natural compounds from Philokalia to return to Kenoma, Deven's home exclave. They weren't expecting any significant threats, certainly not scabs, jackers, and elemental monsters.

Elina was quiet and hadn't spoken since the incident. Sloan laid on a stretcher atop the carry-all. Terri, Deven, and Kaiden conversed away from the rest.

"You'll see it through," Terri said. "Take Sloan and Deven, escort the cargo. Agosta and I will take the girl."

"Where?" Deven asked.

"Corvos…the exclave is due to intercept us if we split from you now. One of our own runs the hall there. We'll be in good hands. You can complete the mission and meet us by week's end."

"Corvos is more than two days away," Kaiden said. "You'll draw a watcher if you stay out here too long."

Kaiden looked back to the Agosta with Elina. Supply packs were being affixed to the shell's back.

"It's because the girl is a metron," Deven said.

"Corvos can accommodate her," Terri said.

"So, can Kenoma."

"It's not political, Deven. Corvos has the best university, the best scientists. We have a guildhall there."

"And you being from Corvos has nothing to do with it."

Terri was honest; it truly wasn't political, despite Corvos being her home exclave.

"I took the oaths," she said, "same as you. I don't need people toeing the line. I need ideas. Solutions. Everything that could go wrong on this expedition has. It's a miracle we haven't lost anyone."

"Sloan may disagree with our fortune," Kaiden said.

"What are your thoughts, then?"

"We missed our rendezvous," Kaiden said. "Rescued a metron, got attacked by what all measurements appeared to be a pissed-off trash compactor. This was considered a low-risk assignment. The best course of action would be to continue to Kenoma as a single unit."

"We've risked the cargo more than we should, and if we divide, there's a better chance one of us will make it."

"Splitting up is literally the worst thing ever," Deven said. "Literally. Every book ever written cursed characters that separated."

"Agreed. This is not a good idea," Kaiden said.

"You and I concur that whatever attacked us targeted the girl," Terri said. "Am I wrong?"

"Seldomly."

"Which means to ensure the success of the contract, which according to the charter takes paramount, we need to draw any threats away. Without the carry-all, Agosta and I are faster. We can hasten days into hours easily.

"We shouldn't be splitting up," Deven said.

"We're not…we're cutting dead weight," Terri said with a smirk. "Take the cargo, get paid, see to Sloan. Kenoma and Corvos will cross in a couple of days, and we can meet up." Terri stared with conviction at Kaiden, who was still weighing the ramifications of disagreeing. "I respect both your opinions."

"But you don't care," Kaiden said. He wasn't accusatory; it was a statement of fact. He knew Terri admired him, and they'd known each other longer than she knew her parents. Terri would often credit him for her accelerated advancement, but in Kaiden's eyes, all he needed to do was not get in her way.

"You're right; I don't," Terri said with a half-smirk.

"Terri—" Deven said.

"—No…she's right," Kaiden said, his attention still on her. "All we can do is advise, offer counsel. My intuition believes dividing is misguided…and I'm wrong. Ultimately, the decision is hers, and I'd follow her to the gates of Vothragna if she asked."

Terri's smile grew.

"Thank you," she said, "…but Kenoma will be enough."

Deven realized he might have overstepped and firmed his lips.

"We'll deliver the cargo, complete the mission," Deven said. "Thank you for your entrusting us with it."

"You make a good proctor; don't let your people hold you to tradition," Terri said.

Deven nodded.

Meanwhile, Agosta and Elina were prepping the suits. Elina finished strapping another pack to the back of Agosta's crutch.

"What's a metron?" she asked him. Agosta was confused by Elina's awareness of the term. "I overheard." Agosta's attention shifted to the remaining lance against another tree, ten meters away. "It's not that strange; I've got excellent hearing."

Agosta continued packing while he tried to explain.

"Within a tiny percentage of the population, there are individuals capable of understanding the ways of this vessel, of harnessing its…still…unseen engine and drawing on its power. Everyone believes it possesses abilities beyond what can be explained by modern science."

"Like?"

"Like…where's the power source? How is it distributed? How can the vessel generate gravity given its unusual shape? How can it alter its internal structure? We're protected from solar radiation by a strong magnetic field, but no one knows how that's being generated. It's almost as if this…place…exists outside our perceptions. How the vessel can wirelessly channel energy may be how it can somehow channel power occasionally to people."

"And those are metrons?"

"At some point in their life, specific individuals discover the ability to listen to the ship, acting as a conduit. This could be intentional or accidental. It may be an evolutionary leap, the culmination of this ship's purpose. They call it psyntience…p-s-y, not s-e-n."

"I wasn't aware of either of them. Is that what I can do?"

"Metron is the more common of the two. It develops from birth or puberty, with a nearly uncontrollable psychokinetic ability to alter reality. The other is called a maker, someone who has mastered their psyntience in a specific field or application. All makers began life as metrons but received training or learned to focus their abilities through diligence and repetition. Some are even proctors."

"With us?"

"No, no. But when we reach Corvos, we'll introduce you to one, a full-on maker. And they'll explain everything and offer you a choice."

"What kind…to be a proctor?" Elina perked up. "Like you? I'd totally do that."

"Just…wait until you read the fine print. It's not as exotic as it sounds. The last few days have been somewhat of an outlier. Most times, it can get tedious."

"Look at what my life was until you found me."

"Yeah, you got me there," Agosta said as he finished locking the last bundle on the rear of his shell. "Our maker will present options, remain a metron, or undergo the rites and rituals to become a maker."

"You talk as if it's magic."

"For the lack of a better word. I think it's more accurate to envision this vessel being capable of altering reality and potentially offering the keys of that ability to those it sees fit." Agosta leaned against his shell, occasionally glancing at Terri as she made her case to Kaiden. "What you did yesterday…had you done it before?"

Elina's attention fell away as she contemplated her memories.

She whispered. "On occasion…I've wanted something to happen…and it did. It was always small. Fire. Wind. I could build things by thinking about them. My family knew. Jackers wanted my power. They threatened my family. Kept me in line. When my parents died, I wanted to kill them. Something else beat me to it."

That comment concerned Agosta, and he leaned in to ensure only she could hear him.

"Was it the same thing as yesterday?" he asked. She nodded. "Do you think it answers you?"

"It tried to kill me," she said. "Jackers got in the way. I let it tear them apart, and when it came for me…I sent it away." It was a complex topic for her, and Elina never told anyone this. Not even her family knew the extent of what she could do. "When I make things happen, I feel…something…answering me. This didn't. Terri's right; I'm a threat to your mission."

"Which is why we're taking you to Corvos. We'll figure it all out—"

"I don't want to be out of control. People have been trying to control me my whole life. This power…most times, won't listen to me. I want that control, to run my own life."

Most proctor guilds boasted at least one maker, some a family. The Staplegunners were not a particularly large affiliation, with its only gifted member operating out of Corvos.

"Proctors don't answer to anyone but themselves," Agosta said. "We have a code. They won't control you…but there will be rules. If you want to manage this power, if you want to no longer give in to the chaotic nature of this life, it will involve discipline, training, and from what I've heard, considerable hardship. With the help of a master, they will allow you to bend that energy inward…effectively altering your own body, your own reality."

"I can change myself?"

"With help. In the process of becoming something able to control your power, you gain the opportunity to change everything about yourself. It's called tuning. You alter your biological and psychological composition to better train your psyntient abilities. In essence, with the help of your master, you construct a new individual made from the old you."

"Can I be a redhead like Sloan?" Elina asked with genuine interest.

Agosta laughed. “From what I heard,” he said. “that’s one of the easier things you can do.”

“Can I be taller?”

“If you want. You could change anything about yourself. You could rewrite your identity…even change your gender if you were inclined.” Elina was getting more absorbed by what Agosta was offering. “Tuning is not a pleasant experience from what I’ve heard, so I wouldn’t make any slapdash decisions right now.” He noticed Terri finishing her conversation with Deven and Kaiden.

Elina offered Terri a half-hearted smile as she returned.

“Are we good?” Agosta asked.

“Unfortunately,” Terri said, glancing at Elina. “Just us three. We’ll have to expedite our journey. Carry her. Go like lightning to Corvos.”

Elina perked up upon hearing, and she resumed securing supply packs to the outer skin of Agosta’s shell. Terri coaxed Agosta aside, assumingly out of hearing.

“And Noah Bennet said I was lucky getting this commission,” she said. “We’re sticking our neck out for this girl.”

“I thought you didn’t trust her?” Agosta said.

“Should I? Trust is earned, takes time. You believe, and that’s enough for me. I just don’t know why you do.”

“Because that familiarity runs both ways.”

“If she’s a metron, you’d have to acknowledge the distinct possibility that she possesses the power to alter your perceptions. Even your memory. That familiarity might have been implanted.”

“If she were that powerful, she wouldn’t have been a slave.”

“An account we take on faith. She might be lying about everything.”

Agosta nodded, smirked, then whispered back, “By the way, she can hear everything we’re saying.”

“What?” Terri turned to Elina, who waved back from Agosta’s shell.

“It’s not that strange,” Agosta said. “She’s got excellent hearing.”

* * *

They were nearly ready to separate. Agosta climbed atop the walker to check on Sloan.

“Best seat in the house,” he said.

“I’m faking it,” Sloan coughed a laugh through her stitches, “don’t tell anyone.”

Agosta smiled.

“Probably won’t even leave a scar,” he said. There was genuine concern on his part, but he remained stoic.

"Darn. I heard they're sexy."

"Don't look at this as a sign of weakness. You're the strongest proctor I know. And I respect the hell out of you."

"It took me almost being eviscerated by a trash tornado for you to finally admit that."

"I've always appreciated you. I vouched without ever having met you. Your record was all that was required." She remembered and smiled. Agosta cocked his head like an inquisitive puppy. "What is it?"

Sloan's thoughts were interrupted by the nearby tree casting out a powerful current of electricity, which bounced between three other peaks. The destination roared in overlapping voices before dissipating. A kilometer away, another display ricocheted between a dozen trees. The illumination over them changed from yellow to blue to green. When it finally subsided, Sloan spoke her mind.

"I never knew where I came from. That rig defined my life."

"Oh, don't worry about those scratches. Two days in the yards, tops. Besides, people define your life, not machines."

Sloan chuckled, ignoring the familiarity she felt with what he said.

"If that's the case, why do we spend all our resources customizing and upgrading our crutches?" she asked. "Bespoke parts. Tailored paint. Personalized flair. Don't get me wrong; I love my rig. But when it was being torn apart around me. I wasn't thinking about it."

Agosta could feel Terri staring at his back. They were wasting time, and it was of the essence.

"What were you thinking about?" Agosta asked.

"People," Sloan said.

"As it should be. Plural?"

"No."

Agosta smiled back. He checked to see who else was watching, then placed his hand over hers. He held it tightly.

"I'm generally not one for sentiment," Agosta said.

"Too bad," she answered with a responding smirk, "I usually have a lot to share."

Agosta's smile faded.

"What is it?" she asked.

"Just odd...sounds like a conversation we already had."

"Given the circumstances, you'd think I remember."

He released her and stepped back down.

"If you're feeling up to it, meet us in Corvos," he said.

Sloan nodded.

As he walked away, she whispered to herself, "I won't forget…"

CONESTOGA

Of course, it would be proctors that would carry such a legend. No one outside believes one of their lances managed to reach the front of Conestoga and return. I mean, is there even a front, or is it just an end? The Covenant Regulars maintain the myth each chance they get, and all the proctors believe them, but if there's evidence, they've never told any of us.

Of course, they got a slew of conflicting stories about immense chambers, control rooms, and exclaves that no one else has seen. But the one aspect none of them disagree on is what they found when they reached the end. It was damaged, shredded, almost looking like it had broken off something larger.

Could the Conestoga only be a smaller segment of a larger vessel, and if so, where is it…and how big would the complete structure be?

Dr. Joachim Raddad
Corvos National University.

Noah's eyes snapped open. He probably drank more than he should have. The overhead lamps simulating dawn slowly brightened on within the habitat. Some exclaves featured a battery of oscillating lights to simulate a sun, while others boasted a single moving globe; this was the former. He rubbed his eyes, then glanced to his right to see Syn asleep.

Her slender arm was draped over his chest. They had embraced. While there was concern over the other members of the lance spying on them, it didn't discourage her from straddling him as they kissed. They managed ten minutes before she was forced to don her mask.

Both knew they were physically compatible but didn't test that theory despite Syn's initial encouragement. Noah was too entranced with exploring the lines of her face, the curvature of her neck. He remembered feeling a moment of regret, like a missed opportunity with someone he had only known a few days, a past neither of them shared, but both seemed to evoke. Had he made a mistake? She forgave him for the tea and the initial indelicate discourse, but there was something more, a memory further back, a mistake Noah hadn't made that he felt he needed to make right.

He didn't want to make the same mistake once.

He rolled her hand away and stood, still fully dressed. He examined the camp, noting the fire had died, and there were no signs of either Machus or Carthan.

Endolon consciousness was like a switch, and Syn opened her eyes quickly and sprung up, alert. She looked about the camp, realizing what had happened. She approached behind Noah.

"They left us?" Syn said.

"They broke proctor code," Noah said as he kicked over the fire. They had to have come back at one point. Given how long Noah had been asleep, they would be several hours ahead of them. Syn was trying to gauge Noah's level of alarm. He appeared more angry than worried.

"How many are there?" Syn asked. She was concerned but didn't want to show it.

"A lot, but this one's in the top five. Number three, I think. They'll be out of the guild by the time we reach Corvos. I'll burn every string they think they can pull."

"Why would they do this?"

"They're gambling we won't make it back alive."

Now Syn was worried. She and Noah orbited the walker, noting the numerous storage hatches opened and emptied.

"They took the food and water," Syn said. Noah wedged his head inside the larger engine hatch.

"And they disabled the matador," Noah said. "Took out its power cell. That'll earn them prison…assuming I don't kill them first."

"How far do we have to go?"

"We'll have to check for anything we can salvage," Noah said as he pulled his head from the engine bay. "Two days maybe. Food is easy. Water not so much."

"I do not require as much as you. Take whatever there is." Hydration was hard to come by in the endolon's natural habitat. Their physiology hindered moisture loss through sweating, panting, or urination.

"You're the priority," Noah said.

"Stop! Being such a…proctor," she shouted. "We both need to survive."

At least the power cell on Noah's dodger was functional; it was alarmed and would have woken him if triggered. Machus and Carthan were at least that smart.

After loading what they could, Noah and Syn left the matador in place. Despite appearing like a military organization, the proctors never sabotaged, destroyed, or locked anything left behind. Even permanent shelters they abandoned are left open for refugees, nomads, or other proctors to use when needed. Potentially another proctor guild would claim the matador on a future expedition. There was always the possibility that jackers would steal it, but the positives outweighed the negatives.

The exclave gateway sat at the base of the hill. Upon reaching it, Noah tapped a few sigils he remembered that accessed this door. Thankfully, his dodger was small enough that he could use his own hands to access it. However, the pedestal chirped back in an alien tongue, and the pedestal holograms converted to blue.

Noah repeated the code.

"Coro, Fignas, Sylo, Fignas, Maldi, Praxid, Praxid, Garoo," he whispered.

"You speak their language?" Syn asked.

"I know the words, but no one's fluent. I'm the lead xenolinguist in my guild." Noah glanced at Syn, noticing her jaw slack, slowly forming a smile. "Yeah, I probably should have mentioned that sooner."

"You think?"

"Well, now you know."

"Where were you educated?"

"Everywhere," he said as he resumed tapping at the alien panel. "Mostly in the shadows and spaces between worlds. I got offered a teaching position within the guild once…but…I didn't want to stop. What good would I have been if I said yes." He focused on her. "Where would I be?"

Syn stared deep into his soul.

"You still surprise me," she said.

"And you never stopped."

"If I wasn't troubled by our current crisis…"

The panel beeped again, and Noah kicked the pedestal.

"Shit," he said.

"They locked us in?"

"I don't know what they did. These consoles are indestructible. They must have activated a security feature. Probably on a timer….my guess a day, maybe two." Noah looked up at the sky, through the doom to the stars beyond. He moved back to the gateway and rested his hand on the stone. "We altered course. Probably twenty-five to thirty degrees."

"We'll miss the rendezvous."

"We'll be fine," Noah said. It was a lie. "They won't be when I get a hold of them. I just need to think."

They stepped from the gateway back into the natural terrain of the exclave. It was a paradise but also a death sentence. Syn's rebreather can last weeks. Noah's wouldn't manage more than a few days. It wouldn't matter as all the fruit in this habitat was poisonous.

Noah's attention was still absorbed on the gateway while Syn's concentration shifted outward. Then she noticed something, something she had seen previously.

"These habitats can sometimes possess several gateways," Syn said.

"That's a good point."

Syn squinted, then pointed to a narrow valley.

"I think it is this way."

"How do you…did you see something?" Noah approached Syn's position and looked into the valley, but there was only a scattering of trees, exposed crags, and colored moss. Syn reached and took Noah's hand, interlocking her fingers with his.

"Do you trust me?" she asked.

"Syn, what did you see?"

"Do you trust me?"

He firmed his grip on her hand.

"Of course."

* * *

They trekked through the valley, walking in the shadow of the slope. The plant life was stranger than usual for Noah's liking. The grass was blue compared to orange atop the hill, with ferns of red blades and speckled mushrooms half his size.

The valley terminated in a bluff overlooking an expanse of yellow moss leading to a forest of green conifers. With the aid of telescoping vision, Noah could finally spot the tip of a single black stone pylon. They both sighed, but Noah shifted his relief to alarm.

"How could you have seen that from our vantage."

"Can we get in?" Syn asked.

"Assuming the security lock is isolated to just the one. We'll need to hustle; every minute takes us further away. I know it's crass to ask a girl her weight, but with hollow bones, you should be light, correct?"

"As a feather," she said.

"Because my dodger has flight capability," he said.

"Carrying someone my size may be clumsy. I can run."

"How quickly?"

"The arrangement of my joints places my top speed well over yours. At least forty kilometers."

Noah approached and came behind her, gently placing his augmented artificial hands on her shoulders. This close, he could finally appreciate the inches he had over her when in his suit.

"I can fly faster," he said, "and there's no time to argue. Are you afraid of heights?"

"I have never been in a situation to test that," she said.

Noah lowered one hand, preparing to sweep her into his arms.

"Step four of the scientific method," he said as he cradled her. She latched onto his neck firmly. "Wow…you *are* light as a feather." Without the need to surge power, Noah's dodger coughed a jet of plasma exhaust and leaped into the air.

He reached a cruising altitude quickly, just a few meters over the trees. The velocity felt faster this close to the surface, and Syn firmed her grip, not that Noah could notice. Syn had her eyes closed for the first few seconds but eventually braved the wind and elevation to take in the view.

She had never seen such an expanse of color and vegetation, a rainbow foreign to her home. She was spellbound only an instant before noting her distance to the ground.

"Yes!" she shouted.

"Yes, what?" he asked.

"YES!"

Noah laughed.

"Don't worry; I won't let you go."

Syn braved her newly discovered phobia to appreciate the oscillating terrain, exchanging forests for glades dotted by sapphire ponds. The trees passed under them, opening into a massive lake that cascaded over a cataract. In an island of mist beyond the falls sat a pedestal dotted by grass and an obsidian obelisk marking the gateway.

"You see," Noah said. "Could never have made it by foot."

"I only saw the tip, not the entire structure. It is beautiful."

"I've seen better. If you're ever curious why your kind becomes proctors, remember this moment."

They approached the obelisk. Noah descended headfirst, bringing a scream from the endolon before the dodger's legs swung forward, and his thrusters slowed their descent. He released her, and she stumbled slightly upon touching the ground.

"How could anyone grow accustomed to his life?" she asked. "It is almost too much to take in."

"Like I said, eventually, even the amazing can appear mundane," he said as he approached the obelisk. The pedestal was untampered, and he went to work. The standard code worked, and the obelisk elevated to expose a much smaller gateway than the usual entrance.

Syn stepped back as Noah deployed *Lucy*, the larger one, a kinetic pulse rifle over a piston ejector. The weapon unfolded and expanded, revealing multiple targeting lasers and barrels. He entered the gateway, shoulder spotlights activating the instant he passed into darkness. She followed closely behind.

"Why *Lucy*?" she asked as they left the exclave.

"Which one?" Noah asked.

"Either…or both."

"The big one was named after my mother, the other after my sister." Syn nodded though Noah couldn't see it. He considered his next thought before articulating it. "Brenda."

"What?"

"Her name was Brenda."

It didn't take long for Syn to realize who he was referring to.

"Thank you," she said.

* * *

It deposited them in a smaller corridor a few hundred meters from the main avenue and a few kilometers from the main gateway into the exclave.

"Ummm…" Noah whispered to himself.

"I would not judge if you did not possess some idea on where to go," Syn said. "My fondness is not in jeopardy. That being said…I really hope this moment of uncertainty is just that."

"Unfortunately, it is," he said as he approached the blood and metal fragments speckling the hallway. "That's fresh." Noah found a few more drops indicating a direction. A scanning unit on his arm blossomed, and he examined the hallway. The blood was only minutes old and hadn't completely dried. A trail led in a particular direction Noah began following.

"Wait, do we want to follow this trail?" Syn asked.

"If they fled, they would do so towards the nearest habitat. They're not going to double back to us, so they'd have no choice."

"What caused this?"

Noah ignored her and took the lead. They moved hurriedly but cautiously as he employed his scanning equipment, checking for heat, movement, and radiation.

"Should I have a firearm?" Syn asked.

"Have you ever used one?"

"No."

"Then that won't change. Firearms held by the inexperienced are a greater danger to friends and feet." Noah slowed his gate and looked back at her. "But would you feel safer with one?"

Syn considered it briefly.

"It would only be a feeling. Safety with you is fact."

Noah smiled.

His sensor net picked up the object before seeing it, the mound of twisted metal. Noah kept Syn behind as he approached the wreck. It was once a crutch, and Noah recognized who was still inside.

"Machus!" Noah said, kneeling against the mangled armor. Noah wasn't going to kill a man already so close to death, but he wasn't going to speed his demise. Several jagged spikes had driven into his torso and legs.

Noah recognized the weapon.

Machus's one good arm grabbed the edge of the dodger's collar.

"Damn you," Machus said through his groans.

"You save your last words for that?" Noah asked.

"It…followed you."

Noah quickly surveyed his surroundings, checking his scanning gear. Carthan was nowhere to be found, likely still ahead.

Noah picked up movement. From the branching hallway, Carthan appeared. His crutch's secondary arm had been severed, though his was still intact. The remaining secondary held a needler shotgun which discharged a dozen hand-length sharpened rods to an unseen opponent.

It emerged.

Syn fell back, petrified in dread.

Noah raised his weapon.

To see a watcher was to see one's worst nightmares incarnate. A self-repairing biomechanical machine that patrolled through the vessel's corridors, watchers attacked anything that didn't belong. A medley of organic and mechanical parts mixed with knives and multiple eyes. It was constructed, but no one knew what came first—the poor creature transfigured by technology to become a weapon or the demented machine with living tissue grafted.

How one selected and tracked a target to the ignorance of all other concerns appeared mechanical and unemotional, but watchers also took pleasure in tearing targets apart. Victims were not devoured—the monsters simply desired to see living things destroyed.

The sound was all too familiar. The grinding snarl. The ticking clock. The rattle of a massive dot matrix printer. The deep-tone air siren.

Syn had read of these monsters. She had even seen a picture of it before but had no idea how fast and voracious they were.

Noah instinctually pushed her back and tried to gain a bearing where his shot would strike the monster, not Carthan. Despite what the man had done, Noah wasn't about to cross that line. His only priority was ensuring Syn was safe.

Carthan fell back and was pinned by the beast's saw tail.

Noah fired fruitlessly to severe the watcher's grasp, but the creature took its time slowly tearing Carthan apart.

First, the legs, then his arms, finally placing the proctor's head in its jaw and gradually biting down.

Noah's plasma bolts were landing, and damage was being inflicted—portions of the beast were melting off.

Machus struggled to a knee to aim his drill launcher.

He got one shot off, the round burrowing deep into the creature's flesh, before the watcher's tail lashed out, tossing Machus to a wall and Noah back to where he pushed the nearly frozen Syn.

Noah flipped himself over to focus on the terrified endolon. He tore his helmet off.

"Syn," Noah shouted. "Syn!" Noah pulled her to her feet and coaxed her to run down the hallway. "You need to run!"

"What? No!" Syn said.

"I need you to go."

Machis was unable to move as the Watcher stalked him.

"You can't destroy it…it's too powerful!" Syn said.

"It hasn't met Lucy," Noah said. "…well, the other Lucy."

"You'll die!"

Noah stepped closer and pushed her away.

"This is my job. I swore to this. Your life was the mission."

Machus, trapped under the creature, fired his weapon at the beast's underbelly.

He was inflicting damage, but the beast ignored it and slowly opened its jaws toward the human's face.

Its drill tongue emerged.

"You are more than that, and you know—" Syn said. Her kind didn't shed tears, another facet of their biology to conserve moisture.

"Follow the hallway to Corvos!" Noah said. "It's a major habitat; there'll be guards. My guess is only a few kilometers. Given how fast you run, it should be a breeze without me holding you back."

"No!" she said.

"You can make it."

"I am not leaving you!"

"Take the book and go!"

Syn stepped back but didn't run.

Noah gave her one final look.

"Noah," she whimpered.

"GO!"

She didn't want to do it, but Syn ran from the fight.

Noah approached the beast as it centered on him, Machus's blood rolling off its jaws.

"Come at me!" he said.

Syn stumbled but regained her footing as she sprinted; the screaming and grinding of metal echoed behind her. She held back her emotions the best she could but broke when she heard his screams.

"Is that all you got! God damn it!"

A shriek of pain rang out.

Syn forced herself forward, faster, further.

He shouted again, "Come on! You bastard! That's nothing!"

Another cry of pain, and another.

Then silence.

Syn closed her eyes and concentrated on her feet, trying her best to maintain a swift pace. The last thing she heard with a muffled whimper.

"I'm not done with you, mother fucker."

It was followed by more clicking and horns as the noises diminished into whispers she could no longer discern. Syn couldn't help but stop to gaze back into the darkness. Even the hisses and distant groans fell away. Her heart sank, and Syn resumed her committed escape from battle.

PARADISE

The legend of Umbra is bigger than Umbra herself. She was the greatest cutter, a master abecedarian. She began with small creatures, then added to her portfolio until she had dozens. She was an artist, you see. It was not about how effectively they could protect her. Umbra held a secret obsession. I followed her legend for half a lifetime. It was a museum dedicated to her whim. Only a handful were ever alive at any one time; the mystery was figuring out which ones were staring back. And yet, that was the cursory hobby when the maestro wanted to relax. Her real drive was to recreate life itself—to shape her clay, stone, or iron into conscious intelligence.

She wanted to create sapient creatures. Outsiders would call her a monster that sired monsters. But I knew of her loss and desire to create life when the natural process was denied. Her obsession pushed everyone away, everyone except those submissive pets. That would have been the end of it, but she refused to let that fixation go; she used her madness constructively.

Then, one day, she did the impossible. She achieved godhood by creating life from nothing. She then released that knowledge to fortify her name and establish the legend. Also, did I ever tell you that her fortress was a golem in itself?

And those we call gods are fools to think she died of old age.

Unidentified

"Let's take a walk," Agosta said to Kabdila in the latter's royal office. Kabdila stood.

"You know, I am still a prince," Kabdila said. "You can't just order me around."

"Fine…then take *me* for a walk."

Kabdila held back a chuckle, shook his head, and followed his friend out.

They paced along the castle's outer wall, avoiding guards that could overhear them.

Philokalia had nearly passed the city and was continuing its orbit east. Life was slowly returning to normal, but there would still be periods of extended darkness until the world finally disappeared over the horizon. Uno had just risen, gifting the city with only a few hours of light.

"Your fool of a father killed her family," Agosta said.

"I'm sure he didn't do the deed himself—" Kabdila said.

"You think that?"

"He has more than enough blood on his hands to flood the Dagos. I'm just saying he probably didn't swing the sword. Not that it matters. Whoever it was, they were thorough. Probably Varant Price; he razed that city to ash. I can't imagine she would've been spared, held here for ten years. Father probably didn't know she existed until someone betrayed her. So, who was it…who turned her in?"

"Wouldn't have been any of the families loyal to Volani. The Aegis ordered the hierarchy of those lines executed."

"I admit that might have been an overreaction on my father's part. I'm relieved we don't have that blood on our hands."

"The vilest stains are the ones you cannot see."

Kabdila stopped short of the castle green under the shadow of the Salt Tower. He was somewhat irritated.

"Excuse me?" he asked.

Agosta stopped and confronted the prince, now loud enough for nearby gardeners to hear.

"I kidnap your child," Agosta said. "I give that child to my son to raise. You find the child after I've passed. Would you punish the son?"

"Yes." Kabdila didn't need to consider his answer.

"Exactly. Would you do the same if it was not a child but a family valuable, a jewel or ring? At the very least, you'd expect it back. We were responsible for this before we even knew she existed."

The two resumed their walk, passing the officer barracks next to the barbican.

"Why are you so heated?" Kabdila asked. "A failure of your network?"

"We were too young to appreciate the magnitude of what your father did. Well, you were; I was gifted with the virtue of apathy. She was a child, and she knows more than us."

"I guess it doesn't matter," Kabdila said. "What a waste." Agosta realized that Kabdila was formulating his solution. "Why do they care? She's one girl. Never believed in prophecy. Maybe it's something else. Maybe that rumor, that they're…what do you call them?"

"Daemons," Agosta said.

"Right. Angels wrapped in human skin. Have you ever seen one?"

"Probably, that's the point."

"Maybe we should go back and check."

"You're not taking a blade to the skin of a child," Agosta said bluntly. Kabdila grimaced as if Agosta's opposition was a simple inconvenience. The only information he had on the myth claimed that nagomjii weren't the only non-humans living among the general population. Daemons, eidolons, both names for creatures hiding in plain sight, and both declared profane by the Ascension with commandments to ensure their uncovering and extinction.

"Regardless," Kabdila said, "they put a hefty price on her head. Ascension gets what they want. Is this why they held back my father…because they knew?"

"He probably wanted to use her as leverage."

Kabdila kept silent as he deliberated options, despite already having decided. Agosta knew this as well but wished his prince would surprise him.

"Thoughts?" Kabdila asked.

"Volani has always been a threat to Ascension authority," Agosta said. "How one girl is still a danger is beyond me. I could understand when they were a family and a house, when they commanded the largest army and the planet, but now…feels petty."

"I wave a title under your nose, and now you get understated."

Agosta paused and cocked his head as he read his friend's implication.

"Clearly, I didn't feed you the answer you wanted," Agosta said.

"One child for one planet. We've made easier choices. Regardless, I won't make such a decision now…but when I do…I need to know I can depend on you to do what's necessary."

Kabdila didn't bother waiting for an answer and made for the central keep, unaware of the concern that washed over Agosta's face.

* * *

Agosta wandered the roof of the inner bailey, offering a view of the curtain wall and the city beyond. The city gates were closed until the first proper morning in three days. The stars embedded in the heaven rings of the Solokring slowly flickered on as Uno reached the horizon of Bythos.

Agosta had always considered history essential to understanding but tricky to navigate. The industry of propaganda exercised by the Aegis and the Ascension was thorough. He ignored what he knew to be false. If he were going to be asked to do what he believed his prince would, Agosta needed to understand why.

And how he somehow recognized that girl.

His best guess was that she was allowed out of her cell at some point, and he had seen her wander the grounds under guard. But something that obvious would have been recorded. He would have remembered. He knew much of Volani history, which most people were unaware of.

If Elina were executed publicly, the mob would demand an explanation, and few would understand the severity of the action. For the life of him, Agosta couldn't conceive why the king would destroy a kingdom but curse his legacy on the soul of one girl. Maybe when the final Volani heir was found, the king could finally confront the greatest threat to the Aegis and be confounded by the hidden power this girl possessed. Perhaps she was living evidence of the folly of gods.

"Why did they create stars?" Mannah asked.

Agosta was not surprised by her appearance but by her attempt at communication, expecting her to pass silently. She was due to return to her world earlier but remained to ensure the absolution of her kingdom. A handmaiden and two royal guards adorned in the colors of Hydranis—the snake on their crests—followed her. She approached him; her hands interlocked behind her back.

"Excuse me, your majesty?" Agosta asked.

"The stars…what are they?"

Agosta focused back on the view. Etiquette would generally insist that Agosta kneel or bow, but he knew she wouldn't expect it.

"Hidden messages from the gods," he said. "A helpful way to navigate. Pretty lights so we don't get mesmerized by the emptiness of oblivion."

"Don't get maudlin," she said.

"I thought you would've left for your kingdom, your majesty."

"Shortly…and you don't have to keep using the formal address; I find it tiresome."

"Yes, ma'am."

Mannah leaned against the stone parapet, unlocked her fingers, and rested her elbows on the edge, certainly staining her ostentatious attire, which she didn't care about.

"Thank you for sharing your intelligence Mr. Pike," she said. "You exonerated my people." Agosta nodded. "Even though you lied."

"Excuse me?" Agosta asked, genuinely intrigued.

"Your report indicated witnesses seeing the shaper emerge from Haverglade Forest," Mannah said, "but we both know it came from the city of Fontaine."

"One of yours."

"They're all mine."

"To be blunt, ma'am, most witnesses started to believe the lie. Half of them claim to have seen the dragon."

"If I had a dragon, Mr. Pike, I wouldn't need to bear the arrogance of lesser men."

"You openly threatened an Ascension cardinal, ma'am. You're not doing a very good job."

Mannah smiled. She appreciated the banter, which she rarely encountered outside her inner circle.

"Still," she said. "I appreciate your regent easing the pressure placed upon my kingdom."

"He doesn't know," Agosta said, eliciting genuine shock from the queen. "Exposing you benefits no one but the church. If I believed you were genuinely responsible, I'd want motivation before confrontation."

Mannah was impressed.

"Then it's you I offer gratitude," she said. "Plan your favor accordingly, Mr. Pike. That *is* the currency in which you trade?"

"Better than any gold," he said as they watched the planet and its hundreds of lights pass over them. "Your world was once divided…before the Hallesegro. You were of Hydrus, and Fontaine was of Phydranus. The regalia, which you lost, merged your houses to form Hydranus, the double-headed snake. Fontaine…is owned by your political rivals."

"Interesting," Mannah said sarcastically. "I'm curious; what else do I know?"

"Why didn't you throw them to the fire? They'd be vulnerable, strengthening your grip on their people."

"We are one people, Mr. Pike, and we can't afford to pull the curtain."

Agosta considered how accusatory he would be allowed to be.

"Meaning you know more than I previously expected," he said.

Mannah smiled.

"You can't afford those secrets, Mr. Pike," she said.

They watched the mechanism of the universe work, something everyone took for granted. Philokalia was still dominating the sky, but deep into the waning sunset, they could see Kenoma, the furthest world directly connected to Bythos, moving along its ring.

"What's he like?" she asked.

Agosta offered only a half glance as he answered. If Kabdila became king, the past dissolved promise would be entertained again. The new king would insist for numerous reasons, mainly because Mannah was the most attractive noble worthy of the station. Agosta knew his friend didn't care for intelligence, which in Agosta's eyes, was the queen's strongest attribute and one that would prove the most problematic in the future if the two royals were to be married.

"He would keep concubines private while expressing fealty with every public breath. He doesn't subscribe to violence in the bedroom and discourages eye contact during sex.

"Should I ask how you—"

"No…He is well educated and balances shrewd acts with veiled aggression. He has never gone to war, but I imagine he wouldn't second guess a call to it. He enjoys aggravating pomposity and discourages chauvinistic, dogmatic, or bigoted acts. He is power-driven, and if you stand by his side, he will champion you to the very gates of heaven. You'd be shocked what you can get away with. Wear trousers. Tend a private garden. Take on lovers on the condition that he watch."

"I don't know if I should be disturbed or impressed at the level of trivia you possess about him."

"I'm his shadow. I'm there even when he's not aware."

"Having said all that," she said, focusing on him, "…Is he a good man?"

"Do you want the political answer or the honest one?"

"Well, political, obviously."

Agosta rolled along the ledge to confront her.

"Aurago is the most powerful nation on Bythos and, by extension, the entire universe. You could not ask for a more advantageous coupling."

"And what is your honest answer?" she asked with a smirk.

Agosta took a deep breath to prep for a long-winded answer.

"No…" he said.

"Why do you say?"

"Because despite your common ambitions. Despite public displays of loyalty and even affection. He will never love you."

"Do you think that matters?"

"It'd matter to me."

Mannah glimpsed the impatience of her handmaiden. They were on a schedule, and the queen's distractions were fickle.

"Well, I appreciate your answer," Mannah said. "You did your research to offer such a blunt response. You're quite…pragmatic. If you ever feel the need to take a vacation, consider visiting my world."

Agosta smirked, well aware that Philokalia was not the safest place. Unlike Bythos nagomjii, those on Philokalia have allied and interbred with a population of grimgods, creating an organized force that raided caravans and villages. The number of growing bandits, given the stretches of ungoverned land and the rise of alien raiders, made Philokalia one of the most dangerous areas in Paradise.

"Too bad it passed the city," Agosta said. "I can't afford a conestoga like some people."

"Well…there are other routes. The offer is on the table, Mr. Pike." Mannah turned to leave but added, "You appear a man of conscience. A shocking discovery given your vocation. Don't kill that part of your soul. When you excise integrity, malice fills the void."

As she walked away, Agosta felt compelled to ask, "Ma'am…can I…ask for advice?"

Now with her entourage, Mannah spun with a half-hearted laugh.

"If you're as good at your job as I believe, you should know my opinion on something you'd ask."

"Maybe I just need to hear it."

Mannah stood her ground despite her handmaiden's frustration.

"What steps would you take to expand your kingdom?" he asked. "What extent would you reach to scale a few steps higher on that ladder, to be that much closer to the gods?"

"Mr. Pike, my family and my kingdom hold stewardship of an entire world. It may be wild at times, certainly dangerous, but it belongs to us. It might be notably smaller than yours, but we hold dominion. That is something few can claim. There resides a strange obsession you on Bythos possess, this…need to expand, to dominate. Perhaps because we operate no borders on our world; we can't conceive of this aggression."

She took a few steps back to him, and the handmaiden nearly threw her hands up. The guards remained stoic.

"I know what you'll say to that," Mannah said. "*Hydranis history speaks to the contrary*. If the Aegis hadn't insisted on twelve kingdoms when the Covenant was signed, the world of Philokalia could've and would've been two kingdoms. My ancestors assumed the throne and kept it for more than five hundred years, but I know discontent grows. Still, regardless of who controlled what, the desire to expand past our world never occurred to us. Doesn't to me."

"But let's propose your house did arrange at least a…political matrimony. You'd leave your world and act as its emissary here. And if the possibility arose for further gain, either or both in power and land, what would you advise?"

"There lies this conceit that royalty answers to no one, that they offer their ear to gods and no other. Their supremacy and judgment are uncontested and unquestioned. It's reckless to ignore history; it's a harsher judge than any deity. I have people that love me; others despise me. I know which is which and why. I'm always aware of my legacy and the people offended or killed to achieve it. Consequence…holds dominion over us all."

Agosta nodded and measured the action he was prepared to take.

"Even kings and queens?" he asked.

"...Even gods," she said as she departed.

* * *

"The regent sends for you," the guard told Agosta. He had been lying on his bed, eyes fixed on the ceiling when he heard the knock. It had been not even an hour, and the sun still hadn't set.

He knew Kabdila too well.

He knew what he was going to be asked to do. Any other time, it wouldn't have been a problem. Agosta met his friend in his royal office, alone. It was almost as if he wanted it to be semi-official. Kabdila sat behind the desk and waited for the door to close.

"What price would you pay?" Kabdila asked.

"I'm not as sullied by economics as you might think," Agosta said.

"You've done worse, we both know that...maybe not so young and beautiful...or...unarmed...but this is the cost. You believe every deal you inked didn't have a value in blood? Every act you commit, whether by words or blades, eventually ends a life."

Agosta stepped forward and kept his tone quiet, just above a whisper.

"Kab, throughout all of this, no matter what you wanted, no matter what act I carried out, it was always justified. We did what we did because we knew we were in the right. I never killed nor ordered the killing of anyone I felt didn't deserve it. You were the heart; I was the hammer. No one dictated our actions. But this...we're both tools of a higher power, enacting their wishes regardless of justification."

"And this is the ultimate mark of loyalty...the first of many we'll be forced to commit to secure our kingdom. Correction...our empire." Kabdila stood and circled the desk. "We were hoping it wasn't a life, but in our minds, we both knew it had to be. No artifact would justify it. This was inevitable. She knows that...even if she doesn't. Be certain she's facing that inevitability right now, confronting the truth that she'd been on borrowed time since the fall of her house. If it were an elderly man, there'd be no hesitation." He placed a hand on Agosta's shoulder. "Make it quick. Painless, we've done enough; she doesn't have to suffer a clumsy kill or the perversions of a male monster." Kabdila smirked and off-handedly added, "but remove the head, keep it clean...burn the body. If you require help or would rather task it to a kingsguard, they'd be happy to do it...but I figured this would be something more suited to someone with authority."

Agosta whispered, "I did what was necessary to keep your hands clean. Everything I did, I knew you would have done, but I took on that burden to protect you. Are you saying you would do this?"

"You know perfectly well I can't…it's not a subject of willingness. I'm going to be emperor within week's end. I can't afford to have this holding me back. You're my shadow…this is what you do."

Kabdila departed, leaving Agosta alone to ponder his next move.

* * *

Agosta stormed into the barracks, confronting the two dozen imperial officers distracted by cards, dice, and pints. They all knew of him and stood to attention.

Agosta scanned their faces and pointed to two of them.

"Katona. Serenda. Out," Agosta said before leaving. He didn't bother checking if Sloan and Deven heard or were following, though they were.

Outside, they found Agosta wedged in a corner in the shadow of the bell tower. He didn't mince words and talked with a low enough tone to ensure no one was overhearing.

"Let's dismiss pleasantries, you two," he said, pointing to Sloan. "Katona, you have no history or family? No estate?"

"No, milord," Sloan said.

"I'm not a lord." His eyes shifted to Deven. "Serenda, you're part of the Kaelum royal family."

Deven was taken aback and could only afford a disquieting, "Uhh…"

"It wasn't a question. Thirteenth in line," Agosta said.

"It's no longer recognized," Deven said.

"And who stripped them of that?"

Again, Deven was unsure how to respond, offering another, "Uhh…"

"I can't wait for you to think of a diplomatic response," Agosta said. "It was Aurago. Sloan…what are your aspirations?"

"Milord?"

"I'm not a lord. I'll be blunt. Is this a gender thing? Are you seeking to stake your claim? Prove yourself on equal footing to people like Deven."

"I don't have any aspirations," she said.

"That's impossible. They offered you the inner circle. You didn't take joy in that?"

"I wasn't given a choice to say no."

"She's…" Deven said, then trailed off. "We're about to…"

"I need you to finish a thought." Agosta talked swiftly as this diversion was costing him time from a still-developing plan. He then pointed at both of them. "Are you two…?"

Sloan jumped to attention.

"Oh, my gods, no!" she said.

"Nooo…" Deven said.

"We've been friends for years."

"Years?" Agosta asked.

"Fifteen," Sloan said.

"You're both attractive; what am I missing?"

"It's nothing, milord," Deven said.

"I'm not a lord, and it clearly isn't…one or both of you keeps a secret the other protects." He stared at them, reading their eyes, how they puckered their lips. He put it together but most was still guesswork. "Okay, it's both of you. And it's not the same secret."

"Milord," Sloan said, "if I may?"

"For the love of the gods. I'm not a lord; stop calling me that."

"Sir—"

"Plated in peasant armor and acting as a sentry will certainly keep eyes off you, but if you enter that castle and don the regalia, you'll fall under Coulter of the Fall. Among asshats, he's king cockbag. Any secrets you keep will be revealed. How dangerous are they?" He scrutinized them as Deven stepped back, worried that guards would encircle them. "Humiliation? Worse?"

"We've admitted to nothing," Sloan said, standing her ground.

"You certainly haven't." Agosta addressed Deven, noticing his stance. "You both need to settle; no one's getting arrested." Deven relaxed, but only somewhat. "I'm here alone. I'm gauging your personalities, your dedication, and loyalty."

"We swore allegiance to the diadem of gold and blood," Deven said, quoting the pamphlet. "We vow—"

"Yeah, I know the creed. In what order does that loyalty lie? The king would claim him over the land over its people. The church would place its word over the king. Imperial sentinels are expected to place themselves at the crown's service, loyalty to no one else…not even each other. If gold and title were waved, how far would loyalty last between you two?" Sloan and Deven stared at one another. Agosta immediately picked up a platonic devotion between the two. Whatever secrets they kept, it solidified their bond. "Your hesitation speaks volumes. You two are loyal to one another. And you'd place that loyalty over the monarchy."

"Sir—" Sloan said.

"I like that," Agosta said. "I want you two manning the northern outer gate." Agosta made for the central tower.

"Uhh…When, sir?" Deven asked.

"Sunrise," he shouted as he quickened his pace. "Remain there until noon."

Sloan and Deven were still stationary, weighing the context of their conversation.

"What was that about?" Deven asked.

"Do you think he knows?" Sloan asked.

"If he did, I'd be excommunicated…and you'd be dead."

* * *

Agosta noted the pronounced echo his feet made as he scaled the tower's steps, how louder and deep-toned they were compared to the handmaidens living there. He could quiet them, but he didn't. He even slammed his feet a few times to foretell his approach.

He slid open the shutter to find Elina asleep, with one hand under a pillow and an exposed leg rising between the sheets. Agosta chuckled to himself before unlocking the door. *Smart play*, he thought.

He pushed in and approached quietly. He noticed the black bristles scattered under a chair.

Pure soft skin, bare almost to the waist. She rolled her head to see him but didn't cover up. He sat on the bed beside her.

"I got the impression given you looked," Elina whispered.

"Anyone else would have fallen for it, but in the time you can pull that sharpened hairbrush from under the pillow, I could disarm you and stab you in the heart with it," Agosta said plainly. Elina's attention darted about the room as she attempted ambivalence.

"I-I-I don't know…what y-you're—"

"Princess, your average guard might have fallen for your slipshod seduction, but I've killed generals."

Her exposed leg fell back, and Elina began to shake.

"Settle your nerves; I'm not here for that…also…ewww," Agosta squirmed as he stood back up. "Good gods, what are you, fifteen? And besides, it's not like there's a convenient water slide at the base of the tower that would spit you into the river for an easy getaway. There are guards at the base, scattered across the yards. The gates are locked. Sewers are grated. It's not supposed to be easy to enter or exit. It's a fucking castle."

Elina noticed the door was still open, an invitation or a test, she thought. She kept under the sheets. Agosta intentionally diverted attention from her, but he knew where she was and what she was doing. She wouldn't be dumb enough to make a break for the exit, and she wasn't.

"Are you here to—"

"If I were going to, we wouldn't be talking," Agosta said. "I'm considering options."

"I'm assuming just leaving me here isn't one of them."

"No. What was it like, being here. Any visitors?"

"I've been trapped in this room for longer than I can remember. His father brought me books. We discussed the world. History."

"Why?"

"The education or the incarceration?"

"The latter."

"Guilt?" It sounded like a question, and Elina was guessing.

"Doubt that," Agosta said.

"Leverage."

"Then it backfired."

"Perhaps he was waiting until I fully matured."

"Then he's blind, as you passed that point some time ago by my guess."

"I assume he's dead. His health was failing last we talked."

"Moments away, by my guess. Succession waits for no one."

"My instinct tells me your prince lacks the empathy of a king that ordered the killing of an entire people. So, he sends you. What are your options?"

Agosta turned to her as he brushed his fingers across a few trinkets on her dresser.

"The first being what the prince ordered—your death by my hands."

Kabdila was right; she had been facing that inevitability. Confronting the truth still unnerved her. Her hand inched closer to the sharped implement.

"If so, despite your confidence," she said. "I'll make sure to give you a scar to mark the killing."

Agosta offered her an authentic grin.

"I like that," he said. "Not the scar…but your fearlessness. You're not tearful, not accepting your fate; you're still weighing your odds in a fight. Good. Never lose that. Prey caught in the jaws of a predator give up; they let themselves be devoured. Reserve your last breath to curse your fortune. But don't worry, that's not going to happen…by my or anyone else's hands." Elina wasn't sure what to do, and neither did Agosta. Elina wondered if he was waiting for her to say or do something, but Agosta took the silence to foster the bravery required to do what he had decided.

"I haven't walked out of the door you left open," she said. "you'd have to explain how I got out."

"You'd be correct; I figured I'd let you cut me above the eye, have you lock the door; I left the key in…but you wouldn't make it across the yard. You could descend into the oubliette, cross the prison into the catacombs, but assuming the guards don't catch you, you'd still never navigate the labyrinth, even with a map."

"No matter what you do, you're betraying your friend," Elina whispered. "Why?"

"I'll have to guide you through the catacombs myself," Agosta said while nodding, formulating his betrayal, "kill whoever intervenes, and get you into the hands of the nagomjii caravan parked outside."

"You still didn't answer me. It can't be honor or sympathy, not for this. Why are you helping me?"

"Because…if you can believe it, I somehow feel responsible. Not sure why or how…but I need to get you out of here."

Elina was understandably confused.

"Do I know you?" Elina asked him.

"I'm sure you'd remember," Agosta said.

"I think I certainly would. So?"

Agosta still couldn't comprehend his motivation. Truthfully, he'd never taken the life of anyone that wasn't armed and awake. That alone would have warranted a stern objection. But to do what he was considering, what he had in his heart already decided, would cross a line believed unbreakable. He never conceived of a situation that would justify such a betrayal, and now, his actions felt as much as impulse as it was calculated.

"Agosta," he said. "Agosta Pike."

TORUS

To understand it, you must know it.

To control it, you must ask it.

The moment you appreciate its power, the more it will offer you.

You must respect it, and maybe it will respect you.

I've seen it possess a vagabond and refuse a cavalier. I've seen a master fumble on a cantrip, and a novice wipe out an army. It's not so much about harnessing the power as it is coaxing it to do something in your favor. Smoke is alive. It feeds, it desires, and it hates.

To put it simply, it has to like you.

Master Pero Garius
Scrolls of Gnosis
450 AC

"We should ignore it," Kaiden said as they all observed the wrecked train.

"There may be survivors," Mannah said. "Have a heart."

"Don't have one; don't need one."

The Vanderov had slowed when Deven spotted the grounded train just under a kilometer away. Everyone had scaled to the top of the cab to garner a look. Deven still held the scope to his eyes.

"What can you see?" Terri asked.

"Medium-sized hood-class military train," Deven said. "a carrack."

"Is she still armed?"

"May I remind you that carracks are popular with pirates," Kaiden said.

"I can't see this being a threat," Noah said.

"How long do you think she's been beached?" Terri asked.

"My guess, couple days, tops," Deven answered.

"What took her to ground?" Noah asked as he descended back into the train. His eyes weren't as good, so most everything was blurred at that distance.

Deven offered Terri the scope, which she accepted and peered through. For a second, she saw *it* again, blurred but standing atop the train. Terri twisted the thumbwheel. The locomotive fell into focus, but the silhouette proved to be just a trick of the light. Terri discounted the illusion and centered on the engine, noticing it on its side with wrecked cars trailing behind. It had been painted a dark green, and unlike the Vanderov's carbody class, the hood was narrow, allowing walkways on the outside of the locomotive.

"Beast. Pirates," Kaiden said.

"Noah, find me a parallel line," Terri said.

"Way ahead, skipper," Noah said as he opened the map table and lightly placed a hand on the outer hull of the train. "Five hundred yards to a siding, a hundred to another, and you'll be two lines aside."

In its prime, the derailed train was angular and gaunt to the Vanderov's sleek shape. It took several minutes circling wide until the train finally approached the wreck. There were no nearby connecting lines, and the Vanderov slowed to a stop with two sets of rails between them and the grounded carrack.

From the opened side door emerged Kaiden brandishing his 10-gauge coach gun. Terri's flintlocks were holstered, same with Deven's percussion revolver rifle and Noah's nine-barreled pepperbox pistol. Mannah followed unarmed.

"You coming, Tooley?" Deven asked.

"Carracks require six tank hydrocells, same as us," Mannah said. "You'll need me to extract them."

"Very good. Be a dear and lock up, please," Terri said.

Mannah closed the hatch and locked the train.

The group crossed the tracks towards the fallen carack. Noah found a few stones on a rail and instinctually brushed them off out of respect. He stopped and felt the iron. There was a vibration he couldn't identify. Something felt odd, but he didn't know why. He stood quickly, staring deep into the tracklands.

"Noah," Terri said as she stopped. "You just perked your ears like an alarmed pet."

"Thought I felt something," Noah said.

Terri shrugged.

"Keep 'em perked then," she said.

The grounded carrack was in poor shape, with dozens of scores and grooves along the locomotive. It had fallen on its side with its nose still on the track, but there wasn't a skid trail behind it. A carrack boasted eight weapon turrets, four per side, not counting the heavy mount on the nose. If there had been weapons, they had been destroyed or removed. Deven scaled atop the train to inspect the damage.

"Got a name, skipper," Deven said. "It's the Kansal Crawler."

"Well, it's not a pirate car," Terri said. "I know the Crawler. That's Tomlin Ackerman's stock."

"You know him?" Noah asked.

"Of him. Hadn't seen him in years, but that's the life."

"What's with this surface damage?" Deven asked.

"Wear," Kaiden said as he circled the train. "Passed through a storm, maybe."

"No storm this severe," Noah said. "I think she drove through a blender."

"Three cars," Kaiden said. "Last one's shredded."

"I remember her having more," Terri said.

Noah climbed up to join Deven, and they examined the scene from their vantage.

"I don't know what derailed her," Noah said, "but I do know what it wasn't. No bends or catch points in the line. I don't see a derailer."

"Impact?" Terri asked.

"Outside of surface damage, no. It's like something just picked up the train and tossed it off its track."

No one was happy hearing that theory, and an uncomfortable silence passed before Terri finally approached the locomotive door. It had suffered so much damage that forcing the lock open was easy. Terri dropped into the cab while Mannah followed. Broken parts lay scattered through the interior, and Mannah had to push aside obstructions to access the engine. She pulled open a few hatches and found the ten-kilogram brass spheres still wired to the engine.

"Tanks are intact," Mannah shouted.

"Okay, get them out," Terri said. "Let's not stay any longer than we have to."

Noah dropped in and investigated the train's interior along with Terri. Mannah knew how to handle hydrocells, but Terri was still unnerved as her tooley casually rolled the expensive batteries out of the engine bay.

"Skipper!" Noah said from the back of the train. Mannah focused on her work while Terri ran to Noah, noticing the body lumped in the corner.

"Shit…get Deven," she said.

All too often, loginoids and zodiacs were associated, but while the former was a product of technology, the latter was a product of magic. Both featured metallic shells, though the loginoid was composed of thousands of floating parts, and the zodiac, like the one Terri was staring down at, sat within a bespoke powered suit it relied on to survive.

A zodiac was more closely related to an effigy as they were both powered by magic and were likely echoes from the past, though it was a lot more noticeable with the zodiacs.

Legends persisted even today regarding how advanced the Iokon Caliphate was before being struck down, claiming that they had achieved more before the Collapse than the survivors had in the subsequent fifteen hundred years. This was all but confirmed, given the rare out-of-place artifacts scattered everywhere.

The most astonishing relic from that forgotten age was the zodiacs. Terri had seen them before but was aware most of her crew hadn't. So, it was not a shock seeing a dead human kept alive via a combination of magic and technology within a suit of powered armor the soul was permanently trapped in.

It was known as a scaffold—a cutting-edge augmentation suit developed by the Iokon military in a conflict against an opponent no one could remember. The zodiac was intended to keep living soldiers alive in dire combat situations.

The technology was perhaps a bit too good. After dying, either through combat or natural causes, the scaffold kept them alive, the smoke having imbued into their bodies and melded them to their exoskeleton. The armor would now have to be surgically removed and, if so, would undoubtedly kill the human within. The scaffold was committed to keeping its host alive at any cost. While keeping a target brain alive, its capacity to regenerate physical wounds was limited, proven by the state of the corpse lying in the carrack. Its face and body had shriveled like a fruit in the sun. The derailment must have severed their arm, and it was lying bloodless next to the body.

It was relatively easy to judge how much action a zodiac had seen by the state of its contained body. She had seen them with only scars while another paraded about as little more than a skeleton with a preserved brain.

The scaffold adapted the best it could. This one had hooked skin to keep it tethered to the body and drilled braces into bones to prevent the skeleton from collapsing. While some scaffolds covered the internals, even offering a tinted helmet to conceal one's identity, this one presented the withering corpse within. A long beige leather duster would have provided some cover if the creature had been standing and alert.

This scaffold was flush to the zodiac's skin, partially merged with the body's remains. To say a zodiac's appearance could be terrifying was putting it mildly.

Terri barely flinched compared to Noah, who was still startled when he received the order to fetch Deven. When they returned, Deven's response was predictable.

"What did you need, skip—holy SHIT!" Deven said, staring at the partially shriveled corpse resting on the floor of the conductor's office at the back of the train.

"You're a doctor; treat him," Terri said plainly.

"I'm a medic—" Deven said.

"Close enough; treat him."

"Are you serious? This man is dead."

"Well, that's racist," the corpse announced.

Deven's jaw fell slack as the zodiac clutched his open, dry arm stump.

"Figured you were still ali…operational," Terri said.

"I'm fine; I can walk it off," he said.

"In Iokon's name!" Deven said, stepping back from the living dead.

"First time?" Terri asked jokingly.

"I'm not a mortician!"

"You're a doctor—medic—whatever, the best we got. I trust your talent to work miracles."

"Are you seriously shitting me, skipper? I-I wouldn't know where to begin."

"I'm not expecting miracles," the zodiac said.

"Ok…I just have…one question." Deven examined the body. "What did you look like before?"

"Just attach the arm," Terri said.

"Yeah…sure…I guess I'll… sew it back on."

"Sutures will work," the zodiac said. "The scaffold will do the rest."

"Are you part of Ackerman's crew?" Terri asked while Deven went to work.

"Wisekjii," they said, "their ashcat. I was inside the drive when it happened."

"And Ackerman?"

"By the time I crawled out, gone. All of 'em."

"Did you see what happened?"

Deven didn't bother using antiseptic and had to ignore that the hand of the severed limb was gesturing while Wisekjii talked.

"I just remember something jostling the cab," Wisekjii said, "then it felt like I was in a tumble dryer."

"A tornado?" Noah asked. His tone conveyed familiarity, like something he had heard before but wasn't sure where.

"Fairly specific strike for one. It sucked all the air out of the can."

Terri stuck her head out of the office as Mannah kicked another tank hydrocell from the train.

"Tooley, is she salvageable?" Terri asked.

Mannah brushed the dust off her coveralls and approached, entering the cabin.

"Potentially, I mean—oh cool, zodiac—anyway, if we get her back up on her rails, potentially. Most cars are lost, but we'd have to call for a hook. We don't have the hardware to lift something as big as this."

Terri turned back to Wisekjii as Deven finished stitching his arm back into the scaffold. The living machine ejected tiny metallic tentacles that wove into the limb to fasten it back to the body and inject life into it. Deven stepped back.

"Repairable if you want to claim it," Terri said. "We'll abandon our right."

"Skipper?" Mannah asked.

"It's in the code. Not much to salvage from the three cars, mind you."

"Appreciated," Wisekjii said as he struggled to stand. "But no. Take what you can. And if possible, me as well."

Out of anyone's perception, Noah spun quickly as he heard something no one else could hear. He stalked across the train, knelt, and felt the base of the derailed carrack

"Are you sure?" Terri asked. "Kansal Crawler's got a reputation."

"I'm muscle, not a conductor," Wisekjii said.

"Very good," Terri said. "We'll take you back to Corvos at least. We'll decide then."

"Skipper!" Noah said. "Problem." Terri stepped out and approached Noah. "Incoming."

"On this line?" Terri asked. She screamed out of the train. "Kaiden. Get out the flags! See if you can stop her."

"Too heavy to be corsair or caravel," Noah whispered. Something didn't feel right. The vibration didn't make sense. It used the rail, but it didn't feel like a train. It was a monster on wheels.

"Let's move," Terri said, "Deven, see to Wise—Wisek—the zodiac. Get those tanks out of there, Mannah!"

Mannah dove back into the engine bay and rolled out another hydrocell.

"Leave the rest, Mannah; we need to go!" Terri said.

"There's only one left!" Mannah said.

Terri climbed out of the carrack with Noah and Deven helping Wisekjii from the train.

Terri pulled Deven's scope from his belt as he passed and peered down the track.

There was no horizon given the curve of the Torus, but there were still limits on what one could focus on, with distortions caused by heat and weather.

But Terri could see what should have been impossible.

"In fuck's name," she whispered to herself.

"What do you see?" Noah asked.

"A demon from the underworld."

Volani, the builders of nearly every groundmover, claimed the Colossus was seen on the tracks before the population ever left their ark. Its design appeared antithetical to common or even archaic practices. An iron-clad black wedge-shaped engine trailed by fifty cars and none with windows.

"Time! To! Go!" Terri shouted back into the cab. Noah, Deven, and Wisekjii reached the ground and bolted across the rails.

"What is that?" Deven asked.

The Colossus was a legend, appearing without anyone noticing a destination or a point of origin. It had been seen pulverizing buildings and pushing through rockslides.

With no brakes of any kind being found, it was clear the Colossus was not meant to ever stop or even slow. Some considered it a ghost train or the devil if assuming Nimbus was a God. Myth claimed the Colossus only manifested once every few years. The last attempt to board resulted in the expedition disappearing, save one survivor who claimed they heard voices from inside the train speak their names before being jolted off. When the survivor came to, his team and the Colossus were gone.

"Only one tank left," Mannah shouted as she removed the last hydrocell.

"Out of there, Tooley!" Terri said.

"She's not slowing skipper!" Kaiden said as he cleared the tracks, leaving only Terri and Mannah still on the train.

"She won't. Mannah!" Terri shouted back into the train. Mannah appeared and threw the tank out of the door. Terri could feel the vibrations of the Colossus. The tremors carried a sound akin to an animal's growl.

Mannah climbed but slipped as she tried to use the conductor chair as a step. She fell back with the chair breaking and falling upon her. Terri glimpsed the lightless, lifeless stygian juggernaut screaming towards them, juggernaut screaming towards them, five times the height and twice the width of the Vanderov.

"Just go!" Mannah shouted as she desperately tried to push the chair off her. Terri dropped back down into the train. "What are you doing, skipper?!"

"What anyone should do," Terri said as she dragged the chair off her. She yanked Mannah to her feet and pushed her up to the open hatch.

It wasn't a gentle stock; the Colossus was a ten-storey-tall, fifty-thousand-ton battering ram attached to a skyscraper that unsettled rocks and vibrated railroad spikes from the ground.

Mannah reached the top of the carrack, finally staring at the behemoth as it encompassed her entire vision. She was nearly frozen in fear.

"Damn it! Get out of there!" Noah said.

Mannah snapped back to reality and reached into the train to grab Terri as she leaped up.

The growl had escalated to a deafening roar.

The two jumped from atop the train, then bolted across the track.

The Colossus forced its way past them, tossing the carrack off the rail like a toothpick.

The train toppled nose over tail like a toy, tearing free from the cars behind it.

The group had fallen on the side of the track watching the Colossus thunder by.

"Son of a bitch!" Kaiden said.

Mannah couldn't help but giggle.

"How is this funny, Mannah?!" Noah said.

"We're alive, aren't we? Another story to tell our offspring." The group stood as the last car passed them.

"The devil makes its presence," Deven said. "Our journey is cursed."

"It's merging with our line," Noah said.

"We should take another route."

"I'm not one for superstition," Terri said as the Colossus distorted in the heat of the desert. "…but…maybe in this situation, it wouldn't hurt taking a longer course. Noah?"

"There's a siding one kilometer along this line," Noah said as he felt the rails around him. "Take that. Merges with a tangent that will take us to Corvos. Adds a day, maybe two."

"I'll take it," Terri said as she returned to the undamaged Vanderov. "Better than tailing a curse."

"Well, we will pass through the Graveyard of Black Church."

Terri stopped and swiveled back.

"Aaand we're back to tailing the curse."

"I'd rather roll the dice with the devil I don't know that tug the tail of the devil I do," Wisekjii said.

The rest of the group all stared confusedly at the zodiac.

"What?" Deven asked.

PARADISE

Alchemists would be easy to spot if the ingredients included eyeballs and virgin blood. Instead, many of the expensive components set their price from simple scarcity.

I heard of one potent concoction requiring something called actinium-225. It's hard enough to find ginseng in this world. To complicate matters, the alchemists never implemented a standardization of vernacular, and a system was only finally enforced 550 years ago, with some traditional mixers still employing the old names.

Every blasted ingredient has to be "of" something. It's called lead, you fools. Stop adding syllables.

Doctor Hennessey Faulkner.
The Proto-Pharmaceutical

It was certainly an interesting few days for Terri. When the herd migrated to the Luminance of Deos for the royal procession, she couldn't help but follow. Afterward, ignoring that brief moment where she endangered herself by forgetting to kowtow, crowds dispersed to celebrate under Philokalia's shadow. She took the afternoon to acquire needed supplies for the hours of study she was expected to finish in a sewer basement.

The festivities were interrupted only temporarily by the deafening boom of an explosion. Terri had been shopping in the adjacent market when it happened, and like everyone else, she ran out to investigate what had happened. It wasn't long before she discovered the handiwork of the purgitans; despair diminished slightly when word rang out that one of the Episcar Knights had perished in the blast. Merriment returned within the hour, as no one would be denied their recreation.

Later that evening, Ascension-approved fireworks brightened the market, dancing picked up, and the revelry didn't subside until morning. She was young and lively but never one for large gatherings. Before she retired, Terri heard a final announcement shouted by a local newsreader, his booming voice proclaiming that the cable cars between the two worlds would cease functioning within the hour.

When she awoke the first morning after Passover, Philokalia had nearly cleared the city, continuing its predictable migration eastward. In a few months, it would cross near the pillar of Nubuwwah that led to the minuscule world of Kerberos before entering the Mara Dagos, the immense ocean the single landmass of Bythos sat within. Before that, sometime in the next two days, mount Astran, taller than the Philokalia pillar, would skim by the top of Mount Klairapliedee, and the two worlds would be only a few meters apart.

Terri knew when the shadow finally passed, every corner of the city would be illuminated again, and it was best she return to Corvos by the end of the week. She wanted Kaiden to accompany her and never fully understood his desire to remain despite what he had told her. *Something was compelling him to remain*, she thought. Terri had decided to make one final plea to convince him to return with her.

She had been away since the previous afternoon. More guards stood outside the church entrance, though the alley was still open. Terri kept close to the walls, acted casual when in the clear, and ducked past the corner as attention diverted away. The hatch was still sealed.

Kaiden was notorious for being stubborn. His family line also carried blood to royalty tied to the kingdom. His mother had married into the Sivoy state, previously a member of the Aedis family, currently controlling a namesake coastal town bordering the Body of Tyrus. Aedis was once in control of the entire Kingdom of Aurago, losing it to the House of Raddad when the Ascension determined that Raddad had the greater claim to the throne when the Aedis king died. Kaiden wasn't for politics, so pride certainly wasn't an issue.

Sadatoni was more interesting, she remembered him saying. It was his commitment to bear witness to what he thought would be the crumbling of an empire due to the weight of logic. As if the Aegis would ever let wisdom prevail in a kingdom as insane as Aurago.

It wouldn't matter.

The bags of supplies gathered from the previous day fell from her grasp.

The laboratory had been torn apart, desks shattered, and paperwork was strewn everywhere. Shelves had collapsed. Terri couldn't make out a square inch of ground under the debris. She let herself be taken in by shock for only an instant before desperately pawing at the rubble.

"Kaiden. Kaiden!"

Despite Kaiden's previous warning that the lab was soundproof, she was as loud as she would allow herself without alerting those above. Most of the artifacts Kaiden had recovered were still present, scattered, and broken across the mess.

She found the book, first noticing the cover—the five-pointed star sitting within an expanding spiral. It sat among the rubble. Terri cleared it from the debris and inspected the damage.

It had taken a deep cut on the cover. From corner to corner, all the way through the leather. The interior was still intact.

Terri whispered to herself, "it doesn't make any sense."

She was correct; purgitans would have taken everything, not destroyed the entire room, and leave the garbage to be recovered. And nothing had been taken.

Then Terri found him.

She was hoping he had escaped or been away. Terri first spotted a bloodied hand from under the debris, half under a fallen bookshelf. She collapsed next to him, pushed the shelf off, then cleared what was covering him.

Kaiden Sivoy's body was carved with a thousand knives. Terri fell back but quickly recovered. She knelt forward and verified what she already knew.

A dozen random thoughts flooded her mind. Had she inadvertently led purgitans here? Did the rector in the church above them follow her? Did the nagomjii execute him for crimes only they knew he committed? Terri even entertained the possibility that Kaiden had done this so to himself—an experiment gone awry. Perhaps the shaper had come alive and butchered him. She had yet to locate it.

No, she thought. *This wasn't an execution.*

This was savagery like a wild animal had run rampant through the lab…a beast that somehow made it inside and left without leaving a trace other than the damage it had inflicted—no tufts of fur or broken claws.

Terri was not entirely proficient in the criminal sciences, but she could tell immediately that whatever killed Kaiden had done so not long after she had left the previous day.

One thing she knew, her arrival was not a coincidence. Her academic background had to consider the possibility that it was. It could have been blind chance. But Terri couldn't believe it. There had to be a correlation; she just needed to find out what it was.

"What in the gods happened here?" Noah asked.

Terri's head twisted to find the Ascension lacky standing at the door. She jumped to her feet and approached aggressively.

"Did you do this?" she asked. "DID YOU DO THIS!?"

Noah kept his composure and stood his ground.

"If I did, would I stand here alone?" he asked.

Terri knew she wasn't armed, but Noah likely was, though the latter offered no indication he was reaching for anything. Instead, Noah raised his hands, and Terri stopped.

"Your people," Terri said, "even when your hands are clean, they've got blood!"

"They would have taken everything of value and burned the rest. Parade him before execution, not butcher him and leave."

"Doesn't explain why you're here."

Noah lowered his arms.

"Elise Price, the diaconate rector above you," he said.

"Son of a bitch!"

"I'm here alone. I wanted to investigate this privately. They found a faulty lens, part of a microscope, in the trash. You didn't lead anyone here; it was filed two weeks ago."

Terri turned back to Kaiden's body, knelt beside him, and closed his eyes.

"A genius and a fool," she said.

"…who thoughtlessly tossed forbidden knowledge in the public refuse," Noah said, which prompted Terri to jump back up. Noah stepped back and threw his hands up again. "Hey, I'm not overlooking his obvious intelligence! But keeping secret knowledge does entail a modicum of precautions to be observed."

Terri's hostility faded slightly, and she exhaled. Noah examined the destruction around the room.

"I'll ask again—" Noah said.

"I don't know; it was like this." Terri wandered the room again. "I only arrived moments ago."

"What was he doing?"

Terri confronted Noah, still with a measure of belligerence.

"He was learning," she said. "Something you wouldn't understand."

"I assume you'll spot the difference between a purgitan and a proctor. I don't destroy knowledge; I seek it."

"You hoard it. Keeping proof that your gods don't hold dominion over everything."

"When you're curious and clever, they don't offer a lot of options. Be punished or become a proctor. Trust me; I understand more of this universe than you can ever care to forget."

"Doesn't alter the fact that you became a sycophant for zealots and despots."

"I joined to escape a life of violence."

"I call that irony."

"Call it what you will. I won't apologize for the choices made. I wouldn't expect likewise."

Terri wandered through the wreckage until she found an appropriate cover, a blanket from his unkempt bed. She draped it over her friend. She knelt beside him and softly placed her hand over his head.

"I'm sorry," she whispered. Noah let Terri have her moment and kept his distance. She eventually stood back up and wiped a tear from her eye.

"I'll ensure his remains are respected," Noah said.

"Before his name is tarnished," Terri said without facing Noah.

"We can avoid that. Whatever happened here destroyed most evidence anyway. I can guarantee—"

"I'll take his body back to Corvos. It wasn't his home, but it's where he'll be respected."

"We can arrange that."

"*We*? Why help?" she asked.

"I'm a proctor, not a purgitan," he said. "I can respect a man's pursuit of truth."

"But I saw you with an entourage. Where are they?"

"Seeing to the church above. Interviewing, paying respects. Accepting tax."

"Bribes."

"They've no idea. I noticed you ducking into the alley." Terri hadn't seen Noah. She had been so careful. If Kaiden hadn't been killed, she still would have presented him on a platter. Despite the situation, it still upset her. "Trust me; anyone else would have missed it. But…I saw you during the parade. Call the rest instinct."

"Why?" Terri asked.

"I felt maybe we'd met before."

"I wouldn't have remembered."

Noah orbited the room, placing his steps carefully while Terri watched. Noah noted the gashes and slices across the brick walls. Terri approached her dead friend, the glint in his firmed grasp— catching her attention. He had held onto it despite losing two fingers defending himself.

Terri peeled the remaining fingers back and removed the shaper. It looked undamaged, pristine, without blemish, let alone blood.

"A shaper," Noah said. Terri wasn't about to hand anything over, regardless of the situation. She was ready for a fight.

"Don't even think about it," she said.

"We've got at least five in the crypt. Not sure of their type. That would have been enough to convict him." Noah threw out a hand. "I'll take that."

"Oh, you will, will you?"

"Your best and wisest course of action would involve you leaving, alone, empty-handed. Let me document this. I can confiscate the lot and take it back to the vault. Nothing will be burned. You can book a whale back to Corvos, and I'll ensure his body is delivered before you depart."

"I'll just hang onto it," Terri said as she dropped the sphere into her jacket pocket, leaving a very telltale bulge. "He left this knowledge to me—all of it. You best go back up and say you found nothing. Lie, I'm sure you're good at that."

"Are you willing to at least believe me when I say I wasn't responsible for this?" Noah said. "Feels like a mild overreaction on anyone's part. This is not some measured response. This was pure rage."

Noah had noted cuts in the brick walls but only then discovered it was on every surface. Every shelf had broken, every beaker shattered. Many of the cuts on Kaiden's body were post-mortem.

"A spell, perhaps," Terri whispered.

"Was he an abecedarian?" Noah asked.

"Not while he was in Corvos; he certainly was capable."

Noah kicked over a few books and knelt to scrutinize a few, rifling through scattered papers. No point organizing any of this now. He lobbed a few tomes aside to dig further in the mess. Lots of notes in the native tongue. Schematics, many he recognized, most illegal.

"I don't see any cryptions," he said. "No albums. Nothing indicative of proto-script." Noah hoped he would find something, not for incrimination but for study. He had heard of mages able to master the magic that broke the reality of the great machine. But perhaps it wasn't a failure; maybe it was the plan, something the Aegis resisted? He knew of the name before joining the proctors. Abecedarian. It had a scholarly origin. Noah's life might have been different if they had found him before the church. There were numerous volumes and cryption albums from executed spellcasters within the crypt, and Noah read them when opportunities presented themselves. However, the practice required ingredients, specific papers and ink; as those were vulnerable, most were destroyed rather than entombed. It also necessitated a teacher, and those were few and not open to advertise.

Noah spotted that one book Terri kept under her arm. It was the single most significant book in the room and was in the best condition despite recent damage.

"What's that?" he asked.

"It's called a book," Terri said, both of them initially ignoring the fluttering papers in the corner of the room.

"That almost looks like—"

"An Iokon Apoc, I know. It's not. It's something more."

"May I?" he asked. Terri was not about hand over anything. She just gave him a dead stare. Noah shrugged. "Look, in an even fight, I'm fairly certain you can take me."

"Do you want to test that?" she asked.

"Given the situation, I'd rather not to be a victim if your misplaced aggression. But with the book, at least from my vantage, it appears he held it up to defend himself. Such a clean-cut, it had to have been a quick strike or a very sharp weapon. It certainly wasn't a claw or bite, if you're curious."

It started as twirling chunks of garbage—broken plates and torn books.

As the entity formed, it gathered the broken beakers and writing utensils.

Noah noticed it first and took a step back.

He grabbed Terri's shoulder to draw her attention.

She followed Noah's eyes, and they faced the thing as it had gathered enough errant garbage to form an irregular torso, then a head occupied by an oversized circular maw of spinning blades for teeth.

"Shit," Terri mumbled.

"Let's get out of here," Noah whispered.

"What is that?"

Noah, with quicker reflexes, pulled Terri away as the creature formed an arm and lunged forward.

The limb of constantly undulating debris connected with the broken desk and torn it to shreds, the fragments being drawn inwards to bolster the body.

The two fled from the laboratory.

They took only a fleeting glance back as the entity absorbed more of the surrounding fragments of broken machines and forbidden technology, though leaving a nearby potted plant undamaged.

They escaped to the ladder.

Noah pushed Terri in front, and they scaled quickly as the living vortex of garbage came around the corner.

Neither of them bothered to look back.

Terri pushed the sewer hatch off, tossed the codex on the pavement, and leaped from the entrance.

She spun back and pulled Noah from the tunnel.

They both pushed the cover back and stepped away, waiting for something to leap from the ground.

…but nothing did.

Noah pulled Terri away, and they raced to exit the alleyway. Terri diverted to grab the book.

"What in the name of serious fuck was that?!" she said.

"I don't know," Noah said. "I'm an archivist with Altair, so I've seen documents on everything that's crawled, swam, or flew across every world, and I've never read about anything like that."

They reached the alley's exit, and Terri fell back against the wall to relax. It was minutes past dawn, and Philokalia's mass had mostly eclipsed Uno, blanketing the city in shadow for the last time. It wouldn't last as a sliver of light was still jutting from the planet's western crest.

For Terri, she couldn't help but acknowledge what Noah had said, that there was something familiar about him, even when she first spotted him at the parade.

"There's something wrong here," Noah said.

"With what, that my close friend was just murdered by an animated pile of garbage or the fact that I just happened to have been caught red-handed with heretical technology by the one faithless priest in Sadatoni?

"Once again, I'm an archivist, not a priest. I don't quote scripture and can't remember the last time I prayed."

"Did you take an oath to serve the Aegis and enforce the policy of the Ascension? If so, then I find it difficult to differentiate. You should turn me in…why aren't you?"

With the planet above finally moving on, many others were visible—Kerberos, Grimaldi, and Abraxas, the latter being the mirror world where their supposed gods resided. The heaven ring it rode across was visible. Noah observed the mechanical universe around him. In time, Philokalia would soon block the godly sphere again as the latter ascended into the sky.

He was faithless…at least he was per the definition classified by his seniors. He navigated the system the best he could. He fell into the crypt and found purpose. He would find, or they would present, a mystery. He would document it, categorize it, and even on occasion, solve it. Many proctors were like that, even those he answered to. There were exceptions, those witless radicals that toed the line. They were buzzkills at parties.

For the rest, as long the proctors sequestered dangerous devices and prohibited magic, they were offered a generous amount of leniency. And the more successful you were, the more flexibility and freedom you were allowed. Once Noah discovered this, it became his doctrine.

He had signed off on some of the crypt's most dangerous artifacts. Duro's Chalk of Annihilation. The Choker of Bontrager. The Gomji Herald. The Human Slayer sword. The Periapt of Elsewhere. Prymula's Skeleton. Seward's Thumper. All his, and not all were simply procurements. A few required the aforementioned violence he was so much against.

"Because ignorance is the greater danger," he said. And I will not be a tool of the zealotry."

TORUS

Has anyone asked why it's called Iokon? The Ascension ruled the Metropolis, and recovered documents refer to the ancient "Iokons."

Were the members of the Ascension these Iokons, or was the entire population considered that? My comrades and I agree that the Ascension was populated by regular people, but was there a hidden class above them, and were these the Iokons?

If so....where are they?

Dr. Nicol Corella
Corvos University
1403 AC

Elina cracked one eye open and smiled upon seeing Agosta and Sloan sleeping with partially interlocked fingers.

The sun had crested from behind Nimbus and was diffused through the graveyard's fog. The light cast virtually no shadows across the city save for one that encroached upon the skip.

Elina was the only one awake. She turned and smiled.

"Hi, Shadow," she whispered.

The other two awoke.

Agosta felt Sloan's fingers pressing against his only briefly, then jolted, noticing his daughter was missing.

"ELINA!?" he said.

Sloan flinched awake and jumped to her feet. Agosta's attention was on the city.

Sloan's attention temporarily shifted down and spotted another illustration Elina had made—that same shadowy figure.

"Elina! Elina!" Agosta said, leaping out of the skip. He ran down the tracks.

"I thought she no longer did this?" Sloan said as she followed him.

"Damned graveyard, Elina!"

Agosta was breaking down, fearing the worst. Sloan was acting more composed and was carefully scanning the environment.

"I can't believe this!" Agosta said, grabbing his head. "Not again! Elina!"

Sloan pulled Agosta close and held his face, staring deep into him.

"Hey. It's going to be fine. She left under her own volition, or she would've screamed. We'll find her." Agosta slowed his breathing and settled. He placed his hand over hers and nodded.

They focused on the environment and scrutinized what they could see, limited by the haze and blocked by the crumbling ruins.

"Have to assume she would continue ahead and not backtrack," Agosta said as they hurried down the rails, eventually reaching a fork in the tracks. They stopped. "We may have to split up."

"I don't think so…" Sloan said, staring down one of the tracks that descended over the hill.

"Elina!" Agosta said to the silhouette in the distance.

As they approached, the figure rotated.

"Hey, Dad!" Elina said.

Agosta reached her and hunched over from fatigue.

"What are you doing?!" he said.

"Waiting," she said.

"Waiting for what?"

"Your guardian?" Sloan asked.

"No," Elina said, "he's gone."

Agosta held his daughter firmly.

"It's not safe out here," he gasped.

"We weren't, we aren't, but we will be," Elina said.

"So, you did see him," Sloan said. Elina nodded. "You found your boogeyman and made friends with it. Did it tell you to wait here?"

"This is where it was standing when it vanished," she said.

"You probably saw something in the fog that resembled the creature in your drawings," Agosta said. "It could have been a predator, a bandit.

"I think I'd know the difference, Dad."

"But was it worth the risk?" he said.

"Compared to the risk of not following its advice, I thought we've been through this."

"She's got you there," Sloan said cheekily.

"Are you taking her side?" Agosta asked.

"Yes…I am."

"See?" Elina said.

Agosta pointed sharply at Sloan, ignoring his daughter.

"You're not helping!" he said.

"She's got a gift," Sloan said. "Put some faith in her."

"It's not about faith or gifts; it's about keeping her safe."

"Bickering parents," Elina said, "you're two are adorable."

"We're not—" Agosta said.

"Bickering," Sloan said, staring at Agosta with a swelling grin. "That was it, right?

"This track leads us down the wrong path," Agosta said, then pointed behind them. "We need to be headed that way; otherwise, this was all a waste of time."

"Was it?" Sloan said, goading.

"We have to wait," Elina said.

"For?" Sloan asked.

The bellow of the incoming train intensified. It was approaching fast. Elina pointed down the tracks.

"That," she said as a red and gold bullet-shaped carbody burst from the distant haze.

Agosta pulled Elina and Sloan aside as the train locked its brakes and skidded to a crawl, drifting slowly past the three of them until finally stopping by the CIC cab.

Agosta and Sloan slowly stood up. Elina was practically giddy. The adults let their eyes wander down the clean lines of the exquisite machine. It had suffered some surface damage but was loved by its owners.

A door swung open, prompting Agosta to unlatch his firearms.

Elina placed a hand on his.

"It's okay, Dad," she whispered.

A dark-skinned woman emerged from the cab, unarmed but unimpressed, given her executive officer had enacted the sudden break without warning, causing her to spill hot tea on her shirt. The stain was apparent and hot.

"Hello!? Agosta shouted to carry the distance between them and the open train door.

Terri unceremoniously held her soaking hand out in the open, trying to dry off. A hand connected to an unseen crew member handed her a towel, which she accepted.

"Morning!" Terri said.

"Captain Agosta Pike, Corvos. Switchmen Union!"

"CIC Terri Zahn, Independent Transport Union, Vanderov Express! RBX-888! What the nine hells are you doing in the graveyard?!"

Sloan and Elina stepped up beside Agosta.

Sloan smirked and sarcastically shouted, "Oh, is that where we are?!"

"We derailed!" Agosta said. "About two days back, on our way to Ragged Hollow!"

"We're not heading to Ragged Hollow!" Terri said. "No one purposely heads to Ragged Hollow!"

Sloan whispered to Agosta, "You were going there to drop me off."

"Are we still?" he asked back without looking at her. She stared impassively back.

"What do you think?" she asked quietly.

"Corvos happens to be our destination!" Terri said.

"That's fortunate if you're willing to be charitable!" Agosta said. "As you might be able to tell, I'm not endowed with an overabundance of currency!"

"Wait," Sloan whispered. "where's the rest of my compensation?"

"I'm not including that among my assets."

"Mitigating circumstances; we may not have an alternative."

"We seem to be in the habit of procuring stragglers!" Terri said. "If you pull your weight, you can ride on gratis! It's better than staying here!"

Agosta nodded.

Behind Terri, Kaiden approached. Agosta noticed the bizarre sight of a loginoid crewmember but didn't articulate any reaction.

"You trusting them?" Kaiden asked. Terri shrugged.

"Do I have a reason not to?" Terri asked out of the corner of her mouth. "I got a feeling." She addressed Agosta again. "Just to be clear, it's just the three!? Who was the CIC of your train!?"

"Machus, of the Loch & Serpent!" Agosta said. "I didn't get his full name!"

"Don't think he has one!"

"Neither he nor his train survived!"

"I know him…it's no loss! You'll need to surrender any weapons! If you work hard, you can play hard! But just like a boat, don't make any waves! If you upset the balance, we offset it by throwing you to the ground! This train's reputation, like its engine, is ironclad! We don't abide rust! Understood?!"

"Understood!" Agosta said, and he and the others made for the train.

"That's a great speech; you nailed that one," Noah said from behind Terri, who turned back and whispered.

"Didn't have time to practice it. It felt a little flat."

"No. Not in the slightest."

"This is unexpected, skipper," Kaiden said. "First, the zodiac. Why the generosity?

"It's a character flaw," Terri said.

"Hardly...what is it?"

"Nothing," Terri said, "…just a feeling."

"If this is going to be a pattern moving forward," Deven said from further back in the train, "can we get a pet?"

The rest of the crew ignored him.

The three boarded through the rear cab door, and Agosta counted the strangers awaiting him.

"Thank you, CIC," Agosta said. Terri nodded. "I appreciate the hospit—HOLY SHIT."

"I get that a lot," Wisekjii said.

"This is," Terri said but trailed off. "…how do you pronounce your name, again?"

"*Wi-zek-jee.*"

"This is a zodiac."

"Sorry," Agosta said, "Just…not expecting—"

"Dad, don't stare; it's rude," Elina said.

"It's a reasonable response," Wisekjii said. "It's why I avoid mirrors."

"Mr. Serenda," Terri said, "why don't you make room in the spare cabins?"

Deven nodded and left the car.

Then came the awkward silence as they all stared at each other until Terri finally broke it with, "your weapons..."

Agosta nodded, unlocked his belt, and handed his firearms to an accepting Kaiden, who held out his hand to Sloan, waiting for the sword. Sloan simply stared back.

"Hi…" she said plainly.

"She's effigy, Noah," Terri said. "She can keep her blade." Noah nodded, then departed to lock the weapons in the safe. "And the rest loosen up; it's not a classroom. Mannah, get us moving. Captain Pike, we'll talk in my cabin."

* * *

Terri started another pot of boiling water and didn't ask, setting cups for her and Agosta along with sugar and milk. Agosta nodded without saying anything, sitting next to the cup while Terri prepared the tea.

"Nice stock you got here," Agosta said, looking over the build. "Old but…classic. Knew how to build them. Brass Traction Railworks, carbody X4?" Terri nodded. "She about a century?"

"One hundred and fourteen," Terri said.

"I noticed the plaque, Vanderov?"

"We just call it the Van."

"What's the origin of that?"

"I got no idea," Terri said with a chuckle. "Someone probably thought of the nickname and worked backward from there." Terri let the silence simmer before changing the topic. "As for you…no shortcut justifies cutting through Black Church unless you're incredibly dumb."

"*You* found us here," Agosta said.

"We're incredibly dumb, but we have a train and a *go-to* attitude."

"Once we reach Corvos, I'll have access to additional funds."

"I offered gratis, but I certainly won't decline donations."

"It's appreciated," Agosta said as Terri placed a bowl of loose leaves and a pair of infusers in the center of the table.

"By the way," she said, "you don't look like you're from Corvos."

"Ignoring the discriminatory wording, your talent for the obvious is without reproach."

"I'm from Corvos."

Agosta spooned leaves into his diffusor.

"Could have fooled me," he said.

Terri smirked faintly.

"I should introduce you to my first mate; you two would get along. But we're not discussing me," she said. The kettle whistled, and Terri filled their cups with hot water.

"Semantics?"

"Just trying to judge character."

"And my origin matters?"

"Honesty matters."

"I've lived there since I was five. It's called moving."

They both removed their infusers. Agosta added several spoons of sugar and a drop of cream, which Terri watched but didn't replicate.

"What were you doing out here?" Agosta asked.

"Contract. Retrieval." Terri said. They began drinking.

"Me too."

"Should I ask…or rather should I know?"

"Family."

"She doesn't look like you," she said.

"Don't miss much, do you…is that required?"

"Point," Terri said. "Custody spat?"

"Kidnapping."

"Extortion? Slavery?"

"Both."

"Bad guys."

"Very."

The radio clicked on with Mannah announcing, "CIC, engine—cruising at notch four. Everything's in the green. Going to eat."

Terri reached over and activated the intercom.

“Confirm. Make sure the kid has something. And don’t touch my sandwich.”

“Yes, on the first, no promises on the second.” The radio clicked off.

Terri had another sip, simpered, then reached into a nearby cabinet for a flask of alcohol. She topped up her cup and offered it to Agosta.

“Shit. Yes. Thank you,” Agosta said with a chuckle.

Terri filled their cups.

“So, that explains you and the girl. What of the effigy?” she asked.

“Trustworthy,” Agosta answered.

“Are you typically this cagey, or do you always phrase your answers in less than three words?”

Agosta took a slow deep sip and savored as he swallowed.

He exhaled.

“It’s been a week.”

“For everyone.”

“My daughter was kidnapped by bandits with intent to sell her to slavery. I hired the effigy to help me rescue her. Machus provided transport. We were lucky; he wasn’t.” Agosta refrained from mentioning the critical fact that his daughter was fucking magic.

“So, you’ve known the effigy—”

“Sloan.”

“For only a few days. How can you speak on her behalf?”

“How can you trust me with my account? I could have fabricated my story.”

“The girl doesn’t appear in distress, and with both of you in our custody, the balance of power sways in our favor. But the effigy—”

“Sloan—”

“Can move without restriction. An uncontrollable variable.”

“For someone with a loginoid and a zodiac as part of her crew, I’d expect you to be more inclusive.”

“Inclusivity isn’t part of this discussion. I’m talking about someone who could very well be in this room listening to us, and I have to consider such a fact.”

“She’s the most honest and genuine individual I’ve ever met,” Agosta said. “I’d trust my life and my daughter with her.”

Terri nodded.

“You’re very confident,” she said. “Effigy are known to forsake friendships on a whim, so I hope for your sake you’re not left disheartened by this effigy—.”

“Sloan.”

Terri didn’t immediately answer.

“…Sloan…” she said.

“She goes, we go,” Agosta said as respectfully as he could.

"You're very direct."

"Yeah, I get that a lot."

"You swear to the loyalty of those around you. You have my respect, Mr. Pike." Terri nodded and continued drinking.

"Outside of following the code, I'm still a little foggy on your reasoning for bringing us on board," Agosta said.

"I've recently learned to lean more on my instincts," Terri said. "Plus, I think we met once."

"I got that too. Aikenhead? In the Tokol Basin?"

"Never been there. Grimaldi, Philokalia?

"I was in Devil's Gate, never in Grimaldi."

"Okay, so we don't know each other," Terri said

"Doesn't look like it," Agosta said.

"Then why do I think we should?"

They both took a drink together; following that, they observed the environment outside the window, limited by the haze they still found themselves trapped within.

"Worlds a big place," Agosta said.

"You ever conduct a train?" Terri asked.

"I was brigadier captain. Two hundred men. I never commanded a train, but I did my share of tours on military vessels. Looks like you managed a pretty good ride yourself."

"Can't complain," Terri said as she finished her drink. "Wait…you were heading to Ragged Hollow. That's not where you were walking. In fact, there was nothing in the direction you were walking except for us."

Agosta swallowed the rest from his cup and placed it back.

"My daughter," Agosta said, "…she saw something."

"Couldn't have been us, not in this soup," Terri said

"I'm suddenly in the habit of taking risks with people."

"Likewise."

"Fine…but this will sound…outrageous."

"Then I know it'll be true," Terri said. "Liars try to make their falsehoods credible. No one starts a fib with a warning that I won't believe them."

* * *

"Mannah, what in the hell are you doing!?" Terri said.

Mannah wasn't eating Terri's sandwich, but after offering food to Elina and preparing a meal for herself, she decided to show the child a rather expensive and heavy book.

“What? She was curious,” Mannah said. “It’s just a book.”

Elina stroked along the edges of the black, near featureless tome, noting the cut blemishing the cover and the brass latch keeping the book locked. Oversized, it was as big as the girl’s torso.

“A book worth more than your life,” Terri said. “I thought I had it locked.”

“You did. What’s the big deal,” Mannah replied. “It’s not like she’s going to know how to open it, so what harm could it—”

Elina flicked the latch open after studying it for only a few seconds. She heaved the massive book open.

Terri’s jaw dropped.

“She’s—” she said.

“Yup,” Agosta said.

The three of them gathered around Elina and the opened book. She flicked a few pages without caring for the contents, stopping at a few illustrations, one showing the torus they all lived in, another a world shaped like a peanut.

“What kind of book is that?” Agosta asked.

“I’ve no idea,” Terri said, “but it was enough for us to travel across the Mare Dagos to retrieve.”

“Can I keep reading?” Elina asked.

“No, honey, give it—”

“Yes,” Terri said. “Yes, you can.”

“You sure, skipper?” Deven asked.

“At this point, what harm could it do.”

“Thank you,” Elina said.

“Just don’t release any curses,” Deven said.

* * *

Agosta opened the door to his cabin. He assumed he would be sharing one with Elina. He found Sloan’s sword resting by the bed on its own. The realization hit him suddenly.

“Oh shit,” he muttered a second before Sloan materialized with a crooked smile sitting on the bed.

Agosta realized that he hadn’t seen Sloan since his meeting with Terri. He didn’t need to ask; he knew she had been listening to every conversation on the train.

“I just lied to the conductor,” he said.

“How do you mean?” she asked.

“Well, you heard everything.”

“Mostly,” she said.

He closed the door, leaving them alone.

"What's your judgment?" he asked. "Do you trust them?" She nodded again and stood from the bed. "Well, I'm glad they didn't suspect—"

"Thank you," she said as she stepped closer.

Agosta nodded.

"Meant every word," he said. "Like I told her. It's been a week."

She stepped closer again.

"So, what happens next?" Sloan asked.

"They'll take us to Corvos. Straight shot."

"Looks like my job is over," she said.

"Looks like," he said. They remained at a comfortable distance. Sloan studied her weapon and heard the various charms rattle off one another.

"I'm always moving," she said.

"I hate staying in one place," he said.

"I'm irritable."

"Matter of opinion."

"I dislike dependency."

"I consider that a selling point."

"I can't bear children."

"Already got one."

She smirked and glanced back at her sword. She held it up and tossed it to Agosta, who caught it the instant after she vanished.

He was speechless…holding her soul in his hand.

She appeared inches from his face, pulling the sword beside her.

She kissed him.

"That was…convincing," he said.

She reached behind him and slid the lock closed

"Shut up," she whispered, pulling him away from the door.

CONESTOGA

I know the words. One of them told me. They disclosed it so straightforwardly that I knew there had to be a catch.

I shared it with others who didn't return from an engagement with a beast. Of course, I might have been lied to, but I don't think that's the case.

I believe it's more than reciting the words; you have to know them, like really know them. You must be fluent in the language; somehow, the beasts know. Your proficiency cannot be limited to a muddled understanding—you must be eloquent. It must be effortless.

I also think the specific phrasing can change based on subtle indications given off by each watcher, which doesn't help either.

Proctor Ward Marshall
Order of the Cenotaph

He opened his eyes; it felt like weights were holding his lids down. The lights were dimmed but still blinding. He had tubes pushed in holes and bandages covering limbs.

Nothing was locked in a cast or missing, so that was something. He blinked his eyes one at a time to reassure he had both.

There was a shape in front of him.

A head.

A face.

A woman.

It was recognizable. He cracked his mouth to speak.

"Terri," Noah groaned.

Terri smirked and nodded.

"Welcome back to reality," she said.

"Am I dead?"

"Yes. Welcome to the afterlife… I'm here to judge your soul."

"Shit," Noah coughed, "all that potential debauchery waisted."

"You're lucky we got to you."

Noah tried to push himself up, but Terri easily coaxed her friend back to the bed.

"How is she?" Noah asked.

"Lucy and Lucy are fine—"

"Not my guns," Noah said, then shrugged. "…well…okay…yes, thank you."

"The endo?"

"She make it to the university?"

"No…"

Dread washed over Noah, and he fought against Terri to stand.

"What!?" he asked.

Terri pushed him back down.

"Actually…she's outside." Terri offered a reassuring nod, and Noah relaxed. "Apparently, you left an impression. We got questions."

"Anyone else?" Noah asked.

Terri shook her head.

"You delivered the cargo alive," she said. "The contract praised your efforts with assurances of a positive evaluation submitted on behalf of Bythos and the endolon nation. Honor has been upheld. Despite losses, the local hallmaster has personally sent their regards. You may even receive a condemnation. At the very least, you can etch a watcher kill on your shell."

"I killed it?"

Terri laughed.

"Remind me to never get on your bad side. We had to carve into its corpse to pull you out. And good luck cleaning all the…juices off your shell."

"It was either it or me."

"I've seen soldiers succumb to the certainty of their death. Fearless fighters go as placid as a sleeping child when the inevitability of mortality presents itself. You'd think when your life is on the line that you'd give it all, hold nothing back. Most just accept it. Prey accepts their fate when in the jaws of a predator. But put one's offspring in jeopardy…or a loved one. That's a level of grit I'd never want to confront."

"Never abandon your charge—first commandment."

"Bullshit."

"That's what I'll tell the grandmasters."

"Okay, that they'll believe. We recovered what was left of Carthan and Machus. Identified by DNA. Anything you want to share about them?"

"They gave their lives to ensure the safety of our cargo," Noah said. "They deserve full honors."

"Also, a good story. Any idea why the watcher would attack you, given your proximity to Corvos? They generally won't get so close to an exclave unless drawn there…and as I said, you were the only survivor."

Noah was unsure about what Terri was implying.

"We'd been pushing our luck for three days," Noah said. "Why? Do you think someone lured it there?"

"If so, I know it wouldn't have been you."

"She's guiltless."

"Are you sure—"

"Yes—"

"Then how—"

"My guess it was the book," Noah said. Terri stepped back and checked the emergency room in case someone was listening.

"If you're saying the watchers followed you because they were tracking a book, best you don't mention that in your report."

"It's cursed."

"Or that. It sounds a little far-fetched."

"We live in an alien spacecraft," Noah said. "Stranger things have happened. Wait…what are you doing here?"

Terri smiled.

"Well…strange things happened," she said.

* * *

A lavish and colossal iridescent arbor draped in various flowers dominated the center of the Corvos botanical park. Agosta passed under it on his shortcut to the local proctor guildhall. Rings of herbs radiated outward within the physic garden. He could see a crowd gathering at the nearby amphitheater to listen to a lecture. Others, along with automated drones, tended the various floras of the grounds. It was bright and natural, unlike the garden he had encountered days prior within the catacombs.

"Kab!" Agosta said, greeting his friend as he emerged from a forest of deciduous hardwood into a nearby glade. "Kabdila Coriolanus, as I live and breathe. I'm thrilled the rumors were correct."

Kabdila approached in his proctor uniform. He was tall, with broad features and a chiseled physique dominated by short, wavy dark hair and week-old growth surrounding piercing blue eyes.

"Agosta!" he said. "You look good…What are you doing here? I mean, I know you're standing, and I appreciate the visit."

The two paced each other as they toured through the mountainous plants of the alpine garden.

"Corvos was nearby," Agosta said. "Scuttlebutt had you promoted, and I wanted to congratulate."

"It was ten months ago, so let's cut the crap," Kabdila said lightheartedly.

"Crap notwithstanding, it's still a hell of a thing."

"Thank you. There was a call for a strong, charismatic leader."

"And did you know of any?"

"Fuck you."

"Who did you step on?" Agosta asked.

"You always said it's easier to push others down than to climb."

"Pretty sure I never said that. But it suits you."

"It does; I should have you stand on ceremony," Kabdila said.

"My tie is in Kenoma.

"Speaking of, why aren't you there?"

They diverted toward a native forest under-planted with evergreen and herbaceous perennials.

"Peripherical obligation. Sivoy, Serenda, and Katona are finishing the bond. Zahn and I diverted here with a refugee. Ended up rescuing Bennet outside the gates."

"Fortuitous."

"Yeah, coincidences have been abundant recently," Agosta said as they navigated through the garden past other walkers. "I mean it, by the way, my compliments. You're the youngest hallmaster on record. Don't know how you did it?"

"I try to eat right."

Their repartee came from a decade of training side by side in Aquino. Agosta was a resident of that exclave, and Kabdila was an Aurago immigrant.

"It's good that someone I know has moved up," Agosta said. "You're one rung away from leading the chapter."

"Up for a coup?"

"Up for a drink. Baby steps."

"No reason we can't do both," Kabdila said before his tone dropped, and he attempted to be earnest. Their steps moved from stone to wood as they crossed onto a boardwalk perched over a small wetland rich in local wildlife and birds. "Why did you divert? The refugee?"

"Yeah…it's complicated. She's a valued asset."

"Colorful banter aside. You know I trust you. You'd give your life for me."

"Would I?"

"If I move fast enough—the point is other halls would drag the lot of you before the inquest. I just need assurances."

"We picked up the harvester in Kenoma and stumbled into a jacker caravan that had been taken out by an unknown third party. Rescued a captive metron, a refugee from Volani. We'd been dogged by all manners of weird shit since, so Terri and I split to bring the girl here."

"Where's she now?" Kabdila asked.

"Hospital. Just a pass to ensure she's good. I'm heading back there after I check in."

"Bring her to the hall."

Agosta stopped just short of exiting the marsh, mere meters from the winter garden entrance. He confronted his friend.

"She's not an asset, Kab."

"You implied she's a target. Targets need protection."

"And not because if word gets out, Corvos military would swoop in and assume authority."

"No reason we can't do both," Kabdila said as he resumed walking. "What did you mean by an unknown third party? If it's not scabs, jackers, grimgods, or screevers—"

"An unknown third party…if I knew, it would be a *known* third party. We almost lost Sloan to it."

"You almost lost a *rig*? Was it a planet?"

"That I could explain."

"Damn it, 'Gosta!" Kabdila said loud enough to draw the attention of nearby tourists. He stopped and spun. "We're not talking in code!"

"It was like a formless will forced itself to manifest, and it used anything and everything nearby to do it. That will, like any rudimentary intelligence, only thinks to eat. Given time, I imagine it'll think of something else. Follow?"

Kabdila thought it over, then proceeded down another path.

"Not really, but what else is new," he said.

"Once the rest of the unit joins up from Kenoma, we can make everything official," Agosta said as he caught up. "For now, I'm relying on your empathy."

"Your responsibilities have you look down while mine have me look up. You manage the people; I manage the politics. I have to consider all incoming information as either a potential windfall or a threat. We're not stonemasons or a religious cult. We're a people whose nation is defined not by borders but by actions. What do you think those are?"

As they entered the riot of blushes, tints, and shades punctuating the xeno-botanical orchard, Kabdila made a point to avoid any occupied paths. The various flowers were sequestered in stone planters with little else to separate them. The invasive breeds, along with those requiring a diverse atmosphere, were kept in the nearby arboretum.

"Protection," Agosta said.

"Only a fraction."

"Exploration."

"We put those on our posters."

"I don't know, Kab…what?"

"We kill. We have the means and the resolve. Everything we do facilitates that capacity. We don't maintain our independence without it. The moment the exclaves get wind that we let our guard down, they'll push us out. Those who kill command those who can't. It's how the universe oper…" Kabdila trailed off, noticing Agosta had stopped behind him.

"In the land of the weak," Agosta muttered, more than a little puzzled, "the man with the gun…is king."

"Yeah….exactly…" Kabdila stepped closer and furrowed his brow. "Have we…had this conversation before?"

Agosta firmed his lips as he considered his impulses. He felt aggression, a nonspecific hostility, but he couldn't understand where it was focused. Kabdila certainly hadn't provoked him. Agosta bottled it.

"No…" he said as he resumed his walk.

* * *

Noah didn't notice after Terri had left that Syn had entered, still draped in the torn and dirtied attire she had on during the trip. She watched him from the door.

They held eyes, a mélange of beeps, breathing, and bells filled the expanse between them. She wore her mask, but he could still see her face, though reading her emotions was tricky.

"You should be careful," Noah said. "If you hang around long enough, people may mistake you for having empathy." She didn't answer, and the silence resumed.

Noah started to feel awkward.

"That was a joke," he said. "I'm…happy you made it. If you hadn't, I wouldn't have wanted..."

She took a step closer to him, then another, her face expressing ambivalence, or at least the best he could estimate. She took another step.

"Uh…look," he said. "I know proximity can bring people closer. Shared stress can form social glue. I think they call it a trauma bond." She took another step and another until she had reached the foot of the bed.

"Not what I would call a stable foundation on which to build a relationship," he said. "I'm only saying this because if you…at all regret anything that happened between us…and you want me to absolve you of any obligations." He waited for her to say something or convey an emotion of any kind. "I mean, I'm a human proctor…and you're an endolon scientist."

He decided to wait out a few seconds. Syn circled the bed until she was beside him. She looked down at him, he up at her, and Noah could appreciate how much bigger her eyes were.

"I'm…talking a whole lot," he said, "…and you're not saying anything, so…I feel like I'm filling an awkward void."

Syn sat upon the bed beside him. She placed the tome, still locked in her other hand, on a space beside him. She slipped her hand under his and held it tightly.

Noah exhaled.

"That's reassuring," he said. She brought up his hand and kissed it.

"When I reached Corvos," she whispered. "I would not go in. I offered to leave them the book. But they refused. They assumed you had died."

"They were in the right."

Her lips trembled.

"Have you ever felt the bounty of joy within your finger's reach, only to have it ripped away?" she asked.

"As a matter of fact, I have."

"For a moment, it is worse than death."

He squeezed her hand.

"As I felt the beast's weight atop me," he said. "I felt calm. I wasn't afraid. Every second I bought was a victory."

"I had given up. Then shadows from the darkness. Your friends. What are the chances they would find you?"

"I'm not one for divine intervention, but in this situation, a case could be made."

"I wonder if there is something more."

"No need to look too deep into it," he said. "Nothing would have stopped me from seeing you again. A watcher is a minor hindrance in comparison."

Syn smiled and removed her mask. She pushed her face beside his and held their cheeks together. He could feel her fingers twist through his hair. She brought their noses to meet, and she kissed him.

"More," he said.

She kissed him again, though her hand brushed a bruise as she moved closer. Noah squirmed from the pain.

"Sorry," Syn said.

"I'm in remarkably good shape for someone that took on a nightmare."

Syn leaned back and stroked her fingers over his body.

"They give it a day until your release," she said.

"You don't have to stay." Noah nudged the book on his bed. "That's important."

"It can wait," Syn said as she rolled the rest of her body on the bed. She nuzzled her head beside his and draped her arm over him. Her legs stuck out over the foot of the bed.

"They may look down on this," he said.

"Your friends can get bent."

"No, I mean the hospital might take issue with this." He jostled slightly to offer more room, which she accepted. She bent her knees slightly to bring her legs closer, putting one knee over his legs. "Eh, whatever, make it work."

"Yes…I will," she said.

He closed his eyes and felt her fast heartbeat pulse through the layers between them.

Her breath was quick and shallow. Part of her narrow torso was applying pressure to one of his sutures, but he didn't dare tell her, worried she would leave.

Corvos had the best hospitals, equipped with bio-forges and genetic reconstructors. His left index had been removed and replaced, and he was breaking in a new kidney. No rejection, little pain. And cellular sealers provided near-immediate healing without scars. Bruising was a minor inconvenience Noah would have to deal with, given Proctor medical coverage was incredibly generous.

"We are sexually compatible, you know," Syn whispered unexpectedly. Noah's eyes bolted open, and he turned slightly to see her staring back.

"Are we?" he asked.

"We have complementary genitals. Hybridization would not be impossible. It may require a lab, and any offspring would be infertile—"

"Wow, was that not what I was asking." Noah laughed. "That part I get."

"Our evolutionary ancestors probably had to contend with fierce sexual competition as the vaginas of endolon females can tighten, completely closing it off to potential….that was not what you were thinking either."

"No…but I'll admit I didn't know that one. I did know that endolon males have bones in their penises."

"Which are significantly smaller than humans. Here is hoping you are…below average."

Noah stared at the ceiling, his brow furrowed as he processed what he heard.

"Never thought to think about that before." He struggled to sit up. "Can I check out now?"

Syn coaxed him back down.

"You still need to heal," she said, holding him.

"Are you sure? I'm feeling pretty good."

"I am not going anywhere."

He laid back on the bed, and they resumed their nuzzling. Another moment passed before Syn blurted out, "You thought I meant preferential sexual positions—"

"Yes!"

Syn nodded and chuckled.

"That is on me," she said.

"At least we talked it out."

Noah pulled Syn's arm over his chest. They both closed their eyes, and Noah could feel himself drifting slowly to sleep.

"I like being on top," Syn whispered.

PARADISE

"I was born with my eyes open."

A common eidolon phrase.

Psylaxis's face resembled porcelain and was perpetually composed, a fixed point in tranquility decided by its creator. Its armor, the shade of ivory, covered in etchings and designs more suited to expensive tableware, would only occasionally reveal the complex set of muscle fibers and gears underneath when it moved.

The children were initially apprehensive, but the excubitor took a knee, removed its equally ornate pearl and steel blade, and balanced it between its arms, inviting curiosity.

The children cautiously approached, but after that initial brave soul reached out and stroked the cold steel, the others followed and pawed at the weapon and intelligent machine.

Machus had grown impatient at the need to present a positive pretense to the rest of the world. To him, the Ascension enforced gods' will, with disciples expected to fall prostrate with that fact. Adoration wasn't required. This was the state religion; it's not like the public had a choice. It was a political mandate that all nations swear allegiance to the church. The Aegis stood above all, with those like Machus speaking on their behalf. He would commonly reference the four steps of faith, from Aegis to Ascension to government administration to the people. Those like him acted as the glue that held this line intact. Psylaxis was a manifestation of power, just as the hedrons and other living machines were. It was an insult for Machus to have to answer to it.

The carriage broke from the parade after finishing its revolution around the outer courts and had stopped just outside one of the markets. While there were still onlookers and admirers, some pawing at the embellishments of the coach, most of the population were culminating their affairs before Philokalia moved too far away. It was still dark, but Uno would eventually rise unobstructed for the first time in a few hours, marking the end of Passover. Only then would the capital be allowed sleep after nearly a week of festivities. Even now, masses still pushed into the streets for final minutes of merriment. Passing crowds blocked Machus's view of the excubitor, and his patience finally ran out.

He barged out of the carriage and motioned the four guards stationed about the vehicle to escort him through the mob. They initially stared, unsure if they should leave the carriage, but an unyielding glare from the priest convinced them to break from the perimeter and push the crowds aside, escorting Machus to Psylaxis.

"Don't you have more…pious acts which take precedence?" Machus said, with the guards standing behind him. Psylaxis continued tending to the children, though its voice emanated from the back of his head.

"I wasn't forged with the intent to be sanctimonious," Psylaxis said. "That is a human trait." Its voice then shifted back to the children, "Now be careful. It's sharp."

"There are pressing matters to attend."

"If you are referring to the explosion yesterday. I believe the local authorities have it under control."

"Are you alive?" Nekau asked. Psylaxis cocked its head and opened its palm to expose the expanding artificial muscles between the seams of its finger joints.

"Do I seem alive to you?" Psylaxis asked.

"I don't know," Nekau said

"Do I need to be?"

Nekau shrugged as he ran his fingers over the hand of the machine.

"I guess not."

"Then perhaps you can explain why we were sent a proctor from Altair instead of purgitans," Machus said. "There was no artifact, according to my report."

"Must you be privy to all knowledge?" Psylaxis asked.

"Yes."

"Omniscience is a talent reserved for gods…don't presume to measure up."

"Do you smile," a four-year-old girl asked. Psylaxis took its finger and swirled it around its face.

"I'm smiling now," it said.

"Can you run?" Nekau asked.

"Quite fast, as a matter of fact."

"Are you saying the Aegis requested him?" Machus asked, his tone escalating, the guards growing uncomfortable, unaware the carriage nearly indiscernible past the mobs had begun moving.

"By name," Psylaxis said.

"Why?" Machus asked.

"Ask her…if you believe you've earned the ear."

"She asked for him?"

"They hear every whisper. See into every shadow. There was a reason. There always is." Psylaxis accepted a piece of paper from an older girl, maybe eight or nine years old. On it appeared a rudimentary but not unskilled charcoal drawing of the excubitor in a rather dramatic post with its sword spearing the sky above. The machine gently stroked the child's hair.

"That is an excellent likeness," it said. "You know the church is always looking for talented artists like yourself." Its hand moved to its waist, where a previously concealed hatch opened. Psylaxis removed a brass ring etched in similar markings to those found on its body. It handed it to the child.

"Take this signet and approach any chapel, curia, or basilica. Tell them what you can do. They'll do the rest. Do you have duties? Are you in labor?"

"Dad toils me in the tanner," the girl said.

"You'll never need to again." Psylaxis stood and patted a few other youths. "Go on now, children."

They waved and scattered into the crowd. Psylaxis waved back, having never once faced Machus during their conversation.

It finally swiveled to confront the priest, immediately noticing the four imperial guards behind him.

"Why are the sentries with you?" Psylaxis asked.

"Because I bear authority in this city. I'm entitled to escort."

"You left no one to tend the carriage," it said calmly.

"Only a fool would dare—"

"You left no one to tend the carriage." Its tone hadn't changed. Psylaxis waved to the guards to follow as it pushed Machus aside.

"Well." Machus tripped over his words. "I mean, I thought."

They reached where the carriage had been. The guards parted the crowds, revealing its absence. Machus's jaw sank.

"Impossible," he said.

Psylaxis scanned over the heads of the crowds but couldn't see the vehicle, meaning it had turned down one of the winding streets of the labyrinth of Sadatoni.

"Which direction did the carriage go?" it asked the crowds. The tone was loud, but it wasn't shouting.

"Speak or suffer the cleanse of purgitans!" Machus said to virtually no reaction from the crowds, with many choosing to dash fearfully away. Psylaxis approached a group that stood its ground.

"The Aegis reward the most faithful," it said, bringing up a previously hidden silver coin stamped with the Aegis seal. A dozen people pointed down one road. Psylaxis casually tossed a coin to the crowd, who promptly fought over it.

The machine wove quickly through the mob, dodging obstacles and crossing the ground faster than the sentries. It repeated the request to another group upon reaching an intersection, offering a similar coin. Half the group pointed down one route while the rest pointed to another. Psylaxis tossed another coin and directed the sentries down one path while it dashed to another.

Machus stood alone in the crowd that ignored him.

* * *

The lavish and luxuriant carriage stopped by the narrow, dark alley, and Elina emerged from the shadows. She looked up to Agosta in the driver's box.

"Seriously?" Elina asked loudly.

"Not time to argue," Agosta said, waving her aboard. Elina pulled on the handle, but it wouldn't jostle.

"It's locked," she said.

"I didn't hear anyone inside. Just jump aboard."

Elina did so, climbing up and dropping beside Agosta as he lashed the kips to a gallop.

"When you said you were going to acquire transport," Elina said, "I thought a couple striders, a cart maybe. I'd hide under a blanket."

"Judgement call. They weren't a lot of options. Plus, what's a better place to hide other than plain sight." Agosta threw the animals down a smaller alley, taking a shortcut through crowds. As the wagon emerged into another market, dozens of eyes noticed them. Crowds parted but did nothing else.

"I feel…exposed," Elina said.

"Not a single person out here knows who you are."

Agosta whipped the beasts to quicken them, and the carriage demolished a market kiosk as it took another corner.

"Is this the leisure route?" she asked.

"Mobs act under the lowest denominator," he said.

"Their lowest what?"

"The most indifferent among them dictate how they act. No one will stand apart, and the more people see us, the more conflicting reports they will give. I give it an hour at least before someone finds the guards. We got a good lead."

"Then what?"

"Clearing the inner courts will be easy; too much traffic for them to pay us any mind."

"Then what?"

"Get out of the city."

"Aannd, then what?"

"I've made arrangements. A Nagomjii caravan sits just outside the limits. I'm wagering once they realize who you are, meaning if they believe me, they should honor the old alliance your people had with them."

"Aaaaaaannnnnd, then what?"

Agosta gave Elina a somewhat muddled glare.

"Haven't thought that far ahead."

As they reached the main road, cross-traffic had gotten worse, with people shuddering businesses and closing final transactions. Others were rushing to the main gates.

The distant horns from the castle's bell tower resonated between the buildings. Agosta turned his head to better discern the pattern.

"What does that mean?" Elina asked.

"Damn, I thought we'd have more time," Agosta said. "They'll carry that pattern to the main gates."

"Is it a code?"

"To close the gate and seal the city. But that horn won't carry to the wall without intermediaries. Meaning we got about five minutes as lazy guards pick up the pattern and pass it on."

"I remember my city employing striders instead of horns."

"I planned on replacing them with lanterns," Agosta said, but it appears it's not been set up yet."

"Well, aren't we lucky?"

* * *

A commotion had erupted throughout the city. Terri and Noah heard the distant horns echo off walls. A moment later, a tower replicated the call.

"What's that about?" Noah asked.

"Something happened," Terri said, "It's a city alert. They'll probably close the gates."

"Then we need to get moving."

They emerged from an alley and immediately noticed the conclave caravan racing towards them.

"Is that an Ascension vehicle?" Terri asked.

"And I do believe it's being stolen," Noah said as he pushed Terri nearly onto the path of the racing vehicle, which proceeded to ignore them as it raced by. Unlike the mobs attempting to avoid the stampeding kips pulling the carriage, these two jumped upon the vessel's rear.

Agosta threw the reins to Elina, who stared at them in disbelief. Agosta stood and went for the blade at his side. He immediately recognized Noah.

"You!" Agosta said.

"You seem eager to depart this city!" Noah said. "We'll accompany you."

"You're the proctor," Agosta said.

"I know," Terri said. "I'm confused too. We just need to get out of the city." Agosta didn't have time to discern their body language or get into a protracted swordfight atop a speeding wagon. He grabbed the reins back from Elina, who did nothing with them.

"Do you trust them?" Elina asked.

"I shouldn't," Agosta said.

"Why are we heading to the Northern Gate? The Eastern is closer," asked Terri.

"No back seat driving!" Agosta said.

"How long before word reaches the gate?" Noah asked.

"Minutes."

The horns passed over them; Noah and Terri's eyes shifted to a sentry tower and a pair of guards scrambling to carry the alert to the outer wall. Their vehicle slowed as it took another corner and revealed the distant Northern gate, still open and manned by a dozen militia along the wall and two sentries controlling traffic with another half dozen guarding the doors. A nagomjii caravan was just exiting the city.

"Imperial sentries are already here," Noah said.

"Because I put them there," Agosta said.

"That wasn't prudent forethought."

The carriage approached the gate.

"We've gotten numerous reports of missing items over the last few days," Sloan said to the nagomjii doonjii. "We had an accusation of one of your offspring pilfering an aumoniere from an older lady. Burlap with a leather top and the emblem of an eagle."

"I know not of this," Wisekjii said from atop his vardo. He was about to snap his kips to trot, but Sloan stepped in front of the vehicle between the animals and its driver.

"She doesn't care for the coins but inside contained a small diary from her late husband," Sloan said.

Wisekjii nodded and spoke his tongue sharply back into the carriage. A hand then passed Wisekjii the purse. He handed it to Sloan to confirm the book was inside, on its own.

She nodded.

Deven stepped closer.

"They admitted lifting," Deven whispered. "Law decrees we impound the vardo and arrest them."

Sloan cocked her head back.

"You know what they do to them in captivity." She then stepped aside and waved the caravan through.

Wisekjii nodded and beckoned his beasts to move.

The Ascension carriage followed quickly behind, and Sloan jammed her body in the way. Deven followed as they both recognized the driver of the vehicle.

"Katona, Serenda," Agosta said. They were initially confused, but the plan's realization dawned on Sloan, whose eyes fell. "I won't manipulate either of you. I won't imply an insult by offering a middling bribe or threatening you by endangering your families. For one, I know you don't have one." He looked to Deven. "And yours...well, I know about yours."

The horn from the nearby sentry tower finally repeated the pattern, which was evident at the outer gates.

"A call to seal the city," Deven said.

"You want us to let you go before we close the gates?" Sloan said.

"Where did you get that wagon, milord?" Deven asked.

"He's not a lord," Sloan said.

"It is my wagon," Noah said as he stood from behind the wagon.

"He just lied," Agosta said to Noah's scorn. "Wasn't a very good one. Remember the encounter in the hall with the Ascension. And the cost to become emperor. That cost involves the taking of this girl's head."

Elina offered a half-hearted wave from beside Agosta.

"Why?" Sloan asked.

"At this point, does it matter? Would it matter to you?"

"The living king swore to my safety," Elina said. "It's the prince that wishes me dead."

"I dedicated my life to this kingdom," Deven said.

"Serenda, given your ancestors," Agosta said, "I consider that shocking."

Deven turned to Sloan.

"Sloan…you can't seriously be considering this," Deven said. "We were just brought into the inner circle."

"Consider that I'm the Master of Coin," Agosta said, "the prince regent's right-hand office and steward of intelligence in this city. The prince succeeds; I'd sit on the second most powerful seat on Bythos. I'd be viceroy…and I'm sacrificing that by my actions. What's more important… integrity…or loyalty to a man that didn't know you existed until yesterday? Don't take this as a sign of weakness." Agosta then focused on Sloan. "And don't be defined by a kingdom."

Sloan couldn't understand the thoughts she was considering. There was a cognitive dissonance as what felt like both familiar and invading thoughts rushed through her mind. Maybe it was a by-product of her nature. She measured her loyalty to the crown, to Deven, and to this man she barely knew outside of a handful of conversations.

She rolled her fingers across the inside of her palm, harkening a moment when he placed his hand over hers, something she had desired for some time…except that never happened.

Was it a fantasy?

She possessed impeccable memory and could always distinguish a dream from reality. She couldn't resist the emotions sweeping through her as the recollection took hold, regardless of its authenticity.

A half-dozen guards were perched atop the lower wall under the looming massive arch of the ancient barricade that encircled the city. It bathed the smaller barbican in shadow. None of the sentries could overhear the conversation the ground guards, Katona and Serenda, were having with the latest vehicle attempting to depart the city.

They all heard the horns but, following the chain of command, awaited instructions from those below. Between the two, Sloan held the higher rank, the echelon among them. While the gates required physical effort to close, the portcullises were gravity driven. The other guards were growing concerned by the extent of the conversation they couldn't hear.

One of the perched sentinels close to the lever was preparing to release the inner lattice of metal and stone while a duplicate brought a herald horn to his lips, intending to relay the call to the inside of the gatehouse to drop the outer door.

Agosta knew what would be required. Small but accurate, one-handed crossbows hung from the sides of Sloan and Deven. At a mere fifty-pound pull weight, the weapons weren't entirely lethal at this range. Agosta confirmed the plan, ensuring everyone knew their place.

The carriage sprung quickly ahead while Terri followed Agosta's instructions and caught Sloan's bow, which fired to one guard's upper leg with calculated aim.

He fell before he could grasp the lever.

Sloan struck Deven's visor with the side of her gauntlet and pilfered his bow.

She landed her shot upon the herald, the dart passing through both cheeks the instant before his lips met the mouthpiece.

The sudden violence offered precious seconds, enough for Sloan to trip Deven to the ground and leap upon the back of the carriage as it quickly passed.

The vehicle crossed the gatehouse before an alert could sound.

Reserve sentries managed to pull both levers but not in time.

Deven slowly crawled back to his feet to watch his lifelong friend escape with a group of strangers, most of whom they had just met.

The carriage dashed into the dense network of huts and shops radiating from the city wall, preventing aimless arrow fire from the city wall.

Deven lost sight of them as the remaining guards attempted to rally.

*   *   *

Psylaxis and Coulter, followed by a half-dozen guards and double that of city militia, reached the Northern gate to find the doors closed. One imperial sentry and a handful of guards were being helped by others. One held his face from a severe blow while another struggled to still stand. The remaining sentry settled on unstable feet.

"Guard! What happened?!" Coulter said.

"They overwhelmed me, milord!" Deven said. "We had only just received the order to close the gates."

"How long ago?" Psylaxis asked.

"Four minutes," a nameless guard behind Deven said. "One of the sentries escaped with them."

"They are likely with the aliens," Psylaxis said.

"I'll pursue," Coulter said.

"No…we'll need an army."

"All this for a girl?" Deven asked.

"Girl?" Psylaxis asked.

"Before they attacked me, they claimed the alert was due to the escape of a girl set for execution."

"I wasn't aware of the girl," it said. "It's the carriage we wanted."

*   *   *

The carriage, now freed from the city's traffic, accelerated. It crossed the summit of one hill on the way to another. They traversed the Kalian channel, the bridges having been replaced now that Philokalia had passed. As they bounded over the second hill, the city fell out of sight. Looking back, Noah could still see the portcullises down.

Might they not have cared that an Ascension caravan had been taken? By now, a handful of available cavalries could have been sent after them, potentially forcing the nagomjii into a physical conflict. Hopefully, the numbers within the alien caravan would discourage such action. He then considered the second option, that an army would, in time, pursue them.

Agosta kept on the task of controlling the kips at this speed. Elina was still beside him, as was Sloan. Eventually, he'd ask her why, but for now, he was willing to admit his virtually unfounded suspicions were correct. He then placed his palm to his chest as he felt his heart race.

"Are you okay?" Elina asked him.

"Yeah," Agosta said. "Just getting really warm?" Sloan leaned forward as she was feeling it as well.

"You too?" Sloan asked.

"Yeah."

"A spell?" Elina asked. "Is it the Aegis?"

"Aegis craft technology to appear magical," Noah said. "True magic employs talismans, requiring touch. We'll well out of range of that."

"Anyone else?" Agosta asked.

"No," Elina said.

"Not either of us," Terri said, assuming Noah's answer based on his facial expression. That was in error.

"Were you two-shot?" Noah asked as he attempted to concentrate. Agosta felt around his chest. He'd assume an arrow would be obvious, but it could have been an Aegis weapon, which was not limited by the prohibition of technology.

"Not that I can tell," Sloan answered.

"It's probably nothing," Agosta said.

PART FIVE

AFFINITY

TORUS/ CONESTOGA

Does it look like a tower we built? Does it look like a tower at all? I mean, sure, it's tall, but there are no lights, doors, or external apparatus.

A statue? An obelisk?

Maybe. Looks more like that weapon you affix to your firearm. What do you call it—a bayonet. No one has ever seen the foundation.

What if Abraxas is only the spearhead of a larger construct sitting outside the Torus?

Keid Rana
Before his disappearance in the Maelstrom

Agosta fell back on the bed as Sloan pushed forward, pulling down his trousers. He fumbled with his buttons as she tore her boned corset with spirited strength, ripping at the cloth and breaking the brass clasps, taking Agosta off guard. She shoved her face to his, and he ran his fingers through her short black hair.

Syn tugged lightly on her white cotton and polyester collared longcoat; the magnetic fasteners released, and it fell to the floor in front of Noah, revealing a silver latex jumpsuit, an advanced endolon construction that maintained her temperature and closed up over wounds.

Sloan tossed the fragments of her corset on the ground and committed to undoing her leather pants. Agosta reached down to help, undoing one belt while Sloan flung the other. She split the zipper and revealed her lace shorts as her ruffle paisley skirt fell over Agosta's head.

Noah separated an invisible seam along Syn's jumpsuit. It loosened. Syn reached to her rebreather pack and disconnected it to Noah's instinctual rejection. She gently coaxed his hand away as she removed the device from her waist, followed by the removal of her mask. She placed it nearby the bed.

Agosta couldn't help but consider the damage Sloan was inflicting on her own attire, the brutality of it all, her desperation to tear at the clothes she was always cursed to wear. Sloan broke all the buttons of her black collared bustier, and they ricocheted off the walls. She kept a vice-like grip on her weapon, a talent all effigies possessed. She would have to be killed to release it. The charms rattled constantly, and Agosta acknowledged the fortune of a loud rolling train.

Syn bent down and licked Noah's face as he undid his cotton shirt, her sandpaper tongue rough against his cheek. Noah kissed an ear; the arrow tip twitched as it flicked off his teeth, and he heard a high-pitched alien moan. She pulled back and stared at him. He became lost in her dimpled smile, those vast green-blue eyes. Her three-fingered hands brushed the sides of his head as they kissed.

* * *

Noah stroked his index across her naked, shimmering skin, skipping over the soft bumps of her cycloid scales. He caressed down her arm until reaching her three-fingered hand, and they interlocked. She opened her eyes and looked up at him; this close, he could see the oscillating colors within her vibrant eyes. He pulled her closer to him, and he felt her right leg falling inside his.

The artificial sun of Corvos was still due to rise, but the light from the distant star system basked the bedroom in a soft blue hue. The silence was only slightly broken by the virtually inaudible hiss her rebreather made.

He had compelled her to don her mask after she was visibly starting to turn pale. He was worried it had been damaged when she tore it off her face. She was almost embarrassed by the weakness, but he no longer cared about such things.

"Syn…when we first met," Noah finally broke the comfortable silence, "I got the impression, and maybe I'm wrong…that you acted like we had met before."

Syn blinked, smirked, and laid her head on his chest.

"We had," she said.

Noah stared at the back of her head, at her silver-white hair. His eyes followed the curves until they fell over the sheet and further until her legs stuck out from the other end.

"I'm certain I'd remember," he said.

Syn fondled a finger through his chest hairs, a feature missing in male endolons.

"I dreamt about someone…about us," Syn whispered. "It felt as real as this. Not unlike anything I had felt before."

"Did it foresee this?" he asked into her hair.

She arched her head to face him. "It was not a portent of future events," she said, then pulled herself up to sit next to him, drawing her feet back onto the bed. She took his hand with hers. "In fact, outside of us, I did not recognize anything."

"Where were we?" Noah asked. "I mean, what did it look like?"

Syn's attention shifted to outside the window.

"It changed. Each time, we were somewhere else, some other time or place. Occasionally, you were there. But when I was close to someone…it was always you."

"Does one specifically come to mind," he asked.

"The last one, after we kissed in Tokol. I had an image of another world. Like this, manufactured."

"Another ark?" Noah pointed to the window and the distant star system beyond this vessel. "Or a world like those?"

"Not even close. It was…impossible. And those living on them were regressed. Castles. Swords. It felt alien…but also familiar."

Noah caressed her hand—smooth knuckles and creaseless palm.

"Were you…you?" he asked.

"I think I was human," Syn said, rolling her fingers over his, reaching his smallest, the one she lacked. "But we were not the same."

Noah dismissed the thought as he pulled her close to him.

"Just a dream," he said. "Sometimes we fill in the blanks when they present themselves in our mind."

"I told myself that…but despite looking different, I still recognized myself."

"Well, it's your dream; you should."

"That is not what I mean," Syn whispered as her naked body slipped from the bed. She retrieved the book from her desk. She worked the lock, unlatched it, and opened the tome. "I lived in this book for weeks before you arrived, and perhaps that was literal."

Syn flipped to a specific page she knew too well, which displayed an image of an individual. It was a gaunt woman with silver-white hair floating as if gravity held no dominion over her. Her eyes aimed out of the book, and Noah felt its stare.

"That's uncanny," he said, glancing between Syn and the illustration that bore her resemblance. "But it's not you…I mean, it's…coincidence. Right?"

"I honestly cannot remember if I dreamt of her before or after seeing this."

"Had to have been after…I mean, you're a scientist, Syn."

"Science involves rational thought. The easiest explanation is likely the correct one, so I must admit that it probably lies with me dreaming of her after. But that does not explain the resemblance. And part of science includes observation."

"Coincidence."

"Regardless of whether it is or not, observation is first; asking a question is second. Who is she? Forming a hypothesis follows. I am still at that stage. That…is why I came here. Best labs and libraries we have."

"All this time, because of someone you dreamt about?"

"When my dream speaks, I do not know if I am talking or being talked to. I let my rational mind dictate my actions…mostly. I admit with you, emotions somewhat took over."

Noah chuckled.

"Well, I certainly hope so," he said. "You said I was in your latest dream. Who was I?"

"I think you were some kind of religious figure."

"I'm an atheist, soo…irony. I wonder who I worshipped."

Syn smiled.

"I think," she said, taking a breath to formulate her next thought, "you were worshipping…me."

They shared a tenderness of silence.

An understanding.

An unspoken passion.

He grinned.

"Not much of a stretch then…"

Endolons don't blush, so she expressed her affection in other ways.

They said nothing else that morning.

* * *

Agosta surveyed the disaster they had wrought, broken buckles, torn fabric, and buttons skipping off the vibrating floor. His clothes were in much better shape.

"Sooo, about your clothes," Agosta said.

Sloan turned her head to him and smiled. She held her blade up, then tossed it into the air, causing her to disappear from the room. He knew she was still beside him despite no longer leaving an impression on the bed. The mess of ruined clothes about the room vanished with her, leaving only his undamaged garb.

The weight came back as the blade fell and was caught. Sloan appeared fully clothed back in her corset, bustier, paisley skirt, and leather pants. She glanced back at him with a smile. He stared back at the ceiling.

"Neat trick," he said. He felt her hand stroke his, and they interlocked. "Do you see yourself," he asked, "when…"

"Yeah," she said. "It's hard to explain. The world looks desaturated. And I see…things. Shapes. Maybe people. Always just far enough for me to not focus on them. Always assumed they were either other effigy or…spirits."

"You're not dead," he said.

"People call me a ghost."

"You're not cold, quite the opposite, in fact."

"I appreciate that."

"So, your attire is…"

"Fixed…at least I got allocated with a sense of fashion. Just not very combat effective. I've torn my clothes in anger. They've been sliced by swords, stained with blood. Each time, it's a reset. I could have told you, but…it was funnier to read your reaction. I'm more worried someone heard us. I think your daughter was next door."

"Oh, she is," Agosta said as he raised his head. He formed a fist and slammed the adjacent wall. He heard a small, feminine yelp from the other side as Elina fell from the wall. Agosta nuzzled himself back to the bed that was barely large enough to accommodate the two of them.

"She's exceptional," Sloan said.

"Outside of parental pride, you'd be right."

"She'll change the world."

"You think so?"

"Call it a hunch."

Agosta gazed out the window to the rushing landscape as the ruins of a forgotten empire whipped by. He remembered that moment days ago and felt it was time to come clean.

"You were familiar," he said.

"What?"

"I did have the framework of a plan. A sniper and a zodiac guard. There was one group I was meeting at that tavern." Sloan was starting to be alarmed, but Agosta attempted to dissuade her. "I didn't lie…there was determination I saw in those beautiful amber eyes. Conviction. But it was an undefined awareness that had me walk to you…like I had met you before."

"You're too young to have slipped past my memory," Sloan said, "And I think I'd remember you."

"I know I wasn't recalling a memory. It was something deeper." He became absorbed in those eyes that he could have spotted from any distance. He stroked his index along her thumb, and she pulled him close for a long kiss.

"I missed that," she whispered.

"It's been a while?" he asked.

"Very."

They kissed again, and she rolled to face him, rolling her leg over his waist as he gently pulled up on her unfortunately leather-covered posterior.

Sloan pulled away and fell back to stare at the ceiling.

"Damn…" she said.

"What is it?" he asked.

"I gotta take all this shit back off."

TORUS

Considering the range of architecture and age of the various buildings, I've come to two different conclusions—either our ancestors segregated themselves based on ethnic or traditional values (which the Caliphate refutes), or sections of the city were built at different times, contradicting the theory that it was created in one moment by some foolish silent deity

Dr. Lucas Kimbell
United Volani University
675 AC

Agosta exited the cabin first, with Sloan not far behind. Given conversations they heard in the adjoining mess, they had hoped the two could use that as a distraction and integrate without inquiry into their actions.

That did not occur.

Agosta stopped dead upon emerging; Sloan walked past him into six waiting faces, staring and smiling back from the hallway.

"Either of you want a mint?" Noah asked, a hot cup of brew in his hand.

"Shut up," Sloan said as she annoyingly pushed past them and into the mess. Agosta followed and found Elina staring with a wide-eyed grin, like an approving parent receiving a school report.

"What?" Agosta asked her.

"I told them," Elina said.

Agosta glanced back to the cabin, realizing how much the crew heard.

"I thought the engine—" he said.

"Nope," Noah said.

"Walls are really thin," Kaiden said.

"Well, this is embarrassing," Agosta said as he joined his daughter at the table.

"Nonsense," Terri said as she walked out of the room, "about time someone got laid inside this giant moving penis."

"Wanna know who won the bet?" Elina asked her father.

"No," Agosta said sharply, pointing at her, "and about that...Ewww."

"I'm just happy for you," she said, still uncomfortably perky given the subject matter.

"We all are," Noah said, dripping with wit and sarcasm.

"I don't even know who you are," Agosta said to him. "We're not friends." He then faced Elina. "Honey, you shouldn't be so open with strangers."

"They're not strangers, Dad," she said.

"Oh, trust me," Deven said as he departed for the mess to grab lunch, "you passed the audition."

"You act as if this is a novel occurrence," Noah said.

"We once operated a temporary brothel," Deven said, "transporting clients from one side of Vothragna to the other. We've heard it all." Deven snatched a pair of unidentified meals, both wrapped in foil from a cooler packed in ice. He approached the engine compartment and wedged them into the exhaust manifold.

"Mannah, I'm cooking a fowl for you; it's in the manifold. Five minutes," Deven said.

"Thank you!" Mannah said.

"Did you want something to eat, hot or cold?" Noah asked Agosta loud enough for Sloan to hear as she wedged herself to act inconspicuously.

"I don't really need…food," Sloan said.

"But I know your kind enjoys it," Noah said. "We take pride in our catering. Kaiden there is quite the cook."

Kaiden nodded in agreement.

"The loginoid?" Agosta asked.

"An oven cooks but is not required to taste," Kaiden said gruffly, "At least I have an imagination."

"Well, if you don't trust him," Noah said, "We got bags of dried meat, fruit, and hard biscuits. But I'm telling you, he makes a wicked pan de campo with boiled eggs."

"Soft center. With a dash of pepper and red spice." Kaiden said, still with his brusque tone. "I can't taste, but it doesn't mean I don't smell."

Agosta didn't show it, but he appreciated the apparent camaraderie between the crew. He hadn't spent much time on crewed vessels of this size but had heard many rotated their team every year. The Vanderov didn't do this.

"That does sound pretty good," Agosta said. Kaiden pushed himself off the wall and went to work. "Honey?" Agosta asked Elina.

"Oh, I was up before you," she said. "They are good at their work."

"Sloan?"

Sloan exhaled, still a little threadbare from the recent conversation. She shrugged and sat down beside Agosta.

"Why not?" she said. "I mean, none of us have eaten much in three days."

Noah grabbed a pair of steel cups, dropped them on the table before the couple, and poured hot brew in each. It was brown, thick.

"And I won the bet," Noah said.

"Okay," Agosta said between his teeth.

"Made me proud."

"I heard you!"

"Okay, enough from the peanut gallery," Terri shouted from the conductor's chair. "We're not clear of the graveyard left. Too many of you are letting your guard down."

* * *

After the meal, a number of the crew, including Sloan and Agosta, stared at Elina as she perused the book. Terri found it unsettling. The girl was gifted in smoke, and maybe that offered her insight into such an old book. Yet, it had been recovered from an ancient Iokon vault when smoke was virtually nonexistent. Despite it not being particularly good, she sipped Noah's brew.

Noah came up behind her as they watched Elina read.

"Do you believe in coincidence?" Noah asked.

"Yes," Terri said. "Yes, I do."

Noah grimaced.

"You're no fun," he said. "We're all due for Corvos. Us, Wisekjii, those three."

"It was a contract, and Wisekjii is being dropped off. Fairly certain he was heading elsewhere."

"I believe there's something more," Noah said as he lightly tapped his nose.

"Child," Terri said loud enough to carry, "can you…read that?"

"Oh, no," Elina said with a laugh. "I have no idea what it says. Looks like gibberish."

"No language I've ever seen," Deven said.

"It's the images that draw me…heh…that sounds funny. I'm drawn to images."

"And she's not a child," Sloan said. Elina smiled at her.

"I thought you didn't believe in this stuff," Terri said to Noah.

"A conversation with someone in Dust might have swung me," Noah said. Elina flipped page after page, analyzing the images, often connected to nearby slugs of text. She flipped it closed on a finger to mark her place.

"Too bad it's damaged," Elina said, stroking the cut on the cover.

"Yeah," Terri said, "…we don't know how that happened. It was flawless when we found it."

Elina returned to her spot and flipped a few pages, reaching one with a generous brown stain. She stroked her hand over it.

"And this as well?" she asked.

"It just appears to happen," Noah said.

"It doesn't," Elina said as she examined the stain. She smelled it. "Nothing just happens."

"Yeah, it does," Terri said. "Things occur all the time without reason or explanation. It's so prevalent, we even gave it a name. It's called happenstance."

"But you can't have something happen without a spark."

"By that extension, something had to have created that trigger. There's an infinite regression there."

Elina turned a page to reveal an illustration of a steam-trike—a vehicle with two small wheels in the front and one in the back. Several indicators pointing to its construction led to blocks of alien dialect. A page of text was skipped to another image, this time of a creature with a giant copper wheel occupying its torso. Gaps in rusted armor exposed a clockwork assembly of gears, pistons, and synthetic muscles held together by a brass exoskeleton. It was supported by six insect-like legs carved from ivory, and the hair growing from its back resembled broken wires.

"That looks familiar," Sloan said.

"Plagurwocky," Agosta whispered.

Another page flipped revealed an eight-car, olive-colored train with a locomotive encircled with walkways and prefixed, not with a cowcatcher but a massive iron pincer. Another page displayed a tiny mechanical bird constructed from polished steel and brass. Amethyst crystals formed its eyes, and it sat perched on a shoulder.

"Animech?" Elina asked.

"Homonculus," Kaiden said.

"I don't know that word, but it sounds awesome."

"Oxomancers build them as familiars."

"Images of trains," Elina said. "Weapons, machines, the different classes of hydrocell. I don't think it's telling a story. It's trying to explain itself. Describe what these things are."

"An encyclopedia?" Noah said.

"Encyclo-what?" Elina said.

"It's a book containing summaries of knowledge."

Elina continued, exposing a winged humanoid creature enveloped by fur and spines. A small snout protruded under a pair of large black eyes within a canine-like face fringed by massive diamond-shaped ears.

Another illustration showcased a triptych of different views of the same machine, an elaborate technological suit of synthetic muscles, armor plates, and weapons sitting atop a set of leg extensions that made the figure appear to walk on its toes.

"That doesn't look like a herald," Sloan said.

"Herald?" Elina asked.

"A hydrocell-powered armor," Agosta said, "This thing looks more advanced and lacks the smokestacks and steam valves." Elina flipped more pages forward, with more images of creatures and vehicles no one could recognize. The final showed a strange hourglass-shaped object of immeasurable scale.

"Look at the header; it's changed," Deven said.

Elina grabbed another fistful of pages and kept skipping until the header changed again, revealing a new set of illustrations.

"More monsters," Elina said as she passed image after image—a mount walking on towering legs, a colossal winged serpent, a creature with a neck so long, it could reach from the ground to the clouds enabling it to filter feed on small flying creatures. Following those were men, some wearing obelisk-shaped conical hats extending down to their shoulders, others marching in elaborate metal armor topped with feathers and coated in silver. Elina stopped on one image of an individual. The colors were rich and the ink sharp. It was a gaunt woman with silver-white hair floating as if gravity held no dominion over her. Her eyes looked outward, and Noah felt its stare, almost as if she was someone he knew. Elina continued browsing. Floating twelve-sided flying vehicles. Handheld reflective spheres. People made from stone.

"There are three books," Elina said.

"Looks like one to me," Deven said.

"No, I mean…books within books."

"Volumes," Noah said.

"Only one applies to us," Terri said, "The other two must be fiction."

"Actually," Elina said, "I think they all apply to us."

"Except the other volumes deal with people and things that don't exist. That indicates a work of fiction."

"Someone's fiction can be someone else's fact," Noah said.

"That's not how the real world works," Terri said.

"Then," Elina said, "…I guess it's a good thing we're not in the real world."

A short pause felt long as the others pondered that thought, with Deven finally breaking the silence.

"That's cryptic," he said.

"How did you find this?" Agosta asked.

"We were contracted," Terri said.

"By?"

"My ex-girlfriend," Noah said.

"Out here? Was it dangerous?"

"We don't hate each other."

"It was very dangerous," Deven said.

"Then maybe you should reanalyze that relationship," Agosta said to Noah.

"You just got laid while everyone on this train listened," Noah said. "You're not allowed to judge others on dating habits."

"And how did she know about it?" Agosta asked.

"He still loves her," Mannah said as she emerged behind everyone, stepping up from her engine room. "He should make amends."

"That is not even close to being part of the conversation, Tooley!" Noah said.

"He's just lovelorn. Anyone have dating advice?"

"That's…an excellent question," Terri said.

"My personal life is not part of this conversation!" Noah said.

"Agreed, that wasn't where I was going."

"We're asking how your ex-girlfriend—" Agosta asked.

"None of us know," Terri said. "At the time, I didn't think it was important, and I was mistaken."

"Maybe it came to her in a dream," Elina said.

"That's hard to believe," Kaiden said.

"Well, you don't dream, so how do you know?" Deven asked.

"I know reality and dreams connect you to a hidden mind my people lack. Your species foolishly split your psyche for reasons we've never understood."

"But is it hard to believe?" Noah said. "Has anyone else dreamed of places they could never have been?"

The rest shared looks before Sloan answered.

"Yes," she said, centering on Agosta, "Just as you have."

"It's weird," Elina said. "As I flipped through these other two volumes…everything was new but familiar."

"Déjà vu," Kaiden said.

"Déjà vu is a misfiring of neurons," Terri said, "offering the…" She trailed off and lost focus, her eyes drifting to the window.

"What?" Kaiden asked.

"I've said that before," she said.

"It's happening to you as well," Elina said. She and Terri exchanged stares.

"What did you mean about this not being real?" Agosta asked.

"Well, you said this book must be fiction," Elina said, "but our part isn't. And if that's real, then the rest must be. And if they're fiction, then we must be as well."

"It's a book, girl," Kaiden said. "They don't have to follow rules, and if it's poorly written, it doesn't even need to have syntax."

"So, it describes in detail the workings of a world," Noah said. "Three of them. And ours happens to be included. Interesting."

"Trivial," Kaiden said. "How would it in any way possess a practical application?"

"Does it have to?" Noah asked. "Knowledge on its own possesses value regardless of its purpose."

"No," Elina said, "these aren't random. There's a reason why we've been brought together."

"Are you talking about the book," Terri asked, "…or us?"

"What do you think?"

"We admitted to strange dreams," Noah said, "familiarity to novel experiences. This could be why."

"Is everyone discovering this?" Deven asked. "Or is it just us because we're in proximity to the book. Have we considered the possibility it's not a symptom but the cause? Maybe it's what causing this to happen."

"These odd coincidences and familiarities started for me before I ever came on board," Elina said.

"Is it magic?" Deven asked.

"I think we can all agree on that," Noah said. "It's got damage that we didn't inflict. So, they must have."

"Who?" Kaiden asked.

"Have you not figured it out yet?" Noah said.

"I'm not good at puzzles."

"Well, I am…she's saying that each volume in this book connects it to a world that is as real…or as fictional…as ours. And if we didn't damage it…they did."

They shared another silence filled only with the rumbling of the machine.

"Nope, still lost," Mannah said.

"That's why it's valuable," Noah said. "A singular account of worlds from someone aware of them all. Three worlds…three books."

"No…rarer than that," Terri said, offering Elina a comforting smile of sympathy and understanding. "One…between all of us."

"We…are that whisper," Noah repeated what Evora had said to him earlier that week.

"What does that mean?" Mannah asked from behind the group.

"These dreams, moments of familiarity," Agosta said. "They're messages from other worlds. Do they dream of us?"

"Just as we of them," Elina said. "What's real—the dreamer or the dream. In this case…we're both. If we try and think of a beginning…of who came first, we won't find it. We are both the beginning and the end of someone else's fantasy."

"Is this what the shadow was directing you towards?" Sloan asked.

"I think so," Elina said.

"Shadow?" Kaiden asked. "What shadow?"

"You know," Elina said, before flipping a block of pages aside before finally reaching it, the one illustration between books one and two. On Page 314. "…him."

The resemblance of the shadowy figure was disconcerting.

"Would you look at that?" Sloan said.

"Just another legend," Kaiden said.

"That we've seen," Deven said.

Elina glanced at the CIC. Terri stared at the familiar silhouette. She opened her mouth slowly, trying to articulate a response before Noah intervened.

"While I'm open and willing to accept all of this," he said, "I am trying to understand why. Why would someone create it? And outside of being a curiosity, what's the point of it?"

Elina riffled through a few pages and picked one with space on the bottom right side. She then reached into her satchel and removed her pencil.

"What are you—" Deven said as she reached out to Elina, who batted his hand away.

"Trust me," Elina said as she began inscribing.

"What are you doing?" Terri asked as she reached for the book. Elina shifted away and continued to write. Terri didn't force the issue and instead looked curiously at her.

"You're defacing a priceless book," Terri said plainly.

Elina blew on the inscription to scatter flakes of loose graphite. She then confidently closed the book.

"No," Elina said. "I'm saying hello."

CONESTOGA

Just like impetuous aliens such as humans and scrimm, endolons sanctioning violent solutions to problems are often shunned, if not outright ostracized by their own kind. They defend a city that often doesn't appreciate them.

These exceptions often leave their city to protect it in other ways, joining a security company or the proctors. In time, the proctors themselves developed unique crutches suited for endolon builds. These endolons still prefer mediation over violence and will never throw the first punch. However, they will insist that they throw the last one.

Exception Over Exceptionalism
Kalesallow

"Hello," Syn whispered with a curious smile growing on her face.

Noah jostled from the bed and awoke. He rolled to Syn with the open book on her lap. Her face was so close, he could hear the rebreather hum quietly. She was worried that it would keep him awake. In truth, he found it soothing, like a light wind blowing past one's window.

"What?" he asked. "Are you okay?"

Syn had been browsing the tome casually, admiring the illustrations, which were the only thing she could do given the dialect was indecipherable. The sketches revealed monsters she recognized, including the watcher on one page. But others were of creatures she had never seen. Tall, thin-legged mounts. Robots shaped like animals. Diagrams indicated the operation of shells not unlike Noah's, old firearms, and even older melee weapons. She even took time to study her doppelganger.

One page suddenly stuck out.

Syn pointed to the tome splayed across her lap.

"Fine," she said, "the book changed again."

"Another oddity?" Noah leaned in.

"I flipped past this page. I know because I recognize the illustration." Syn's finger floated over the page and ran down to the bottom corner. Noah stared at what Syn was pointing at, and his jaw fell.

"It never left my hand," she said.

"I'm going to take a stab that it never did."

"Regardless. Feels like carbon."

Noah stared at the scribble sketch in the corner. It was written in cursive and spread from the corner onto the text.

"Who's Elina Prescott?" he asked.

"I do not know…observation," she said, referencing their conversation from earlier.

"We must have missed it." Noah wasn't trying to be dismissive; instead, he attempted to act rationally as he thought Syn would.

"How did we cut the cover?" she asked.

"Okay…ask the question. Make the hypothesis."

"I am unsure if I have enough to truly make that."

Noah moved from the bed, but not before offering a kiss. She held him to extend the affection.

"I'm due for debriefing at the guild. Find you at the university later?"

Syn nodded.

"I will be at—"

"Campus of Protohistoric Archaeology," he said. "Research Library. Past the agora. Level six, room B-15." Syn was impressed. "I would've taken you to the gates."

He bowed, smiled, and made his exit.

*   *   *

The illumination of the artificial sun indicated noon. Noah had taken his leisure pace back to the local guildhall. He still walked with a limp, a miracle given his condition when admitted to the hospital.

The guildhall stood apart from Corvos, built from one of the old ruins found when the exclave was colonized over fifteen hundred years ago. There wasn't much left save for a thirty-meter tall ashlar curtain wall coated in plaster, reinforced with buttresses, and topped with crenellations surrounding catacombs that descended over a hundred meters into the foundation of the exclave. The proctors had erected their sophisticated hall utilizing modern construction techniques, denser materials, and superior technology. There was also glass and a skylight large enough to accommodate flying vehicles.

Noah passed the notice board, the briefing rooms, and gyms, recognizing a few faces. There was a scrimm practicing in the firing range. An endolon exception—effectively what Bythos called defectors or citizens that no longer followed the proclamations of the people of Bythos—nodded in appreciation. They must have heard. Certainly, if Noah found them later in the guild tavern, a drink would be owed.

Noah spotted the one individual standing out in the cafeteria, a young girl, probably in her early teens, enjoying a meal while talking to a fellow proctor.

After that, Noah reached the engineering bays. He recognized Agosta's jagger being polished. Another, a torque, was in pieces. No way anyone survived that encounter. Near the end, Noah found Terri Zahn's multi-limbed cage.

Noah noted the significant number of damaged shells in the bay. A lightweight scrimm lola was being dismantled for parts in one stall, and a human prowler had suffered heavy damage from a recent sortie. There had to have been a recent clash between guild personnel and either a jacker caravan or scab hive.

The last stall held his dodger, significantly smaller than Agosta's and in far worse shape. Addressing the damage, the missing plates, punctures, and outright severed components, Noah was shocked how he could have survived.

They'd fix it. He completed his task; honor had been maintained.

"How in the name of Vothragna did you take out a watcher on your own?" she asked from behind Noah's shell.

Noah approached and bent around the dodger to find a dirty-blonde spitfire with perky checks working on the drive cluster of his shell.

"Does this mean I get to add a watcher stamp to my kill sheet?" Noah asked.

"No, I mean seriously, how did you do it?" she asked as she tapped her allkit on the various damaged components. "Your oil pump is punctured. The hydraulic system has completely lost pressure. You got fibrous muscle tears in every limb. Plasma core is breached. Both power cells have been destroyed, which I find especially impressive as they're located behind you, but since you suffered no damage to the dodger's spine, it would have had to have gone through you to damage them. Jump jets are completely buggered, and the sensor cluster in your helmet was crushed—how the fuck did you even survive this? You should be a meat pretzel."

Noah smiled; he knew who it was just by the sound of her bespoke tools. It had been a minute since they had shared a drink.

"I missed you too, Mannah," Noah said.

"Yes, yes, give us a hug, mate," she said as she stood and soiled his cleaned proctor dress with her filthy coveralls. He didn't care. "I heard you and the endolon." She winked.

"Is that common knowledge?"

"No, but *we* all know."

"Great. Who's the kid in the mess?"

"Dunno, some stray they picked up in Philokalia." Mannah resumed working on Noah's dodger, throwing out broken components, and there were plenty of those.

"Jacker?"

"No idea," she said, "but she's important."

Noah circled his machine, realizing the extent of the work ahead of Mannah. He then diverted his attention to the surprising number of other shells and cages in the bay.

"How are you?" Noah asked.

"A lot of damage; a lot of work to be done."

"I noticed…hive?"

"No, and not jackers or watchers or gaunts or demigods. Like I knew what you fought before they told me. Each opponent inflicts pain in different ways."

Noah approached the other crutches. They had all suffered so much damage as to question the survivability of their pilots. They could not all have been as lucky as he. He approached one, an expensive-looking midas. It must have been pushed through a blender, given the number of subsurface cuts scattered over the armor.

"So, something new ambushed this group?" he asked.

"Not a group," she said. "These are individual encounters." Noah was surprised by the revelation. "This ship is nearly ten thousand kilometers across. We've barely mapped out a fiftieth of its mass. Who knows that else can lie out there?"

Noah approached the suit and ran his fingers through the various slices in the armor.

"Still…" he said.

"Hey, I got a dozen apprentices coming this afternoon. You want to join them? You're a hell of a good wrench, your day job notwithstanding."

Noah nodded but made for a distant door.

"Perhaps. I'll be back," he said.

"Liar."

Noah reached the roof level of the hall, offering an impressive view of the flood plains beyond the walls. It was also a point of recreation for off-shift mercenaries.

Noah was still on disability leave and would be stuck in Corvos for the foreseeable future, a predicament he would not object to. Syn had told him she would be consigned to the University for at least a year, putting Noah in the position of potentially sacrificing his commission to prevent reassignment elsewhere. She hadn't asked, but he had made the commitment.

He groaned as his aching muscles strained when he sat down on a bench. He was alone only a minute when a recognizable fellow Staplegunner emerged from the lower level.

Agosta didn't say anything when he reached the railing and took in the view, two bottles of fermented cereal grains in view.

"Agosta," Noah said.

Agosta swiveled to see his friend.

"Nice day, Noah," he said, then approached Noah and offered a drink. Noah quickly scanned the empty roof, smirked, and accepted.

"Quite the interesting last few days we've had," Noah said as Agosta sat beside him.

"Agreed."

"Proctors keep no secrets. I assume you know."

"Not as much as you think. I got the broad strokes. The joy is in the minutia. I'm sorry…about your losses."

Noah threw the drink back; it had been a while since he tasted alcohol. It was good.

"Yeah," Noah said, "I'm not…trust me, you won't take joy in the details of my story. I'm just happy we made it back." There was silence as Noah figured he was expected to extrapolate. "Yes, she and I are fucking."

"I suppose a high a five would be socially improper and disrespectful." Agosta held out a hand, which Noah stared at before finally accepting the offer and slapping it. "I suspected your tastes were unconventional."

"Unconventional…because she's an alien?" Noah asked.

"Because she looks…honestly…a little…scrawny. Thought you'd go for someone with a bit of meat on their bones."

"It's not that bad—"

"She looks like a pillowcase full of elbows—"

"Endolon biology; low gravity homeworld—it doesn't matter. Are we good?"

"Copacetic, you have my blessings," Agosta said.

"Appreciated," Noah said. "And you? Terri told me you guys had to split up. How is everyone else?"

"They should cross our way in a day or so. Hoping they made it…I mean, it's Kaiden, Deven, and Sloan. They'll be fine. They ensured delivery, I'm sure."

"So why did you divert? I thought you were on a milk run to Philokalia? What gummed up the works?"

"She did."

"Who…that kid?"

"Elina Prescott," Agosta said, taking a drink. "she's a metron."

Noah nodded.

"Well, we could use another in our ranks," he said. "They're worth more than…wait." It finally hit him. "What's her fucking name?"

* * *

Syn had finally delivered the book to the waiting archives of Protohistoric Archaeology. There, she would be closely involved with the study of the book, and she had access to the whole of human and alien knowledge.

An expert in paleography would aid in analyzing not the words themselves but how the language was written. Accelerator mass spectrometry would be able to estimate the age of the manuscript. Syn could call on a staff of linguists specialized in codicology representing every culture on the vessel. Stemmatologists would compare the book against the millions of others in Corvos to find a connection. The ink's chemistry, the paper's composition, and how the text was applied would be studied under the most advanced machinery.

She was responsible for it all. Syn was the custodian of this single tome, and everything had to go through her. At the beginning of each day, it would be unlocked from its vault and eventually returned and logged. Syn was especially interested in monitoring any physical changes the book underwent. The other researchers didn't fully understand what Syn meant, but she didn't want to extrapolate.

It was the late afternoon, and Syn had the book under a soft UV light, searching for hidden information. She flipped a page, and she gazed at her double. No one had asked about her yet, and Syn didn't know what she would say that wouldn't sound crazy. Syn gently caressed the page, rolling her fingers over the illustration.

"I feel like I know you," Syn whispered.

You know yourself.

Syn examined the room, even though she knew it wasn't a voice she heard. And unless she developed a psychological condition, she was sure the voice was not hers. When someone listens to the voice in their head, they generally know who is speaking. Syn leaned closer to the book and stared at the illustration. Despite not possessing any evidence, there was a connection between the two.

"Are you real?" she whispered, unaware if a vocal response was required.

As real as you.

"Then am I real?" Syn waited and heard, or rather felt, nothing else. She stared at the image and considered that this was undoubtedly not an inner monologue. Syn had read that the scabs had no inner voice and that scrimms' manifested in ways they couldn't entirely explain. For endolons, it acted similar to humans, except her people never got songs stuck in their heads.

That is the more important question.

"How is this possible? Am I thinking these thoughts?"

In a way.

Syn noted the distance of colleagues and their potential to overhear. Observation, hypothesis, she thought to herself. Syn stepped away and approached a nearby window overlooking the agora, well away from the book.

"What are you?"

Another possibility, another variation. One that would have never found you if it wasn't for our connection.

"And did I recognize Noah from you?"

No, that was another. But I am the only one able to reach further. Our third lacks the connection to talk back, but she will in time. As related events occur, this connection will strengthen.

"So, how can you do this now?"

I'm unique, with an insight most lack.

"Intuition."

Prescience. I feel ideas that dictate my actions. Noah came to you. I had to bring him to me.

Syn returned to the book on its underlit table and flipped a few pages, passing illustrations of machines she had yet to identify.

"He is with you?"

He's not aware, but yes.

"And you can influence people…through dreams?"

It's only us I can reach for obvious reasons. We can influence each other in ways we can't immediately perceive. As our connection grows, what divides us will diminish.

"Meaning we'll become more alike."

It's happening even as we discuss this.

"I don't understand."

You will.

"So, what does your prescience tell you now?"

It tells me…that the smoke is a lie.

"What does that mean—"

And love him…because he won't be with you much longer.

Syn became alarmed and flipped the page to confront her doppelganger directly, a safe assumption.

"What does that mean?" Her tone had escalated. She waited but received no response.

"Hello?!" she shouted loud enough to alert researchers in the adjacent room. Some attempted to ignore her, assuming it was a momentary outburst from a frustrated scientist.

"What does that mean?!"

Now everyone was looking, and Syn didn't care. She wanted to tear that page out of the book as if that would do anything. Syn fell back on her chair, aware eyes were still watching. Everyone around her was human, and some were inexperienced with her kind. Perhaps this is just how they act.

"Love him…" Syn whispered to herself.

PARADISE

Aegis rarely disclose their names to strangers and prefer to remain known by their title. This doesn't work when away from Abraxas for extended periods. Their actual names are singular, multi-syllable, and wholly unique. Some believed these names are assigned based on position and that Aegis possessed a more straightforward, private name known only in privileged circles (this is, in fact, correct).

Tepheron Octoginta

Psylaxis, Machus, and Coulter occupied the royal hall. They were spread apart within the room and almost yelling at one another when Kabdila burst in.

"What the FUCK is going on here!?" Kabdila asked.

"Your court has been compromised!" Machus said as Kabdila circled the group and his royal chair he refused to sit in.

"I wouldn't believe that, even if it were true."

"Your so-called *Master of Coin*, your spy, has absconded with our carriage. Who does he represent? Does he act in your name?"

Kabdila stopped and confronted the purgitan, pushing deep into his personal space.

"Are you seriously that stupid?" Kabdila asked.

"How dare you?" Machus said with a growl, though a slight stutter uncovered a flaking veneer of arrogance. "We may have to put half your circle to flame to rout the heretics."

"My imperial sentries outnumber your people, so I'd like to see you try." Kabdila's tone settled as he approached his royal chair but didn't sit. "My court has not been compromised; I have the expected mix of sycophants, fanatics, and warmongers."

"I am calling on both orders of Silantine and Episcar."

"Let's cut through the deception; you danced around the issue, but my father found the last scion of Volani, and you implied, rather outright affirmed, that her death was the price of my kingdom's ascent." Kabdila could read Machus's confused face from across the city. This close, it was apparent. "...And holy shit, you didn't know."

"I certainly—"

"One thing Agosta taught me was how to spot a liar. I'm no longer going to address you. I'll be addressing your owner." He pointed but didn't look.

"I speak for myself—"

"Very well," Psylaxis said calmly as it stepped forward. Machus opened his mouth, but the machine stared at him with that fixed, composed facade.

"Your carriage was sitting outside the northern court," Kabdila said. "There's an iron access near one of our catacomb grates. He fled through there. It's called fortune. I'd claim the gods were involved if said gods weren't actually involved. Your wagon happened to be available. That is all...and why was it unguarded?

"Is your army gathering?" Psylaxis asked.

"Yes, I called on the knights, the sentries, and whatever militia I can spare with enough to operate the gates and towers. We'll be able to leave within the hour. You've claimed to be indestructible; why didn't you chase them down."

"I am not as impatient as you may think. Strategy is paramount."

"More than likely, we can't allow outsiders to discover you're not indestructible. And why haven't the gods been informed? I mean, if this is such an offense to steal a carriage, why haven't they mobilized? They should be faster at this than we ever could. Send a demigod."

"Philokalia is blocking our eyes to Abraxas," Psylaxis said quietly enough so the room's peripheral guards couldn't hear. "Gods are silent until then."

Kabdila groaned and almost coughed a laugh.

"Wonderful claim, omniscience, isn't it? Then it falls on us to chase these criminals down. We might have avoided this if you had informed me directly about this child when I assumed the regency. Leave it to the church to be evasive."

The distant massive iron and wood entrance doors groaned open, and a lance of city guards marched in with Deven Serenda in the lead. Kabdila marched down to confront them, several outer guards moving to support him.

"I've got a mind to execute the lot of you," Kabdila said. "Care to explain what happened?"

One guard behind Deven dropped to a knee and begged, "Please, my king, spare me for my failure!"

"Stand up, you idiot," Kabdila said, "let braver men talk." He then focused on Deven and perked a brow.

"Lieutenant Katona and I were assigned the outer gates," Deven said. "A nagomjii caravan was leaving when I caught one of the younger creatures attempting to pilfer a bag from Katona. I ordered the brood arrested and jailed. Katona disagreed. She believed the child would not survive incarceration."

"She's right about that," Kabdila said. "Did Agosta and the others employ that as a diversion?

"Until they were right on the gate when the call came through. A representative from church was present." Deven then sneered at Machus. "A proctor."

"Aaaaaa!" Kabdila pointed and gloated at the purgitan. Kabdila was going to enjoy this. "And fuck you too."

"He claimed to command the carriage," Deven said, encouraging the prince's diverted rage. "There wasn't an assumed authority. I do believe he was in this very room."

"Your inner circle," Kabdila said to Machus.

"Damned proctors," Machus grumbled to himself.

"I was suspicious but was assaulted by Katona," Deven said. "They breached the gates before the men could close it."

"Why would she do that?" Kabdila asked.

"Maybe she was seduced, your highness."

"Maybe they all were," Kabdila said as he returned up the steps and spoke to Psylaxis. "You lot want to offer details? The Pogrom's goal was to erase Volani from the map and ensure their lineage was annihilated." He lifted an index. "One child survived. One child! How is she a threat? Is she gifted in some way? Is she a daemon as I suspected?"

"If you can believe it," Psylaxis said, "gods keep secrets even from their people…and their creations."

Kabdila confronted Deven.

"You get a good look at the conclave caravan?"

"As best I could," Deven said. "Two women, two men, one child."

Kabdila circled the room again.

"Perhaps that legend of their gift to enchant the masses was true. She charmed my father to act against his best interest, and now she enthralled those closest to us. Imagine what she could do to a city or an army."

"Are you seriously entertaining that theory?" Machus asked.

"If true, it could exonerate everyone involved, save face, and justify a public execution of this last scion."

"The alternate is that Mr. Pike, who is clearly intelligent, also possessed a modicum of empathy," Psylaxis said. "Given my impressions of the man, I would venture that also a possibility."

"—The bastard could've had anyone and anything," Kabdila said. "Women. Men. Little boys—animals, I didn't care as long as he was loyal." The room was silent, and Kabdila gathered his thoughts. "I've known my spy for years," he said. "One does not share his perversions without sharing other tastes. You get to know a man. This is not like him." Kabdila made for the throne he had been neglecting. He sat upon it and rested elbows on knees. "He won't travel south because there's nothing but ruins and nags. The timing couldn't have been worse."

"From what I overheard," Deven said, "their plan was to travel north and try to reach Aquino or Corvos."

"Recovering the carriage must take precedence," Machus said.

"Why?" Kabdila asked.

"It must."

Kabdila's eyes widened as he grasped what Machus was not saying. He stood back up and approached Machus slowly, pointing firmly as if a sword to run the purgitan through.

"You acted in response to the wagon," Kabdila said. "You didn't know about the girl, and it was you that issued the alert. You had no idea she was being abducted. You only cared about the vehicle. Why?"

Machus looked to Psylaxis, as blank as ever. The priest dared not speak and waited for the machine to reveal the true extent of the situation. The delay revealed to Kabdila what he hadn't considered until that point.

"Where is the Aegis?" Kabdila asked.

Machus and Psylaxis both turned to face the regent.

Kabdila's jaw unhinged and fell slack.

"Are you shitting me?" he said.

* * *

A hundred soldiers had gathered with Deven in the lead. Coulter paced in front and barked at them.

"Your orders unwavering," Coulter said, "unfaltering, with no lenience to failure. We have heretics and deserters making their escape from the empire in possession of not only invaluable intelligence but holy relics from the Ascension, which they mean to sell to our enemies. While our gods could certainly intervene, this opportunity falls on us to prove our fidelity. We stand to gain considerably by their grace. There can be no mercy given to these traitors. Our success shall be nothing less than eradicating these infidels and those accompanying them. And from the spoils come the blessings of plunder, rank, and faith."

The soldiers banged their shields as Kabdila stormed out from the fortress. The men kowtowed, and Coulter bent a knee, but the prince had none of that.

"Coulter! Work these dogs to a froth. Deven, a word."

Deven separated from the rest of the group and dutifully approached the future king.

"They don't know the truth, your highness?" Deven asked quietly.

"Of course not," Kabdila said. "What we reveal to the grunts would spill to the mob; there'd be chaos. No one will know of the missing Conclave or that the Aegis are currently blinded by the very machines they maintain. Outside the inner circle, those who know will face purgitan flame."

"Understood, your highness," Deven said, leaving a lingering question unanswered.

"Two tasks befall you, and you cannot return until both are seen to completion," Kabdila said. "One involves this proctor and his…bizarrely foolish act of heresy, and the safe recovery of the Conclave coffin and who resides inside. Second is the hunting of this…traitor…the one from our inner circle…but I hope he might have been enchanted. If you are given the opportunity, offer him the chance to recant. If he seeks to pad his pocket, I'll consider it. But for you, I can offer considerably more."

"I understand, your highness," Deven said stridently.

"Were you and Sloan lovers?"

"No, your highness."

Kabdila offered a double-take, surprised by the sudden answer.

"Well…why not? She certainly wasn't ugly. Does she butter her bread on the other side?"

"Not to my knowledge."

"Do you?"

"Sir—"

"Don't answer; I shouldn't know. How well do you know her? Do you believe her capable of these actions?"

"I thought not, your highness, but it appears we were both stupefied today."

"Where's her home."

"She doesn't have one."

"Everyone has one. How far to the throne are you?"

"I'm just a ranger, your highness," Deven said.

"I don't have men enter my hall without knowing everything about them. You're part of the Kaelum royal family, are you not?"

Deven stepped back, unsure how to respond.

"Thirteenth in line, your highness," he said, "but the ancestry is no longer recognized—"

"Our future expansion as an empire depends on the elimination of the last scion of Volani. With that power, all other threats become inconsequential, including the various other challenges of power. I know Draggo and Aquino forged an alliance because of the threat of Imperial patronage. After all these years, what is there to gain by keeping Kaelum and Eridius underfoot? Depending on your actions in this matter, I'd make a decree offering you an office under royal command—a baron regent of Kaelum. You can marry an Aurago relation and subsequently have that child assume the throne as the first Kaelum royal in two hundred years. You'd still be taxed and blood-allied to Aurago...but your people would have their kingdom back."

Deven couldn't initially respond. It was a safe assumption that one in line of succession would sniff any throne of someone able to ascend someone's position. Deven lived his entire life aware that his people lacked direction and were nothing more than vassals. He could achieve something that no one in his family had been able to accomplish for over a century.

However, Deven was also aware the obliteration of his ancestors occurred at the hands of gods and requested by Aurago. Deven firmed his lips and stood indomitable.

"I'll find them all, your highness," he said.

"And that's how I earn loyalty," Kabdila said as he walked away. "By the way, Serenda...it's your majesty now. My father is dead."

Coulter had been listening. He glared at Deven, then intercepted his prince before reaching the court gates.

"Your highness, did you just promise the nobility to an imperial sentry?" Coulter asked.

"I dangled a spud on a branch in front of livestock," Kabdila whispered. "They'll follow something they'll never achieve. The trick is not showing the stick."

Deven stared as the two men conversed quietly.

He knew what was being spoken despite not hearing it.

There was also that lingering question that was neither asked nor answered—was Deven part of that inner circle?

Agosta had prepared him...

...and Deven could see the stick.

TORUS

They may parade articles of agreement, but most pirates only abide by them when their CIC is watching. Plus, each corsair crew operates with their own code, some contradicting other articles operated on other trains. Each one shares a few similarities. Most crimes are punished with exile, often in areas where a criminal will face hardships.

Weapons must be locked except in cases of raiding. They don't tolerate stealing, cheating, or assaults against their kind, common sense sort of stuff. I played the part on three different trains, each with its articles to memorize. The Arrowhead didn't allow women. The Crescent Star prohibited onboard gambling. The Number Seven insisted fealty to Communion, though I couldn't find any connection to them.

I never personally saw these private yards, but I know at least the names of two of them—Acadia and Concordia—with rumors that there may be a half-dozen others. I also heard about the Silver Bullet, but no one has ever personally spotted it.

Florence Mesdag
A Canton of Pirates

"Wait, you were sleeping?" Noah asked.

Terri straightened herself in her CIC chair as she woke. Noah was unimpressed.

"No," Terri said with a groan, "...I was paying attention—"

"I was ranting for ten minutes!" Noah said.

"I got the gist." Terri gazed out the window to see the Vanderov was finally exiting the Graveyard of Black Church. Several lingering ruins passed, most decayed and reduced to rubble.

"Okay, what did I say?" Noah asked.

"You think endolons look weird," Terri quietly said as she attempted to orientate herself.

"No, I didn't; I said...wait, what?"

"What?" Terri just blinked a few times, ignoring what she said.

"What's that?"

"What's what?"

"What's an endolon?" Noah asked.

Terri opened her mouth, then closed it. For a moment, she thought she understood the world. She checked through the window to confirm where she was. Everything fell back into place.

"Nothing…I don't know." Terri leaned forward to her desk. She was in the engine cab on her CIC chair in front of the controls. She and Noah had shared a drink and gotten to ranting about recent events.

"Are you okay?" Noah asked.

"Certainly. You have thoughts about our passengers?"

"You were sleeping," Noah said. "That's what I was ranting about."

"Right…"

"For ten minutes."

"Right."

"You sure you're okay?"

Terri glanced out the window.

There it was. Again. Between the ruins. She didn't indicate shock or confusion. She didn't direct Noah. Terri had good eyes, making out the dark, gangly figure hundreds of meters away, facing her window. Neither she nor the figure reacted. It never did, and she had gotten used to it. A second later, it vanished behind the building.

"Yes…" she said.

"What is it?" Noah asked.

Terri shifted from the window and focused on her drink.

"Do you ever get the feeling… not that you've done something before? More that you remember something you couldn't have done?"

"What the girl said got to you."

"Even before we brought them on board, and it's been getting worse. Like we're all moving towards something."

"Yeah, Corvos."

"No…Not a place…"

Noah gazed out the window, but all he could see were the scattered ruins dotting the desert. The dense tracklands pointed to buried memories of an abandoned empire, sand and monsters where a city once stood.

"We're out of the graveyard," Noah said, "but it's going to be a while at this speed before we clear the Dagos."

"A couple if we're still stopping at Ragged Hollow," Terri said. "It may be prudent for us to resupply."

"Drop off our passengers?"

"Those who want to go. I've got a feeling they may remain. I mean, he's got military training from Corvos."

"He's not from Corvos."

"Now, now, let's not judge a person on their skin," Terri said, remembering her conversation with Agosta the previous day.

"It's not that," Noah said. "Part of his attire is outdated from the Aurago navy. Probably served on a Ziggurat or privateer."

"Maybe it's scavenged."

"Fits too well."

"And she's Volani," Terri said.

Noah took another drink.

"Sympathetic soldier," he said, "rescues an orphan and abandons his responsibility due to a newfound sense of empathy and responsibility. It's an…old story."

"Is it?"

Noah just shrugged. Terri kept her attention outside her window, expecting to see it again, that shadow that parents claimed hid under beds, the one that would abduct children if they were naughty. The one she'd seen a dozen times in the past two weeks.

"We're the product of someone's else fantasy and the creator of another," she said. "I mean, that was the point she was trying to make. We may have a few questions for your ex when we finish the contract."

"Dad! Sloan!" Elina screamed from the mess room. "Everyone else who's not…Dad or Sloan!"

Noah and Terri exited and ran into the next car to Elina in front of her book. Sloan and Agosta entered from the opposite side.

"They answered!" Elina said.

"More defacing," Noah said as the group crowded the girl. She flattened the Codex and pointed to a page halfway through the book.

"I didn't see it happen. I just flipped a page…and there it was" They moved closer to see the inscription where Elina was pointing.

Hello Elina. I'm Syn.

It was written with a graceful hand, neat, not cursive. Whoever it was, they were making every effort to be legible.

"Your ex?" Terri asked Noah.

"Another…time?" Agosta asked.

"Another place," Terri said.

"Which one?" Noah asked before addressing Elina. "You are using a pencil, right. Just want to make sure we can erase this if need be. Is she? Can we erase it?"

"Looks like it," Elina said.

"She was always a smart one."

"Let me remind you that this is not your ex-girlfriend," Agosta said.

Elina flipped a few pages before and after in hopes of spotting something else, but when she returned to the original, the previous inscription had been revised.

Sorry for the stain.

"Well, that explains that," Terri said with a smile. "Also, it appears the Codex won't change while you're looking at it."

Elina grabbed her pencil and inscribed under Syn's message.

"What are you writing?" Sloan asked.

"Honey, perhaps you should…" Agosta trailed off as Elina ignored him.

Did you damage the cover?

Elina put the pencil down, crossed her arms…and waited.

And waited.

Everyone kept quiet, exchanging awkward stares. Elina then flipped a page and back. Nothing. Then again.

I did not.

"So, it was the other one," Terri said. Elina flipped the page and back, and it had been added too.

Is Noah there?

"Yes, I am," Noah said.

"She can't hear you," Elina said.

Noah leaned in and reached for the pencil.

"May I?" he asked.

Elina nodded. Noah took the pencil and wrote below the question.

Yes.

"You know I could have done that, right?" Elina said before flipping.

The smoke is a lie.

They exchanged glances, confused by the statement. The writing style was consistent between the entries.

"What does that mean?" Agosta asked. "Something about your abilities, Elina."

Elina couldn't conceive how smoke could be a lie. It doesn't speak to her. While it seemed to choose people, it never manifested any motivation or objective.

Elina wrote, *Am I there?*

They waited.

Elina tossed pages and scanned for any alterations. Nothing came through. She even tapped pages as if the other side could hear.

They waited.

"Are these connections temporary?" Elina asked.

"Hey…don't worry," Terri said. "Baby steps. You're talking to another universe. Be glad they speak our language. Let us know if something changes" Terri walked past them, towards her room, then shouted, "Noah, you're on the chair!"

* * *

It was an hour later. Noah was the conductor on duty. Terri was in her cabin, lying on her bed, staring out into the Mare Dagos. Uno was due to swing behind Nimbus within the hour, but she wasn't tired. The tracks here were uneven and often half-buried in sand, but the Van's dashpots absorbed most of the vibrations, offering a somewhat smooth ride. Terri couldn't sleep right unless she was moving. She needed those vibrations.

Not a place, she thought to herself. A small glass half-filled with alcohol with the color of dark ochre sat between her hands on her chest.

The rolling dunes were almost hypnotic as they oscillated and bowed like waves in the window. The odd set of ruins were islands of death in a sea of iron. The Vanderov's near-pristine red and gold body stood out against the near monochromatic landscape.

A soft knock sounded from the door.

"Come!" Terri said. The door slowly creaked open, and Elina's head poked in. They stared at each other without a word. "Yes?"

"Do I need a reason?" Elina asked. Terri let out a huff and fell out of bed. She welcomed Elina to the opposite seat and sat down herself. Terri placed the glass in front of her. Elina waited, and Terri could read it on her face.

"Too young for alcohol?" Elina asked.

Terri smirked, nodded, then grabbed another glass and emptied half her drink into it. She offered it.

It was strong.

Terri usually didn't water her drink. It was still a little much for Elina, who almost gagged.

"Uch! Why do people like this?" she asked.

"They don't. They pretend it's good," Terri said. She opened her hand, expecting Elina to return the glass, but she held on, stubborn. "They use fancy words and claim the unpleasantness is part of the appeal. They'll make the case that drinks that taste like dirt and train oil are preferred. Just an excuse to offer prestige to the disgusting avenue to inebriation."

"Then why do you drink it?" Elina said as she tried to take another sip. The second was worse.

"Because on occasion, I need a disgusting avenue to inebriation."

Elina forced down a third sip. Alcohol tasted of peat moss, wood, and disinfectant. The buzz hit her, and she giggled. Terri knew she might have to answer for this to her father, but she drank it straight when Elina was her age.

"He's not my real Dad, you know," Elina said.

"I wouldn't have guessed," Terri said, dripping with sarcasm.

"We crafted a family. Sloan too."

"Didn't you just meet her?"

"Dad likes her."

"Yeah, I think we all know. Sorry you had to hear that."

"Like I don't know those things. Dad and I move a lot. He couldn't keep everything a secret. I'm older than I look."

Terri cocked her head, not sure if she was concerned or impressed.

"Fourteen," Terri said.

"I'm sixteen."

"You're fourteen, your father told me."

"Damn it."

"Maturity is a state of mind," Terri said after downing the rest of her glass like a boss. "I've been riding the rails since I was six. When I claimed the conductor's seat, I commanded men twice my age."

"Must have been fun."

"Not always. You think someone like me with a train like this happens overnight. I didn't fall prostrate or let anyone have their way for it, regardless of gender. It wasn't luck. Attempts were made, and there's a line of scars on those that underestimated me."

Elina's smile was certainly augmented by her minor intoxication, and she reached halfway through her drink while Terri poured a straight shot for herself.

"I'm going to be an oxomancer," Elina said.

"From what I've been told, you're certainly capable."

"I've been practicing since I was a child, before I even knew there was a name for it. Trying to focus on the basics."

"Don't push yourself. The big spells need regulators."

"I've heard. Simple stuff."

"Show me…"

Elina cackled and placed her cup back on the table. She stared at it attentively, establishing its place on this table, in this train, in this world. She came to understand the composition of the metal and the deformations made by a lethargic forger. Terri couldn't see from her angle, but Elina's eyes had changed. Tinted fumes wafted as the girl blinked. The liquid started to shake, and the metal cup folded out of existence, refolding a foot closer to Terri, next to her glass. The fluid didn't shift, and it promptly splattered on the table.

"Shit," Elina said.

"…I mean…that kind of worked," Terri said as she reached for a towel and cleaned up. "You drank too much anyway." She wiped the table and took the glasses back. "Shown anyone else that?"

"Only works on objects, not people. Sorry I spilled your—"

"On trust me, I'm still impressed. How big have you gone?"

"Hatbox."

"How far?"

"Couple dozen meters."

"Hell of a start, though…We'll get you a trainer." She was more talented than Terri thought, and oxomancers were a gifted and rare sort. It explained Agosta's safeguarding. Perhaps having them join her crew wasn't such a bad idea.

"We…are you part of the family?" Elina asked.

"Your dad is not my type, and I think he's taken."

"Family is what you make it."

"I know too well…The family you choose is stronger than the ones given." Terri drifted her attention to the window, expecting to see her phantom for that fleeting second before vanishing, but there was nothing. "Elina…that shadow. The illustration in the book. Have you seen it? For real?"

"Yeah," Elina said, "it marks where I should go, who I should trust. I've seen it since…well, since my parents died."

"Most assume it's just folklore. Marked more by graffiti and stories passed between generations. Actual accounts are few, made by people who claim it an omen. No one alive ever sees it twice."

"But you have…haven't you?"

Terri had issues answering. She wanted to be honest but had accepted keeping such a secret close to heart. No one knew about it, not even her crew. She opened her mouth to answer but was interrupted by the radio chiming with a somewhat annoying but short-lived alarm. Terri reached over and clicked the intercom.

"CIC," Terri said.

"Contact, 195, 1500, and closing," Noah announced.

"What is it?" Terri asked.

"Privateer…maybe?"

With that, both women exited quickly from the room.

* * *

The olive-colored, iron hood-class locomotive with a dozen mismatched cars trailing emerged from behind one of the ruins. It was holding pace with the Vanderov, if not slightly faster, as the track it was riding closed the distance between the two trains. The locomotive was encircled with walkways and prefixed, not with a cowcatcher but a massive iron pincer.

The top hatch of the Vanderov's locomotive flung open, and Terri emerged with Kaiden. He used his impeccable augmented vision while she extended a vintage telescope.

"That's familiar," Kaiden said.

"And not menacing at all," Terri whispered.

"They came behind us the moment we left the graveyard."

"Those are privateer colors."

"They're popping smoke…It's green."

"Okay," Terri said, then shouted back down the ladder, "Noah get Mannah to reduce to notch 3; let's see what they…" Terri trailed off, then whispered something to herself.

"Skipper?" Kaiden asked.

"*The smoke is a lie*," she said louder, then shouted back, "Delay that. Hold speed." She peered through her scope and scrutinized the details of the incoming train. "I don't know this one, you?"

"Negative, skipper," Kaiden said.

"Agosta?" Terri shouted back into the train.

"Yes," Agosta said as his head popped into view.

"You served on privateers."

Agosta was somewhat taken back

"Okay, we sharing now?" he asked.

"Come up, see if you recognize this one."

Agosta scaled the ladder and squeezed beside the other two, accepting Terri's scope. He examined what he saw.

"Almost looks like the Mourning Star," he said. "That's m-o-u-r-n-i-n-g, by the way."

"Are you sure?"

"I'd say 95%."

"Noah, flash them," Terri said. "Tell them we are on a medical mission and can't slow down."

Noah opened a panel on the car's roof and winched up a signal lamp. He activated it and flashed a coded message to the other train. He waited, then repeated the transmission.

The approaching trained popped green smoke once again. It accelerated. It switched to another line that would eventually bring them to parallel by only a few meters.

"Rail code dictates we slow," Kaiden said.

"I don't buy it," Terri said before shouting below. "Tooley! Can we outrun her?"

"On a normal day, absolutely," Mannah said, "but full steam could gurk the regulator, and then we're completely scuppered!

"What'd you say?" Agosta asked.

"We're in the backseat on prom night!"

"Is she having a stroke?"

"It's fine," Terri said. "I need everyone to go red!"

"Your crew know how to defend themselves?" Agosta asked

"We know a thing or two," she said as she descended back into the train. "Kaiden, open the lockers, get this man his weapons."

Kaiden descended and made for the rear of the locomotive.

Noah followed.

"I'll prep a greeting for our guests," Noah said, followed up by patting Deven's shoulder. "Are you up for a fight?"

"No," Deven said, "but when has my vote counted for anything."

PARADISE

MACHINA

A dark world entirely covered by storms that hangs off an orbit ring between Kenoma and Philokalia, Machina was once the steward of Draggo. Even though the kingdom's flag transferred to Bythos, they still consider Machina their home. The people and the royal line have attempted to break the "curse" plaguing their homeland but to no avail. Machina has a single moon, Skaras, still green and lush, though virtually inaccessible. Machina connects to Bythos through the pillar Basilica.

Orbital Period. *360 days*
Satellites. *1 (Skaras)*
Rotational Period. *18 hours*
Major Semi-Axis. *7,200 km*
Equatorial Circumference. *1,500 km*

PHILOKALIA

This intimidating world orbits Bythos so closely the two worlds are only a few meters apart at their highest peaks. Philokalia rides along a groove (the Kalian Channel) running along the equator of Bythos and is controlled by Hydranis.

Orbital Period. *300 days*
Satellites. *None*
Rotational Period. *10 hours*
Major Axis. *3,441 km*
Equatorial Circumference. *315 km*

Encyclopedia Titanica
Corvos

The group couldn't see Sadatoni, but the positioning of Philokalia above indicated how far they were. The nagomjii wagons had gathered outside the forest, the ones that had escaped the city and the ones they were meant to rendezvous with.

The stolen conclave carriage sat nearby. The trained kips were still resting from an hour of constant running.

"Looks like the nag tribal chief is allowing sanctuary," Noah said to Terri as they gathered near a tree and away from the others. It was a strange alliance, but right now, she was the only one he trusted. He wasn't aware, but she felt the same. Neither fully understood why.

"What about the others?" Terri asked, motioning to the carriage.

"Some older fellow and a girl that stole the carriage. A sentry from the gates. A rather eclectic sort of expatriates."

"I mean, will the nags offer sanctuary to them as well?"

"Unsure as of yet."

"What's their story?"

"I imagine we'll find out. He's the prince's spy."

"Pardon?" Terri asked.

"They called him the Master of Coin. He's Aurago's magistrate of intelligence. Not sure how much he knows, but he was atop an echelon high enough to attend every royal gathering. He spoke out of turn, talked back to Machus, so…I like him. But he did so without fear of repercussion."

"Maybe this is it."

"Doubt it. You don't climb that high with impatience and arrogance. Someone crossed a line."

"Have you considered this is part of a plan to shame the church?"

"I can think of simpler ways."

Terri leaned against the tree, both nervous and calm. They had to consider their following actions and couldn't risk remaining too close to the city for too long.

"How did you win over the nags?" she asked.

"They remember every kindness, every crime," Noah said. "Wasn't expecting to come back so promptly. From what the doonjii said, Katona and Serenda allowed them to cross the gate despite calls for detainment."

"He's feeling generous," Terri said, her experience with aliens being extremely limited. They were welcome in Corvos, but they generally avoided the universities.

"They don't feel the way we do," Noah said. "By sparing his people from punishment, their culture imposes a debt upon Wisekjii. He was obliged to offer refuge, and we would have insulted him if we rejected that."

Noah looked to Philokalia; he knew by now the planet would have crossed the city below and that Abraxas would soon emerge overhead. Uno was between them and would appear for only a moment.

"They'll come for all of us," Noah said.

"Well," Terri said, almost triumphant, "you're a faithless proctor now; can't have that knowledge public."

"My motivations are…complicated."

Terri reached for Noah and tore the Ascension emblem from his vest. At least she tried. It took a few good pulls, and a moment of awkwardness later, it came free. Noah didn't stop her as Terri tossed the patch to a nearby creek.

"They don't need to be," Terri said.

They approached the carriage and found it still locked. An unkempt girl with matted hair and torn clothes leaned against a wheel, holding her hand, likely covering an injury. At the same time, the older man, still adorned in expensive fabrics, examined the vehicle, still trying to figure out how it was supposed to open. That left the imperial sentry attending to the kips, ensuring they wouldn't take off.

"How did you steal a Conclave carriage?" Noah asked. The man immediately walked in front of the girl as she stood.

"No one was using it," Agosta said.

"And you are?" Terri asked.

"Unimportant."

Noah offered a wide berth to the two and circled the carriage.

"Have you checked the carriage for anything of value?" Noah asked.

"It's locked," Elina said from behind Agosta.

Noah approached the rear of the carriage. It had a traditional Aegis lock, meaning it did not employ a key but rather a security measure that prevented outside access outside of Ascension personnel. Noah hoped his handprint hadn't been revoked yet.

He gripped the handle, and a chime rang out. Noah twisted the handle, and it unlocked the carriage.

He looked inside.

The color from his face fell away. Terri walked back to see into the carriage as well.

"Holy shit," Terri whispered.

"We're all dead," Noah said.

The conclave coffin was still secured at the back of the carriage.

Noah stepped in and moved to the control panel next to it.

"Well, that's familiar," Terri said. "I pulled that out of the wreckage when the conestoga crashed."

"Please be empty, please be empty," Noah repeated to himself as he tapped a few buttons on the side of the machine designed to appear magical to the uneducated. It sent out a deep below, followed by a sequence of beeps. A gust of air echoed out, and the coffin cover disassembled.

Within rested a frail feminine figure with white flowing hair, suspended as if in water. Her features were almost withered but not disheveled. She was pale white, with loose white fabric that flapped across her skin. It was the Aegis Syn, a living god.

"You've got to be kidding," Terri whispered.

Agosta noticed the two frozen in disbelief and joined them. He stared at the, unfortunately, kidnapped Aegis and shook his head.

"Well, looky here," Agosta said with a broad grin, "someone threw away a perfectly good deity."

"Have some respect," Noah said.

"No thanks, got my own," Agosta said before speaking to Elina. "We're leaving."

She nodded.

"Where?" Terri asked.

"Better you don't know," Agosta answered as he gathered what supplies he could and encouraged Elina ahead of him.

"Probably west," Elina said. Agosta threw up his arms.

"Was it this level of foolishness the cause of your capture?!" Agosta said.

"I like her. Besides, we're all in this together."

"When prisoners escape a jail, they don't hang around, and they don't remain together. Why the sudden loyalty? We've known them for an hour."

"A forest starts as a seed."

"...And takes time we don't have."

Noah stared at Syn, and a compulsion swept over him to touch her, but he fought against it. Syn smiled, and he couldn't help but return the favor.

She recognized him, and she wasn't afraid.

"An army will be coming!" Terri said.

"I know, and not just for that thing," Agosta said.

Noah stepped back as the Aegis floated quietly in her coffin.

"Wait," Noah said. Agosta stopped. "You're a servant of the regent, inner circle...is this under his command?"

Agosta glanced to Elina and then back to Noah.

"He'd execute us both," Agosta said. "Rather, more specifically, there's not a kingdom in this universe that wouldn't murder the lot of us for what's in that carriage."

"Corvos wouldn't," Terri said.

"While I appreciate your loyalty, my experience points to the contrary."

"Regardless, we need to formulate a strategy. For one, we can't linger. The nags will help."

"Will they," Agosta said, "when hundreds of fanatics all wishing to sow favor with their gods come storming over that hill, will they be as friendly?

"Thousands!" came the shout.

Everyone looked across the hill as a single guard walked toward them. Agosta stepped up to form a line with Terri and Noah.

"Deven!" Sloan said, almost spooking the beasts of burden. She ran out to meet him, and they embraced. "Did it go according to plan?" They two met up with the rest.

"You were right, milor..." Deven said to Agosta. "About everything."

"Told you," Agosta said.

"You know about the Aegis?" Deven was practically out of breath from running. He tried stealing a strider, but the opportunity didn't emerge. He could have shed his armor, but something told him he'd be needing it.

"Yeah," Agosta said.

"You picked the wrong carriage," Deven said.

"All it did was accelerate their response. Their reaction would've been equally brash when they discovered who I was with."

"But now the machines are after you as well."

Agosta hadn't considered that. Armies must move from water to water in their pursuit. They must stop, rest, and prepare. Psylaxis was not required to do any of that.

"Yeah, that could be an issue," Agosta said.

"I told them what you told me, heading north. What direction are we going?"

"Apparently, since we're all sharing, west. But I never agreed to a fellowship. What's our timetable?"

"Ten, maybe fifteen minutes behind me," Deven said.

Agosta turned and walked past the others to meet Elina, still holding her arm by the carriage. He reached for her hand to check the extent of the wound.

"How bad is that?" he asked.

Elina recoiled from him. He hadn't touched her once and was initially concerned; her response pointed to past trauma, but body language indicated that wasn't the case.

"Nothing," she said. "I just cut myself during the escape."

"Let me see."

"It's nothing. It'll heal quickly." She almost fought him off.

"At this point, can you afford to keep secrets?"

Elina took a deep breath and, against her better judgment, revealed her arm, the inch cut on the outside below her elbow, and the bright splinter of white light spilling from it.

Agosta immediately covered it.

"Okay, keep that cover—" he said.

"Holy shit!" Sloan said as she noticed it as well.

There went that idea.

"You, shut up!" Agosta said.

"At this point, can you afford to keep secrets?" Sloan smirked back. She would have to explain how she could hear him so well at some point.

"What is it?" Terri asked.

"She's a daemon," Sloan said. There was no reverence in her tone. She recognized another outcast, like herself.

"Angels of Paradise," Deven said. There was a slight hint of reverence in his voice.

"She's walking around in a human suit?" Noah asked.

"Not exactly," Elina said as she accepted a cloth from Agosta and wrapped herself. "That's how I prefer to look. And I've been wearing this face since I was born."

There was a byzantine and thunderous greeting from the nagomjii tribal chief who noticed the new arrival. Wisekjii pushed past the wall of humans to embrace Elina. The tribal leader spoke in his tongue.

"*They who inherit the universe.*" Terri translated, "*You are given peace.*"

"Okay?" Elina said, still in the grip of the alien.

"Sanctuary," Wisekjii said back through a thick accent.

"You speak our language?" Terri asked.

"Words belong to no one," Wisekjii said. "We know the ways of men. Their actions speak through the ground. Predictable. I knew you would gather. You call luck; I call fortune. Take everything and follow us. We know forests. Will disappear."

"They suspected that," Deven said. "It might not be a good idea."

Wisekjii returned to his people, ordering them to pack up.

"Do we leave the Aegis?" Terri whispered to Noah. He nodded.

"Yes…for the best," he said. "It'll appease the Ascension and may cut the legs of the army in pursuit."

"Oh, I don't think so," Agosta said. "We just proved a god could be kidnapped. They can't allow any of us to live."

"I'll accompany you," Syn said as her coffin drifted from the back of the carriage; she still floated inside. Her voice was soft, almost a whisper, yet it carried to all of them. "It's imperative that I do so."

The group stared back, a mix of shock, annoyance, and enervation. Without a word, Agosta walked away. Noah stepped closer to the Aegis.

"You were the one that called for me," Noah said. "By name. Why?"

"Because familiarity begets coincidence," she said.

"It's a risk…they'll chase us to the ends of worlds for you," Noah said.

"I'm worth it." Another smile from her instilled Noah with emotions he couldn't understand, like if a lover and a beloved parent both smiled for something he had done. Was this part of their power, how they instilled adoration and worship in the masses? Was it genetic? Was he inhaling contaminated air radiated from her or her coffin? Or was it magic?

Agosta approached Wisekjii.

"We appreciate the shelter," Agosta said, "and we mean no disrespect. But that army will approach. They will catch up. You may hide from a few, but not from many. And if they find us in your care, no matter your weapons, numbers, or the power of your voice, they will kill every one of you. If we leave now, you can do as much to assist by offering a diversion. You can let them think they're with you. Take the carriage. Claim it as salvage. Let them search it. They'd die to capture us. They won't die for deception. Make a stance…be strong. But be innocent, and you'll be safe."

Wisekjii understood what Agosta said. The alien considered the obligations he was compelled to follow. He nodded in agreement.

"We take carriage. You take vardo. Fair," the alien said. Agosta agreed though the idea of controlling a small house intimidated him. He revisited the group, still gathered near the coffin and the Conclave carriage.

"Our plan is to travel west," Agosta said. "Splitting still feels viable."

"East and west while the nag move north," Sloan said. Agosta nodded.

"They're taking the carriage and will use it as a diversion," Agosta said. "They offered a vardo. It's clumsy, but the kips are strong. We'll need that for what lies ahead."

"But if we split, who's without it?" Noah said. "That coffin is heavy and sluggish under its own power."

"To compound matters," Terri said, "there's not much west. You'd have to circumvent the Body of Tyrus. I assume your destination is Corvos, and I'd normally support that, but you'd have to pass through Eridius, and you'll find no allies there. Unfortunately, east is our best shot. And one direction equates cooperation."

"You may have a point," Noah said. "We're surrounded by kingdoms that share no love for Aurago, but I can't see any of them providing sanctuary. That being said, Draggo and Pyxis lie to the east, and last I checked, they were both at war. That may provide a distraction…lure armies into conflict."

"My plan was not to lead us into a crossfire," Terri said.

"What was your idea then?" Agosta asked. Terri took a step closer.

"You finally agreeing with the child that we're all in this together?" she asked.

"I'm not a chi—" Elina said.

"Don't care," Terri said, still facing Agosta. "Not five minutes ago, you said we were all on our own. I'll also add that you've yet to prove your motivations. This child is an unknown variable. I've no idea what she can do."

"I'm…standing here," Elina said as she threw up her damaged but bandaged arm.

"And what are your intentions with her?" she asked. "It was a fortunate coincidence we met up but did you seriously sacrifice one of the most powerful positions this universe had to save someone that evidently you just met?"

Agosta considered it. It was madness, and yet his resolve never faltered. He knew the difference between right and wrong in life, and when given the opportunity, he would encourage the nobler option with those who listened. When the time came to do the adverse, there was regret but not apprehension. But this was different. She was.

"I'm as surprised as you are," he said.

"Division would divide the army," Sloan said. "Split three ways between us and the nags; we've got a better chance for survival."

"Split three ways still swings overwhelmingly in their favor," Terri said.

"I did say thousands," Deven said.

"Together or apart makes no difference," Terri said.

"Listen to her," Syn whispered, a statement which threw Terri off, who just stared blankly before shaking herself back into focus.

"Sure…okay…" Terri said, "thanks for the vote of confidence…god?"

"I'm sorry, who are you again?" Sloan asked Terri.

"At this point, does that matter?" Terri said. "Our destination is the same, regardless of our motivations. We need to work towards that, and looking above, we're getting pressed for time."

"Wait, what are you thinking?" Agosta asked.

"Crossing the Sufferance War was never my idea. That is." Terri pointed to the east. Just under the slowly moving world of Philokalia stretched a peak from Bythos. Noah and Agosta both leaned it to follow her aim. "Mount Astran."

The group stared, and the realization dawned on them.

"Oh, FUCK THAT!" Agosta said.

Noah threw up his arms.

"Why not?" he shouted. "If you're falling to your death, might as well flap your hands!"

"That's suicide," Agosta said.

"Only if you plan on dying," Terri said.

CONESTOGA

Cenotaph. *The only noteworthy inhuman artifact within Corvos is a large monument at the center of the Citadel. It is not particularly tall at five meters, but it has been respected by those who built the city around it, offering a wide berth of trees and tended grass within a large park. Initial archeological investigations have determined that the Cenotaph continues down into the ground for as deep as surveyors have attempted to dig, potentially to the base of the exclave, but only the portion above contains any writing, a strange dialect that matches most of the others seen across the Conestoga. The Cenotaph can also be adjusted through a series of rotating disks that comprise its top half. Each disc contains a sequence of glyphs, but despite centuries of examination, no arrangement of symbols has ever revealed a purpose or function to this puzzle, and it remains unsolved to this day.*

Corvos, An Unabridged History

Within the engineering bay of the proctor guildhall in Corvos, Mannah concentrated on repairing Noah's dodger. She was exceptional, but this shell was in moderately poor shape. She decided to work late, not that she considered it an effort. Occasionally, she'd sit alone in her apartment with servos and mainframes she had brought and toil away to keep her hands busy. Her loyalty tied her to the Staplegunners, but she'd see to the other proctor crutches if she had time.

Her focus completely disregarded the swirl of parts in a stall across the bay. Behind a wrecked prowler, a wrench, a numatter cell, and the dismantled pieces of a wide-beam ion cutter floated and swirled around one another. The twister grew in size and strength as it peeled off the armor plates off the shell.

The barrel-like torso broadened, and a pair of tornado-like appendages formed from the torso.

* * *

Noah had gathered them after telling Syn about Elina Prescott's existence at the guildhall he was residing at. Syn insisted on meeting them and ran from the University before dinner. She'd never seen inside a proctor guildhall before.

It was...unremarkable, filled with engineering equipment and a modicum of creature comforts. There were no libraries or laboratories, and she became impressed with how Noah found an education in one of these. At the upper level, below the observation deck, Noah guided her to a private meeting hall accented with fake wood, comfortable chairs, and a glass wall with views over the rest of the exclave.

Kabdila sat at the head with Agosta, Noah, Terri, and Elina encircled the table as Syn dropped the codex in front of them. Noah was used to an endolon, their appearance, and how they moved, but the others were uneasy. Elina had never seen one before, and she stared with wide-eyed curiosity.

"It's one book," Syn said.

Everyone just stared, attempting to conceal their confusion.

"We...can see that," Terri said.

"It's the Plex Codex."

"How do you know that?"

"I don't...I'm just...calling it that. I'm sure it has its own name."

"We're all just...sitting here," Kabdila said.

Syn pushed the book to Elina, who acted like a parent had just bestowed a bike to her.

"Thank you," Elina said.

"What are you doing?" Agosta asked.

"Familiarity begets coincidence," Syn said.

"Syn, how do you know this?" Noah asked.

"It's a primer, a type of book that teaches you how to learn and read. It can be used to decipher a language." Elina opened the unlocked book and tossed pages. "And in this case, it's also telling a story."

"About what?" Terri asked.

"About us," Syn said. Elina flipped through the first book with illustrations of fantasy creatures, castles, and sorcerers. "And them?"

"Why...what's the point?" Noah asked. "Does it exist for the purposes of existing? Is it warning us about something?"

"I need to go back a few steps, so please keep up." Syn and Elina exchanged looks. "I just finished a conversation with your double in the other reality."

"Is she nice?" Elina asked as if the comment's implications were a matter of fact.

"I have no idea. It doesn't matter. I tried to glean what I could from the other two, and I've determined that they are not as gifted in science and technology as us. This is especially prevalent in the illustrations provided in the other two volumes of the Codex." Elina frantically flipped through the codex, stopping at the most dramatic illustrations.

"Syn?" Noah asked. She turned to him. "You're talking different."

"Am I?"

"You…don't notice."

"No…should I?"

"Never mind, not important. So, three volumes, three realities."

"You said that as if you understand what she's talking about," Terri said.

"I do." Noah glared at everyone. "I couldn't have been the only one that used proctor resources to further my education."

"Did you just goad us to go back to school," Agosta said. "Because I did, and I hated teaching." Now the stares had shifted to him. "What… it was English."

"You were able to carry a conversation with someone," Terri said. "How?"

"Through the book," Syn said.

"Is there a…radio?" Kabdila asked.

"Not exactly." Syn leaned in, which was easy as the table was leveled for humans, and she flipped a few pages in front of Elina until she reached the Aegis image. "She reached out to me, my double in the first book. Then I reached out to the second, and…well." Syn pointed to Elina. "She answered." Syn grabbed a clump of pages, flopped them over, and then a few more before reaching Elina's inscription. Elina was practically glowing.

"How?" Agosta asked. "How is that possible?"

"I believe this is one book," Syn said.

"Once again," Terri said, "that appears obvious."

"You're not getting it." Syn was used to discuss matters with scientists, those of open minds that could fill in the blanks.

"It's one book shared between three realities," Noah said. "One book, three places…at the same time."

Syn and Noah shared an understanding. She smiled.

"I fucking love you," she said. Noah winked back.

"Really!" Elina boisterously said as her attention darted back between the two. "AWESOME!"

The door to the hall opened, and three more proctors entered. Their arrival was a surprise to Syn but not anyone else.

"*Who Dares the Void*!" Kaiden said.

"Sloan!" Agosta jumped to his feet upon saying her name. He ran to her, and they embraced, to the shock of everyone, including them. They released and pushed each other to an acceptable distance.

"That was…unexpected and appreciated," Sloan said. She grimaced from a few bruises, but as suspected, she didn't even have a scar to mark her trauma.

"Yeah…thanks," Agosta said, almost embarrassed. "Kind of spontaneous there."

"Can I have a hug?" Deven asked with a grin.

Agosta stared at the scrimm, then shrugged.

"Sure," he said, then hugged Deven, who was initially shocked but eventually settled into the humorous affection.

"Delivered, paid, contract settled," Kaiden said to Terri. "Another win for the guild."

"Excellent, venerable work," Kabdila said.

Agosta patted Deven on the shoulder.

"So…decided to stick with the guild?"

"No," Deven said. "I decided to stick with all of you."

"Aww…my hero."

"Are we…interrupting?" Kaiden asked.

"Not at all," Terri said. "Syn, who Noah escorted from Bythos—and they're fucking, by the way—was just explaining how we're sharing this book with three different alternate realities and can employ it to communicate with one another."

There was a pregnant pause, and then Kaiden answered it.

"Oh…"

"Yeah, it was just getting interesting."

"Like a parallel world?" Deven asked. "Us after making different choices?"

"Something of that," Syn said, "but a smidgeon more extreme."

Deven took a seat beside Agosta, and the others followed.

"Well, then, color me interested," Deven said.

"One book, three realities," Sloan said.

"That being said, there are variations," Syn said.

"You just said—"

"I believe the theory still holds that this Codex connects our realities, but the arrangement of the individual books does appear to change. I'll show you what I mean." Syn leaned again and pointed to the inscription. "On this page, when she says *hello*, see how it carries onto the text. Initially, I just figured if written by a child, they'd disregard what they were overlapping."

"I'm not a child," Elina said.

"Of course not…which confirms my thought, not so much a theory, that she is writing on a different page…but the same page."

"That makes no sense," Kabdila said.

Syn pointed at him suddenly.

"No, it doesn't!"

"English isn't your first language."

"She is writing on a different page at the same position, but I believe the arrangements of the books inside each variation are different."

"I follow," Noah said with a nod.

"I don't," Kaiden said.

"We're book one in this Codex," Syn said. "I'd be willing to bet in their universe; they're book one."

"So, none of us is last," Terri said.

"Well, that is a guess, but..." Syn said, trailing off. "Yes."

"For an endolon, you talk very human," Deven said.

"I agree...and it's probably because I'm not an alien in the other two realities."

"Same with me?"

"I'd imagine so. It's entirely possible some of you aren't human as well. There are illustrations of different bipedal creatures. Humanoid machines. We could be any of them."

"How do you know we're all represented?" Kaiden asked.

"I don't. But I know Elina is, and I am...and I confirmed Noah is as well."

"If what you are saying is true," Deven said, "what would happen if we tossed this book into a fire."

"I wouldn't suggest it, but if it could be destroyed and the damage does indicate it could, I imagine it would cease to exist in the other two realities."

"And somehow, we can communicate through it," Terri said.

Syn nudged her chin towards Elina.

"She already has."

"That is something I'd do," Elina said, taking full credit.

"Technically, we've been doing it for days. The tea stain, the cut on the cover, Elina was just more direct. And for that...I very much offer my appreciation."

"You're welcome."

"How do we know it's not an imposter, someone posing as her?" Kaiden asked.

"I recognize my handwriting."

Agosta smiled and firmed his grip on Elina's shoulder.

"That's why she used cursive," Agosta said with an approving grin. "You truly are special." Elina had only known him for a few days, but she had already accepted paternal praise from Agosta.

"So, wait...is this your handwriting?" Terri asked, pointing at another inscription on the subsequent page.

"I wanted to be clear," Syn said.

"You've been defacing a priceless book?" Kaiden asked.

"You said a smidgeon more extreme?" Noah asked, trying to refocus the conversation. "How different are we talking?"

"Look at this second volume," Syn said. Elina followed the lead and switched pages. "The illustrations. Assuming they're accurate representations, and I believe so, given the drawings in our volume, they paint a picture of an exceptionally regressed society. Castles. Beasts of burden. Swords. And…" Elina reached a page of a woman floating inches off the ground with a collection of floating pieces of pages swirling around, each inscribed with glowing sigils. "Some kind of…magic?"

"Magic? How?" Kaiden asked.

"Hello?" Elina squeaked as she raised her hand.

"We've been studying metrons for years," Syn said. "The best we can determine is that something is allowing them to alter reality. We've assumed it's been this ship. The world presented in this book…comes off as borderline fantasy."

"Knights, Kings," Agosta said.

"Princesses," Elina said.

"That leaves the last," Syn said, prompting Elina, "where I was talking with the other Elina. It comes off as a midpoint between the other two. Not as technologically advanced. Trains. Older firearms. A couple centuries behind us but with some abnormalities based on what appears to be some form of alternative power source."

"And whatever *this* is coming out of this dude's face?" Deven asked, pointing at the yellow-tinged smoke emanating out a duster-donned, grizzled man's eyes.

"Magic," Elina said.

"My guess is the ratio of magic balances that," Syn said. "You need magic in a world of fantasy."

"Well, this stopped being scientific," Kaiden said, pushing himself from the table. "Need I remind you that observational data ended about five minutes ago."

"I know…I know," Syn said, "And I appreciate you rooting me."

"So why…why is this happening?" Terri asked.

"Haven't you all felt it?" Noah asked. "The familiarity we've all been encountering. Meeting people for the first time and recognizing them."

"And I believe these occurrences will increase," Syn said, placing her hand upon Noah's, disregarding the judgments of those staring at the affection. Endolons were supposed to be reserved. "We may eventually pick up the thoughts or memories of our doubles in these other realities."

"Assuming we're alive in them," Kaiden said.

"To what end?" Kabdila asked.

"I have no idea," Syn said. "My twin in this world said something that didn't make sense. I passed it onto the other reality hoping it would resonate with them."

"I see the conversation between you and Elina," Sloan said as she loomed over Elina's shoulder, "where is the one between yourself?"

"It wasn't written. I heard her…in my head."

There was another pause, an uncomfortable one, that Kaiden broke.

"You know that could be excused as mental illness?" he said.

"Back off, Kaiden!" Noah said.

"As a scientist, she has to entertain that possibility!"

"The evidence is right in front of you, damn it."

"She said as related events occur," Syn said, throwing her voice between the argument, "meaning despite our differences, coincidences between our worlds are bringing us closer together…in a…metaphysical sort of way."

"Like us…meeting each other," Noah said. "Existing as we do in each of these worlds."

"There must be an infinite number of worlds with us in them," Kaiden said, "realities a lot closer than these three. There must be something more."

"Well…there are three books that exist as one," Elina said. "Just a hunch."

"I entertained that idea," Syn said.

"Except I was experiencing these moments before," Agosta said, "I never saw this book until now."

"Precisely, we rescued Elina and brought her here," Terri said.

"It might be an anchor," Syn said, "…or it could be a key."

"Or a warning," Kaiden said. "Even a weapon."

"How far can these interactions go?" Noah asked. "Could they disrupt each other?"

"We're dealing with a crisis that has never existed in the history of this universe," Syn said. "We've no precedent for experimentation. No laboratory can test for it. I wouldn't even know where to begin."

It was all a bit too much for the group to take in.

Sloan exhaled.

Agosta leaned back in his chair.

Noah firmed his grip on Syn's hand, aware that she would have never opened herself like this a week ago.

Terri crossed her arms, not to be belligerent; she was just attempting to process. The only sound in the room was the nearly inaudible wheezing from Syn's rebreather.

"Assuming all this is true," Terri said. "…Every work requires a creator. An author had to have written this book. And if we're extending this line of thinking, it would be someone capable of perceiving time and space beyond the limits of our reality."

This was the part Syn wasn't looking forward to.

"I suspect an answer, but you aren't going to like it," she said. "Check page 314, between books one and two."

Elina was almost precautious as she browsed the book. She slowed as she reached the page. And then there it was.

It occupied the entire left half of the tome, a tall, undressed, emaciated figure with extended limbs and digits. Its elongated head held no eyes, just a broad, uninviting smile of needle-like teeth. Its arms were outstretched as if the creature had been crucified. Deven leaned back, unwilling to delve too deep.

"I've suddenly lost all interest in this subject," he said.

"The only illustration not contained in any of the three books," Syn said.

"The operator," Sloan whispered.

"We've been telling stories about him for as long as I can remember," Agosta said. "My father told me when I was young, passed on from his father. We've got inscriptions and references to him."

"But all share the same claim that he was a legend, a fable," Kaiden said. "What you say to scare children."

"I saw him!" Deven said, glaring at Kaiden. "Do you believe me now!?"

"Technically, I never said I didn't," Kaiden said.

"You called me an idiot!"

"And you still are, but an honest one."

Deven tried to stand, but Agosta held him down.

"You also called it a myth, Kaiden," Terri said.

"We found the girl because of that," Sloan said.

"Really?" Kabdila asked.

"Deven saw it; we investigated. Found the jacker caravan, which we wouldn't have seen if we hadn't done that."

"The codex may detail our relationship," Syn said, "but perhaps the operator is the one creating coincidence. He's the one bringing us together."

"Why?" Terri asked.

"I don't know…you'd have to ask them."

"I'm still shocked we all have the same names," Kaiden said.

"Perhaps that's part of the coincidence."

"Hell of a happenstance, same names, maybe even the same faces. The odds should make it near impossible."

Noah gaped at Kaiden, hanging on to what he said.

"Impossible," Noah said slowly, centering his thoughts, staring at Syn, who repaid the fondness. "Near is still conceivable. Impossible is like infinity. When you hang a modifier, it becomes as far from impossible as is a certainty." His eyes moved to Terri, then to Syn, "A fantasy world is impossible, part and parcel. These two realities cannot exist. So, if there's can't…neither can ours. This vessel, this…ark, we all reside in. We've never found a power source. We don't know how it generates a magnetic field or gravity. It's close to a powerful singularity that we can see, and yet, it doesn't appear to affect us. Our world…is impossible. It cannot function based on the very rules it appears to govern. It's unrealistic."

"If this is not real, then why do we accept it?" Terri asked.

"Because it's in our nature to do so," Syn said.

"The more I live in these moments," Noah said, "the more I start to wonder. We call these *realities*…Maybe we're using the wrong word."

Most of what Noah said went over their heads, save for maybe Syn and Terri. Kabdila broke the silence that endured.

"Well, this has all been lovely. Firstly, this conversation is going to be isolated," he said. "No one in this room will discuss what was spoken or even mention the existence of this book to anyone outside our chapter. We clear?" He didn't wait for a response. "Secondly, I want to be informed of everyone that has seen or worked on this that is not present in this room. I hate to get legal, but paperwork will be involved."

"This is more important than union claims," Terri said.

"If this gets out, it'll get political. Bureaucracy will snake in, muddy the waters and clog the gears. I'm not just thinking of recompense; the fewer voices involved at this stage, the more that can be done. Doctor, was that all that you discovered?"

"No," Syn said. "I found one other pattern, one aspect I found repeated, an illustration in each—"

The claxon hanging from the corner of the room blasted an oscillating horn far too loud for the room. Deven and Syn cupped their sensitive ears. Everyone except the endolon jumped from their seats and ran from the room.

They skipped steps and amalgamated with other proctors from other chapters on site. The crowd flowed to the engineering bay. As the group flooded the entranceway, the first few proctors stumbled over the shredded bodies of those who got too close.

They could see Mannah cowering behind Noah's still intact dodger.

"Mannah!" Terri said as she approached. "What is, whoa!" She jumped back as it emerged from another stall.

The thing emerged as a massive walking cyclone with a towering torso that stretched up and fell in front to create a tunnel-shaped head occupied by nothing but an oversized circular maw of spinning teeth.

One proctor had attempted to get to his suit, but the beast had pulled him away, and he lay trapped, spinning inside the limb. The blender of blades closed in, and the other proctors couldn't help before the victim was visibly torn to pieces, blood and limbs scattered to the edges of the room.

The creature's deep-toned roar sounded closer to an internal combustion engine trying to turn over. An oscillating grinding growl; it was a smooth periodic wave of quiet rumbles and earsplitting grunts intermixed with sucking air as it vacuumed the debris surrounding it.

"Trash tornado," Sloan said before bolting from the room.

"Sloan?" Agosta shouted to her back as she disappeared.

The few proctors that were armed launched various shell and pulse weapons at the monster.

While most of the physical projectiles were absorbed into the machine, a few others managed to flake off fragments of the living storm.

Plasma weapons fared better, but most of the energy passed through rather than impacted.

Agosta's jagger was closer, and he pushed himself to the wall and kept his distance from the beast as it was distracted by the incoming fire.

It launched an arm forward, catching another proctor and sucking him into the monster's body where he was slowly taken apart, while another arm reached into the bay, shredding the parts off a broken cage and swelling its own body as a result.

"We need to get this out of the bay; it's devouring everything," Terri shouted.

Syn reached the entrance to the bay and was stunned by the creature. She recognized it and was about to tell the group about what she had seen before the alarm was raised. The only illustration repeated between all three books.

She'd have to tell them later.

"Elina, if you have something in you," Terri said, "best let it out now!"

Elina frantically tried to avoid the shuffling of proctors and weapons. Terri kept the girl behind her as she tried to move her into cover in one of the other stalls. Her cage was too far away.

"I kind of just did it by reflex," Elina said. "I'm not sure how!"

"Lay back, then. Don't put yourself at risk."

The storm had grown enough that its torso started to split in two. A second head formed.

"This just gets better and better!" Kaiden said.

Agosta's jagger sprung to life as he locked himself in.

His lightning rifle expanded, opening its strange cross-shaped barrel and three laser sights.

He immediately fired, a bolt striking fragments inside the storm, arcing to others and disintegrating them.

It was by far the most damage anyone had done by that point.

Another shot severed the tip of the creature's arm as it captured another nameless proctor.

The debris fell like broken glass, and the injured but alive individual fell to the ground.

The storm focused on Agosta, but crossfire from Deven's emerging shell along with the other proctors proved too much.

It forced its way to the door of the engineering bay, which opened in a moment of poor timing.

It was still trying to finish dividing, the two torsos beginning to split.

The proctors, in and out of crutches, followed the beast out. It made for the exit of the base but was stopped by a giant yellow and black monstrosity that slammed into the ground in front of it.

The rig's colossal plasma weapon fired, taking off the second head.

Sloan switched to another weapon which unfolded in her shell's arm, a bizarre large-barreled gun that didn't fire as much as it bellowed in a massive sonic concussion wave, one that shattered the windows of this side of the complex but smashed the legs of the monster, blowing debris into the bay.

Another visible shockwave from the rig reduced the monster's mass, and it fell, trying to reform to a shape a quarter of its previous size.

A final blast blew the rest to pieces, a single handful of metal fragments swirling in the place of where the beast once was.

Sloan took a step and stomped on what remained.

The rest of her unit caught up as the other proctors stood in shock.

"Why was that outside?" Kaiden asked.

The hatch to Sloan's suit opened up. She hadn't bothered to don her helmet.

"It can't fit in any of your bays," she said.

Agosta approached and circled a curious cobbled firearm.

"Soo…where were you hiding this?" he asked.

"After our last encounter, I felt I needed something with a bit more… kick." Sloan opened the rest of her rig, and she stepped out. The other proctors were skittish and searching for any further movement. Mannah finally stepped out from behind Noah's dodger.

Syn guardedly skulked from the entrance to scrutinize what she had witnessed. Most everyone else was tending the dead and the wounded and the expected long process of cleaning up garbage that now covered the whole engineering bay.

"It was devouring everything and attempting to reproduce," Syn said as she kicked through the debris on the way to Noah.

"A monster," Noah said.

Syn considered what she had seen

"Like a virus," she whispered.

The rest of the guild gathered together, surveying the damage done to the bay.

"I've seen that thing before," Noah said.

"We've all seen it before," Agosta said.

Noah's eyes then rolled over.

His head fell back as his limbs went limp, and he collapsed at the entrance of the guildhall.

"Noah!" Terri shouted as the group gathered.

Syn said nothing as she crumpled beside Noah, holding his head as he fell. Deven exited his shell and ran to retrieve his medical equipment while the others gathered.

Syn stroked Noah's cheek, remembering what her twin had told her.

"Not yet…not yet," she whispered.

TORUS

They parade the Letters of Marque and Reprisal, but ultimately, they're all just mercenaries. The Torus is mighty big, and the arks lack the resources to operate the fleets boasted by old Iokon. But out there sit thousands of restless railrunners and their desire to keep moving.

So, the arks built and sold them the means, carracks, cutlasses, corvettes, and cutters. Buy one from an ark and be contracted to that ark for the life of the train…supposedly. The crew would be responsible for maintenance and yard work. It wasn't perfect, but the arks felt they could control the ring without spreading themselves too thin.

Then the freelancers emerged, those with bespoke trains able to hold their own against the factory models. They refused to fall in line and took contacts as it suited them. Despite signing the government license and gaining permission, the arks distrust most of them and would prefer the only privateers to be those with lifetime commitments.

As for the privateers themselves…well, some of them believe their profession dignified, even noble. They parade their superiority, but in the end, the only thing separating them from accusations of piracy is a piece of paper.

Golo Volco
The Age of Rail

The Mourning Star approached the Vanderov. It was still puffing green smoke from a spout at the back of the locomotive. It began accelerating, gaining ground, and the line was bringing them parallel.

The Vanderov hadn't changed its speed, and the upper hatch had closed. No one was visible.

The Mourning Star came up the side; the Van appeared fast and sleek, but it was dwarfed by the enormous hood-class iron juggernaut. It jetted steam from either side of its nose like a heated taurus, surging and gaining ground as both trains crested a hill, on course to a gathering of ruined and collapsed buildings.

The Van offered the impression that it was abandoned, like someone had set the throttle and jumped off to leave the train to its fate. There was no movement within its windows as the parallel vehicle matched velocity.

A door on the second car of the Mourning Star slid open, revealing a dozen men and women armed with various archaic rifles and a single pintle-mounted net launcher.

It fired a mesh of micro-explosives attached in a circular pattern against the hull of the Vanderov's second car. It was connected via an umbilical to a detonator within the grasp of one of the pirates.

They counted down.

A previously hidden hatch within the side of the Vanderov revealed an impressive 1-gauge punt gun.

The weapon was braced against the outer hull of the train, but Wisekjii, well aware of its recoil but unsure of how secure the weapon was, still braced against an inner wall when he pulled the trigger.

The blast from its barrel shook the pirate train and blew out a hole on the other side of the enemy car.

The net gun had practically vaporized along with two poor souls next to it.

"Wow, that thing kicks," Wisekjii said.

An upper hatch on the third pirate car opened, and a dozen armed individuals spilled out.

Side panels on the car flipped up, creating a wide bridge between both trains.

The pirates crossed onto the Vanderov.

Under that same car, Deven heard the cue of footfalls over him and pulled levers next to the outer wall.

A panel concealed in the car's roof flipped outward like a gymnast's vaulting table.

One pirate stopped short as the panel slid back into place.

He wasn't aware there were other plates, and another catapulted him off the train to the sand.

Some plates launched left, while others right.

One by one, a few unfortunates were tossed between the two trains.

While one landed on the bridge that connected the two vehicles, another slid down the side and fell under the wheels of the pirate train.

The remaining pirates jumped back onto the connecting bridge or pointed their long rifles and shotguns downward, firing through the armored hull that could withstand small arms fire.

Deven dove for cover as a few rounds made it through.

He removed a grapeshot caplock pistol and attempted to find a target.

"Deven," Kaiden said as he seemingly appeared next to Deven.

"Holy shit!?" Deven jumped upon seeing the loginoid beside him. "How are you quiet?! Aren't their bells in there?!"

"Captain needs us in the cab; let's go!"

The enemy train accelerated, attempting to get in front of the Van.

"Do I push it?!" Mannah snapped from her engine bay.

"No, hold speed!" Terri said back.

Sloan, Agosta, Elina, and Terri discussed strategies in the locomotive's cab.

"What are they doing?" Sloan asked.

"They're trying to get in front of us, force us to stop," Terri responded. She clicked his radio, "Noah, how good are you with that void rifle."

"Good enough," came the reply over the radio.

Terri then patted Agosta on the shoulder.

"I have a plan."

While Terri spoke to him, she was focused on Elina. Agosta was not impressed.

"Not a good one," he said.

"You don't even know what it is."

"It involves my daughter; call it a hunch."

"It won't put her in danger." Terri addressed Elina. "I've seen what you can do. I have faith in you."

Elina nodded but was keeping her apprehension internalized.

"I can help," she said.

Wisekjii loaded another round. There wasn't much room to aim, but it wasn't like the Mourning Star could evade.

He fired again and punched another significant hole in the side of the train, tossing out a pair of pirates in its wake.

In response, the opposition opened a door and revealed a six-barreled revolving cannon.

Wisekjii glanced through his scope to see the weapon training on his position.

He jumped from his seat as the cabin was lanced by a hundred rounds in a matter of seconds.

Several shots struck the pun gun, cracking it in two.

Kaiden and Deven ran into the locomotive's cab.

"Let's see how well you earned that commission you deserted," Terri said to Agosta after they had finally settled on her strategy. He was not entirely sold on it, as it jeopardized the two people he cared about the most.

Terri and Agosta made for the exit of the cab, passing Deven and Kaiden.

"You two, look after the girl," Terri said.

"I can take care of myself!" Elina shouted.

"I know; I was referring to the train. Hold her at notch five. Keep them…both safe."

"No heroics," Agosta said as he pointed to Elina. He exchanged expressions with Sloan that communicated her commitment. She would die protecting Elina, and he wouldn't trust anyone else.

The trains were moving faster than the suggested speeds for the tracks they were running on.

The sand had buried most of the lines, and sharp bends could derail a vehicle moving fast enough.

Within the second car, Noah braced an elaborately decorated long-barreled rifle plated in gold but tipped with an inscribed brass plate blocking the muzzle. He pulled on a pair of matching goggles with a swingable lens. As he dropped one in front of another, his view of his train's red wall gave way to the outside of the pirate vessel, then inside the enemy locomotive.

He scanned the inside of the vessel, counting the virtually endless number of pirates the Mourning Star was boasting.

Noah shifted his attention to the conductor, who assumed he was safe surrounded by locomotive and engine. He didn't resemble someone in charge, probably just an underling, but that didn't matter.

Whoever they were, they didn't see the bullet as it materialized in front of their face before the projectile entered him.

Those around the target were understandably surprised.

Two cars back, another door slid open, and brigands within had fired magnetic explosives to the Vanderov's windows, blowing several out.

Grappling hooks fired, connecting the two trains.

Pirates spilled in and were immediately met with gunfire from Agosta and Terri.

A bandit ducked for cover and returned fire to cover the arrival of allies.

In the locomotive, Elina was sheltered with Sloan and Kaiden while Deven controlled the train. Sloan held her blade out to Elina, who was concentrating on the weapon.

"This can work?" Kaiden asked.

"Don't break her focus," Sloan said. "You can do this, Elina."

"Sorry, I'll try to be—" The loginoid showed little emotion as they spotted one pirate had hurdled the distance from one train to the other, landing at the cab window.

Before he could lob an explosive device inside the cab, Kaiden directed their 10-gauge coach gun and fired. They didn't need to aim as the spread pattern removed the train's window and shoved the target onto the sand, their grenade detonating a second later and rocking both machines.

Kaiden's perception reached beyond those in the cabin, and without swinging their head, they pointed their weapon up until it was flush with the roof of the train. They fired again, and the four looked out the opposite window as another body fell.

Deven nodded approvingly as he prepped his six-shooter percussion rifle. "I'm glad you're on—"

"Don't break her focus," Kaiden said as they reloaded.

Elina squirmed and strained. She held onto the totem with Sloan opposite her holding the sword. Sloan smiled without pressure.

Elina's eyes changed.

A wisp of smoke wafted from her nostrils.

Elina concentrated on the object and the destination.

Sloan's totem folded into itself, disappearing, with Sloan instantly following.

Within the Mourning Star's second car, the bladed totem materialized and fell on the floor between a half-dozen pirates that had surrounded the revolver cannon as it continued to strafe alongside the hull of the Vanderov.

Only one noticed the weapon and bent over to pick it up. They brought it up to analyze the magnificent blade. One of the other bandits must have dropped it.

And then Sloan materialized.

Terri fired a shot from one of her flintlocks.

Two others sat empty on the ground.

The projectile passed through one pirate and into the metal wall behind him.

Terri flicked a thumb and commanded the shot to reverse its course through another pirate that got in the way and returned to the barrel of the gun that fired it.

Terri dove behind cover and refilled the powder in her firearm.

Agosta emptied his cylinder, taking out two bandits.

One of them pulled off a shot.

Agosta rotated his weapon, and the round deflected off the barrel.

He then retreated around a corner, glancing at Terri.

"That was cool," Agosta remarked as he reloaded his weapon by rolling this cylinder across his bandolier, the bullets being pulled from the belt into the gun.

"Not so bad yourself," Terri joked. "We going to compare enchantments?" She stroked her finger across one brass inscription on her firearm, which glowed yellow with a puff of smoke wafting from it. The barrel then ignited in a small flame.

Terri smiled and aimed her weapon at the distant canister of train oil.

Her shot became a ball of fire that impacted the tank and detonated it, spilling flaming crude onto those nearby.

"Oh, it's on," Agosta said as he finished reloading.

He caressed a similar inscription on his weapon and tossed the entire firearm to the back of the cab, in the middle of the remaining four bandits.

Terri was understandably confused.

Agosta silently counted in his head.

On one, an explosion rang out, and those pirates not taken out by the explosion were struck by one of the bullets.

"Well, that was a waste of a perfectly good firearm," Terri said.

Agosta smirked and snapped a finger.

The weapon, sans drum and bullets, flew back into his hand.

"Okay, then," Terri said.

Sloan broke into the cab of the enemy train and braced the door lock behind her. She found the conductor dead on the ground with the train still accelerating.

Sloan increased the power to its maximum and pulled a lever to switch to an outgoing track.

She opened the side cab door and cut through two men firing weapons from the outside walkway.

Unfortunately, by this point, the pirate locomotive was well ahead of the Vanderov.

Sloan climbed atop the faster train and ran across its roof, jumping gaps, trying to reach the nose of the Vanderov.

Kaiden appeared between the locomotive and the second car. Noticing Sloan running the Mourning Star's length, Kaiden climbed to the top of the Vanderov and ran to the front of the engine.

They reached the curved nose, twisted their arm into a tentacle, and held firmly onto a railing.

The other he held out for Sloan, who was desperately trying to reach them.

Kaiden pulled matter from their legs to extend their reach.

Without another option, Sloan leaped from one train to the other.

She held out her sheathed blade as she fell short, and Kaiden grabbed it by the scabbard's nose.

Sloan swung down the side of the locomotive and clutched onto the side.

She climbed up with Kaiden's help.

The Mourning Star angled away from the Vanderov, stranding the few remaining pirates promptly removed under protest.

The majority of the crew of the Vanderov entered the cab.

Agosta embraced Elina, then searched for Sloan.

"We may have a problem here!" Kaiden shouted from above.

Terri opened the top hatch of the locomotive and reached Sloan and Kaiden atop the train. Kaiden pointed to the now out-of-control Mourning Star as it continued moving away. Terri followed the line the corsair was riding on. It swung back to cross perpendicular with the Vanderov's track less than a kilometer ahead.

"Pilot down!" Terri said below.

Mannah threw the levers, Deven and Agosta pulled the chains, the front of the train opened, and the arrow-shaped cowcatcher fell in front of the wheels.

Terri, Sloan, and Kaiden dove back below.

"Grab something!" Terri said.

Everyone held what they could as the engine of the Mourning Star crossed in front of them.

Car after car passed.

The bullet-nosed Vanderov pierced through the middle of the last car, splitting it in two.

The cars tumbled off the track, including the locomotive, which was pulled off its line. It spiked hard into the sand, causing it and other cars to topple over one another.

Still with momentum, the train cars slammed into the ruins of a nearby building, causing it to collapse over the wreck.

The Vanderov heaved from the impact but remained on its rails, emerging from the cloud of debris it created.

The crew protruded from opened windows or the top hatch to see the destruction behind them.

"Holy…shit," Noah whispered.

"Mr. Pike," Terri said, "You, Sloan, and your daughter are welcome to stay with us as long as you need. If you want to keep moving, we never stop."

Agosta nodded.

"Thank you, commander," he said. "I'll discuss it with them…but…" He gauged Sloan's facial expression; she smirked at him. "…I don't see them objecting to hanging around."

"Although felicitations are rightly deserved," Kaiden said, "does anyone see what I am seeing?"

The group focused on the Mourning Star's smoldering wreck. One of the cars jostled. Flecks of paint flew off the hull. Metal bent, wood snapped, and the car imploded. Debris swirled in a vortex. The dust cloud from the falling building obscured much of everything else.

"More of those creatures!" Elina said.

"Screevers?!" Deven said.

"Something worse," Agosta muttered.

Earthquakes were not a risk here—the rumbling was from something. It was gaining in intensity.

"Must be thousands of them!" Sloan said.

From the fallen building erupted what could only be described as a snake-like tornado filled with garbage, a 300-hundred-meter-long torrent of gyrating debris creating a circular mouth of twisting blades.

As it bent to face the train's rear, the crew could see almost through the entire length of the monster. The living whirlwind roared as its body slammed back onto the surface.

Like glass, the beast shattered, scattering its body of a billion parts across the ground.

A moment later, the parts drew themselves back.

The beast pulled in surrounding rubble and debris off the destroyed Mourning Star as the snake twisted itself back into shape, the torrent spinning faster as the creature of semi-sentient garbage slithered towards the train.

"No!" Agosta said. "Just one."

PARADISE

Houses of Hydranis

Costrian. *Once a great house, Costrian lost most of their holdings in conflict with Eldenberg. Although technically allied with Hydrus, Costrian only do so out of necessity. The only keep they maintain control of is Faldersall, one badly needing restoration.*

Eldenberg. *A house of some prominence, Eldenberg's value remains with their numerous fortresses, though most have been turned to ruin. However, they still have their home castle of Redcrow in good condition. Eldenberg was a powerful house under Phydranis, but the kingdom's rule under Hydrus reduced Eldenberg's reputation. They remain loyal but believe the future of the kingdoms stems from the alliance and not petty conflict, which they believe no one on the planet can maintain any longer.*

Hydrus. *Hydrus and Phydranis have close blood ties but remain in bitter conflict. However, thanks to a unified political front, Hydrus has maintained the throne for the past 500 years.*

Phydranis. *Phydranis is considered by many the more powerful house between them and Hydrus, thanks to a larger standing army. However, petty family squabbles and the lack of a unifying voice prevented Phydranis from making ground. After Hydrus assumed the throne 500 years ago and maintained it since, Hydrus has struggled with internal conflict over deciding who should rule the house.*

"What is that?" Terri shouted to Wisekjii, pointing at the drawing hanging inside the vardo. The nagomjii had cleared out most of the valuables inside the carriage as that was not part of the arrangement, and most of what was inside would be useless to non-aliens. The interior of the barrel-shaped vehicle was punctuated by gilded red-painted wood, extravagantly carved banisters, and a pair of single beds, though the mattresses had been removed. They even removed the curtains. Thankfully, Nagomjii vehicles benefited from a suspension that would rival even the Conclave's most expensive carriages.

The image was pinned to a wall, and Wisekjii was removing it when Terri noticed.

“That,” she said. “THAT! That drawing?” She approached inches from the alien and tapped the image so there wouldn’t be any misunderstanding. “What is that?”

Bipedal.

Pale.

Thin.

Needle-like teeth.

“The Shallow,” Wisekjii said.

“I’ve heard it called the Outsider,” Terri said.

“Then why ask?”

Terri ignored the comment and hung on the name; it had many.

Wisekjii rolled up the image and removed it as the rest of Terri’s group loaded what they could into the freed spaces.

“You’ve seen it?” she asked.

“Guides us,” Wisekjii said.

“Does it direct your caravan? Does it tell you where to scavenge?”

“Guides everyone.”

“Terri!” Noah said. She ignored him, staring at the alien, who smirked the best he could, then offered the image, which she accepted. “Terri! We’re a little pressed for time.”

Terri held onto the drawing.

Wisekjii offered the shaper, which Terri had previously believed was in her pocket.

“Don’t lose again,” Wisekjii said.

Somewhat vexed at being pilfered, Terri took the shaper. Wisekjii winked, then returned to his people.

Noah and Deven finished loading the Conclave coffin into the carriage. Everyone else piled inside or atop the vehicle.

“This vardo is not what I’d call a nimble instrument,” Sloan said as she climbed aboard.

“It’ll have to do,” Agosta said.

“This is suicide,” Noah said as he closed the doors of the vardo with him, Elina, Deven, and Syn inside.

“People have tried it—” Terri said as she climbed up to join Agosta.

“And they’ve failed,” Agosta said.

“Not all of them. And they didn’t have faith. Isn’t that what you’re good at.”

The group took one final look as the nagomjii caravan vanished into the forest, large tracks and grooves telegraphing their path. Agosta beckoned the kips to a gallop to crest the next hill before seeing anyone behind them. Wisekjii had offered the caravan's two fastest beasts, and the kips proved shockingly quick as the vardo bounded over the grassy hill.

The group could hear the low rumble of eight thousand hoofs slamming on the ground. Mount Astran appeared closer than it was. Agosta looked up to the world of Philokalia above them, a planet they were racing against.

Terri knew that Mount Astran's softer gradient faced them, and before that was a low hill with an advantageous downward angle they could use to pick up speed. Terri knew everything except the math, and she didn't have much time to run the calculations in her head.

"I imagine the army will have caught up to the nagomjii by now," Sloan said a few minutes later.

"You think they're going to be okay?" Elina asked.

"Nagomjii are defined by their survival," Noah said. "They'll be fine."

Elina nodded, then asked another question.

"Will we be welcome?" she asked. "Is this lesser of two evils or the evil of two lessers?"

"Corvos is too far away. This is our only option," Noah said.

"But what will happen if this works?" Elina asked.

"You ask questions when you're nervous, don't you?" Noah asked.

"Is it obvious?"

"Not really."

"I'm not against this course of action," Deven said. "Well, okay, I was, but apparently, my vote didn't count. I'm only observing that we haven't thought of what we will do *if* this plan works."

"Have a drink. Do a dance," Noah said.

"Take the victory," Agosta said loud enough to be heard from within the cabin. "We'll have earned it. Sloan, do you have a comment on this?"

Sloan was laying on the back of the jolting carriage, gazing upwards, and wasn't paying attention.

"Hmm?" she asked.

"You appear calm for someone in this position."

"Just staring."

She had never taken an opportunity to stare at a world like Philokalia, a miniaturized variant of Bythos with rivers, hills, deserts, and cities. It rotated on its column, rising from the lower world, keeping Kurzel ever facing down, a castle cursed to benefit from the light of Uno for only a few hours each day. But there was life, hundreds of fires and lanterns scattered across the towns. The capital benefited from a relatively regular daylight schedule as it was fixed on the opposite side, with its castle tower perfectly centered at the axis. Sloan had even heard rumors that the tower rotated in the opposite direction to counter the planet's spin. She would very much like to see that.

"So close. So far," she whispered. "Do you dream?"

"Of course, I do," Agosta said.

"I wish I did."

The wagon stopped suddenly, jostling everyone, as Terri pulled the reigns. Some stood atop the wagon while others exited out the back. The entire group settled on the distant peak, Astran, not the most prominent mountain by any margin but possessing a singular, unique attribute.

From the opposite surface on Philokalia stretched out the equally unassuming Mount Klairapliedee. Both were insignificant peaks barely tall enough for a title, except once a year, for a single instant when the summits of Klairapliedee and Astran crossed within a few meters of each other.

"I think I hate you," Agosta said.

"It's been done," Terri said.

"Alleged."

"Why," Noah asked, "...aren't we moving?"

As the mountains grew closer, the clouds swirled into a vortex.

"Timing is critical," Terri said as she stepped down and reaffirmed the backstrap and girth on the kips. Noah rocked the vardo to check stability.

"Starting to agree this is suicide," Deven said.

"That's two of us," Noah said, "but it's a little late to conjure up an alternative."

"I think it's fortunate," Sloan said. "Any other time, it would be impossible. The gods are smiling."

"Our god," Agosta said, "if you can call her that, is in the back seat...what does she say?"

"Only that she'd accompany us," Noah said.

"So, she can watch us fail, likely die," Terri said. "Those coffins are practically indestructible. She's probably gambling we'll fall off a cliff, and she can be rescued from the wreckage."

"You'd be mistaken," the Aegis said as she stepped out from her coffin at the vardo. Her frailty presented as she struggled to stand and held tightly to the side of the vehicle to prevent her body from collapsing. "Which I admit would be a rare occurrence for you, Terri Zahn."

"You shouldn't be outside your coffin," Noah said as he sprung to Syn's aid.

"I am because it is a coffin," she said. "Given the speed of your beasts and the angle of the hill, you will need to spur the animals to a full sprint in exactly thirty-five seconds. The chief swore these were the fastest kips, which are known to pull a vardo like this to a maximum velocity of seventy-five kilometers per hour."

Terri took in the information and failed to admit that she hadn't thought of every parameter. She thought they'd have more time. When she examined the angles and the distance, she determined Syn was likely correct.

"Why are you doing this?" Noah asked.

"Because I have to," she said. "Besides, if you noticed, my previous accommodations were rather…uninteresting."

"You want to join us because it'll be more fun?"

"Good enough reason for me," Terri shouted. "Everyone, secure yourself and toss anything that could weigh us down!" She directed Elina to follow Noah and Syn back into the wagon; she did so.

"Twenty seconds," Syn said as Noah guided her back into the wagon. She gestured to the coffin, and Noah begrudgingly pushed the pearl-shaped capsule onto the dirt.

"When I give the word, start shifting!" Terri shouted as he took the lead atop the wagon.

"I already am," Agosta whispered as he sat beside Terri and Sloan.

"Shifting. Shifting! Shift your weight from left to right, synchronize to get this wagon leaning."

"Ten seconds," Syn said from within the vardo.

"Will this work?" Elina asked.

Noah stared at the beaming Aegis, a subject of worship for the universe, inches from his face. He could still feel the indoctrination, insisting he fall prostrate or at least avert his eyes.

"I guess you just have to have faith," Noah said.

Noah glimpsed out the back window to notice the pursuing army had emerged over the hill behind them. Upon spotting the vardo, they increased their pace.

"Five," Syn said, "Four, Three, Two—"

"Close enough!" Terri said as she whipped the reins.

The massive animals roared and dragged the wagon down the hill towards Astlan.

The vehicle accelerated, and the immense animals, known to have no known top speed when unrestrained, exhibited no signs of exhaustion as they raced down the incline. A significant dust cloud emerged behind. Despite possessing an advanced suspension, even the vardo had trouble with the rough terrain.

The cavalry of Aurago reached the hill's crest. Prince Kabdila assumed the lead in front of Machus, with Psylaxis running alongside.

"What are they doing?" Kabdila asked.

"They're attempting the Astran leap," Psylaxis said calmly.

"They'll never make it."

Psylaxis didn't wait for the king's command and sprang ahead of the army, running faster than any human could.

"Chase them down!" Kabdila said, with the army following his lead.

"Lean left!" Agosta said.

The group transferred their weight to one side of the wagon, and the vehicle lurched.

"Right!"

Everyone threw themselves to the opposite side, causing the vehicle to heave back.

"Keep doing it!"

Sloan gawked at the approaching planet above them.

"Damn, that thing's big—" she said.

"They're right behind us!" Noah said.

"Left!" Agosta said.

The kips could move no faster as they raced up the hill towards the expected cliff.

If the gravity of Philokalia missed them, they would plummet to their deaths back on Bythos. The peak of Klairapliedee approached close enough to touch as it passed over them.

The vardo was approaching the edge. The kips had been whipped to such a fury they ignored any other concerns, even their own lives, as their feet left Bythos.

"Grab something!" Terri said.

"Right!" Agosta said.

The beasts leaped from the precipice.

One failed to be drawn by Philokalia.

It snapped from its tack and fell back to Bythos.

The other twirled in the air as it was suspended briefly in freefall, a feeling experienced by everyone else.

Inside the vehicle, Noah and Elina flailed like they were drowning.

Syn swam within the space, gently placing the two others back into place.

The wagon soared and floated, then rotated from the group's leaning.

The wheels came around as the wagon fell towards the smaller world of Philokalia.

It was not a graceful landing, and the back wheels broke off on impact.

The front axle came down next and buckled.

The drum-like construction of the vardo offered a durable shell, but it crumpled as it landed.

The vehicle lurched and twisted out of control. Terri pulled on the brake handle, but it did little to stop the carriage as it tossed itself down the opposite hill of Klairapliedee.

One wheel locked, and the vardo leaned, fell on its side, and rolled.

Terri and Agosta fell out of the driver's seat.

The roof came down upon jagged rocks and caught Sloan in between.

The impact split the vehicle in half, cracking it like an egg and spilling the contents onto a grassy incline near another precipice.

Psylaxis reached the bluff but stopped short, realizing he would never make the jump. Machus, Kabdila, and his army came up behind shortly later. A few arrows could cross the expanse, but with the random wind and gravity, there was a chance a bolt could strike the Aegis, and no one was going to take that chance.

Agosta had fallen forward and pulled himself beside the surviving steed, grimacing at the blood running down his arm.

"All right, everyone okay?" Terri asked.

Noah saw to the Aegis.

"Are you injured?" he asked her.

Syn smiled and shook her head.

Agosta couldn't find Sloan and inspected the wreckage, worried she might have fallen back to Bythos. She hadn't, and he found her feet under part of the vardo. Fear swept over him, a connection to this individual that felt stronger than it should have. He desperately pulled the heavy chunks of wood off. A conscious Sloan helped until Agosta pulled her from underneath the vardo, uninjured. She exhaled in relief and sat up.

"Sloan?" Agosta asked. "How did you?"

"What?"

"That should have crushed your ribcage…and your head. Probably the rest of you too."

Sloan inspected her body, then shrugged.

"Ow…?" she said.

"That's convincing."

"What can I say," she said as she stood, "I'm lucky."

"Lucky would have avoided injury. You broke the wagon's fall."

"Nope…I'm good," she said as she patted his shoulder, then discovered his injury. "That looks…painful."

He glared at her.

"Nope…I'm good." The motivation for her escape registered with him.

Someday, he would have to be more direct with his questions.

"Everyone," Terri shouted, "welcome to Philokalia."

She surveyed the group, inspecting injuries, and watched their attention shift toward Bythos. She joined, noticing Psylaxis at the edge of the Astlan summit glaring at them as the two mountains drifted from one another.

"If it could show emotions," Terri said, "I'd wager it was pissed."

Kabdila was close enough to see Agosta, who glared back, offering neither emotion nor motivation for his betrayal. Kabdila was enraged and confused, and he said nothing. No witticism or snide remark.

A moment later, the light of Uno exploded between the two worlds, blinding the soldiers still watching Philokalia, which became nearly invisible in the rising sun's glare.

Kabdila and Machus dismounted and approached the still Psylaxis. Machus, masking anxiety, approached the machine. Psylaxis lowered its head to face the cardinal, expressionless as always.

"We'll call for the hedrons," Machus said. "They'll hunt down these heretics. This is only a minor—"

"Archbishop of Aquino, Exclave Superior. Cardinal vicar and head of the palatinus of purgitans," Psylaxsis said almost methodically. "Within our covenant, those of title found guilty of desecration would be held responsible for their own punishment." Machus took a slight step back. He cracked his mouth to object but remained quiet. "Your progenitors ingested poison, fell on swords, and immolated themselves." Psylaxis stepped closer to the frozen Machus. "How would you judge your actions this day?"

Machus felt a mix of dread and overconfidence. He shared the hierarchy with six others under the Sovereign Supreme, credited with executing more heretics than any other in five centuries. He was feared by the Ahkdanate, spurred armies to crusade, and assumed the voice of the Aegis when their own could not be heard. He shouldn't have to answer to a machine.

As he thought this, he realized he had been standing before the machine for several seconds without responding. He considered his response carefully, taking into account a proper mix of pageantry and intimidation. The fear subsided as he spoke.

"I—"

With inhuman speed and lethal force, Psylaxis swung his flat, opened hand towards the cardinal's neck faster than anyone could blink, let alone respond. Despite not being edged, the velocity and power of the chop severed the cardinal's head, leaving the body still standing, a spray of blood covering Kabdila. The corpse then slumped with the skull rolling downhill.

Kabdila blinked, half his face doused. He stood his ground against Psylaxis and its bloodied hand. It hadn't even bothered to draw its sword. It said nothing more and walked past the prince.

* * *

Half of the vardo stirred as it resumed its tumble down the hillside. It rolled towards Syn, but Noah wasn't having it. He pushed the surprisingly light frame towards Agosta, who caught the Aegis before the wreck slammed into Noah. The force knocked him off his feet, and he slid down the grass to the edge of the nearby cliff.

"Noah!" Terri shouted as she ran to him.

There was nothing to hold, and Noah fell off the edge. As his feet bounded from the rocks, his head fell back, and he could see a green valley a dozen meters below. For a moment, he considered his odds were pretty good he could survive the fall.

Alas, there were rocks.

CONESTOGA / PARADISE / TORUS

From across the Solokring, within a darkened launch haven of Abraxas, a single red light illuminated. A signal processed by the central thinking machine is translated.

- *COMMENCE—Ascension Cardinal Machus distracted by Psylaxis while two unknowns commandeered the carriage containing Aegis Syn.*
- *BETAPHONE—The carriage tracking system was damaged in the escape, and last contact had it leaving the city.*
- *GAMMAPHONE—Launch hedron GXL-4999 to conduct reconnaissance. Locate Aegis Syn. Analyze threats, request reinforcements.*
- *DELTAPHONE—Command Psylaxis to assume authority as a replacement.*

The clamps upon the hedron released. The machine coughed a mechanical growl and floated from its cavity. A few electronic groans later, the haven doors opened, and the hedron launched towards the planet below.

Script Epsilon
Verse 56
Plex Codex

"He's alive!" Deven said after injecting Noah with a bio-electric reconstructor, which knitted the torn middle meningeal artery in his head.

"Noah!" Syn said, stroking his face. His eyes remained closed.

"Come on, snap out of it! You're making me look bad," Deven said as he coarsely struck Noah's face, causing the latter to open his eyes, followed by an explosive scream.

Everyone else fell away from the outburst except Syn, who Noah pushed away as he pawed desperately to move away from the strange group.

"What the fuck!" Noah said. His attention darted from the group of strangers to the bizarre mechanical giants looming over him. He looked up to the sky and found pinpricks of light awash in darkness but nothing else. "What happened!?"

"Did he lose his memory?" Agosta asked.

Noah's attention shifted back to the group. He knew some faces but uniforms were foreign.

"What's going on? Where am I?" he asked.

Syn was the only one not staggered by Noah's reaction.

"It's okay," she said softly. She inched closer to Noah as he pushed himself back to a wall. His head arched back to again gape at the wonder of the strange domed lattice between him and the stars, with no mechanism in place to control the universe. "Settle down."

"Where am I?" he asked her.

He recognized her. Not the face or even the body. There was something. Her hair, maybe. Her eyes. Her voice. He stopped shaking, and his breathing slowed as he looked at her.

"Did he take a hit?" Terri asked. "Deven?"

"This doesn't happen," Deven said. "It was an early epidural hematoma. It wasn't even close to starving his brain."

Noah recognized their faces and even their voices, but little else. Agosta. Terri. Deven's voice was familiar, but it was coming from the face of a monster.

"Noah," Syn said again as she reached for his hand.

"How do you know who I am?"

"Because you know me," she said. "Look at me. Look at my face. I'm both known and unknown to you."

Noah was out of place, out of time. But he felt rooted like there was something he could recall, maybe from a dream.

"What's going on?" Noah asked Syn. As he focused on her, he felt himself relaxing, the same reaction as when he first saw her and again in the carriage.

"I understand now," Syn said.

"Who?" Noah asked, his voice trailing to a whisper.

Syn smiled and touched his cheek.

"You're not my Noah," she said.

The group stepped back, stunned by the statement, which she repeated. "You're not…my Noah."

Noah stared back at her, a face he knew.

"No…" he whispered. "I'm not."

*   *   *

The colossal, snake-like twister with a circular mouth and a tempest of floating teeth slithered behind the Vanderov, devouring the line behind the train.

Elina stood with Agosta, Terri, and Sloan atop the locomotive, gaping at the monstrosity as it gained ground behind them.

Aware of his daughter's talents, Agosta knew this beast was well beyond her capacity to repel.

He didn't bother to ask.

He felt her hand grab his.

There was little they could do.

The behemoth devoured the world behind it as it closed in on the train.

*   *   *

Noah's eyes opened.

He could hear the calls of his friends, voices he could distinguish. His eyes inched slowly open, overwhelmed by the unexpected sunlight. His back ached, but he felt no broken bones. He felt dirt beneath him, blades of grass, and a sprinkling of moisture from a splashed puddle.

He had fallen a short distance; a rock towered over him to a scattering of faces that called back.

He must have joggled his ears as their cries were little more than mumbles. He recognized a few of them.

However, everything else quickly took his attention, the world he was in and the universe surrounding him. His mouth fell open as he took in what was impossible.

A full-scaled mechanical model of a geocentric solar system. Heaven rings that supported stars and a radiant but small sun. Other worlds orbited nearby, supported by colossal columns and rings, most disappearing in the haze of the atmosphere.

Noah's fear turned to wonder as he realized where he was.

It was impossible.

But it was also his reality.

POSTSCRIPT

"That is an odd collection of trinkets you got hanging off that sword," he said. "Don't they impede you in battle?"

Sloan's attention remained fixed on the passing desert sand outside the window.

"A price I willingly pay," she said.

The blade was resting on the table between them; Sloan's hand was casually resting atop it, an automatic action her kind had been programmed to do after centuries. As the train rumbled over the rails, it jostled the tea in Sloan's cup and the charms hanging off the sword's crossguard, pommel, and even above the rainguard on the blade.

"That one looks important," he said, pointing to one, and opened the locket with the image of a man, one with steel flecks in his beard under a balding head.

Sloan slid her hand down and closed the ornament. The second one was closed and featured an older blonde woman. He didn't look into or ask about the nearly identical matching locket next to it with a small chain connecting the two.

"Someone I loved dearly," she said.

"Long time ago?" he asked.

Sloan pondered her answer, another vain attempt to pull a memory, any memory, of who it was. All she knew of him was the inscription on the back of the locket: *Love him until the day you die.*

"I have no idea," Sloan whispered.

"Well," he said, "…who were they?

"I don't know," she said.

"Then…how?"

Sloan looked over the inscription…but felt nothing but the mild despair that washes over her whenever she tried to remember what she had forgotten. The inscription on the second locket of the woman read *you were family, protect posterity.*

"It says so," Sloan said.

"You trust it?" he asked.

Sloan got up to leave, not wishing to pursue the conversation further. "I have to," she said as she exited the room.

APPENDIX I

VOLANI PARADISE

Volani was once the largest kingdom in Paradise, with valuable resources licensed to outlining kinhouses. They forged alliances with Kaelum and Eridius through marriages, with cousins once occupying all three thrones. Volani was also an outspoken critic of the church, endorsing a secular philosophy. This, along with other disagreements, resulted in the controversial Aeon Pogrom that erased the kingdom from the planet.

Since then, the enemies of Volani have taken it upon themselves to expunge the history of Volani's contributions to society. They succeeded thanks to the suppression of knowledge endorsed by the Ascension. Unlike other conquered kingdoms, Volani was not allowed to keep its Territory as a vassal to a larger state, and current maps don't indicate old borders.

Initially, it was considered a diplomatic effort by the Ascension to unite the largest nations of man across Paradise. The Aegis had emerged and founded a religious order that swept through the known universe through force of charisma and superior technology. Initial shows of force proved the Aegis's resolve, but soon after, the deities fell behind the curtain of Abraxas, preferring to operate matters through the now established Ascension.

The final direct act by the Aegis was the formation of the Twelve Covenants. This treaty carved up Paradise and handed authority to a dozen of the most powerful families. Regions were named after elements of Aegis mythology with the condition that any house that would claim a throne adopt the kingdom's name. At the outset, it appeared devotion to the church would be uncontested, but despite the geopolitical landscape shifting under the authority of a higher power, the Twelve Covenants failed to eliminate ancient ethnic disagreements or religious preferences.

Instead, culture wars broke out within nations occupied by diverging societies told they were under the umbrella of a single kingdom's identity. The lines drawn looked arbitrary, with numerous rival cultures indiscriminately labeled a single "people" and told to get along. In most situations, these tribes, later labeled houses, would rebel or claim authority over their nearest throne. The Ascension might have intended to create this internal instability to further enforce its influence over affairs.

Volani was the only nation that instilled a unified national identity without enforcing that identity through violence. After 0015, the Volani ruling family of Sahli brought the surrounding houses under their control within their capital Menkar. There, Fatima Sahli Volani negotiated fair trading agreements, demilitarization, political marriages, and a "round table" of rulers known as the Shahs, of which Volani was only a member.

From the High Table of Shahs, Volani established a construction schedule to include universities, docks, and bridges. None of these projects included churches.

The High Table assured that the priority would be infrastructure, and religious representation would follow, though it never did. Fatima had dreamt of a united nation based on cooperation and the sharing of knowledge. Through her position's power and surprisingly long life, she could open her doors to potential rivals. She kept nothing back, and despite initial espionage between the High Table members, adversaries quickly became allies.

It was aided by Volani, possessing incredible wealth in both resources and knowledge, caches the house was open to sharing with others. Another shrewd tactic encouraged by Volani's military authority was that anyone not under the umbrella of Volani was not to be entirely trusted, creating early animosity with the northern neighbor of Aurago, with which Volani shared the longest border.

This strengthened Volani pride, though the encouragement of discrimination was against Fatima's ideology. Fatima married the son of a fellow Shah, Javed Javadi, and their child, Leila Volani, continued in the spirit of her parents. This included a hidden agenda to subvert the canon of the imposing religion. At the time, those in Volani were practicing their own faith, centered around the increasing deification of the Volani ruling families.

A trade and knowledge agreement with Corvos allowed Volani access to the Khronos libraries and comprehension of cryptions and how they were applied. It was during this time when it was discovered that those derived from the first Volani line possessed a strange affinity with cryptions and the emerging discovery of branding, though Volani members themselves were never branded. One from Sahli could harness the power of Paradise in ways no one else could. While believers claimed Sahli possessed Aegis blood, others circumvented this by claiming Sahli, and by extension, the ruling family of Volani, were the true heirs of Abraxas. The Aegis were usurpers.

The Aegis declared that the Sahli must be daemons and ordered their execution, a command no one in Volani followed. Regardless of one's belief, it became a national obsession that one derived from Sahli blood assume the Volani throne. Thankfully, it was discovered this sympathy with the universe did not dilute through subsequent generations mixing outside the family line. This allowed for stronger alliances as Sahli children would be paired off with numerous allies, all wishing to possess someone touched with sanctified genes. Having a religion emerge from this had to be expected.

The Volani royals became known as "The Greaters" in certain circles. Legends of their abilities circulated within the kingdom and the universe. Meanwhile, relations with neighbors became complicated. Those neighbors swearing fealty to the Ascension became openly hostile while the rest beseeched the Volani royals with patronage and treaties.

While Corvos and Volani shared a beneficial trade agreement, the remoteness of the former prevented firm ties. Later, the Treaty of Erskine was signed involving the kingdom of Kaelum. Volani responded to Kaelum's loyalty by aiding them in retaking the throne during the War of Klydes in 0070. In 0105, with land in the south still unclaimed, the Aegis called for the Planitia Crusade.

At the time, the Aegis was still convinced Volani's position would diminish over time and eventually fall under the umbrella of the Ascension. In response to rising concerns of nagomjii in the south, the Aegis demanded a push to claim those lands. The motivation for the Aegis was threefold. They hoped to form a southern kingdom with nagomjii to amalgamate their numbers under the church and create a thirteenth nation to hold Volani in check, fearing they would eventually move south to claim the lands anyway.

The church also hoped Volani would spread itself thin to allow rival Aurago a chance to sweep in to claim rich lands south of the Ordanos river. Volani were given the authority over the crusade hoping that a conflict would ignite, pulling resources from the north and souring public opinion toward the Volani ruling house.

This proved one of the biggest missteps in Aegis and the Ascension history. Volani led the charge into Planitia but kept the brunt of their forces in the north, utilizing armies from Kaelum, Eridius, Draggo, and Pyxis with reserves from Aurago. This prevented an aggressive push south by Aurago and solidified the assumed authority of Volani as they commanded armies populated by other nations.

The Planitia Crusade involved massive armies sweeping across the land, routing nagomjii tribes in a vain attempt to organize the population and establish a cohesive structure. Despite assumptions, no central leadership could be found or enforced. Instead of committing genocide as predicted, the general of the armies, Milad Nazari Volani, attempted peaceful negotiations with the local population.

The nagomjii would be allowed to function independently while the land was colonized by caravans that would follow the armies. The alien population agreed, and

Volani expanded into thousands of square kilometers of fertile landscape uncontested, establishing Volani as the largest nation on Bythos by a considerable margin.

It was midway through the first millennium when the seeds of contempt took root. Volani's influence and popularity within Paradise grew despite propaganda and rising geopolitical tension. The Volani line of succession remained unbroken. Despite Ascension churches being allowed within the Territory under the condition that the immunity against taxation and autonomous governance be eliminated, the faith had yet to overwhelm the local Volinity movement.

Despite the Ascension plotting Volani's elimination, even they understood the political ramifications across Paradise if it was unprovoked. The nation had abided by Aegis regulations and government policy by that time. They paid their levies to the church, a pittance given the nation's worth. The Ascension was allowed an observer seat at the High Table but was banned from operating purgitans.

When cryptions were banned, Volani acquiesced but kept employing brands. After Kaelum's royal family was eradicated in the Minute War of 1395, Volani quickly ran out of allies. Aurago was growing in strength, and it became evident that Aegis tolerance had run out.

By this time, the descendants of Sahli were decreasing in number. Unfortunate accidents, disappearances, and the odd assassination had finally taken their toll, and it was theorized less than a dozen individuals existed with the Sahli gene. During this time, the rumors of the Sahli being daemons persisted, with any evidence of their origins suppressed.

In 1445, the current ruler, Kiana Kazmi Volani, after twenty years of encouraging unbridled cultural development, finally broke the Hallessegro ban on developing technology. Of course, the ban was more of a grey zone, with many nations receiving special authorization for specific projects. For Volani, it was the development of a rail network, and once the project had begun, the Ascension had declared Volani heretics.

Of course, it had nothing to do with the fact that a rail network could rapidly shift resources and military across such a vast nation. The city of Kaitos was obliterated not long after, an act the Aegis claimed. Subsequently, the Aegis increased support of Volani's rivals, mainly Aurago.

Aegis also supported a short-lived alliance between Aurago, Aquino, and Draggo, and this alliance declared war on Volani in what became known as the Aeon Pogrom. The direction was simple—the rivals of Volani would eradicate every ally of Volani. If a soldier raised a weapon, he would be killed, as would his family. Houses with a genetic relation to Sahli would be executed to the last child.

Only families that swore obedience would be allowed to live. The initial fighting was intense, with Volani rivals suffering heavily crossing the Ordanos. Despite this, evidence of the Sahli being daemons could not be exposed. Executed suspects failed to reveal their origin upon death.

Meanwhile, Aegis-controlled conestogas circumvented geographical obstacles to strike primary defenses outside of archaic ranges. Although the alliance was prohibited from employing technology, the Aegis would assign their machines to work alongside them. Despite this advantage, the cult of fanaticism enveloped the Volani house stalled quick victories, and tens of thousands of innocent lives were lost.

After ten years, a poorly handled battle dubbed the Massacre of Primarch Hill gutted the Volani knightly order, leaving the capital of Menkar vulnerable. The city was all but destroyed, and the royal line executed. The Aegis stepped back and allowed the merciless Aurago army to storm in, razing villages and killing nearly every person they found. The slaughter was malevolent, and the alliance to destroy Volani fractured.

Kingdoms that had refused to take part publicly demanded the Aegis halt the war. Draggo and Aquino ceased their crusade while Aurago continued until they were confident the nation of Volani could no longer rise to claim a kingdom.

The kinhouses of Volani had their top royalty executed and passed down to members willing to swear loyalty to the church. Aurago swept through the country and took every square inch. They posted bounties for the heads of any individual possessing Volani blood.

The Pogrom was so costly that Aurago was stretched thin across a massive country. Early attempts to force out the nagomjii proved disastrous, and for at least the time being, it was decided that the prior agreement between them and Volani would stand. There were no kinhouses of Volani. The castles taken were rebuilt to match Aurago architecture. The Volinity cathedrals were destroyed to make way for the Ascension.

Years later, many people tried to pretend the Pogrom didn't exist, as it was an example of how insane humanity could be when told what to do by those posing to be gods.

TORUS

There's no doubt that Volani possessed a significant advantage after the Collapse, blessed with resources and massive manufacturing yards, given the ark's position as the Iokon's leading heavy industry provider. While not designed for aircraft like Pyxis, Volani controlled the Nazari Industrial Complex, the largest train manufacturing yard in the Torus. This proved invaluable after the Collapse as Volani constructed and launched the first Groundmovers to reclaim the tracklands. Before other arks could leave their cities, Volani established cantons about their region, never officially claiming the territory as their own.

Through the groundmovers and later with the first steamliners, Volani established contact with nearly every ark in the Torus, confirming the poor state of the world. Initial alliances proved hopeful, though many would end up being short-lived. Eventually, Volani would license their technology and entire trains to other arks, an unwise decision given later events. Volani was at the forefront of emerging technology involving magnetic fields and energy storage, much of which faded into the wastelands when Volani was nearly destroyed and occupied in 1485 AC. Several cantons now boast knowledge recovered from fleeing immigrants that even arks lack.

For centuries, Volani was a glimmering symbol representing the heights of human achievement during the Iokon era, and it's believed the city-state was one of the wealthiest before the Collapse. The ark certainly appeared to confirm that theory. While not too far removed from the brutalist buildings of Pavonis, Volani appears far more inviting, with gilded buildings that glimmer depending on the lighting. The many towers boast ornate statues and flamboyant stained glass, though the city is primarily dominated by the half-dozen spires that jut from the cityscape. Some locals refer to them as the pyramids given technically; they fit that description, though these have smaller bases than the traditional shape. At 800 meters tall, each pyramid dominates the block, with several skybridges connecting them to nearby buildings. The spires house the administration arms of the various branches of Volani heavy industry, with the ruling council formed from the heads of each division, democratically elected from those below. This creates a cooperative where the branches do not compete but work together to meet typical social and economic demands. After Aurago's invasion, half of these towers were destroyed, with the remaining being employed as management offices for Aurago occupation.

Volani suspected Aurago was looking to employ their military to enforce that claim over larger patches of the Torus. The ark on the exact opposite of the ring was undoubtedly their biggest threat. However, while Volani was fully prepared for a ground assault, it could not defend against attacks coming from directly above. When the siege began, Aurago Ziggurats emerged out of the Stream and rained fire on the city below. Realizing there would be no quarter given, the Volani military instead focused on protecting fleeing trains filled with refugees. While Aurago attempted to blockade these trains and employed privateers to help, Volani still outgunned them train-to-train. Additional support from Corvos ensured many of the fleeing trains vanished into the wasteland, many of which would never appear again. It is assumed they formed cantons across the Torus or found sanctuary in sympathetic arks like Corvos, Draggo, and Eridius. Dozens of vehicles were never seen or heard from again. Today, while Volani still exists, it is a mere shadow of its former glory, operating as a satellite colony tightly controlled by Auragon military. Despite boasting a population of 1.1 million, half of Volani's population was Auragon.

CONESTOGA

When it was active, Volani operated as a socialist democracy. It maintained this and spearheaded the first alliances between exclaves, including the Union and Successor League. They were considered the most influential exclave, the one that penned the name of the Conestoga and the first to break the puzzle keeping humans locked within their exclaves. Volani was the first to create its colony outside of its own habitat and contact another nation. They were the first exclave to initiate peaceful relations with a non-human species, in this case, the endolons of Bythos in 600 AC. Volani was often the tip of the spearhead to push deeper into the Conestoga to uncover its secrets. The exclave was described as "utopian," The habitat edges were mountainous and falling into the plateau where the Volani cities sat mixed with colorful vegetation and crystal-like buildings.

Volani's military focused entirely on defense and exploration, not sustained invasion. This all changed in 1490 AC when Auraga committed what became later known as the "rough raid." Aurago sent a massive invasion force to break into Volani. Aurago had been led to believe Volani's lacked significant firepower and would be demoralized when faced with a superior foe. This proved incorrect, and when the conflict turned against Aurago, and the invasion was broken, Aurago fled. Having lost their patience for the predator city, Volani intended to pursue the army back to their exclave, intending to remove the junta. However, moments before the Volani military left the exclave, a low-yield nuclear device within the habitat detonated, immediately vaporizing half of the habitat's 200,000 inhabitants. Another 150,000 died in the subsequent days as people desperately tried to escape the exclave. Those that did were set upon by watchers, scattering refugees across the Conestoga. Some reached allied nations and were taken. Others vanished into the labyrinth of the Conestoga, never to be seen again. At final count, less than 10,000 Volani refugees managed to find a safe harbor.

Landscape. Regardless of what came before, the Volani exclave is now an apocalyptic wasteland with scorched vehicles, felled buildings, and dead vegetation. Radiation is still dangerously high in places, and the debris thrown up by the blast created a dust cloud that kept heat bottled inside the habitat, increasing the temperature beyond human tolerance. Despite this, Volani had owned valuable texts on the weavers as well as technology only they wholly understood, thus creating a demand for proctors willing to take the chance to enter this hellish landscape. And of course, they are not the only ones, as both jackers and scabs have been found within the region, the latter being more resistant to the environment than humans.

Ramada. Strangely immune to heat and radiation, ramada is an ancient construct formed from white stone sitting on the mountains' southern edge. Those who reached the peak claimed to find a fortress with few rooms and a massive inner chamber locked from the outside, encasing something within. No one has been able to breach this inner chamber, resisting any form of outside attack. To this day, Ramada appears to radiate a soft white glow, making it visible on days from kilometers away.

The Storms. For unknown reasons, on occasion, something will form from the ruins in Volani that appears to possess some intelligent controller. It materializes out of the various wrecks and attacks anything it can see, matching similar descriptions of creatures within the Tokol exclave. It is unknown how the same creatures have appeared in two different environments. Reports of these creatures are more pervasive in Volani, given the number of proctors, scavengers, and bandits willing to enter Volani and steal its secrets.

APPENDIX II

CONESTOGA GLOSSARY

Chimeratanium. A mysterious alloy of atomic-sized machines that can be programmed to permanently emulate other transitional metals in various configurations, chimeratanium can be found within many devices.

Crutch. A crutch is a blanket term for the many powered armors people operate across the Conestoga. First discovered within "The Yard" (see later), a crutch soon became mandatory for many expeditions, with the proctors possessing the most powerful variants.

Driver. A driver is the weapon's engine, dictating the energy core it requires.

Index. This device is attached to a driver to alter its function.

Endolon. These advanced humanoid aliens derive from the exclave of Bythos and maintain good relations with most human nations. They are known for their thin frames and lack of tolerance for rudeness.

Energy Core. Five power sources are available: fuel, numatter, plasma, volt, and cell. The Conestoga supplies all except for the latter, which is built by humanity.

Exclave Science Initiative. The ESI was formed in 375 AC after the formation of the Union and was comprised of scientific and engineering personnel to help exchange information between nations. Despite the Union dissolving in 650 AC, the ESI never folded and maintained their relationship to the present day. Despite possessing a membership from nine exclaves, most of the membership derives from Corvos and Draggo.

Gateway. Each exclave possesses at least one gateway separating it from the rest of the Conestoga. These were initially locked, but eventually, those within each exclave discovered how to open them. An airlock prevents mixing atmospheres, and each gateway is large enough to accommodate Gargantuan or smaller creatures. While most exclaves only feature one gateway dead center of their habitat, others may possess three of four.

Jackers. A religious cult comprised of scavenger/bandits that wander through the Conestoga and several habitats. jackers appear immune to watcher attacks and prey on non-jackers regularly.

Numatter. Numatter is a programmable self-powered nanosubstance used to create simple shapes while also powering the device that requires those shapes. It is related to chimeratanium but is comprised of large molecules.

Processor. A processor is a minor upgrade that only marginally modifies a device in very subtle ways. Each device lists its own available processors. Human engineers have managed some success in producing processors, unlike most other parts.

Rough Raid. In 1490 AC, the predator city Aurago attacked the Volani exclave to overthrow its ruling party and control the habitat. The conflict proved more protracted and bloodier than Aurago had planned. The latter was forced to retreat, but not before detonating a nuclear warhead, destroying the exclave and killing most within, including many retreating Aurago soldiers. Aurago claimed they were not responsible. No one believes them.

Scabs. While two alien (non-human) species within the Conestoga have formed a relatively peaceful relationship with many human habitats, the insectoid scabs are exceptions. These nomadic creatures possess a hive intelligence and are fast learners of whatever technology they encounter. They form nests both within the Conestoga and various habitats and are rarely welcome. A scab's mindset is so alien that all attempts at communication have failed. They seem to want food and knowledge and don't know how to acquire it without conflict. The only exception to this is when a vile emerges.

Scrimm. The other civilized non-human society with the Conestoga, the scrimm are flight-capable egg-laying mammals who value intelligence above all other abilities. Scrimm reside in the exclave of Kenoma and have maintained good relations with endolons and humans.

Status. This refers to Weaver technology's capacity to accomplish an effect it doesn't appear capable of.

Successor League. A trade alliance formed in 700 AC between most exclave nations and their colonies. Unlike the Union, the SG charter does not mandate military and humanitarian aid. It is only in place to enforce policies regarding trade and conflict. A substantial portion was also allotted for regulating the proctors, which the original Union did not perceive as an issue back then.

Trinity. A nearby system is occupied by a black hole (Behemoth), a red dwarf (Avalon), and a neutron star (Axis). This system also contains various planets, with the Conestoga orbiting between the second and third world.

Union. An early alliance formed in 350 AC between the greater nations of Volani, Pyxis, Draggo, and Fornas, which later included later colonies Hydranis,

Eridius, and Kaelum. This alliance was then splintered in 650 AC with the discovery of Aurago and their subsequent invasion of rival exclaves. The Successor League in 700 AC later replaced it.

Upgrade. An upgrade attaches to an operating device and adds a function rather than alters the original.

Van. A standard transport seen in every exclave, the van runs on six spheres instead of wheels and was found as a preloaded design within the Yard.

Watchers. The Conestoga maintains these self-repairing biomechanical machines to prevent unauthorized excursions within the Conestoga. They are hostile to nearly everyone and will pursue targets any distance with only a few exceptions—they won't pursue into medical chambers, botanical chambers, exclaves, or the channel.

Weaver. Only a nickname, this term refers to the unseen alien species that constructed the Conestoga and all technology contained within. Despite attempts, no documented evidence has been found showing what the weavers looked like, how they acted, or why they constructed the Conestoga in the first place.

TORUS GLOSSARY

Ascension. Before their fall, the Ascension, the ruling body of the Iokon Caliphate, was exiled and became nomadic bandits in the wasteland.

BC. The standard unit of currency within the Torus based on brass.

Caravel. Ordinary merchant trains that wander the Torus.

Cavalier. The largest mercenary company in the Torus, the cavaliers is a knightly order tied with Communion leased out to arks to aid in external affairs.

CIC. Conductor-In-Chief, the captain of a train.

Column. The inner portion of the Torus, the "hole of the doughnut," as it can be imagined. It is unclear if the hole is occupied or not, but the region of the Convex facing the inner region of the Torus is known as The Column and is surrounded by Nimbus.

Communion. A technology-based religious order that predates The Great Collapse, Communion possesses knowledge of making hydrocells and employs that knowledge to extort supplies and spread their faith across the Torus.

Conestogas. Custom-built trains are often the homes of those living on them.

Convex. Referring to the interior of the Torus ring.

Corsairs. Pirate-crewed trains.

Groundmovers. The largest trains ever built were employed to clear the tracklands of debris hundreds of years ago and are still in operation today.

Hydrocell. These batteries are constructed by Communion and power all technology.

Logicmarker. A sentient machine intelligence, a logicmarker is believed to be miniature replications of a larger logicmarker at the center of the Torus many people call Nimbus.

Maelstrom. A colossal stationary storm on the outer edge of the Convex, the Maelstrom is believed by many to have been the source of The Great Collapse, dating back to that event over 2,000 years ago. The storm, measuring 500 kilometers across, is impenetrable and is the source of the effigy.

Makers. Independent engineers proficient in brass and smoke can create custom devices employing them both; makers are often found in the wasteland.

Mecha. This logicmarker is believed to be within the center of the Torus along with the vacant city that encircles the Column. No one has been able to enter either.

Nimbus. The city encircling the Column. Although it resembles an urban space, it may be a singular mechanical construct.

Privateers. Independent but ark-contracted military trains.

Sea of Spires. This breadth of the Iokon Metropolis is occupied by hundreds of still-standing towers, resilient despite the surrounding environment's disintegration.

Smoke. A strange dark mist emanates from people and items possessing magical power and maybe the physical manifestation of magic itself.

Steamliner. Massive ark-controlled passenger and cargo trains

The Sprawl. The expanse of mostly abandoned ruins leftover from the original Iokon Metropolis, the Sprawl, covers 75% of all available landmass within the Torus.

The Stream. A ring of swirling clouds encircling the entire Torus in the center of the Convex.

Uno. The artificial star that moves along the center of the Convex, surrounded by the Stream, Uno provides both heat and light.

PARADISE GLOSSARY

Abecedarian. Magic operates very differently within *Paradise*, with its practice prohibited by the Aegis. Users employ "cryptions" that access and alter the reality controlled by Paradise. Masters of this art are known as Abecedarians.

Aeon Pogrom. A short conflict saw the majority of Bythos-based kingdoms unite to annihilate the kingdom of Volani in 1470.

Agathon. The private name employed by daemons to refer to their kind.

Ascension. The "church" of the Aegis. The Ascension is populated by non-Aegis and represents Aegis affairs outside of Abraxas. Only the Ahkdanate (cardinals) have been to Abraxas. The Ascension is populated by the curia, the Diaconate, the

Ordinariate, proctors, rectors, the Silantine Guard, Knights Episcar, and the purgitan inquisitors. Like all those not Aegis, "most" members of the Ascension are prohibited from using technology.

Commandments of Enlightenment. A book released by the House of Palak in Corvos before the installment of the House Republics (also known as the "Comlightment"), the Commandments are a series of directives about how Corvos should be run, including basic laws and ideological visions for the house and peoples to follow. They demand the recording of all history, the neutrality of the nation, and the refusal of any state religion. The Commandments prize intelligence, creativity, and love above all human values. They denounce the blind worship of anything, not just including religion but any ideas or objects. Beyond these general demands, more specific ones condemn murder, slavery, and the harming of children. The Commandments have been the subject of condemnation by the Ascension.

Crematoram. A plague that broke out in 0045 that only affected humans, the Crematoram, is rumored to have occurred thanks to a non-fatal virus from the nagomjii that jumped species and decimated much of the human population of Bythos. Several outer worlds quarantined themselves for up to fifteen years until the last case was recorded. Crematoram was spread via respiration, and even though initial symptoms resembled influenza, the later stages of the virus involved rashes that simulated burned skin. Crematoram had a 15% fatality rate and is theorized to have killed nearly 250,000 people. The virus vanished by the end of that century, but there are conflicting reports of how it disappeared. Claims range from the Aegis offering the cure to a treatment developed and disseminated by Corvos. A more straightforward theory claims the virus simply burned out after the population developed natural immunities. However, the damage had been done. The plague crossed borders and social ranks, with nearly every house suffering casualties. In the case of the kingdom of Aurago, Crematoram decimated the house of Docarab, removing them from the line of succession. Race-based attacks against the nagomjii continued decades after the virus disappeared.

Cryptions. Cryptions are pictograms written in an alien tongue employed by Abecedarians to create effects that can appear magical as they alter the reality controlled by Paradise.

Culling of Agathon. At the same time as the signing of the Twelve Covenants in 0015, the Aegis revealed that a secret humanoid species was living among them. The Aegis accused them of being fiends and ordered their elimination upon detection. The agathon, as they called themselves, were in hiding, with many people oblivious to their existence. Over a thousand daemons were exposed and executed in the hundred years that followed. Only Corvos and Volani refused to enact the policy of detection and elimination.

Daemon. The term daemon refers to a mysterious race of humanoids that hide among the general population. The Aegis declared them profane and ordered their annihilation. Among themselves, they are known as the agathon.

Eidolon. Another term for golem in Paradise—artificial creatures powered by magic that is constructed by magic users. Some have achieved sentience.

Farris Union. An ancient alliance between Draggo and Aquino that saw them both controlled by a single monarch, Olden Farris, the Farris Union was meant to counter the influence of the Forthwind Guild. Even with this alliance, Farris couldn't make a discernable impact on the Guild monopoly. It is commonly known that all pirates able to sail at that time were funded privately by Farris. After the Guild proved too influential, Pyxis and Corvos aristocracies concocted several incidents at sea, forcing conflicts between Guild members. They then used this excuse to disband the Guild, believing that even fragmented, Pyxis and Corvos could still maintain control of the Lacus. It did not last as Aquino and Eridius pushed hard into the area, and the entire region has been volatile ever since.

Forthwind Guild. A trade alliance between Pyxis and Corvos meant to monopolize control of the Lacus Major. The Farris Union was formed in contrast.

Golden Shield. Also called the "Pyxis Totem Foedus," the Golden Shield is a charter of rights and treaties created by the crown of Pyxis and applied to all the kingdom's flags. It ended most of the internal conflicts in Pyxis and assisted in enabling national pride.

Hallessegro. The council of kingdoms under blessing from the Aegis. All realms pay homage to the Aegis. There have only been a few times the Aegis have called all the kingdoms of the Hallessegro together. Once included the terms of tribute demanded by the church, another was the conquest of Planitia in 105.

Honors of Kings / Regalia. As part of the Twelve Covenants and as a condition of establishing a kingdom, the Aegis insisted that each realm prove its validity to the throne by possessing a specific valuable relic. These can include weapons, shields, orbs, or simply rocks. To lose the honors is to lose one's right to the throne. In the case of Kaelum and Eridius, the honors were taken by Aurago and placed alongside theirs. With Volani, the honors went missing at some point in the Aeon Pogrom's final days. Rivals to a throne believe no claim can be validated unless they possess the honors, though it takes more than holding the honors to claim a throne. The honors are worth more to different kingdoms. Corvos keeps their regalia under security but more out of national pride and not because of any condition to be a kingdom. Alternately, Hydranis houses fight bitterly to claim the honors, over and above direct attacks on rival houses. It is common knowledge to many that the regalia are magical.

House Republics. Corvos operates a strange republic system where the people vote for a ruling royal house from more than a dozen available. The first time this was put forward, the house of Palak imposed it and then took themselves out of the running, allowing the rise of the house of Anugati. Each time a ruler dies or a specific time elapses (whichever comes last), a vote is called (although it can be called earlier, it never has). Despite this system, after Anugati came to office, they rarely left. Although accusations of corruption in the voting system have been raised, no proof has emerged. There was only a brief moment when Anugati had no viable heir of proper age, and the throne fell to Kisau for three decades. It soon fell back to Anugati due to the hugely unpopular policies of Kisau (they attempted to overthrow the Commandments of Enlightenment.

Incanetics. These magical prosthetics are the resulting hybrid of brands and golem construction. While desired by those with limbs, the Ascension had prohibited their acquisition.

Khronos Libraries. Khronos was an ancient order of record keepers attempting to reconstruct the missing history of humanity during the dark ages. They could verify that society, at one point, possessed knowledge now forbidden by the Aegis. Although dedicated to history, Khronos also trained students in the arts and philosophy, producing generations of enlightened thinkers. However, Khronos came under condemnation from the Aegis, and the various libraries worldwide were eventually closed or destroyed. With Aurago, the libraries were overly taxed. The royal guard deposed the chief librarians in Aquino and burned the libraries with the collections still in them. Many books were smuggled out, finding salvation within Volani. When Volani was eradicated in the Aeon Pogrom, most of these collections were wiped out as well. Legend has it the Khronos sect has a private collection hidden from the eyes of the Aegis. There are also rumors that Corvos maintains a secret library, offering sanctuary to wandering members of the fading order.

Mutaform. This technical term refers to the variations of humans that have developed in Paradise. These deviations are far more severe than the minor anatomical, cultural, and genetic differences known to humanity before their appearance. These deviations have been segmented into the kingdoms where they are prominent. They are corvon, kael, erid, and pyke. The nagomjii are considered an entirely different species and are not considered a mutaform.

Nagomjii. A nomadic alien species with no genetic similarity to any other species within Paradise, the nagomjii generally keep to themselves and enter human kingdoms to sell trinkets.

Paradise. The name of the entire universe in the perception of the people within the orrery. It encompasses Bythos, Una, and all the worlds around Bythos. It is mentioned in replacement for the "universe."

Solokring. The outer shell of Paradise, this barrier prevents anything from leaving or entering Paradise. It also operates the heaven rings.

Tepheron. The Tepherons were a religious order that gained considerable traction in Aurago centuries ago and was unofficially responsible for the Aurago civil campaign between the houses of Joachim and Phelhall. Although the houses believed their conflict was over the Aurago throne, many thought it a holy war between the Tepherons and the Ascensionists. Tepheron faith believed the Aegis to be demigods created after the splintering of a greater god, Tephos, and that each Aegis carried within their heart a piece of Tephos. The Tepherons' most considerable dogmatic disagreement with the Ascension was the Tepheron claim that the Ascension did not speak for the Aegis and that the Aegis seen with the Ascension are prisoners. With the end of the civil war, the Tepheron faith declined. With the rise of the house of Raddad, the Tepheron faith was prohibited. It is still practiced in small villages to this day.

POSTFACE

I consider my *Amethyst* series my magnum opus despite Affinity dominating my soul for several years. The idea of telling a story in this format began with Darren Aronofsky's magical realism film, *The Fountain*. I became fascinated by the concept of identical characters in different worlds. I played with a similar idea in a sequel to *Amethyst* (yes, I have planned that far ahead), but the final outline didn't carry that inspiration through.

I was spurred again by reading David Mitchell's *Cloud Atlas* and its six "nested" stories. However, I wanted my narratives to coincide, following a format similar in concept to George RR Martin's *A Song of Ice and Fire* series. However, where those books separate their narrative through point-of-view characters, *Affinity* would divide itself between its three different realities. I was still, at the time, unclear on both the narrative and the specifics of the three settings. However, I had already decided it would involve a different mix of magic and technology, an idea I touch upon frequently (if you hadn't already noticed).

The release of the feature film *Cloud Atlas* was both stirring and frustrating. It resolved several narrative hurdles I had been battling with and then presented its story comparably to how I planned with *Affinity*. That film, my favorite by Lana and Lilly Wachowski (and Tom Tykwer), restructured the Mitchell novel to tell all six stories simultaneously, adding an additional element of casting the same fourteen actors in different roles in each of the narratives.

Affinity would involve three narratives, and instead of representing different times in the same universe, connected through variations of chronicling (movies, diaries, letters, etc.), it would detail three different parallel realities. Characters would share similar descriptions and even their names, but not direct connections, at least initially. These connections would increase and develop throughout the book, creating a greater intimacy than even those implied in *Cloud Atlas*. Characters would inherit feelings and eventually memories from their doubles in their attempt to determine the cause of their converging realities.

Given my love of inserting books in my books, I, early in the story's development, created the *Plex Codex*, which acts as a way for the relative realities to eventually communicate with one another.

As found in Amethyst, whenever I explain an element of my settings, I eventually fall into a nameless voice that doesn't particularly mesh with the neutral voice of a third-person writing style. As a result, I will often transform that digression into a fictionalized "in-setting" excerpt from a nonexistent book. I enjoyed the process so much that it carried into *Affinity*, and now I have somewhat adopted it as an aspect of my writing (it doesn't show up in House of Skye as it is presented as first-person).

The *Plex Codex* was the ultimate manifestation of that idea, a book that would act as a McGuffin and eventually be revealed as a connecting thread between all three stories. Readers that share my love of bizarre and unusual books may pick up inspiration from the intentionally nonsensical art book, the *Codex Seraphinianus*, and I put a few references to the author in the form of the name Tojilfenias found in the book.

Seraphinianus was not the only inspiration for the Plex Codex. Another, the Codex Gigas, is the largest extant medieval illuminated manuscript globally, and its mysterious and honestly disconcerting history provided additional encouragement.

However, by 2013, I was entrenched in role-playing games, a hobby that became a career by the end of that decade. Every novel idea I imagined would first be made into a playable setting. *Amethyst* followed this similar format and would last for eleven years before the first page of the first novel was written. I have often suggested that, regardless of if you play tabletop tole playing games or not, a fantasy or science fiction writer should consider presenting their story as a game setting as it codifies, quantifies, and defines the rules and limits of a setting. Several famous books began as a fictional encyclopedia of defined ideas (Dune and Lord of the Rings being noteworthy examples). As players require definition in their game, creating a tabletop setting book allows writers to keep their setting from running off a narrative road.

Further, it can also create an environment where a writer can test the waters with friends creating characters to develop where a story can go. The hurdle with *Affinity* was that my players were uninterested in creating three identical characters in three different settings. They created one, Paradise, which expanded in a game that only ran five sessions before it (and my entire game group subsequently) collapsed. One issue was that Paradise took so much effort to launch that I hadn't written the other two worlds by that point. I determined that each would be a different mix of magic and technology, involving hard science fiction and the other steampunk. But beyond simple ideas, Paradise was the only one developed.

I regret that my old game group splintered soon after. Although I did run another *Amethyst* campaign, most of the players from *Affinity* didn't carry over. By that point, they had been involved in my projects for over fifteen years. With few exceptions, I talk very little with those players, which wasn't due to age or career intervening. Unfortunately, I had a falling out with two of them, and with their connections with the rest of the group, several others vanished from my life. It happens, folks.

I also met my future wife shortly after, so I am in no way regretful for how my life unfolded in the subsequent years.

For years, *Affinity* sat as one-third of an idea. Only after the successful Kickstarter campaign for my book *Ultramodern5* in 2019 was I able to complete the project.

The original plan had been to take what I had written for Paradise, develop the other two settings, and create a trio of 100-page campaign books. That ended up not happening. *Paradise* finished at 150 pages, a limit I would impose on the other two, assuming they would fall well under that. Then *Conestoga* ended at 200 pages, and THAT became the new limit until *Torus* followed up with 220. I had to return to *Paradise* and expand it, then *Conestoga* soon after.

Narratively, *Paradise* was the longer story, but it became clear the project had grown beyond my initial plans, resulting in the 2021 Kickstarter for *Affinity,* which raised over $100,000. One of the final stretch goals was the novelization, which brings us to this point. I subsequently had to expand the stories for Torus and Conestoga, resulting in the last novel's planned goal of 70,000 words exploding past 100,000. And to make matters worse, it ended in a cliffhanger.

A preface or postface often involves acknowledgments, and I got a few, including both the thousand-plus backers of my *Affinity* Kickstarter and the nearly identical number that supported *Ultramodern5* in 2019. Both those projects allowed me to become a full-time writer, for all that's worth.

I thank my closest friends and family, but most of all, my wife, Nicole, whom I met in 2014, for supporting my career. For those wanting to be writers, here's a great piece of advice:

Marry a bookkeeper.

Seriously, she's been a mountain in the fog, a light in the darkness, and the stars on which I navigate. I wouldn't have been able to have done any of this if it wasn't for her inspiration and guidance.

Chris Dias